MARKINGS OF FATE

THE UNBOUND FATE
BOOK 2

C.J. BLAIRE

For the ones who take what's rightfully theirs

AUTHOR NOTE

Dear lovely readers,

I spent the majority of 2025 writing this book months before I decided to release of book one. My heartfelt gratitude is always extended to my readers, and those who have stuck with me since the release of *In The Dark*. This series exists because of you, and the love and support you've shown me does not go unnoticed.

That being said, Isa's unraveling continues. With that comes unwelcome emotions and making decisions she doesn't want to make, all while discovering who she was before her memories were stolen.

I hope you fall in love with these characters as much as I did while writing them. There are themes of loss, betrayal, heartbreak, and torture in this book. I trust that you, as a reader, know your limits. Thanks for reading!

Content & Trigger Warnings are at the back.

PREVIOUSLY FROM IN THE DARK

Isa's mission transformed when she joined forces with Rydian, the King of Aurelia, to uncover the truth about her missing mother and her lost memories.

As their search led them deeper into the castle's buried secrets, Isa found her resolve and her feelings for Rydian shifting. But it was during their pursuit they discovered that Milena's grandson—the Siphon and second-in-command—still worked for King Elion.

After stealing a portion of the castle's map from King Elion's archives, Isa and Rydian still struggled to locate her mother until Isa realized the map was incomplete. The missing half forced them back into Elion's archives for one final attempt. Upon their final attempt, Ezra caught them in the archives and dragged them before King Elion.

Isa revealed herself as the rightful heir to Elderheim, bearing the royal essence to both realms. She had stolen a crystal behind Rydian's back, and restored her memories through Milena. In doing so, she discovered that she bore two mate marks—one from each realm.

PLAYLIST

Rain - Sleep Token
Give - Sleep Token
Like a Villain - Bad Omens
Death of Peace of Mind - Bad Omens
Just Pretend - Bad Omens
Fall Into - Ally Nichols
The Grey - Bad Omens
Renascence - The Pretty Wild
Secrets - Amira Elfeky
Take Me Under- Amira Elfeky
Ritual Touch - Goddess No Holy
You Should See Me in a Crown - Billie Eilish
Something in the Heavens - Lewis Capaldi
Killing- Ally Nicholas
Killer Looks - Just Pete

MAGIC SYSTEM

Realm of Elderheim
All Aetheri can use elemental magic, leaf whisper, and communicate with animals.

Aetheri Magic
Siphons
Crystal Scrying
Stone Shaping
Herb Weavers
Healers

Realm of Aurelia
All Shadovar can use elemental magic, enter the Veil, and shift their appearances.

Shadovar Magic
Seers
Shadow Shaping
Vision Walkers
Shadow Mending
Death Whispers

1

It frightens me, what I'd do for the ones I love.

Because now, as my fingers twitch for that delicate blade, I know that I'd slit my own throat to protect him.

Perhaps returning my memories was a mistake as despair tightens in a way that leaves me breathless—unsure of my future. It drags me toward two worlds: one I want, and one I desperately want to run away from.

Who am I? I had asked myself that question months ago. Though now, I have no answer. Not as I stare into the eyes of the one I despise most.

King Elion's mocking laugh bellows the throne room air like a warning, its echo reverberating off the stone. Whatever nerves burn through me, I hide and slow my breaths.

Theron, King Elion's personal guard and my tormentor, inches forward in clinking metal. Both Ren and Theron stand beside Elion while Rydian kneels to my right—Witt is still frozen and panting in my grasp.

Slivers of dawn stream through the windows, spilling pinks and oranges along the floor. Colors that are drastically different from the tension hanging in the air.

Yet my spine straightens, my chin held high as I meet King Elion's deadly stare as his daughter. The heir to Elderheim.

And the only thing I don't want to be.

Knowledge I had tucked away for the last couple of weeks in case I needed to use it. Which is now, apparently.

I had only hoped to use it later, after I had time to plan. But after *Witt* caught us stealing in the archives, I'm left with no choice.

Witt's eyes widen, his feet slowly lifting off the ground. Whips of light slither down my arm, eager to touch him—end him, as it begs me to. Only then do I release his body before the light touches his skin. He collapses.

Memories of Witt had flooded me in the archives the moment he had admitted to being the Siphon. Just as Milena said they would. He was never the Ezra from Rydian's memory.

No. Witt had replaced the Ezra I thought I knew, slipping into the innocent boy's position in my memories like a shadow. I should have known, though, with the way he was always so distant— disconnected at times.

The signs were there, like how he could switch emotions in seconds, revealing his true nature. I always thought that it was his training. Except, it was him and who he was deep down. He never even liked me.

My blood boils as it sinks in—*the betrayal.*

He'd been playing me, hiding behind another mask while I blindly trusted him.

Witt stands, his eyes cold, while silently moving to the side of the dais as if waiting for Elion's command. It all makes sense now, and I was the fool who never saw it coming.

I glance at Rydian, still kneeling with his hood lowered. Shadows conceal his face as his gaze rests on the floor, our communication silent and cold. Empty.

Shame skitters down my body, and I wish to know what he's thinking. I'm sure he feels betrayed in his own right. Ignoring my feelings, I force my attention back to King Elion with nothing but a cold, blank stare. Elion's gaze finally meets mine again, and a large grin spreads across his face.

"Heir?" Elion bellows another laugh. "Why would I need an heir when I can live an immortal life as a god?"

I stiffen—*a god?* Dread sinks into my stomach. Witt walks up the dais, standing on Elion's left.

"I've spent the last six decades pulling essences from the Fae," Elion says, "discovering that when they're placed inside crystals, they become pure, concentrated sources of magic. Unfortunately, I can't take it all, otherwise it turns the Fae into a... Well, they are not themselves. Disgusting, withering creatures..."

Is he talking about the Grokees?

Meaning he had begun to experiment with living creatures, turning them into something unrecognizable. Holding back a shudder, I'm drawn to the memory of how I was attacked in the valley, my hand covered in decaying skin and fur.

How Rydian and I were ambushed in the Whispering Woods by those things that looked like Fae... but not.

My gaze snaps back to Elion, nausea settling heavily in my stomach. I can't imagine a realm full of creatures like that taking over. It would be catastrophic.

Swallowing the bile in my throat, I say, "Royalty can only hold the throne for 300 years before passing it to their offspring—"

"Or whoever is next in line; until me. Scrying has allowed me to see snippets of my future. I'll rule all the realms, ascending as a god." Leaning forward, he grips the throne, knuckles white, eyes lost to a lust for power. He's obsessed with it.

"Why would you want to do that?" A scowl slowly spreads across my face.

"Because, *daughter*." His head snaps to me. "Even Fae lives come to an end. Why would I give up my throne for a half-blooded heir when I can ascend in power? All creatures will worship me, build my temples, and hold festivals in my honor."

"You wouldn't be able to do it, not unless you performed a—"

"A ritual, yes." His lip curls. "At first, I wanted to find a way to preserve my essence inside the crystals, so I could pull from it slowly, extending my life over time. But as I've found out with the creatures, you cannot pull the entire essence from a being without sacrificing the body. Then I came across old texts regarding the Veil-stone—the ritual required to ascend. Essences are only the beginning. I'll complete it, and I will ascend, making me the first of my kind. I won't need an heir—not *you* anyway."

As much as I hate him, I can't help the hurt that creeps in. The ache of not being wanted. "Why are you telling me this?"

He glares, waving a careless hand. "Because soon, your mind will be wiped, and you will return to your duty in the Brotherhood."

"Why keep me alive then?" I ask breathlessly. "Just kill me."

He chuckles. "Because what better revenge on your mother than forcing her daughter into a lifetime of servitude? To have you kill off all of Aurelia, slowly, over time, and turn you into a weapon."

My stomach twists. I was right—he's using me to kill off my own kind, but he misjudged me.

I sneer, my anger bubbling over. "You do need me, *father*, and you've clearly underestimated what you created me to be since I can give you what you want."

"And what is that?" He straightens, leaning forward and appearing interested.

"I can give you Aurelia."

Rydian slowly swivels his head toward me, my mind flooding with his hurt and anger—a fiery, furious anger. My breaths halt.

"Don't do it," he warns. *"You will not like what happens if you decide to help him."*

Heart racing, I hold Elion's stare.

"Please, please forgive me," I whisper, barely brushing the edges of his mind before cutting the connection entirely. Ignoring him—pushing him aside—sours my stomach.

"From what I've gathered," I say to Elion, "you need the Veil-stone to complete your ascension. That's what you've been searching for all these years, is it not? That's clearly important; otherwise, you would have already ascended. I can give you Aurelia and help you find the Veilstone. I'm the heir to the realm after all."

He leans closer, a cruel, wicked smirk crawling up the side of his mouth. "I admire the effort, but you are not the heir to Aurelia because you are not a Vaelborne. Only the Vaelborne bloodline can hold the throne unless you are the second-in-command. That is not you. Your mother was not on the throne when you were conceived."

His smirk widens into a grin, as if he's beaten me at his own game. But I've always been a few steps ahead.

A low, bitter laugh slips from me. "Did you know that when a king or queen of Aurelia marries, they also have a ritual to complete? It involves the exchange of blood under a marriage oath, officially making who they marry a part of their *royal* bloodline."

His face goes nearly white, and the shock marring his features tells me he didn't quite think of that.

Upon a royal marriage ritual, the exchanging of essence creates new royalty. Aethralis traditions are different, as they use Siphons to exchange that essence upon marriage, not by blood. While technically I'm not related to any Vaelborne, their magic runs in my veins the same as the Aethralis bloodline does.

"That means nothing," he growls.

"That's where you're wrong. She married King Andre before my birth and completed that ritual while pregnant with me, making me the first Aethralis and Vaelborne between the realms. I am not Isa Valedara, bound to the Veiled Brotherhood. My name is Isayara Elysandre Vaelborne, heir to Elderheim and Aurelia, first of my bloodline and bound to both. You can kill me or wipe my memories, my very existence if you want to, but you won't get the Veil-stone without me."

My hands warm.

Trails of shadow and light cascade down my arms, sparking at my fingertips. If he doesn't believe my words, he should believe the power running through my veins.

He eyes me as the chamber falls eerily silent—not even a breath to be heard. Turmoil circulates, guards shift on their feet and clanking metal echoes in the chamber. Without warning, Elion slams his hands onto the throne, growling in frustration. Angry eyes flick to me before he waves a careless hand at the two guards holding Rydian, as if all of this just set him off.

They yank his hood back, and betrayal and rage blazes behind my eyes. The ache of being lied to—*his* ache.

Regardless, a sliver of relief crashes over me when Rydian's human form glares at Elion, but then a guard sweeps his dagger across his throat. Blood sprays, soaking his tunic, pooling onto the floor as he slumps forward.

My breath catches, my lips parting in surprise as I fight the tightness in my chest. Panic rises—clawing and unrelenting—my head pounding in a way that leaves me to believe he's dead. I know he's not, but my lungs burn as I fight for air.

I blink when our connection quiets, and I force myself to remain planted. Force myself to hold my fraying composure even though my heart cracks with every passing second.

He's not dead. He's not dead.

But now we have half an hour before Rydian heals himself, revealing who he is—the king of Aurelia. Worry pulses my veins. I need to end this discussion with Elion—quickly—to figure out how to get Rydian out of the castle before he rises.

Will the guards dispose of him?

Despite wanting to throw myself over Rydian's body, I reluctantly tear my gaze away and lift my chin. Elion needs the Veilstone, and without access to Aurelia, he won't be getting it. Not without me at least. I'm his only way in, so I let him sit in silence as he strokes his beard, brow set with annoyance.

How badly does he want the Veilstone?

"What do you suggest then?"

I steady my breath, inhaling. "Use me. Lift the border and let me claim Aurelia to begin the search for the Veilstone. We can work together, giving you what you want, and I will swear my loyalty to you."

"Why would you do that?" His eyes narrow.

"Because you could have used me to win them over—to find the Veilstone," I say, my lip curling. "Instead, you created a weapon because you were angry with my mother."

"She betrayed me. She *lied* to me when she was supposed to love me. *That* does not go unpunished. And those *mate marks*—" He growls, the deep sound rumbling from his chest as he grips the throne in frustration. A world of hurt and fury flashes across his face. "I did what I had to do, but I don't think that's your real reason, is it?"

"I want to know where she is." I hold his stare with all the confidence I can muster, my trembling hands curling into fists.

He laughs, deep and loud. "You'll barter an entire realm for someone you don't even remember? You're foolish and no daughter of mine if that's all you want."

He's right, of course, but I have a plan and I'm hoping he doesn't catch my lie. His eyes gloss over, as if he's considering my offer, and he runs a thumb over the arm of the throne. He glances down with a smirk.

"How do I know you won't break my trust if I let you leave? I'm not foolish enough to just let you walk out of here."

For a breath we hold each other's gaze.

"I'll go with her," Ren grumbles beside him and steps forward, a dark expression settling over his features. "Send me with her, and if she steps out of line, I'll deal with it myself—report back as I've done many times before."

My heart twists. What does he mean by that?

A creeping silence lingers as Elion holds Ren's gaze, stroking his beard as if weighing his options. As if calculating the risks of sending me to Aurelia. Heavy and suffocating, the air thickens like static, twisting into something darker—a buzz of royal power. Sharp enough to pin me in place.

Elion's controlled expression gives nothing away.

If Ren goes with me, everything changes. He'll have a way to stay in communication with the king. Not just because he'll be there to keep me in line—to watch and ensure I obey orders—but because he's a direct link back to Elderheim. Now that Ren is Captain, his presence becomes leverage for me *and* Elion. And Ren knows that; he's ensuring I arrive in Aurelia.

Elion turns back to me. "Fine. But you won't be swearing loyalty to me by your words alone, but by a blood oath." He fights a grin. "If you truly mean what you say."

Fuck, fuck, fuck. A blood oath?

My stomach sinks, my eyes darting to Ren, and the briefest flicker of anger marks his face before it settles back into a blank expression.

If I swear my loyalty to King Elion by a blood oath, he will have every ounce of control over me. Any amount of freedom I have would be lost, owned by the king of Elderheim.

Did I ever truly have freedom before?

I inwardly shudder. *No.*

Elion's eyes narrow. "If you successfully take Aurelia and give me information about the Veilstone, I will give you what you want. Once the oath is sworn, you can leave in two weeks, and I will temporarily lift the border at your departure."

"And if I swear this oath, what of the rest of my memories? I want them before I go," I say.

Even though my memories have been slowly returning, memories of Aurelia have yet to plague my dreams, leaving me to believe he has more in his grasp.

His brows lower into a glare. "You're not getting those. Not until you can show me that you can do as I request. Until I get something substantial from Aurelia first—from *you...*" He lets the words linger, and a chill snakes down my spine. "Why else would I give you something that could potentially destroy me? Your memories are tied to your very essence. Aside from the oath, if you want them back, I need something that proves you're loyal to *me*. What will you give me in exchange for fully restoring your essence, hm?"

He hums and descends the dais, deliberately slow, stopping only a foot from me. Then his eyes hold mine, the amber in his irises glowing brighter with every second.

It's like looking in a mirror.

"Is my word—my loyalty—not enough for you?"

"No," he says. "If you want to be whole, I'll need something that proves you're not just spitting pretty words. If you're anything like your mother, you're just as deceitful. For now, a blood oath will spare you from losing any more memories, and after you take Aurelia and give me what I want, I will tell you where your mother is. Do it now. Swear your loyalty to me, and what you want is in your grasp."

He smirks, knowing he has something I desperately want. He raises a dagger, the hard steel gleaming in the morning light, and urges me to extend my palm.

I swallow and fight the urge to flee with a small shake of my head, glancing at the dagger in his hand.

I don't want to do it—I *can't* do it.

Then, a sparkling crystal replaces the dagger in his palm, very similar to my missing memories. It shimmers momentarily before a glowing vision appears right in front of my face. My mother.

Or who I think is her, as she looks the same as she did in Rydian's memories. Her blonde Varethin sits dull at the top of her head. My heart falls as she frantically looks around, held in a stone room, with no windows in sight.

Dirty and alone.

She disappears, and my heart stops. He still has her, and she's alone. Used just like me, locked in the same fucking castle.

"Where is she?" I growl, stepping closer as rage builds behind my eyes.

Elion snaps his fingers, a sound that has me halting my steps, fear tightening in my chest.

Theron steps forward, wearing new, elaborate armor. Not the usual metal for the guards—a deep gold that shimmers as he strides forward, his hateful eyes gleaming from behind his helmet.

Elion raises a hand between us, forming it in the shape of a claw. Within seconds, air is sucked from my lungs, and my breath seizes in my throat. I grit my teeth, enduring the pain, eyes watering.

"You will swear that oath to me if you want to live—if you want your mother," Elion murmurs. "And when you do, Captain Demaris will accompany you to Aurelia in two weeks. If you truly want to serve me, you will find yourself rewarded in ways you can't imagine. But since you currently refuse to cooperate, you're going to have a nice little chat with Theron. You clearly need to be punished for demanding that I cater to you and for stealing that crystal from my archives. Your memories are safe for now… but you are not."

My head spins as I struggle, lungs burning. Then he releases me, and I suck in a sharp breath. Theron prowls forward with a menacing grin as Elion moves back.

He throws his sword to the ground with a clang. The searing heat of magic settles into my hands, and I aim it at his chest. It ripples across his chestplate, fizzling out as if his armor can evaporate it.

My eyes flare, stomach sinking.

This must be what Luke was talking about a few weeks ago—the new weapons and armor for the King. Only this kind is somehow immune to magic—a new problem we don't need at the moment.

I look at Elion, and a menacing grin spreads wide across his face, as if he expects me to put up a fight. *This is a test.*

If I fight Theron, it will look like I'm not loyal to the crown—to Elion—and I'm not willing to risk that. I need to accept my punishment for this to work. Ren cautiously steps down from the dais, eyes solely fixed on me before inching closer, stopping just shy of the King. Then he shifts, as if he's going to stop this.

My throat tightens. For a brief, flickering moment, I cling to the Veil, cling to his mind, and focus on Ren. The Shadovar can speak into anyone's mind, he just can't reply. I only hope that he can hear me.

"Please, don't move. Let this happen."

Ren exhales and braces himself, brows pinching slightly. His eyes flick to Elion, and I force myself to straighten, dropping my hands.

Just as I do, Theron's metal fist slams into my jaw with a sickening crack, sending me crashing to the floor. A heavy boot drives into the side of my ribs, knocking the air from my lungs as I clutch my stomach, crying out.

Pain consumes me as I hold myself, gasping through gritted teeth, enduring each blow, over and over.

Relentless. Brutal.

I helplessly lie there, waiting for it to end. Raging fury settles at the base of my neck, melding with the pain searing across my skin. My body screams in agony, and blood seeps into my eyes, my vision blurring.

Just a few more seconds and it'll be over.

I find myself thinking of Rydian, my memories, my mother—anything to keep me here. Anything to keep me tethered.

As the blows rain down, the minutes drag. I vow to myself that one day I'll kill them—Theron. King Elion. Witt.

The power in my veins slowly dwindles as the punches continue. My breath shallows, and my vision darkens at the edges.

"Your Majesty," Ren interrupts, his tone clipped. "She'll need to heal for the journey. She won't be able to take Aurelia if she's dead."

"She needs to learn," Elion mumbles. "She needs to bleed."

"I agree. But as captain, she's my responsibility…"

The conversation continues, but I hear nothing else as ringing explodes in my ears. I attempt to lift my head to beg Ren not to intervene, but Theron lands one last blow to my face.

Time fades.

Within a few seconds—minutes perhaps—Ren is at my side. A sharp cry escapes me when he lifts me from under my shoulder.

Elion joins him and opens my palm by force. After a moment, a sharp pain bites into my skin. I lift my swollen eyes. Elion cuts his own palm, dropping his blood to the fresh cut on mine.

"Swear your loyalty," Elion demands, the words barely audible over the ringing.

I suck in a shaky breath, my chest rattling. I repeat the words he says to me, my voice barely audible, muffled by the blood between my ears.

Elion grins before a searing, blinding pain scorches my insides, twisting and crawling into something dark. The tingling sensation itches like spiders in my veins.

I drop my head and numbly stare at the floor. Yet for a brief moment, something wild whirls beneath my skin, warm and famil-iar. *Familiar.*

"Keep her in line, Captain," Elion orders. "Witt, come with me and throw that male out near the river," the king orders and then leaves.

My right eye swells, my breaths short and shallow. I whimper when Ren flings my arm over his shoulder, leaving me to dangle in his grasp, my feet barely grazing the ground.

"What have you done?" Ren growls.

I cry out when we slowly begin to move, tears slipping down my cheeks. Lightheaded and dizzy, blood splatters to the floor, puddling at my feet in a whirl of crimson.

"We need to get you to your chambers. Let me carry you and don't fucking protest," he growls again, dipping down to effortlessly lift my legs out from under me. If I weren't in so much pain, I might have dwelled on the concern lacing his tone. The trembling of his hands as he held me.

Or is that the ground?

My pained gasp pulls the air from my lungs, though I focus on resting against his shoulder. With the agonizing throbs searing into my side, I realize that Theron has broken multiple ribs. A sharp pain burns across my jaw as I doze in and out, my head leaden.

"Fates, what happened?" someone asks.

"Can you open the door?"

"Is she going to be okay?" A door creaks open, and then I'm gently set down on something soft, my head falling to the side.

"Bring me hot water, linen, and alcohol. Do it now."

2

———

"We'll be quiet," he says, balancing along the edge of my window as he's done a thousand times before. "No one will notice we're gone. Just for tonight."

I know it's a lie, but with a huff, I quickly find an outfit and strap my favorite daggers to my waist before climbing through the middle window. He always convinces me, regardless of how many times I protest.

It's not the first time I've snuck out, but it's the first time leaving the castle in the middle of the night without a mission. He always does this, though, sneaking in while I'm sleeping.

Does he not know I need my rest? How else will I become an elite assassin for King Elion?

We climb the rise of the castle, vanishing in the shadows with expert stealth. I've just turned seventeen, and he wants me to experience Alvonia at night in honor of my birthday.

A tavern, he'd said. A girl needs to experience her first ale, and he wouldn't miss me having mine.

He throws me a wide grin, the kind that would drive anyone insane, yet I can't help but laugh at the mischief that shines through.

He pulls his hood up, concealed in the shadows as we walk the streets of Alvonia, quiet and stealthy. He always wants me to work on my stealth. I know him like the back of my hand, though, yet our friendship remains hidden, as it has been for the last year.

It's better this way.

As we settle near the back, hidden in the corner, drunk chatter and loud singing fills the tavern air. Couples twirl in the center, dancing around seated guests.

"It's great, isn't it?" he asks, and I scrunch my face in disgust, slamming the glass back down with a thud.

"This is what you wanted me to try? It's awful!" I shout with a laugh. He only grins, sliding me another one, and ale sloshes over the rim.

"Once you have two more, you won't even taste it." He clinks his chilled glass with mine. "Here's to making the most of what we got, even if it's shitty. Happy birthday, wench."

Hours go by, my head buzzing from all the ale, when my arm is yanked back. A searing, sharp pain jolts up from the tightening grip, and I cry out in pain.

A large male with arms the size of my legs gets in my face when I lash out and strike, my throw sloppy. Then a full brawl breaks out, and my friend lunges for the male with precision. He punches hard and fast, square in the male's jaw, before we're running down the streets, our cloaks whirling behind as we race through the darkened corners of Alvonia.

We run until we can't anymore, chests heaving, and end up in a dim alley. Fast and stealthy, just as we practiced.

We always practice.

Our chests quickly rise and fall, pulses surging with adrenaline against our ribs like something wild and forbidden. Laughter bubbles up, us having escaped our assailants with ease, before we finally head back to the castle, making it back in one piece.

Tomorrow is going to drag with training bright and early, but I wonder what tomorrow night will bring.

And regardless of how many times I protest, I'm always looking forward to the familiar tap of his dagger on my window in the middle of the night.

I jolt awake with a quiet gasp, nausea curling in my stomach and drenched in sweat.

For a long moment, I lie still, squeezing my eyes shut as the layer between dreams and my dreadful returning memories thins. The question brands my mind—was it only a dream or a memory? I force my breath to slow, and eventually, the spinning subsides.

Then the pain returns.

Upon waking fully, the events of what happened flood me—King Elion, Theron, the beating... the oath.

Lifting my arm with a wince, I brush trembling fingers over my right eye and flinch. It's swollen shut. My tongue flicks over my lips, meeting the sharp sting of split, tender skin. Still sore.

Still very fucking sore.

I shift slightly, pressing a hand over my abdomen and nearly biting through my lip to avoid crying out in pain. A sharp, unwelcome scent hits me—iron.

With a glance down, I realize I'm still wearing the same blood-stained outfit I had on before Theron beat me senseless. Then the faint, colorless mark on my wrist catches my attention. I sharply inhale.

My second matemark, the one tied to Elderheim.

I discovered its origin shortly after Milena restored my memories... only I have no idea who it belongs to. *If* it belongs to anyone, though the ache that sometimes blooms in my wrist tells me it does.

I look across the room and find Ren slumped back in the chair near the fire, asleep, his arms folded with a stone dagger firm in his grip, even in rest. It's dim. Early morning or evening, but I'm not sure.

How long has it been?

Fire crackles softly in the hearth, breaking up the dreadful silence. I sit upright, and a soft cry finally slips free. My ribs are definitely broken.

Ren stirs, swiveling his head, and is on his feet within seconds. A flicker of worry flashes across his face before he masks it with a clenched jaw.

"Can't you rest for once?" he grumbles.

"I just want… to bathe," I get out, breath rattling in my chest. He mutters something before stabilizing me at the edge of the bed.

"If you didn't look like shit, I'd scold you for having the worst plan I've ever seen. If that was even a plan. What were you thinking?"

If I weren't in so much pain, I might've laughed. But when I lift my gaze, breath dies in my throat. A black bruise blooms around his eye and along the left side of his face. Ugly and fresh, as if he took his own beating from Theron. Or the King, perhaps. Did he step in?

"What did you do?" I say on an exhale.

"Nothing."

"Doesn't look like… nothing." I wince, my jaw screaming when I try to grind my teeth. I swat him away with a trembling hand. "I can do it myself."

"Fine." Ren backs off a step, arms crossed. He watches me wobble and then steps forward again with a sigh. "Will you stop being difficult?"

"No." I glare. "How long has it been?"

"A few hours. You've been slipping in and out since I brought you back," he says, then his voice softens. "They killed Rydian. They tossed him out by the river."

Relief washes over me—Rydian got out.

I screw my eyes shut and attempt to tether myself to Rydian through the Veil—grasp it in my mind. It pulses in dull thuds then fades away like a misted shadow between my fingers. I'm too injured to reach him.

"Isa," Ren says when I don't reply.

I huff, but then a slow smile grows on my face when a thought surfaces. If only he knew about how Rydian cannot die. Not from a regular blade, at least. Though the panic I felt in the throne room reminds me that, for a moment, I thought he did. Watching him slump to the floor had me grappling for control.

Ren leans down, face inches from mine. His hands come up, lifting my chin to tilt my head back. Something flickers behind his eyes—concern and something else I can't quite decipher. I hold his stare and push one of his hands away before I give him a small, knowing grin.

"Did you hear me—" Ren's voice cuts, his brows pinching as if I've completely lost my mind. "Why are you smiling?"

My mouth opens to respond, and I wince again.

"Hold on. I had Silas get healing drafts from the weavers in Alvonia. You'll need another one tomorrow. It won't rid the bruises, but it'll dull the pain. Speed your healing." Ren reaches for a vial on the table near the door.

"Thanks," I say breathlessly. "Would've been nice to know… before I tried sitting up."

He uncorks the vial then gently tilts my head back. The bitter draft burns my throat, and I scowl as it slides down. The pain in my ribs eases a little, and warmth settles in my stomach.

"It wasn't Alec," I rasp, my voice scratchy. "When we killed Rydian in Sylvanor."

"Sylvanor?" His jaw tightens.

I nod. "He showed me his memories. I knew who he was when we killed him." I lift my gaze, refusing to miss his reaction. As I suspected, his face pales. I brand my mind with this memory, a grin tugging at my mouth.

"You should really see your face right now," I chuckle, regretting it as I clutch my ribs.

"You should see yours," he clips before his eyes go distant. He steps away as realization sweeps in. But I wobble again, unable to hold myself upright without him, and he lurches forward to catch me.

Another wince. "When you caught me… by the trees, he shifted into Alec. He can only die by the Veilblade, something we don't have."

"I killed the king of Aurelia?"

"And he came back… then let you live," I breathe. "Puts him into perspective for you, doesn't it?"

He says nothing, only helps me stand, inching me closer to the bathing chamber. I wobble before he leans me against the wall so he can start the bath. He throws in soaps and linens as I finally catch my reflection from across the chamber.

Unease coils in my stomach.

My dark hair is crusted with the blood from my forehead, a gash at the hairline, smeared with blood. As if someone had attempted to clean it. My right eye is sealed shut, a dark black and purple mark forming around the area. Ren was right, I look terrible.

Gods, I *feel* terrible.

It was the worst beating I'd received from Theron, though I'm typically strung up by my wrists. This time, he hadn't held back, and I could do nothing but lie there and take it. Ren takes my hand, guiding me to the edge of the bath, and I groan, limping forward.

"Thank you," I say, brows pinching as my eyes land on his black bruise again. "Why did you do it?"

His brows lower, but instead of answering, he exhales slowly—controlled, deliberate. His eyes skim over my face, as if memorizing every bruise and cut. But when he finally speaks, his voice remains steady.

"I should have done more," he murmurs, but a coldness settles in his eyes, dark and distant. "And by the time we leave this castle, Witt is going to bleed for this—for all of it. There will be nothing left of him to return to."

A shiver runs down my spine.

He doesn't need to elaborate for me to know that he will make Witt's death torturous, carving out every inch of his body until he begs for it to stop. No, Ren will take his time, ensuring Witt feels every scrape of his blade. A reassuring thought, but…

"We can't do it yet." I shake my head. He opens his mouth to argue, but I say, "We can't kill him when we leave, or Elion will keep us here… he'd kill us for it. We need to get to Aurelia." I release another strained breath, but Ren's eyes meet mine, his jaw clenching slightly before he nods. "I didn't want you to step in, anyway. It needed to happen."

Yet somehow, he convinced King Elion not to kill me so we could travel to Aurelia in one piece. So Theron wouldn't kill me. And he did that by taking his own beating.

"I'm sorry for not telling you," he mumbles, and my brows pinch. I assume he's talking about the loss of our friendship—when I couldn't remember. I didn't realize he felt so guilty for not telling me.

Before I can reply, he turns to leave. Unfortunately, I can't move without wincing, and although the healing draft helped, the majority of my pain throbs in my shoulder and ribs. I bite my cheek, hating that I need help—hating that I have to ask. It's not like I have a choice, though, not now anyway.

"Ren, wait," I get out and almost groan. "Can—can you help me?" The question comes out wary, but he stops halfway to the door and pivots toward me with a blank expression. He blinks, and silence permeates the air.

Then he asks, "Can you lift your arms?"

"I... no. I can't lift the left one. I think it's out of place," I grunt, closing my eyes when he reaches my side. He feels my shoulder with prodding fingers, inspecting, and attempts to lift my arm when I let out a soft cry.

"It's dislocated," he says, eyes meeting mine for a moment. "We need to reset it before it causes you more pain."

"Right now?"

A blank stare. "Yes, unless you want to walk around without being able to use your arm."

I sigh and give him a slow, cautious nod, gritting my teeth. He gently grabs the crook of my shoulder and lifts slowly. With a quick snap up, the bone slides into place with a loud pop. My teeth grind, jaw screaming as a blinding red-hot pain shoots down my arm.

"Seriously?" I bite out, rolling my shoulder back, but at least I can move it. Only now, my entire arm is throbbing. He steps in front of me and reaches down, unlacing my pants without a word. His head dips in the space between us.

"Take them off," he says.

Heat rises in my face from embarrassment over not being able to do it myself. I cover it up with a smirk despite the constant pain throughout my body and gently kick them off. I push them to the side, catching a glimpse of his unamused glare.

"Good to know your humor is still there," he grumbles, and I huff out a quiet chuckle. "It's going to hurt, but I think we can lift it over your head." He reaches for the hem of my tunic.

"Just cut the damn thing off already, I'm not lifting my arm again," I clip, bracing myself.

I expect him to draw one of his stone daggers, but instead, he grips the collar at the back of my tunic. With a brutal, swift motion, he rips it down the middle, causing me to wince from the jolt. I catch his gaze over the top of my head. A small grin forms on his lips as my ribs scream in pain.

"A little gentler would be nice," I hiss, holding the fabric in place from the front, but he ignores me.

"Can you get in by yourself?" he asks, and I nod. "Call for me when you're done, and I'll help you."

Without another word, he exits and shuts the door behind him. I glance in the mirror once more, staring at my reflection—at someone who looks like me coated in old blood and fresh wounds.

But my eyes drift to the colorless mark on my wrist, pulsing with the faintest glow, and an ache I can't ignore much longer.

3

My pulse races, and I suck in a few sharp breaths, willing my heart rate to slow. I pull myself out of another haunting memory.

Ever since I left Milena's, they've done nothing but plague my dreams—emotions and feelings pushed back into me as if they'd never left.

Peeling my eyes open, I find myself in my own bed again, dressed in something far more comfortable than the bloody clothes I was previously wearing. Something soft and light.

How did I manage to get back into bed?

The last thing I remember is bathing, cleaning the blood off, and resting my head on the rim of the tub. The healing draft eased my pain, but I must have fallen asleep, meaning Ren saw me—helped me.

Did he dress me too?

I quietly groan at the thought and sit up, still in pain but not nearly as bad. My fingers gently graze my ribs, which are surprisingly not as sore, and my right eye feels less swollen.

Ren's asleep on the floor, and a pile of food sits on the table near the door. Yet his items scatter the room—shirts, pants, his weapons thrown across the chairs.

By all means, make yourself at home.

And as if right on cue, my stomach growls as the scent of sharp cheese fills my senses. It's dark, and the fire is out. A brisk chill blankets the room. I glance outside. The sun rises over the snowy mountain in the distance. It must be early.

Reaching over, I toss a pillow at Ren's head, causing him to jolt awake. He grunts, throwing an arm over his face, his dark hair falling to his temples from the force of the throw.

"Why are you asleep on my floor? Don't you have a room?" I ask, wondering why he feels that it's necessary to sleep at my feet like an animal.

"Did you think I was going to let you sleep in here alone after what happened?" he asks, voice husky from sleep. He turns to look at me from beneath his elbow. "King Elion said you're my responsibility."

My brows pinch in confusion.

"Well, you're not staying in my room for two weeks." I huff. "How long have I been asleep?"

He groans, sitting up. "Two days. And yeah, about our journey. Are you going to tell me what the hell happened the other day? We need to discuss that blood oath you swore."

I swallow, and squeeze my eyes shut. The blood oath. Two days?

Gods, I haven't spoken to Rydian since that night. If he's not already, he's going to be angry when we finally talk. I sit there, palms pushed against my eyes as I process the chaos that's happened over the last few days, and stifle my rising panic. But I worry about him.

Did he heal fully or was his power too drained? Will he even speak to me? The betrayal I saw in his gaze before leaves me to believe that he won't, and my heart cracks.

"*Rydian?*" I push the thought into the Veil and hold onto the familiarity of his presence, hoping he's close enough to hear me. *"Are you okay? Please say something. We're fine. I'm fine. But we need to talk and I'm… sorry."* I wonder where he's ended up, but only silence greets me.

"Isa," Ren says impatiently.

I sigh, opening my eyes to face the inevitable.

"Witt caught Rydian and I in the archives. He brought us to Elion," I confess, instantly regretting the explanation when Ren's face contorts with rage. He steadily inhales, as if fighting the urge to shout.

"You both should have waited." He shakes his head, shoving a hand through his hair. "He risked the safety of both of you when we could have created a plan with Orin and Ivy. What were you thinking?"

"I wasn't, okay?" I snap. "We discovered there was a second half of the map. I know it was a mistake, but I forced Rydian to go. He was the one who told me to wait, but I..." I exhale with a shake of my head and look out the window.

He's right, of course.

Forcing Rydian to go with me was entirely my fault. I was too impatient. *Impulsive.* But I knew my mother was alive—I was eager to find her. To reunite and go to Aurelia to begin my future with Rydian.

Now that plan is shit. Now we're stuck, forced to work for the King and aid in his journey to find the Veilstone on a blood oath. Gods, what did I do?

Ren growls. "You thought meeting with Elion was a better idea than fighting your way out of the archives? I trained you better than that. You would have been able to get out, I've seen you fight—"

"Yes!" I shout, though shame and anger rise in my chest as I fling myself off the bed, my fingers curling into fists. "We discovered the *rest* of his plan. Discovering that felt far more important than waiting around, hoping to find something about my mother. We had no leads, and we'd been sitting around for weeks, burying our noses in that map for nothing. I'm sorry for not waiting, truly, but you're fine and so is Rydian, even if he's furious with me. We'll find him on the journey." My hands tremble with rage as my stomach sinks. I'm afraid to ask my next question. "Did you know Ezra was the King's second-in-command?"

"No," he says with a small shake of his head.

"Did you know?" I repeat, unable to take the ache in my heart if he did. Since the guards in the archives had acted as if they knew Ezra was the second-in-command, I've been questioning who else might've known and kept it from me.

Ren's brows lower. He shakes his head again, his tone softer. "No, Isa, I didn't know. Ezra behaved the same as any one of us. I didn't know he was anyone important until King Elion had me in the throne room that night. I swear."

I turn and look out the window, almost expecting Ire to be perched outside. Only cold, harsh winter winds beat against the glass.

"What you did was selfish."

"I *know*." I groan, turning back. "And it cost us, but at least we know the extent of what Elion is planning."

Ren crosses his arms as we stare at each other in silence, but the anger on his face slowly disappears. He walks to the table near the door, grabs the last healing draft, and hands it to me with a glass of water.

His features soften. "Okay."

"Okay?" I squint, suspicious.

"Yes, okay. And I'm sorry."

I laugh in disbelief. "Are you apologizing to me, brute?"

His serious, gray eyes skim my face before narrowing. "Don't get used to it. We need to devise a plan for the next eleven days until we leave. And we need to discuss that oath."

"The oath," I sigh, nodding. "What do we know about blood oaths?"

He gives me a blank stare, then scratches the back of his head. "There are different types of blood oaths for different... reasons— like marriage oaths, claimings, and fealty bonds. But they all have one thing in common, which is a tie to your essence."

"And the one I swore to Elion?"

He sighs, grimacing. "It can't be broken. When royalty binds their blood to someone by an oath, their essence bonds with the recipient's magic. You won't be able to lie to him or speak of that oath to any one outside of Elderheim. And if he pulls a summons, even across the realms, you have to answer. Your magic will torture you for disobeying and will bend to him if he commands it. You spoke a fealty oath, meaning there are no repercussions for him. You are at his disposal."

Fighting the tears that prick my eyes, I focus on the wall behind Ren, as if every ounce of guilt pounds into me at once. Not just guilt, but shame too, as the oath I swore just ruined any chance of gaining Rydian's trust again.

"He should've just killed me." I shake my head. "He should have—"

"I think you know what would have happened in that room if he had attempted it," Ren declares.

My breath catches, and for a long moment I say nothing. Neither he nor Rydian would have allowed that to happen, regardless of my mistakes.

Regardless of the blood oath I swore.

I only give him a small nod and reach for my water, swallowing the lump in my throat. "I think we should continue what's normal —train and go back to routine unless the King states otherwise. And you do whatever it is... captains do. I want to walk through the castle in the Veil to see if I can discover anything about that armor Elion's making."

Another wince from Ren. "I don't think you should do that."

"I don't think I have a choice at the moment," I say dryly. "I'll be careful. I'll do it at night when it's quiet. I'd also like to see what you can find out as captain. If anyone can easily get information, it would be you, meaning we need to continue to hate each other." Despite myself, a small grin pulls free as I sip from my cup.

If Elion grows suspicious of us working together, I fear he'd swap Ren out for Witt when it's time to leave for Aurelia. So, hating him for the time being seems like my only option.

"Easy enough for me." He gives me a wry smile, eyes gleaming with quiet amusement—the feeling oddly familiar.

My eyes land on his jaw, missing the usual scruff. I sigh after a moment, because despite my many mistakes, he's still here.

"Do you trust me?" I ask.

He gives me a look that says I already know the answer, but he nods anyway. I walk to my cloak, draped across the settee, and reach into the pocket. My fingers clutch the familiar weight that settles there. I extend my hand. "I stole this for you."

His fingers brush mine as he grabs the crystal swirling violently in gray, mirroring the color of his eyes. His expression shifts, eyes widening in disbelief as a lock of onyx hair falls to his brow.

"What is this?"

"It's your… memories," I say, and swallow, recalling my dream of a boy with brown hair that looked a lot like Ren.

Was it a dream or a memory?

It's hard to say, but I know giving him the crystal is the right thing to do. I only hope that whatever memories whirl inside, it's what he needs.

"I suspected they took them at some point," I explain, "especially when you didn't know who Witt was. I looked while I was in the archives."

His eyes snap to mine.

I had spotted the chest near King Elion's desk, containing hundreds of crystals. Yet for some reason, Ren's sparkled the brightest. I knew it was his the moment I saw it swirling in the corner—the only gray crystal out of the bunch—and trusted my instinct.

"Are you… sure it's mine?" His voice drops, though anger marks his face. *Welcome to my world.*

"Yes. I assume the King only suspects that I'd taken my own. I don't think he'll notice yours being gone," I say with a small smile. But I remember all the crystals in that chest, some with names etched onto the bottom and some without—names in the Brotherhood.

Could that be why so many of the guards didn't seem to know Witt was second-in-command? If they knew, someone would have said something… right? Whatever the King is hiding, he must have taken everyone's memories to cover it up.

"Thank you," he says, placing it inside his cloak.

"When we leave, we'll go to Milena and see if she can put them back… if you want them." I shrug.

"What about Rydian and the others?"

"I'll attempt to reach him through the Veil and hope he doesn't strangle me. Maybe he'll listen long enough before attempting it," I laugh half-heartedly, though the joke falls flat. "I'm not sure I want to leave the castle just yet."

Ren nods, placing his weapons in his sheaths. "Elion has ordered extra security—guards on every corner. If you sneak around, you'll need to remain in the Veil."

He swings his cloak over his shoulders, clasping it at his neck.

I stifle my annoyance. Elion knows I could cut down whoever gets in my way. But I won't. Not if I want this to work, so I'll just go along with this little game of his.

I'll use the Veil, but right now I don't want anyone searching for me, and I won't risk Ren getting caught in my chamber—we can't be seen talking unless we're arguing. I sigh and rub my temples. Just one more hurdle to get through.

"Will you train with me?" I ask.

He pushes open my window, the metal creaking, then pivots just enough to flash me a grin over his shoulder. "If it means I get to kick your ass."

I smirk. "I won last time, remember? How's your thigh?"

Our last spar a couple of years back had led to him cutting off my air supply before I ended the intense session by sinking my blade into his leg. At the time, I thought he was going to kill me, but now...

"I let you win." His grin lingers for a moment before he slips through the window and onto the roof on silent feet.

4

Sweat drips from my temple as I jolt left, narrowly missing the fist shooting toward my face.

This morning, Luke and I were ordered to train in combat. All because Xane refused to partner with me, eyes wide and frightened as if I'd attempt to kill him during a simple sparring session. Luke's bronzed skin glistens with sweat, and although he's the Brotherhood's best tracker, his endurance is shit.

It's been five days, and regardless of how often I enter the Veil, how often I brush my thoughts against Rydian's, he continues to ignore me. Not a single word, and it's beginning to terrify me.

But I know he's close by.

I know this because a shiver of cold fury brushes my mind every once in a while, reminding me what awaits once we reunite. Though the silence between us weighs heavier than his rage, coiling tight in my chest as guilt and shame claw at my insides.

A part of me aches to beg, to push until he has no choice but to speak, but another part of my mind whispers that his silence is mercy. That his words would only cut me, and for the first time in a long while, it's a moment I fear the most.

Our boots scrape against the stone as we quickly weave in and out, steps light and nimble. My hands protect my face when Luke throws another combination of punches toward me. Dodging them in a blur of movement, I lunge forward with my fist, barely missing his jaw as he darts back.

The arena easily occupies the space of a small meadow with a path around the perimeter and benches near the back. But today, young orphans sit at the edge of the arena, varying in age, watching us spar to learn new techniques. Their eyes are focused, some with their fists clenched, as if eager to test it themselves.

Theo is nowhere in sight, though, and worry tightens in my chest. I haven't seen the young Siphon since Ren and I delivered him to King Elion weeks ago. Are they using him? Where is he?

Luke and I circle each other when he throws his fist, forcing me to sidestep. I narrowly avoid the hit as my thoughts pull me under. My braid sways with the movement, and I give him a sly grin, attempting to kick his left side.

He grunts and jumps back, sweeping his leg out, an attempt to pull my feet out from under me, but I anticipate the move and leap back. Sven, the lead combat instructor, steps forward and motions for us to stop sparring.

"I hope each of you studied their swift and calculated movements. Pair up," Sven orders, and the orphans begin to pair off, each one finding a place in the arena.

We're drenched in sweat, our temples dripping as we step away and quickly find our flasks. Luke silently eyes me, giving me a slight once over when a knowing smirk raises on the corners of his mouth.

"I'm disappointed the heir of Elderheim didn't put me on my ass," he says with a smug grin. "I also wanted to teach you a lesson, but I don't think your *father* would've been too happy with that." As if that was the reason he was terrible today.

My breaths slow while I quietly assess him, confident and calm, and the gleam in his eyes tells me he's trying to provoke me. Push to see if I snap. I remain silent, refusing to give him that satisfaction.

As the biggest gossip, he's no doubt the reason I've been hearing whispers of *daughter* and *heir* in between spars. Rumors travel fast, but I assumed it was the guards from that night spreading the information. Yet, Luke somehow caught wind of it and is now taunting me.

I give a flat smile, mumbling, "Laugh all you want, they're wiping everyone's memories, including yours."

His lips part, face paling. A long, silent moment passes before his jaw sets, as if everything clicked into place. As if it all just made *sense*. His eyes flick toward the doors.

"Not so funny now, is it?" I taunt.

Ren and Witt walk through the arena doors, both with lowered brows. Ren wears a black tunic that opens at the chest, clad in every weapon he owns. He motions me over, jaw clenched tight as he talks to Witt. His self-control is much stronger than mine, apparently.

Luckily for us, Ren hasn't had an issue with pretending to hate me since he's had so much practice over the last few years. My boots thud against the stone as I approach, and I can't help the sneer on my face as Witt's gaze locks with mine.

My chest tightens as memories of us flood to the surface.

Witt places a hand on his hip, eyes on Ren. "We'll need a few from the Brotherhood. I want Luke and Xane there beside King Elion's guards."

"You needed me, Captain Demaris?" I force a tight smile.

"You are to join the formal dinner tonight as a royal and have orders to visit Karina this afternoon."

The castle's seamstress.

"What?" I say with a rough exhale.

My brows rise, composure cracking over his casual words. I study them as a chill crawls up my neck.

Does this mean King Elion has accepted me as his daughter? Who else knows about my heritage? Up until now, I had only caught rumors throughout the halls. I didn't realize it was official, as there was no mention of it being formally announced. Not that I expected Elion to make those arrangements... but still.

"Who else knows Elion is my father?" I ask hesitantly.

"Everyone." Ren smirks. "You want to behave like a royal, you'll be treated like a royal. So, you'll need to prepare for tonight."

Everyone? What does *that* mean?

Witt shoots Ren a glare and casually sighs, so similar to the Ezra I knew—the carefree demeanor of my former best friend—and my breath catches.

"King Elion reached out to the current ruler of Aurelia, and he agreed to meet," Witt says. "King Rydian Vaelborne will be joining us tonight with a few of his court members to discuss your upcoming travels."

I stiffen, my chest too hot at the mention of Rydian. Granted, I thought we would travel into Aurelia and find him on the journey... but that doesn't seem to be the case. This was never a part of the plan.

And he's agreed to dinner. Fuck.

I look at Ren, but he only blinks, his face devoid of all emotion. Gods, I wish I could read his thoughts.

"Don't look so surprised, Princess; it's just dinner," Ren says casually, arms folding.

"Don't call me that," I snarl, stepping toward him, but Witt puts an arm in front of me, holding me back.

My face whips right. "Don't touch me."

Witt holds my gaze and slowly drops his arm. Ren's brows lower, his hands curling and faintly trembling as he settles his glare on Witt. Barely controlled rage.

A grating silence hovers between us, and I glance over my shoulder. It's not just us who's quiet, but everyone around us as well. Sven quickly gets the orphans back to work before I turn my gaze back to Ren.

"Enough, Captain," Witt growls, then turns back to me. "I'll escort you from Karina's this evening."

"You will not," I hiss, my palms heating. Now that I know the truth about him, a simmering rage consumes me. I clench my fists. "You are the last person I want to be around because *you* are the reason I'm in this mess in the first place—stealing my memories. I'd rather chew fucking glass."

Witt's brows lower a fraction, and I catch the smirk Ren's fighting, watching me unleash my rage on the king's second-in-command.

Ren clears his throat. "Well, it's either me or Witt. Regardless, you'll be escorted by one of us."

"Fine. Captain Demaris will escort me," I bite out. "If that's all, Captain, I'll see you tonight."

Ren gives me a curt nod as anger continues to simmer beneath my skin. Pivoting sharply toward the exit, I grit my teeth when Witt calls my name. Within a single breath, my control shatters entirely, and I'm snarling inches from his face.

"I have nothing to say to you, Witt Dralor." I spit his name like a curse. His eyes narrow, scanning my face as if he's just pieced together something important.

Ren's fingers twitch near his daggers, but he remains otherwise still, almost breathless. He'd fight with me if it came down to it, which is the only reason I don't.

"I may be working for the king, but I want *nothing* to do with you," I snarl.

"Are you going to punish me for following orders? I was just doing my job." Witt practically purrs the words, though his hazel eyes lock onto mine, and I hate the fact that I notice how his hair is cut short again. "You'll have to talk to me sooner or later."

A soft, menacing chuckle escapes me before I can stop it, and I step closer. The movement forces him to take a cautious step back. He eyes me as my tone drops.

"You know, the king wouldn't even mourn you. I could kill you right now, and I bet he'd replace you before you even hit the ground."

Elion had already sat in the throne room, watching my wrath unfold on Witt without so much as a second glance toward him. Witt is nothing—he will only ever be a tool for Elion to use, just like me. Just like the Brotherhood and everyone in this godsforsaken castle.

"You're replaceable," I say, catching Ren's small smile from behind Witt.

Witt looks off to the side, stuffing his hands in his pockets and then clenches his jaw. His gaze slides back to me—slow and cold.

Calculated.

His mask flips, and I quickly realize that I'm speaking to the real Witt. His voice raises the hair on my arms. "I'm sure you'll get your chance to end me soon enough."

I say nothing, only turn on my heel and exit, the door swinging shut behind me as his low chuckle pierces the air.

5

———

This dinner is a mistake.

Regret sits heavily on my shoulders. If I had told *someone* who King Elion was to me...

Perhaps I wouldn't be going to this dinner at all. And that maybe, just maybe, I'd be curled up next to Rydian on a settee somewhere in Aurelia.

Regardless of those feelings, I also know that I did the right thing in the moment, because we're one step closer to getting my mother. But I want my mother and my memories back—aching for them in a way I didn't believe possible.

Ren and I silently walk toward the Great Hall, my emerald gown detailed in gold, sweeping the floor. The neckline plunges, framing my collarbones before reaching the edge of my shoulders. Long, loose sleeves flare to my wrists. The intricate gold bodice sculpts my waist, the long skirt falling off my hips in layers of silk.

Yet dread consumes me; the anticipation of this dinner has had me sick all day. Rydian will arrive with members of his court, and the thought of him being here at all unsettles me. I can't shake the worry that gnaws at my thoughts, hoping that tonight will at least go smoothly. We stop just outside the Great Hall when Ren faces me.

"If anything happens—if something goes wrong, we leave," he says, his voice barely above a whisper.

I nod, saying nothing while I stare at the doors sealing us from what awaits on the other side of them. The moment I step foot beyond their oiled hinges, my life will change.

"Look at me," Ren demands, and my eyes flick to him. "Blood oath or not, we will find a way to leave."

"Okay," I breathe, and he pushes the door open.

The scent of aged oak instantly hits me, mingling with the savory roasted meats wafting from the kitchens. Theron, Witt, and Elion are in a quiet discussion near the head of the table that's centered in the room. Large enough to seat twelve—five chairs on each side with a single chair on each end—which, I assume, are meant for the kings.

A golden runner centers the table, small candles lining its length, and at each place is a dinner setting. Fine porcelain and crystal chalices, accompanied by a variety of cutlery, sit on either side of the plates. To the left is an entire wall made of glass, and connected to it are double doors leading to the front of the castle.

Instinctively scanning the room, my stomach drops at the sight of Ekrin Highcrest in a deep discussion with Caius Kleren, the Duke of Arcan. *Shit.*

The last time I saw Ekrin, I was under the guise of Sensa Blackwyth at the Aurorafest. Sometime between then and now, I had forgotten that the dukes were a part of King Elion's council. Of course, if Rydian is bringing his own members, so would Elion.

But does Ekrin know who I am now?

Surely, or he wouldn't be here. Ekrin's eyes briefly meet mine before returning to his conversation, and if he was surprised, it doesn't show. King Elion pivots only to give us both a once-over. His grimy smirk has my hands curling into fists, but I remain at Ren's side, and straighten my spine.

"Lovely to see you arrive on time," Elion grumbles, striding toward us. "Our guests are almost here. You are to sit and be quiet if you know what's good for you. If they talk to you, you may reply, but nothing more."

He throws a casual glance towards a grinning Theron from across the room, sending a chill down my spine. His body is free of the new armor, and I wonder if it's to hide their latest creation. But if Theron touches me tonight, I can't guarantee I'll idly stand by and let it happen this time.

A guard walks through the large glass door, announcing Rydian's arrival, and my stomach sinks. My palms sweat as my feet pull me toward the doors, trailing behind Elion. Ren walks beside me, both of us stopping a few feet away. I place my arm beneath his to hold me steady.

Elion steps beyond those glass doors at the front of the castle just as Rydian, Ivy, Orin, and two males I don't recognize ascend the wide stairs.

Theron steps beside me, standing a few inches shorter than Ren, and I instinctively stiffen. His scarred hands rest on the hilts of his swords, and his eyes are full of a hate I can't comprehend. I glance up, catching the glare down his crooked nose—features that clearly show he's in his fourth decade of life.

He faces forward, mumbling under his breath. "You're healing so… nicely. It's a shame you didn't scar, even though I tried my best to mark up that pretty face of yours since you can't seem to keep your mouth shut." He chuckles, and I fight the racing of my pulse.

Although the healing drafts have sealed the cut across my temple, bruises still mark my face. The one across my jaw remains sore, and the mottled green circling my right eye still has days left before fading entirely.

Ren stiffens and then casually drops my hand, walking behind me to stand next to Theron. My breath catches when he gently nudges me aside, away from Theron's gaze, but his movements remain casual, as if he were merely speaking to Theron as a captain.

Even if Ren's expression is unreadable, the way his shoulders tighten tells me he's stifling a growing fury. He glares down at Theron before huffing a quiet, menacing laugh. The kind of dark laugh I'm used to hearing on missions.

"Save it for later, would you?" Ren grumbles.

The weight of Theron's presence immediately retreats from my shoulders, a pang of sadness creeping in at Ren's willingness to step in. Witt would have never done that for me—he *didn't* do that for me, I remind myself. Not in the days we were supposed to be friends.

No, friends would have stepped in regardless of the consequences... right?

Theron strides across the room to hold his position near the head of the table, the clip of his boots fading across the marble. I sigh, my shoulders dropping ever so slightly.

"You good?" Ren murmurs.

I nod when he resumes his spot on my right, and keep my eyes fixed ahead.

As Elion greets each Shadovar guest, I fight the nausea twisting low. My nerves burn as they all nod in return. Everyone piles their hands on top of each other, and Elion speaks the phrase that allows each foreign guest to enter.

It feels as if time stops entirely and I hold my breath, hoping that whatever happens, Elion doesn't sense that I've already given the majority of them access to the castle.

He wouldn't be able to notice that... would he?

My pulse races at the thought. Ren squeezes my hand but doesn't move as we watch what could end the entire dinner. And just like that, everyone walks right through the glass doors. Rydian's expression—controlled and uncaring—doesn't falter, as he ignores my presence altogether. Regardless, my pulse flutters with relief at the sight of him.

Gods, he's breathtaking and frightening all at once.

He stands tall in his true form, nothing like the human he presented in the throne room. A long-sleeved crimson-colored tunic sits taut across his chest, and a black cloak of shadows trail behind him. He places his hands in his pockets, subtly scanning the room with the face of a king.

His jaw feathers as he looks around then lingers on Theron, probably a little longer than he should. A black crown sits on his head, and a single point sits in the center of his brow. The other delicate points hold a slew of dark red rubies and amber stones. He glances left, and that's when I notice that his mark is missing. The patch of cut hair is neatly hidden within his auburn strands. If I hadn't known he had one, I would never have noticed it.

Is he hiding his mark?

My eyes shift to Ivy and Orin as they step beside him, both dressed to fight. Though I couldn't imagine Ivy wearing a dress, not here anyway. The two unknown males stand behind them.

"This is my daughter, Princess Isa, and Captain Ren Demaris," Elion says.

"I'm sorry," I say finally, pushing the thought out as I had for the last few days.

His eyes momentarily flick to me, his body stiffening slightly, before he gives me a subtle once-over. It takes everything for me not to cower under his gaze. He reaches out to shake Ren's hand, jaw tight.

"Captain," Rydian says, giving Ren a firm nod and his own once-over, lingering on his face. On the bruise there.

Then Rydian's fury abruptly scorches my thoughts, and my breath hitches, my chest so hot from the invasive emotion that it creeps to my face. For the first time in five days, his voice enters my mind.

"Who did that to you?" The words come out smooth—calm even— but there's a warning in his tone.

An underlying promise of a future punishment for whoever marked my face. I find myself unable to answer. I stand beside Ren with my lips slightly parted, spine straight as he intently holds my gaze.

"Answer me before I tear this entire room apart."

"Theron," I say quickly, blinking as Rydian turns the other way.

Elion continues his introductions, motioning to Witt and the two dukes next to Ren. "These are members of my council: Ekrin Highcrest, Caius Kleren, and Witt Dralor. Ekrin and Caius are the dukes of Alvonia and Arcan, and Witt is my second-in-command."

I assume the Dukes of Nymara and Eldryn weren't able to make the trip due to the last-minute plans. Rydian hardly acknowledges them before sliding his controlled, icy expression back to Elion.

Ekrin's brow arches, his eyes flicking from Rydian to me and glinting with amusement. My pulse skips, recalling how he discovered me by scent alone as an Herb Weaver. He's likely scenting Rydian and the other Shadovar's blood now. He wouldn't be able to scent me *on* Rydian... would he?

"Let's sit, shall we?" Elion briskly walks past in a swift breeze to the head of the table.

Luke and Xane are armed and positioned by a few guards in the back with Theron hovering nearby. Ren's grip gently tightens on my arm, guiding me firmly to the section where we'll be sitting.

Orin claims a seat on my left, leaving an empty chair between us. The young silver-haired male slowly lowers himself into a chair across from me, seating himself next to Witt. The air grows thick as everyone settles, scraping their chairs against the floor.

Rydian leans back, his movements slow and deliberate, almost lazy. His elbows rest on the arms of his seat, his hand drifting up to graze his jaw while he assesses each person carefully. His calculating gaze sweeps across the table, authority radiating like an uncontrolled blade.

He doesn't speak, but he doesn't need to.

A heavy silence settles, and after a moment, Elion flicks his wrist and lights the candles in the center.

"Let's get started," Elion says casually, gesturing to the maidens to bring out the wine, as if he didn't wage a battle with Aurelia a few short years ago.

"You claim she is the missing princess," Rydian says, his voice deep and resonant, carrying the weight of each word.

"Business before dinner?" Elion asks, brows lowering before leaning forward. "You haven't even introduced your council to me yet, but I see you're missing one."

Rydian shrugs with a careless wave of his hand. "I'd like to get to the point." Then he casually points to each member of his council, starting on his right. "Orin Mikara, Ivy Salaric, Eldric Linov, and

Wayd Blackfell. Members of my council, the other one couldn't make it."

Wayd—his name echoes in my thoughts, a brush of familiarity. This must be who Orin mentioned before they left with the map.

Elion's lips press into a thin line, and the faintest flicker of annoyance crosses his face before he exhales.

"Very well," Elion says, though tension simmers beneath the surface. "I'd like to discuss the bargaining for the missing princess."

Rydian's gaze narrows slightly, and his eyes flick to me before landing back on Elion. "The *so-called* princess you *claim* to have," Rydian drawls, letting the doubt in his voice fester. "Since there's no confirmation that it's even her. You called her your *daughter,* after all. She cannot be the Princess of Aurelia if you claim her as your own," he points out just as dinner is placed in front of us. Still, I remain quiet while the others begin to eat.

Elion chuckles. "Ah, yes, the only important question. Allow me to explain, and I'll make sure it's worth your while."

"Worth my while or worth the risk of being played a fool like the last time you struck a bargain with Aurelia? We haven't forgotten. I was there." His tone remains calm, but his eyes are cold yet unreadable as he drums his fingers on the arm of his chair.

The room seems to hold its breath, his words delicately hanging in the air when Elion finally replies. "You've been looking for her, have you not? You look like a smart male, so tell me, did you know Elynor was pregnant when she left my castle before marrying King Andre?"

"The king you murdered? Where *is* Elynor?" Rydian leans forward, elbows resting on the table, his stare holding Elion in place. Shadows skim his knuckles, dark wisps of night twisting in escalating fury.

The table stills, and Witt shuffles across from me as if waiting in anticipation, a dark gleam shining in his eyes. Rydian's council members remain calm and quiet, yet I have no doubt they're communicating in the Veil. Yet, for some reason, my heart twists at the thought of being excluded from that.

"Safe... for now," Elion says, his lip twitching in annoyance.

"King Andre was a pawn, caught in the middle of something to which he didn't belong. He was a casualty, nothing more."

We all know that's not true; he was intentionally targeted that night during the battle. Otherwise, Witt wouldn't have brought the Veilblade. Rydian's fingers curl into fists as unresolved grievances surface.

Rydian growls, "He was a better king than you will ever be, but let's not stray from the original point. How do you intend to prove she's the missing princess?"

There's a hitch in my breath as everyone's gaze lands on me. I grip the cold cutlery in my hands, fixing my eyes on my plate and slicing into the delicate meat. I sneak a glance at Rydian, whose jaw clenches in restrained fury.

It's clear this isn't just about me—it's about the war, the betrayal of the treaty, and everything that came with it, including the death of King Andre. Including Elynor. None of it has been forgotten.

Just then, Elion snaps his fingers. I freeze at the sound, my blood turning cold, knowing precisely what it means as Theron strides forward.

"I have no reason to lie to you." Elion waves a hand. "Her mother completed your little marriage ritual before she gave birth, apparently, making Isa the heir to both realms. She just so happened to be in the way when we captured her mother—I have no use for her here."

Theron thuds to my side of the table, and my head jerks left. The bite of my hair being pulled forces out a sharp cry. My cutlery drops, clanking against the porcelain. Theron exposes my auburn mark to Rydian with more force than necessary.

It's always more than necessary.

"See," Elion says coolly. "The missing princess. She wears a mark of Aurelia."

Within a beat, chairs scrape across the floor as I'm held in place, but then the pain stops. I'm quickly released, left panting into the table with my hands braced on the ends. Silence hangs in the air.

My eyes open, locking on Witt, Wayd, and Ivy who stands across from me. Witt has his weapons drawn as Wayd stands next to him, a smirk on his face, his finger wagging in warning.

My stomach drops.

Ivy's hands hover over her weapons and skims the room. Orin takes a sip of his wine with a raised brow, as if enjoying the show. He throws me an amused sideways glance.

"Who do you think would win?" Orin pushes the thought to me.

I narrow my eyes. With a glance to my right, Ren clenches his jaw, eyes a raging storm of gray. My breathing stalls at the sight of a dagger firm in his grasp, resting on his lap.

What the fuck is happening?

Ekrin and Caius smirk, and the guards near the back inch forward. Finally, with a small glance over my shoulder, I find Theron held by his throat in Rydian's invisible grip.

King Elion casually leans back, drumming his fingers along the table, a smile playing on his face as if this has become the most amusing event of his life.

Theron's boots scrape across the cold, stone floor as he's dragged closer to Rydian, his body jerking helplessly like a puppet on invisible strings. He halts abruptly, inches from Rydian's face, his breathing ragged and desperate.

"What's your name?" Rydian's voice drops.

Theron's scarred hands claw at his neck, blue lips parted as he struggles against the force tightening around his throat. A sharp gesture from Rydian allows him to rasp out a response.

"Ther—Theron," he croaks.

Rydian's hand hovers between them with its palm open and steady, blue eyes searing into Theron in an unforgiving glare.

"You knew she was a princess," Rydian calmly states. "Yet you dared touch a hair on her head, causing her *pain*. That..." Rydian chuckles, the sound so haunting it raises the hair on my arms. "That was a mistake."

Theron flinches, breaths shallow while he hangs there, gasping for air. It's the first time I've ever seen the guard terrified for his life. An unexpected smugness settles in my chest.

But I know the real reason Rydian has Theron in his hold—for the bruises that mark my face—and when I looked into his eyes earlier, they promised death. And death has come to claim the soul that's rightfully his.

"Did you think I wouldn't care?" Rydian asks, head tilting to the side. "Her life is worth more than yours, and yet you gambled it away with arrogance right in front of *me*."

No one dares to move, let alone breathe, as the scene unfolds. Elion chuckles softly, breaking the silence.

"Well," Elion says. "It seems our dear Theron has finally learned the price of his ignorance and will learn to be... gentler in the future. Don't you think that's punishment enough, King Rydian?"

Rydian doesn't look away from Theron, his lip curling into the smallest sneer before he whispers, "No."

Theron's eyes widen, lips parting in a silent scream just as his neck cracks, twisting into an unrecognizable angle, right before he crumples in a heap on the floor.

6

____

The guards in the back stride forward, weapons extended, just as seated members shoot to their feet.

Ivy twirls her twin swords as Wayd grips a black whip and faces Witt, who's holding his own weapon. Adrenaline floods my veins, and my fingers twitch as I reach for the daggers hidden in the folds of my gown. Ren places a hand on my forearm. He gives a gentle shake of his head and mouths, _wait_.

Rydian tilts his head to the side, a challenge sparking in his eyes. Elion only sighs, raising a hand and halting the guards behind him. They all skid to a stop, their armor clanking in unison.

"You know... I _liked_ him," Elion says. "But I see you believe that I have the missing princess now, or was that all for show?"

Rydian leans on his hands, his palms pressing into the table. "I believe she's the princess."

"Great, now let's continue eating. No need for the food to get cold," Elion snaps, acting as if he didn't just lose a personal guard. My blood goes cold.

He issues us more wine while guards pull Theron's lifeless body out of the room. Slowly, the tension eases, and everyone conceals their weapons, sitting once more.

Rydian just killed Theron. *For me.*

Still, my pulse races, shocked by the turn of events as Rydian didn't waste a single second enacting his vengeance. I can't help but feel a little relieved, but also… terrified.

"That is an intriguing weapon you have. Wayd, is it?" Elion asks, pointing down the table at his whip. "What made you choose such a weapon?"

Wayd's dark emerald eyes contrast with his silver hair, cropped short on the sides. If I were to guess, I'd say he's around Rydian's age. Wayd leans back, stroking his jaw that feathers beneath his hand, a small, tight smile playing on his face.

"I like the versatility it gives me during a battle—the ability to wield and strike my opponents from a distance," Wayd says, his voice carrying a gravelly edge. "It was a gift from my aunt."

His eyes shoot to Rydian, a look I'm familiar with in silent conversations. Rydian shakes his head, a subtle warning for him to remain quiet. Wayd looks at me once again.

"It's nice to finally see you again, Princess." He blinks, waiting for me to respond, but I don't recall ever knowing him. A wrinkle forms between his brows. "Does she… speak?"

"I speak," I clip, and narrow my eyes before setting my wine down with a soft thud.

He smirks, clearly unimpressed. "Oh, good. I was beginning to think you were a mute."

My lips curl into a faint smile, deceptively sweet. "Would you like for me to remain mute while I cut that insolent tongue of yours clean out of your mouth?"

"Isa," Elion warns, but Wayd only chuckles, holding my gaze.

"Don't provoke the tamed beast," Rydian says calmly.

I have a feeling he's speaking of me and not Wayd. Regardless, I lean back and sip my wine, staring at Wayd across the table.

"So, King Elion, what do you propose? Forgive me for thinking that this all seems too good to be true, but why are you willing to part with her now and not before?" Rydian asks as our plates are removed from the table, leaving nothing but our glasses.

Elion sighs. "I must admit, the battle I waged against Aurelia was sought in anger. Taking Isa was not originally in my plan, as my issue was solely with Elynor at the time. I know I said some harsh words about King Andre, but he knew about Elynor's relationship with me, including Isa's heritage, and decided to keep that knowledge to himself. It needed to be taken care of. What's done is done."

My pulse skyrockets. How could he have known about what King Andre knew or not? Unless he's lying about it, needing an excuse...

Rydian's eyes narrow. "How can I trust she's not truly in Aurelia as an informant when she was raised here in Elderheim? Her loyalty would be to you, not to me. How can I trust you won't go back on your word like the last time we had a treaty?"

"I had a feeling you would feel that way," Elion chuckles, "but I would like to return her as a way to honor our last agreement, and repay what loss I've caused to your realm. I believe Isa is best suited for Aurelia, where she can fully thrive learning the Shadovar ways after having spent the majority of her life here in Elderheim." He nonchalantly waves a hand in the air.

"That's not enough." Rydian clenches his jaw.

"Oh? And what would be enough for the King of Aurelia?"

Elion's fingers click against the chair, but Rydian remains silent, as if debating whether he should answer. Then he smirks and leans back, clasping his hands together.

"If Isa's lineage is tied to both of our realms, as you say, this makes her an ideal candidate for uniting us, don't you think?" Rydian asks. "But I want her loyalty."

My eyes widen, and I fear his next words.

"I agree." King Elion strokes his jaw, eyes flicking to me for the briefest of moments. "What are you suggesting?"

"A marriage alliance would remove any doubt of divided loyalties. As you know, I need an heir to carry on the lineage, and since she's Vaelborne, she'll be able to fulfill that. I want Elynor too."

The table falls silent, and my lips part in surprise. I grip Ren's hand under the table to keep the rising nausea at bay. Marrying him would be… impossible, wouldn't it?

As much joy as it would bring me to be Rydian's queen, it's just one more choice that will be stripped from me—forced into something I can't control. It should be *my* decision, not theirs.

If anything, Rydian should be on his fucking knees proposing to me, not bargaining my hand over dinner. Bitterness coats my tongue.

I'm nothing more than a pawn.

But if I bear two marks and am bound to Elion by a blood oath, surely one of those issues would become a problem. I force myself to swallow, to stifle the urge to retch up my meal.

This isn't happening.

"You can't be serious," I say finally, my stomach dropping to the pits of the Fates.

Everyone remains utterly calm, save for me. With how Rydian's council has maintained their expressions, it's as if they already knew this was coming. A cold dread settles in my chest as realization dawns on me—this was always Rydian's plan.

The only ones appearing remotely shocked are the dukes, their eyes flaring momentarily. I swallow the rising lump in my throat, my heart racing.

"Normally, I would consider such a proposal, but Ekrin Highcrest has already asked for Isa's hand in marriage. I'm obligated to keep her tied to Elderheim in the future for our own heirs." Elion smirks. "And I'm not quite sure I'd be willing to part with Elynor just yet."

I'm already bound to him by a blood oath, and I know firsthand that Elion has no interest in heirs, so what is he planning? What more could he possibly want from me?

Rydian shifts his calm, yet lethal attention to Ekrin. His pale green eyes meet mine across the table, and an oily smirk tugs at his lips. He swirls his glass, the red wine crawling down the rim as it settles, and an agonizing silence buzzes in the air.

Then his eyes dart down the table, holding Rydian's smoldering gaze. I begin to wonder if Ekrin will be the cause of Rydian's control fracturing tonight, especially given how tightly his jaw clenches at Ekrin's deliberate silence.

After a long moment, Ekrin dramatically sighs with a wave of his hand.

"I'd be inclined to withdraw my proposal for the sake of the realms. I'd hate to be the reason there can't be peace; though I still believe she would make an excellent duchess," Ekrin says almost sarcastically.

His smug grin pricks my skin, and I growl, slamming my hands onto the table. "I won't be marrying anyone!"

Wayd's mouth tips into a knowing smirk, though Ivy remains completely neutral. Then Eldric, the older male next to Ivy, quietly assesses me before shifting his attention down the table. He hasn't said anything since arriving, only watched as the conversations unfolded.

Elion's gaze shifts to mine, and a slow, cold grin spreads across his face. But I catch it—the faintest flicker of frustration sparking in his eyes. He doesn't like outbursts, and I've spoken without being spoken to. Then a crawling sensation infiltrates my blood, forcing me to bite my tongue to prevent a cry.

Forcing my silence. *The oath.*

Rydian's wry grin cuts through the tension. He's seemingly unaware of my pain, though his smug amusement only forces my anger to rise. His brows lower, shadowing the sharpness of his eyes as a dark thought seems to take root.

"Well, there you go," Rydian drawls, his voice laced with mockery. "Looks like Ekrin is kind enough to withdraw his proposal for me. What do you say, King Elion—would you like to unite the realms?" A low chuckle escapes him, as if he finds this all delightfully ironic.

Elion leans forward, though, hands clasping on the surface of the table as he studies Rydian.

"I have a couple of requests before I agree," he says smoothly, raising a single finger. "I'd like your firstborn heir to ensure her loyalty isn't just to you but to me as well; she is my daughter after all. I would also like her to aid me in tracking down the Veilstone once she leaves here. I believe she has the power to end the realms' feuds once and for all, don't you think?"

Shock barrels through me at his confession to search for the Veilstone so casually. Yet my chest heaves as he finally reveals the bargain he's wanted all along—the Veilstone.

And my heirs, apparently.

It's as if he suspected Rydian would suggest a marriage bond. But to finally release me to Aurelia, he wants another bargain. A willing participant. What could he possibly want with my future children?

Rydian's smirk falters slightly, a grim expression settling over his features as he becomes eerily still. He strokes his jaw, as if thinking it over.

"You're still looking for the Veilstone," Rydian says. Elion confirms with a small nod. "And you'll give me Elynor?"

"Absolutely not!" I grit my teeth. "I will not be bred like some hound for any reason!"

Binding myself to Elion is one thing, but giving up my own children is something I won't do. He already *has* me, why would I give him more?

"I need Elynor a little while longer, and then I will return her to you," Elion mutters, fingers drumming.

Ren's composure falters, and he leans back, assessing everyone. He's pissed, mirroring my outburst, but no one pays any mind except for Ekrin who also leans back in his chair with a smug grin.

My hands curl into tight fists as I glare at both kings, but they don't so much as flinch. They don't even acknowledge me.

"Don't agree to that," I plead, tethering myself to our thread in the Veil that seems to fray as more time passes.

He ignores me, and the weight of Elion's requests linger.

Promising heirs to another king is no simple gesture—it's binding. Fae children, whether Aetheri or Shadovar, will always remain sacred. They are our legacies, woven into the fabric of our kind, and to promise them to someone is no mere agreement—it's as grave as a blood oath.

Would Rydian really give up our heirs? Why is he considering it?

Forcing my breath to steady, I lean back, crossing my arms to hide the uncontrollable trembling in my hands. The fracturing pieces of my heart.

"So, King Rydian, do you agree to the terms?" Elion asks calmly. Rydian looks to me for a moment, and the deep blue eyes I once sought comfort in betray me in a single breath.

"I agree to the terms. We can leave tonight if you wish," Rydian says, eyes still fixed on me.

"*Why would you do that?*" I ask, tears threatening to fall. Still, he ignores me.

"No, not tonight," Elion declares. "Princess Isa's been... misbehaving as of late, but I'll allow her to leave in a week. In the meantime, we can prepare her for the journey. I also demand that Captain Demaris accompany her. I'll have the agreement ready by the time you arrive to pick her up."

"I'll allow it," Rydian nods, standing. "We'll be in touch."

My fingers tremble as we all stand, and the kings formally clasp hands. Rydian pivots to me and grasps mine, bringing it to his lips. He kisses the top with a menacing smirk, his council quietly waiting by the doors.

"I can't wait," he whispers, eyes burning through me, then leaves without another word.

Elion snaps his fingers, ordering everyone out, even the guards. Ren, whose eyes are as haunted as mine, quietly exits the chamber with a quick look over his shoulder.

I whirl to King Elion. "Do you think I'm going to marry him? I will not—I'm not going over there to be wed and bred like some animal. I already swore a blood oath to you; I didn't agree to that."

Elion takes two calm, deliberate steps toward me, expression darkening as rage hardens his features—not a single trace of kindness.

"Yes, you will, if you know what's good for you," he says, and shoots out a hand, dragging me to him by my neck. I stumble from the force, baring my teeth. "This is what you'll give me in return for your precious memories and that mother of yours. You will also provide me with information on that legion of theirs. Is that clear? You said it yourself: *anything for the realm.* Or have you forgotten? Let me make one thing perfectly clear: you are nothing more than a weapon for me. Do your job."

Dread sinks in my stomach, his sharp words cutting into me like a blade—words repeated back to me from the Aurorafest, after Ekrin requested my hand in marriage.

I only thought I was playing the part.

"And what exactly will I be giving you? My heirs?" I hiss in his grasp.

He chuckles. It's then that I realize that he's been planning this since the day I stepped forward and claimed myself as heir to Elderheim.

"Everything." His tone sends a shiver down my spine.

He forcefully releases me with a sneer, lip curling, and exits the Great Hall. I blink, staring after him until he disappears beyond the doors. Isolated and alone, I'm left standing there, just as it's always been.

I swallow the ache, though—force it down even though I feel it bubbling to the surface, seconds from combusting entirely.

After a few deep breaths, I manage to walk back to my room, the click of my heels echoing in the empty halls. Disbelief quickly floods my veins—my thoughts—accompanied by a searing anger from how tonight ended. I'm already fighting for control, fighting the betrayal of my heart as I watched two kings pawn me like a game of chess.

Something to be played and used.

I'm left wondering if Rydian's behavior tonight was merely because he felt betrayed by me in the throne room, or if he's only playing into his reputation as the Dark King of Aurelia.

Unfortunately, I can't decide.

My jaw grinds in frustration—the next seven days are going to be agonizingly brutal.

Guards line the perimeter as I turn the corner, every inch of the courtyard taken up by someone in clinking, shining armor. I enter the door to my stairwell, my eyes colliding with the guard in the archway before I round the banister for the stairs.

But the moment I step foot in my chamber and my door clicks shut, a familiar *whoosh* breaks the silence. I whirl around with wide eyes and my daggers outstretched.

7

"Rydian." I exhale his name as he stalks forward from the shadows, brows lowered and furious. *Shit*.

In a flash of movement, he lunges for me, and my daggers clank to the floor. My hands are trapped in his grasp while his other hand curls around my jaw, backing me against the windows. My head thuds against the glass. No fire roars beneath the mantel; only flecks of moonlight stream in behind me. And we're alone. My pulse races at the thought.

"Not much of an assassin if you're so easily disarmed." His voice comes out as a low growl, raising the hair on my neck. I'm clearly speaking to the King of Aurelia.

"I let you," I snarl quietly, my voice shaking with anger. If we speak any louder, the guards in my stairwell are bound to hear us. "What was that? You made a bargain you had no right to make. How could you do—"

He chuckles, the sound devoid of humor. His grip tightens. "You lost the right to be involved in decisions when you left me out of a very important one."

Guilt claws at my chest at that, my breath faltering as I fight the sudden tears pricking my eyes. "I'm sorry, Rydian, I never meant to hurt you."

"Should've thought of that before you lied to me. But we—" He chuckles again and then hums, releasing my hands to move a stray hair from my face. For the briefest of moments, his expression softens before it disappears. "—we have a lot to discuss when you get to Aurelia, don't we, Princess?"

The implication of his words has me stiffening in his grasp, my lips parting, my chest tightening with confusion and...

My stomach drops.

For the first time since meeting Rydian, fear consumes my entire body in an unwelcome shudder.

"Are you frightened of me?" he asks.

I say nothing, unable to answer, my lips flattening to a thin line. Words dissipate off my tongue as fast as they arrive, only my quick breaths filling the space between us.

Then I let out a small gasp as the coldness of his shadows circles a path below my jaw, squeezing my neck. I know he would never hurt me, but still, the possibility of him snuffing the air from my lungs prickles my skin.

"You killed Theron," I say finally, though the words stumble out on a breath, and my eyes squeeze shut. That's what I choose to say? He's angry with me, yes, but he killed Theron after seeing the bruises on my face.

When I open my eyes, he leans in, his lip curling into the faintest of sneers.

"I would kill more than a measly guard for you, Isa," he says inches from my mouth, and a chill snakes up my spine. "No one touches what belongs to me. I would wipe this entire fucking realm if it meant keeping you safe—if it meant that you got to come home with me. Because that's what you promised, isn't it? Or was that a lie too? What is it going to take for you to realize that you're stuck with me? Who do I have to kill for you to understand that you're mine?"

"I'm not yours," I hiss, and a slow, creeping smile lights his face in the shadows, the faint sheen of the scar across his lip a harsh reminder of what he'd sacrificed the last twenty years.

"You tell such pretty lies," he says, and his thumb runs over the seam of my lips before his grip tightens again, enough that I whimper.

Then the window sways open beside me, metal creaking on its hinges. Rydian's eyes flick to my right, and I don't need to swivel my head to know who's perched along the ledge.

"Let her go," Ren mutters.

His boots thud hard against the floor as he drops into my room. Another whoosh breaks the silence, and just past Rydian's shoulder, Wayd steps in from the Veil. His silver hair somehow gleams in the darkness, but his attention is fixed on the knife picking his nails.

Has he been here the whole time?

"Remember who you're talking to," Wayd warns, but his eyes casually graze mine before flicking back down.

Rydian huffs a quiet breath and smirks, releasing me. The emptiness of his touch burns my skin like a hot knife. He takes two large steps back until he's swallowed by the darkness blanketing the right side of my chamber.

"Why are you here?" Ren asks, his elbow brushing against my arm. The coldness of his blade grazes the tips of my fingers. Ren steps forward, daggers held tight in his grasp.

"I'll be back in seven days to retrieve you," Rydian says, looking to Ren before landing on me, his expression unreadable.

My mouth falls open only for me to close it again, because I have no idea what to say now that he stands here. I sigh, shoulders dropping. "We have to go back to Milena's to restore Ren's memories."

"Of course you do." A dark, disbelieving laugh brushes the air, and Rydian shakes his head. "Then I'll meet you here and we'll Veil there together."

He studies me once more, silence permeating the air as we all awkwardly stand there. I have so much more to say, secrets to confess, yet nothing comes out. Not with so many in the room, and it kills me.

"Why didn't you kill Witt?" I ask just as he's about to step into the Veil—as darkness swirls around him in wisps of shadow.

Neither me or Ren can kill Witt without repercussions, but Rydian could. "He was right there—"

"There will be no quick death for him. There will be pain, and I will ensure he suffers," Rydian interrupts, nodding to Wayd, who then disappears beyond the Veil. "I'll see you in seven days... I hope you're ready."

His words come out like a warning before the Veil consumes him, and within a span of a single second, he disappears from my chambers. I hate how cold it feels without him here, yet all I can do is stand there and blink in the darkness.

Ren pivots, flicking out an angry hand to light the hearth with a spark of fire before running his fingers through his hair. Though no amount of flames can warm the emptiness I feel, where a gaping hole currently sits in my chest. I know that I'm the reason for this, all of it, and if I had just said *something*...

"Isa." Ren studies me near the settee with a pinch to his brow. The same settee he perched on after my trip to Milena's. "Are you okay?"

Whether from the moment or my overwhelming sense of my failure and loneliness, my composure cracks, and a sob slips out. Three little words fracture years of restraint—the carefully buried emotions I was taught to swallow.

As I stifle my broken cry over my colossal fuck-up, Ren stalks forward and silently pulls me to his chest. Something I'm not sure I've ever truly experienced until now—the feeling wholly unfamiliar yet familiar all at once. His chin rests on the top of my head, his arms wrapping tightly around my shoulders, and his hand threads through my hair.

We stand like that for a moment, silent and still, until my breath slows and shame consumes me for crying in the first place. For leaning into him when I know I shouldn't. Ren's body trembles against mine, as if this entire night has him fighting for control too.

Only then do I realize the stone quaking beneath our feet. I step back with wide eyes. Ren exhales through his nose, hands opening and closing into tight fists as he turns from me.

"Is that you? Are you angry?" I ask breathlessly, glancing at the trembling walls, the rattling whiskey glasses, the creaking windows. "Calm it before someone notices."

"Yes, I'm angry, Isa. How could I not be?" he growls, and then the shaking of the stone subsides as quickly as it came. He sighs, placing his hands on his hips and shaking his head. "This entire night was fucked, from start to finish. He should have never made that bargain. What the fuck was he thinking?"

No, he shouldn't have, I want to say. Instead, all I can do is nod at his turned back. I take a shuddering breath, calming my racing heart.

"At least Theron's dead," I say, fixing my eyes on the flames, the crackles distracting me from my thoughts. Yet my head pounds as if someone has taken a rock to my skull, and I squeeze my eyes shut once more.

"Yeah, well, I wish I could've done it myself. I'm glad he did it, though," he says finally and turns to me with a disgruntled huff. "I'm sleeping in here tonight."

I hardly hear him as I step around the settee and sit, still dressed in the gown from earlier. I pay no mind to how it bunches around my waist as I draw my knees up to my chest, the bottom pooling to the floor like a puddle of melted emeralds.

"If I had known how much trouble this all would be, I wouldn't have gotten my memories back." I shoot him a glance, but he's already studying me. He sits, leaning forward to rest his elbows against his knees, only he's changed from his earlier attire.

"What did you find out from Milena? You never told me," he asks.

I shake my head, not ready to discuss it. At least not until I can talk to Rydian about it. Though I can't help my thoughts from stirring in the thin layer between dreams and my returning memories. All they've done over the last few weeks is confuse me.

"I don't know what's real—what my memories are," I admit, rubbing at my temples. "Every time I close my eyes, I'm thrust into this never-ending nightmare of trying to decipher them. It makes my head pound. There are moments when I know something is real by the emotions that stir upon waking. I can't help but wonder if they are only a figment of my imagination."

That's been the hardest part, though Milena failed to mention how utterly confused I'd be as my past infiltrates my dreams.

"Maybe I can help." Ren suggests after a long moment, his eyes flicking to his hands clasped between his knees. But when I open my mouth to ask about his locked-up memories, he quickly says, "By telling you if they're real or not."

I lean back with a sigh, studying him, and wonder which one to ask about first. My brows rise a little as one pushes its way to the surface—the mark on my wrist, pulsing with memories I haven't fully retrieved yet. Only slivers spring forward, broken fragments lost in the corners of my mind.

"Did I have a... thing with Malrik?" I ask, my pulse thundering with dread. Ren actually snickers, stifling it with his hand in an attempt to quiet his amusement. My eyes narrow. "What?"

"No." He holds back a smile, leaning back. "No, you never really liked Malrik... or Luke, for that matter. That was definitely a dream."

"Thank the Fates," I say sarcastically and sigh, though a grin tugs at my lips. "But I... used to sneak out when I was younger. Was that real?" I ask, and he nods, eyes fixed on the wall behind me before settling on my face. "And the brothel? Have I always..."

"Gone there?" He chuckles. "Yes, that's real. You've always gone to the brothel."

"That's what I thought." I let out an unamused huff. "But I don't think the ones returning are from the Painted Bird, the place looks... different. The inside is, anyway," I get out, sifting through the broken fragments I can't quite seem to grasp fully.

Ren wrings his hands and then clears his throat. "King Elion will most likely hold a meeting among his council tomorrow—plan for your departure. I'll probably be there."

My stomach drops, my thoughts snagging on one thing in particular. "Do you know what the Veilblade looks like?" I ask, and he shakes his head. "Could you... keep an eye out for anything that looks unique? Once we get to Aurelia, I'll have to tell Rydian about the—"

The words burn on my tongue, my blood crawling in a way that has me wincing, fear singeing my spine.

Silenced.

Like my own blood knew what my intentions were by a mere thought. Gods, what did I do?

"You won't be able to discuss it with him." Ren reminds me, letting the implication of his words hang in the air. But even as defeat sits heavily on my shoulders, a thought blooms.

"Maybe not… but you can. The oath doesn't say anything about *you* keeping quiet, did it? I could learn everything about Elion, and if I happened to tell you things in passing, or even if you…" I trail off, letting the undercurrent of meaning dangle between us.

He blinks before a small, knowing grin forms across his features, head shaking as the thought slides into place.

Technically, I wouldn't be lying to Elion if I stayed out of it, letting Ren do all the talking. I wouldn't be betraying Elion if Ren told them everything we know; he's in the Brotherhood after all. I have every right to trust him. Elion wouldn't suspect Ren, not if he's been loyal all these years.

"Would it work?" I ask, hope rising for the first time since I made the oath.

"Yes, it would… but we will have to be careful on how we do that," he says to himself, resting his elbows on the arms of the settee as he leans back, lost in his own mind.

"I need you to tell him," I say. "If I can't do it, I need you to tell him everything." His eyes flick to me before he slowly nods, his eyebrow lifting almost curiously.

"We should get some sleep. We have a long seven days ahead of us," he says and stands, dimming the fire in the hearth so that only a soft orange flickers along the walls, spilling onto the floor.

I walk to the bathing chamber to undress, only stopping once I get to the doorway and turn as Ren tosses a few pillows to the floor, unaware. For a moment, guilt settles in my chest for letting him sleep there, but I allow myself to appreciate his willingness to do it. He doesn't have to, yet he chooses to stay.

"Ren," I murmur, and he turns, facing me. "Thank you."

He blinks. "For what?"

"For staying." I give him a small smile, choosing my words carefully, so as to not make this any more awkward than it already is. It was just weeks ago that I hated him—wanted nothing to do with him, actually. But I've come to appreciate his loyalty, his friendship, even though I don't deserve it. Even though I don't remember anything.

"You make me feel... less alone," I add with a teasing grin.

He immediately grunts, turning from me, and grumbles under his breath as he lays out a quilt. I hold back a chuckle, amused by how flustered he is by my gratitude, and click the door shut.

8

A shiver runs down my spine and my hands tingle in anticipation of tonight. The sun is low across my chamber—an hour before setting entirely—and a particular type of adrenaline floods my veins. The same energy that consumes me before starting and completing a grueling mission.

Only this one is different.

After intentionally walking by many guards on the way to my chamber—ensuring they see me—I lock the door with a variety of runes, sealing it shut. Arcan is mine and Ren's set destination, one of the many cities that forge weapons for the king—something we desperately need information on.

Yet over the last four days, my fury has risen to a simmering heat as I sift through those promises Rydian made. And the more I think about it, the angrier I become. I've tried finding ways out of them only to come up empty-handed every single time.

Still, even if it was to get me to Aurelia, he had no right to bargain with my heirs. Even if he's angry with me, he overstepped. Promising heirs to anyone is not to be taken lightly. It's an outdated tradition, yet he agreed to it with hardly a second thought.

And marriage? Gods, I want nothing more than to be with him, but what if his mate or mine steps into our lives after our vows are made? What happens then?

Another shiver—I have two mates. *What a mess.*

My thoughts whirl, the minutes dragging when finally, my window creaks open and a familiar set of boots perch on the edge. Ren quietly drops into my chamber, closing the window once more with a soft, groaning snick.

His hood sits low over his brow, the cloak concealing every weapon he owns. Only slivers of his jaw peek out, the tip of his nose, and the subtle curve of his lip. With his spine straight and a menacing air of confidence, he's a sight that would typically invoke fear in others.

Regardless, I release a sigh. "No one will come looking for you?"

"I thought that since you lost your memories, certain things would have faded," he grumbles. "Yet you still question me."

A small grin. "I suppose some things can't be wiped."

"Clearly." He huffs. "Are you ready?"

With a flick of my wrist, I choke the fire in the hearth and pull my hood up. I reach for his hand and for a breath, my magic roils beneath my skin, dancing and expectant. I latch onto the Veil, still inexperienced in traveling with others, and intently focus on our destination.

The only way to travel, apparently.

Weightlessness consumes me the moment we vanish, my vision darkening, head buzzing as the forested city tangles in my thoughts. Vivid and clear. Within seconds, we arrive in the forest just outside Arcan's city of ancient trees, housing the king's metal forgers, Fae, and many, many humans.

As our feet touch the ground, Ren's face pales before turning an odd shade of green. He yanks his hand from mine, braces both against his knees, inhales, and then groans. From pain or nausea? Likely both.

I stifle a chuckle, remembering my own experience after traveling in the Veil my first few times.

"Don't look now," I say, bending over him. "But a menacing assassin was just taken out by the Veil."

He groans again, weakly shoving me by the shoulder before straightening, brows lowered and clearly unamused. Another minute, and he's successfully stifled the nausea, color seeping back into his face.

We walk through the forested expanse ahead.

This time of year, the vined road is covered in a blanket of thick, powdery snow. But along that road are webs of others, leading further into the trees, shops, and homes of the Aetheri, halflings, and humans. Light, clean air brushes my cheeks, bringing with it the rich scent of smoke.

Bonfires, many of them.

Orbs dance lazily near the low-hanging branches above, the size of marbles, appearing more insect than magic as they glimmer in the fading sun. But beyond that, Fae and human children sit on the thick tree limbs, feet kicking as they peer down with little smiles. We press forward, but a smile of my own tugs at my lips.

Arcan is home to more humans than the other cities in Elderheim, most choosing to work in the farmland, bakeries or forges that specialize in traditional metals rather than the intricate stone weapons created by the Shapers.

Jobs are what they're typically after, and since the king is creating new weapons and armor, we believe that Arcan will have that information. Something we're eager to learn—anything regarding that new armor and where exactly they're getting it.

Many of the thick ancient trees remind me of Milena's cottage. Only here, pointed, glowing amber windows stagger upward on a few, showcasing their many levels.

Despite our effort to hurry, two hours go by quickly, having scouted and questioned four forges for any sign of that golden, shimmering metal that was able to repel my magic. Each one we subtly inspected led us to no answers and more questions.

"You might want to ask Alloris at the market," a woman named Charlotte says, tossing a dirtied rag over her shoulder and wiping her sweaty brow. Soot marks her pale features. Behind her, a young boy bellows air into the forge as angry flames flick upwards. "He typically sells there every week and has been here the longest—

works closely with those up north. He would know more. The last shop on the left."

"May the—" *Fates be with you*, I want to say.

But humans often take the saying as a curse, not a blessing. The Fates are worshiped as gods, said to have shaped the realms and each noble bloodline that rules them. Some people still revere them. Others blame them for their suffering—humans most of all.

Unlike the Fae, most humans refuse to worship the Fates, pushing them aside with nothing but distaste. The Fates once walked our realms, but rumor claims they linger in the Veil now—unseen and unheard for centuries.

Not since before our realms were split.

But if I'm honest, I often wonder if they're real at all... or if they're simply a myth we've been taught to endure.

"Thanks for your help," I tell Charlotte instead, and quickly step into the heart of the square where Ren leans against the ancient trunk, assessing the city. He has let me do all the talking, considering he's frightened each forge we've stepped into.

"Off to the market?" he asks without looking and pushes off the trunk, his boots crunching against the packed snow.

"Looks like it."

We weave through the clustered crowd, most in groups of three or four. Buzzing chatter fills the market air, and I catch the faint scent of roasted stews, sickly sweet treats, and the sharp tang of ale. All of which apparently send me into a feral hunger as my stomach grumbles.

Shops blur beside us, and after a few minutes of walking, we pivot left, arriving just outside the forge Charlotte sent us to. With the door wide open, the wild scent of burning embers and hot steel hit my nose, followed by the sharp clanking of metal on metal. It pierces the air a few times before we step inside.

Ren tugs his hood down, ducks, and follows me in.

We step into a red-brick forge with many sharpened blades of every size hanging off the walls. Daggers, swords, axes, and hammers.

At first glance, they're only mundane pieces, but upon closer inspection, etched symbols line each one. Some along the handles, others along the delicate blades. To my surprise, the symbols resemble the runes we use for infiltration in the Brotherhood. I arch my brow when Ren's knowing gaze meets mine, surely thinking the same.

The man near the forge has his back to us and pounds a large hammer into the scorching red metal before him. Shirtless and damp, his muscles strain with each blow—quite literally forged by steel.

Though he doesn't seem to hear us when we call out. Ren grumbles in annoyance and then bangs against the wooden work table with the handle of his blade.

The man turns, his brows shooting up when he spots Ren. He swivels his gaze to me before discarding his items. He walks toward us, resembling someone in his late thirties, and runs a hand over his shiny head. Upon approaching, he lights a pipe between his lips and inhales.

"May I help ya?" he drawls in the local dialect, then tugs off his thick gloves.

"Yes, actually," I say, leaning against the counter with an elbow. "We're in the market for some new blades. Are you Alloris?"

"Aye," he grumbles. "What can I do ya for?"

"I'm looking for something specific, but my eyes caught the beautiful blades on the wall over there." I point behind me. "The sigils... are those runes?"

Alloris casts wary eyes between Ren and I. "Some. Protection and strength runes—helps the wielder deflect blows, have swifter swings. Simple magic. Others are merely just designs."

I've never seen that, not really.

The forges we've visited so far had only simple blades, but if these runes provide strength to humans who can't wield magic... They could be using a Siphon to pull strength into the rune. My stomach sinks at the thought. It's possible.

"Interesting." I grin.

Ren says nothing, but I notice the way his eyes skim the forge while Alloris's attention remains fixed on me. "There's a specific metal I'm searching for. Not common, but recently discovered. We heard rumors that someone in Arcan had been forging some for the king and wanted to purchase something."

If I hadn't been trained to notice it, I would have missed the little twitch of surprise in Alloris's gray brow, the flicker of tightness along his jaw, or the sudden tension in the air. Thick and uncomfortable.

Despite that, a persuasive smile lines his lips before he exhales a puff of smoke with a quiet chuckle. "Not sure where ya heard that, but that's not here. What's it called?"

Without so much as a word, Ren tosses a heavy pouch of gold onto the counter with a clink and a rustle. Ren holds his gaze before flicking his eyes down, a menacing smirk tilting his lips. Alloris reaches for it, but my hand darts forward first, the leather groaning in my grasp.

"Answer some questions and it's all yours," I say, holding his gaze in challenge.

His hand hovers, the silence stretching, and Alloris's chocolate eyes flick from us to the gold. He gnaws on the pipe as if he were thinking about it. Another beat passes when he says, "This won't come back to me?"

I smirk. "No one even knows we're here."

"Aye. Follow me," he grumbles, turning into the corridor past the forge and veering right. "Kallen, man the front!"

After a moment, we enter an office of sorts, and Alloris clicks the door shut. Papers spill off the desk, some in neat stacks and folders, others in disarray. He sits behind it, and I take a seat, though Ren remains standing behind me with his arms folded.

"What are ya seeking, exactly?" Alloris asks.

"Just what the metal is," Ren says, voice gruff. "Where is it coming from?"

"North, from what I know." He inhales again, brows drawing close together as the pipe between his lips glows red. "Nullium steel, mined at the Veil's Edge."

The Veil's Edge—the land where our realms meet, west of Eldryn and high into the mountains. However, it doesn't make sense, as I haven't heard rumors of humans or Fae bringing anything to Arcan. They'd have to pass through Alvonia.

"How can it…" I trail off, unsure how to explain it. "Repel the magic? Who's mining it?"

Alloris huffs in disbelief, leaning back. "Humans been minin' it. Shapers been unsuccessful with it. Herb Weavers, too. Somethin' about it repellin' the use of their magic to mine. Not sure how it repels, I only know where it is." He shrugs. "At least the humans have a job, I suppose."

"And you've been making the weapons and armor yourself?" Ren asks, his voice a little quieter. I only assume it's not to frighten Alloris as Ren continues to tower over both of us.

"Aye, some," he starts, mouth falling open before closing it again, brows furrowing. His pipe droops between his fingers. "I helped get it started. After a few forgers learned from me, they sent em' to the legion. I assume that's where they make the rest."

A chill snakes down my spine, acutely aware of what little information we know about Elion's plans, regardless of what he shared with me in that throne room. Silence lingers, leaving me to lean back, my mind racking through scenarios.

"Thanks for your time," I say after a moment and stand, turning for the door. Alloris clears his throat, a wry smirk tilting his lips when I glance over my shoulder.

"The gold?"

A small smile. "Right. Here's a little more for the trouble," I say and toss it to him with a few extra. "We were never here."

"Nope. Now get out," he says, dumping the contents and sifting through each coin with a flat smile.

"Well, that can't be good." I gripe as we pass through the forge again. "Why does Elion need any of that?"

Ren huffs. "I have a few ideas, but at least we have some answers."

Some answers, yes, but way more questions.

We exit, and I veer left, itching to leave Arcan and head back to the castle, my nerves burning with a sudden anxiousness. We've been gone for almost three hours, and the longer we stay, the more my skin crawls.

My brows furrow—only silence follows me. I turn to find Ren walking in the opposite direction, and skid to an abrupt stop. My breaths billow out in an annoyed huff.

"Where are you going?" I call out, and then groan when he doesn't reply, walking away as if he doesn't hear me.

Or perhaps he's ignoring me?

With no choice but to follow, I grind my teeth as he weaves through the thick crowd. He towers over every single person in the market, making it easy to track his movements until I reach his side. I shoot him a fleeting glance, though no expression marks his features, just set determination for whatever reason.

"You choose now to venture into a market when we've been gone for hours already?" I glance around. Random, curious eyes flit to Ren, passersby quickly moving out of the way as he walks down the center.

"None of the guards have tried to knock on your door this late in the afternoon for the last four days. I think we're fine."

"You've been watching them?" I ask, my brows shooting up. I didn't realize he was doing that. But he's right, none have knocked or checked on me recently like they had been doing.

"That's what captains do." A small, knowing smirk tilts his mouth. "I might have ordered the laziest ones to man your stair-well. We should be good for a while."

He stops just outside a stall, the one I scented on the air earlier. Roasted stew hits my nose with such force it causes my stomach to grumble again, and I stifle a groan.

The human woman fills two clay bowls and hands them to Ren in exchange for a few pieces of gold. My eyes narrow when he hands me one, hot and steaming.

"Your stomach was becoming quite annoying," he says and brushes past, quickly finding a nearby table with stumps off to the side.

Slightly dumbfounded, I blink and watch him sit.

Tiny, twinkling orbs hover above the table, light dancing along the wood when I sit on the stump across from Ren with a small scowl. Regardless, I take a bite, and a burst of flavor explodes on my tongue. Savory. Exactly what I needed, apparently, as my stomach settles in satisfaction.

I've been to Arcan many times, though now it feels familiar in a way I can't quite explain, leaving my brows to furrow. Ren takes another bite, solely focused on his food.

"What was your first mission?" I ask as a group of Fae walks by. Some with smooth bronzed skin, the others pale like my own. They wear a variety of layered linen to ward off the chill. He straightens a little, brows pinching. He scans my face, and I almost cringe, realization sweeping over me. "You've told me before, haven't you?"

"Yes." For a brief moment, his features harden as if a memory pulled him back before his expression smooths. "It was the thief who killed my parents."

My stomach sours at the thought, dread pulsing in my veins. I hate the fact that he's told me this before, forced to relive it. I grind my teeth, frustration holding me hostage.

I still haven't recovered the memories of my own first mission, the images broken and tangled. I know it's there, though, I just haven't quite pulled it to the surface.

He glances around, then clears his throat. "When Elion recruited me, I thought it was my chance for revenge—to learn the skills I needed to track him down. Elion somehow knew what had happened, and because of that, my first mission was that thief."

With my heart racing, all I can do is stare, my stew forgotten in my grasp. His eyes remain fixed on the mingling crowd, and then he takes two heavy breaths before looking at me.

"For the longest time, I felt like I owed Elion because it felt like a gift. I realized that he just liked information, using what he had. I became a weapon that day." He exhales, the sound almost exhausted, and pushes his empty bowl to the side.

A beat of silence settles, leaving me at a complete loss for words. Yet for some reason, I reach across the table and squeeze his hand, knowing that whatever spills from me would mean nothing.

He stiffens for a brief second, eyes fixed on our joined hands. I only huff a laugh and pull back to finish my food, knowing how uncomfortable he likely feels.

We linger for a few minutes, and Ren watches the market with casual vigilance, elbows resting on the table. Then he tosses something carefully wrapped in parchment in the center.

My brow arches when he unfolds it, the crinkle of the paper breaking the air, and reveals two berry tarts that ooze on the sides. Deliciously sweet, burnt sugar sears my nostrils, as if it had been warmed beforehand.

I hold back an amused chuckle. "Did you steal those?"

He scoffs quietly. "I only steal from the king." Then he slides me one and takes a bite of his own. My face warms when he holds my gaze, as if he's urging me to try it. "You'll like it."

I pause, now unsure whether or not I should eat it. Despite myself, I take a bite, my eyes widening momentarily, and hold back a delightful groan. It's really fucking good.

"Told you," he chuckles, finishing his in a single bite, though his eyes glimmer with quiet amusement.

"Satisfied?" I grumble.

He just watches me eat with intense focus—something that has me fidgeting, my skin warming as his eyes drag down my face. A slow smirk rises, as if he's eager to make this more awkward, when a fluttering leaf appears beside him.

He stiffens, spine now straight with duty. My heart stops, as I know exactly where that came from. Luckily, leaf messages are sent with intention to the recipient, so there's no chance for the sender to know his location. My pulse drums beneath my skin.

"Who's it from?"

"Witt," he says, and his jaw tightens before he lights it with a small flame, turning it to ash. It drifts down, lazy and slow, dusting the space between us. "Rydian will be at the castle tomorrow."

I swallow, stomach sinking with eagerness or dread or fear? I hate that I can't tell the difference.

"He's two days early."

"Yes," Ren murmurs. "He is."

9

I thought I'd be used to the adrenaline of a mission by now... Yet despite my calm exterior, I'm forcing down the bile rising in my throat now that I'm prepared for our departure to Aurelia.

It *feels* like a mission—bound by my oath to Elion.

Ren and I stride down the corridor, twisting and weaving through the halls with nothing but the scuff of our boots breaking the air. Guards track our movements with every turn, and a glance to my right tells me Ren is no happier about this than I am: his eyes fixed ahead, his face taut with tension.

Rydian is here, and I was summoned just minutes ago, shortly after rising for the day. Ren was already waiting outside my door when I finally opened it, though hardly a word has been spoken between us. I had spent the remainder of last night tossing and turning with a sourness in my stomach.

The throne room doors swing open, and I fix my gaze on the singular table in the center. Rydian faces Elion, his hands formally clasped behind his back. The air is stifling, musky, and dull as if mirroring my own feelings.

Packed with only the essentials, the leather handle of my pack groans as my grip tightens with frustration.

On the other side, along with Witt and a new personal guard, a scholar in a long dark robe stands next to Elion, reciting the agreement in a low mumble. Elion must not have been too upset about losing Theron if he's already replaced him.

I hold back a scoff.

Ren and I approach and stand a few feet away, watching and listening in silence. My anger bubbles.

The scholar carefully sets down his scrolls and reaches for a small, delicate blade on the table. Rydian stands tall, his back straight, when he extends his hand—palm facing up. The scholar pricks his finger, and blood beads before it drips into the quill's hollow top. It trickles into the nib.

My stomach twists, and I swallow as he grips the blood-filled quill and signs the parchment in a quick, careless scribble. He places a bloody fingerprint beside it. It shimmers something wild— blue, violet, red.

I grind my teeth, my face flushing, breaths quick as betrayal sits heavily on my chest. I don't know why, but I was hoping this was all some... ruse to get me to Aurelia.

That thought quickly vanishes.

Without another word, Rydian shakes Elion's hand, tight smiles lining both the kings' faces. Elion's eyes flick to me, a slight smirk spreading on his face, downright menacing. He says nothing, just watches in silence before the prickle of my blood has me fidgeting. Elion grins—a silent reminder of my duty in Aurelia.

Rydian turns sharply and extends both hands for us to grasp, refusing to meet our eyes. Disbelief floods me.

Is he serious?

I glance at the parchment with the scribbled signature and a bloody fingerprint. The faint stench of iron and ink sears my nostrils, melding with the old scent of aged parchment.

"Let's go," he clips.

My jaw clenches, fury scorching my veins as I take a deep, calming breath and attempt to graze his thoughts. Nothing. Not even a single chill touches mine.

My eyes narrow. The ink hasn't even dried yet, and he's treating me as if I'm no more than an item to possess. A *thing* of his to own.

Even if he's angry with me, the Rydian I know would never treat me that way, not really. Then the faint scent of him drifts by, forcing me to swallow a surprised gasp, and square my shoulders.

I place my hand in his without a word, biting my tongue, and we enter the Veil. Within a moment, we're standing in the Whispering Woods, perhaps a mile from Milena's cottage. The air is brisk and cold against my cheeks.

"I hate the Veil," Ren groans, bracing his hands on his knees, and takes a few deep breaths. Surely to keep from vomiting. Ignoring Ren, I whirl to face Rydian, my eyes narrowing once more.

"Where is he?" I ask breathlessly.

Whoever stands beside us is not Rydian, but someone who's taken his form for today, and Elion didn't notice. The figure stares at me and blinks before rippling, quickly melting into Ivy.

She wears a tight bodice and leather pants with a cloak resting upon her shoulders. And as always, she's secured twin swords on both hips. Her almond-shaped eyes casually skim the forest. As if binding herself to Elion—signing her life away—wasn't out of the ordinary but a duty.

My stomach sinks, the realization of it all sweeping through me. It *was* a ruse. Rydian never planned on handing over our heirs, but... Ivy forged an agreement as his second.

Is that even possible?

"Rydian sent you to sign those papers? Why did he—why would you do that?" I demand, stuttering in absolute disbelief.

Her face snaps to mine. "Because I have nothing to lose, that's why. As his second, I take responsibility for protecting his realm—especially when the princess is involved," Ivy clips, and I'm now feeling as small as a grain of salt. "I won't be discussing any more of King Rydian's plans, so if you want to know more, you can ask him yourself when we arrive at the border." Her tight braids cut the air as she briskly walks past, boots crunching in the snow.

Guilt tightens my chest. I was the reason she bound herself in a contract to King Elion—to ensure I arrived in Aurelia. A sacrifice she was willing to make for the sake of the realm. Now *I* feel sick.

"He couldn't even pick us up himself," I say softly, watching Ivy descend the path, and swallow my rising emotions. "Did you hear that?"

"Yes," Ren groans, straightening with a glare.

Despite myself, a chuckle rises at his discomfort and pale skin. He takes a deep breath, rubbing the back of his neck as color floods his cheeks again. Snow settles on his black cloak, fur halting at the middle of his back, and the remaining thick canvas-like material brushes the ground.

My eyes find Ren's in the gray light of dawn, and my shoulders droop in defeat. He nods in Ivy's direction, urging me to follow. I sigh, pull my scarf over my nose, and begin walking. The closer we get to Milena's cottage, the more my palms sweat as a sudden anxiousness takes root.

A few minutes go by before we stop and look left.

A low growl permeates from beyond the trees. A massive howler emerges from the shadows, dark yellow eyes staring back at us, snow dusting his fur. Though I recognize Grim, one of Milena's companions, Ren braces himself with a dagger in hand.

His brows lower as Grim prowls forward, paws hitting the ground in low thuds until they come nose to nose. Ren says nothing, only twirls his dagger with a small smile as if preparing for it to escalate.

Grim snarls, the low sound raising the hair on my arms. *"I don't want to eat her, Stone Shaper. But you're starting to look like a decent snack."*

My eyes widen, and the way Ren slowly scans Grim leaves me to believe that we both heard him. Grim snaps his jaws, but Ren only smirks. Then Grim's attention momentarily shifts to Ivy standing a few feet away. His eyes narrow.

I step around Ren with a sigh, tugging my scarf down. "He wants to know if his memories can be placed back like mine were a few weeks ago. Can we see Milena?"

No sooner than the words leave my mouth, seven pups come

into view, stopping near the trees in the distance to watch the exchange. Only they don't look like pups, easily reaching my thigh in height though only a few weeks old.

My mouth falls open when six come running, and I reach down to greet them. Grim quickly snaps his jaws, so they cower and I snap my hand back. My smile falters.

"Do you not learn anything?" Grim growls at his pups. *"You are to observe, not engage."*

Grim steps away from Ren just as his mate, Nisha, pauses at the treeline, watching him correct their offspring. Her eyes glow in a mix of crimson and amber; a contrast to her dark coat. Another dark pup eyes me from Nisha's front leg, the only one at her side and resembling her in color.

The pup stands tall with a menacing air of confidence warping around its dark coat, wild yet restrained. We hold each other's stare, its golden gaze burning mine, and admiration washes over me. Even young, the pup's stare is almost intimidating.

Grim glances at Ren one last time before he huffs and steps through the glamor just off the road, revealing Milena's cottage at the edge of it. She waits outside with her arms crossed, a tight smile lining her lips, and her hair in a loose bun.

"I should take your head for bringing him here, you know," she scolds, glancing at Ren as we approach.

"We can trust him. His memories were siphoned," I explain.

She holds my gaze a moment longer before nodding, motioning us inside with a wave of her hand.

"I'll wait outside," Ivy says, and crosses her arms as she leans beside the door. Annoyance floods me, and my chest tightens as I hold back a frustrated remark.

Instead, I push past, ignoring her altogether.

As we step inside, freshly baked bread greets us, and the fire crackles on our right. I've come to love Milena's home and welcome the familiarity of it. Shrugging our cloaks off, we place them on the rack by the door. Ren rolls his long sleeves up to his elbows.

"Can I get you anything?" Milena asks, resting her hands on the back of a chair, but I shake my head.

"We're not staying," Ren says, digging the crystal from his pocket to pass off to Milena. "We're headed to Aurelia, so we need to leave shortly after."

Her brows rise. "Aurelia?"

I nod. "To the border after this, so we won't be staying long. Just long enough to get Ren's memories back, if that's okay."

She nods. "I can do it now if you'd like."

Milena doesn't argue when Ren sits instead of lying down, and I assume it's only natural given his size. He rubs his wrist before wringing his hands together.

I know the feeling all too well.

His eyes lock with mine across the table before shifting to Milena, who studies the gray crystal she holds firmly in her grasp.

"May I touch your forehead?" she asks, and he nods.

Placing her hand on him, she closes her eyes. The gray crystal drains of color after a few seconds, ascending her arm and exiting out the other, flooding his temples in a bright light.

As soon as the twisting swirls of grey light enter his mind, his eyes frantically dance behind his lids. He exhales, breath quick and uneven, his hands splayed on the table.

Ren's eyes fly open as he shoves away from the table, and the chair shoots back, clattering to the floor. Frozen and wide-eyed, Ren's hands curl into fists, tight enough that the tendons and veins bulge in his forearms. I swallow, watching his usual calm exterior crack.

Whatever he just recovered, it made him incredibly angry.

But then my stomach drops, as I know what it feels like to gain those sensitive memories—something that should have never been stolen in the first place. I reach for him, but he shakes his head and pivots, stalking toward the door.

I call out, but Milena extends her arm to stop me as he flings it open with a loud grunt. A gust of snow falls to the floor, entering the cottage before the door slams, leaving me with Milena at the table.

"Leave him. He needs to work it out for himself. Give him a few moments," she says and then hums quietly. "He must have gained a lot of memories at once. Important ones, anyway."

"That happens?"

"Yes, if there aren't a lot. You can either get all of them at once, or some, and recover the rest over time when an event triggers the memory. I've seen a mix between the two," she says, pushing her glasses back up her nose.

I sink back down, but guilt claws at my chest. He never knew what he lost, and now to have everything come crashing down... well, I know exactly what that feels like.

Milena offers tea and then packs us food, wrapping the items in a cloth. With a gracious smile, I accept the offer, packing them away before reaching for Ren's cloak and darting out the door.

"What happened?" Ivy asks, her tone laced with curiosity as my boots touch the cold ground. I hold back a scoff.

"Memories... clearly." I sigh with a quick look around. "Where did he go?"

She nods past me, toward the creek in the distance. Ren sits near the bank, elbows resting on his knees with his head down. I weave through the trees, stopping behind him, and toss his cloak across his legs. He doesn't stir.

"Thank you," he says, and I'm unsure if he's thanking me for the cloak or his memories. I sit beside him.

"Do you want to talk about it?"

He lifts his head, fixed on the stream. The edges of the bank are covered in a thin layer of ice and snow. Winter blankets the realm, yet the current remains wild and strong.

"Witt killed my brother," he says finally. "I didn't even know I had a brother until now. He wiped it from me."

"I know." Though my brows pinch, unsure of what to say. I know nothing will soothe the ache in his chest. Not now, anyway. Anything I want to say would only make it worse.

Shortly after Witt had revealed himself in the archives, memories of the real Ezra came rushing back to me. That the boy at the orphanage in Rydian's memories wasn't Witt at all, but Ren's little brother.

Ezra happened to be my closest friend at the time, which was why Witt becoming Ezra was such a believable story.

The real Ezra had been killed and replaced by Witt as part of an assignment to monitor me—to become my shadow. To ensure I remained unaware of who I truly was. And apparently, the only way to do that was to kill Ezra and replace him with the king's second-in-command, leaving me to believe that I was raised beside him for the majority of my life.

Ren and I both witnessed him die that day, right before Witt snuck up behind us and took our memories. Elion had taken Ren's to keep him from retaliating, forcing him to forget his brother, while I lost mine so I would go along with the lie they spun.

"I'll kill him," Ren says softly, so quiet I almost lose the words on the wind. His anger dances between us. "If I go back, I will burn that castle to the ground. I will destroy everyone in it."

He trembles with rage, clenching and unclenching his hands as if attempting to control his building fury. Rock and sediment tremble around us when he finally looks at me, his expression a mix of rage and heartache.

I know that he would do it—kill everyone in that castle without so much as an apology. I expect to feel disgusted by the thought of him harming innocent lives inside that castle, yet all that surfaces is understanding. I would do the same.

I quickly realize just how similar we are, aching for retribution for the lives that were stolen from us. The memories. And now that we've gotten them back, all that remains is heartache.

How far are we willing to go to get it?

The thought tumbles around, leaving a whirl of emotions. Perhaps being raised in the Brotherhood has its repercussions.

"I know. I'll be there when you do it." I glance at my hands. "Ezra's life deserves to be remembered, though. I'm sorry he's gone."

He only nods, facing forward again.

Something moves in my peripheral and I glance over my shoulder, eyeing the dark pup from earlier. It stands at the edge of the trees, watching us.

"I'm sorry you had to find out this way. We'll make it right," I assure Ren, facing forward once more.

Reaching over, I give him a gentle squeeze and stand, but he places a hand on my arm, and lifts his eyes to mine. My brows pinch before understanding what he's too proud to ask outright. I sink back down.

We sit a moment longer, a comfortable silence settling between us as we listen to the quiet rush of water hitting the rocks. When Ren finally stands, he offers me his hand.

"We need to leave," he says, raising me to my feet, then turns for the cottage. He strides past Ivy, through the doorway, and retrieves our packs.

We stand outside Milena's home as she bids us farewell. Ren quietly thanks her as she hands us more food. Even though I shake my head, she shoves the items into my hands with a smile.

Surprisingly, Grim and Nisha stand shoulder to shoulder, dipping their heads as the pups trot forward. Then Nisha pivots, grabs the dark pup by the scruff, and drops him at my feet.

"Fates, Nisha, what the—" I stumble back in shock.

"He's yours," she says.

"No, he is not. I can't..." My lips part, utterly speechless.

"What did she say?" Ivy asks warily, eyes locked on the ebony-coated pup near my feet.

"That he's mine."

Ivy immediately shakes her head. "He cannot come with us."

The moment Ivy's words leave her lips, Nisha steps forward with a low growl, paws crunching wet leaves and ice. Ivy is forced back a few steps, her palms raised and her eyes widening.

"That is not up to you, halfling," Nisha growls as if she could hear her, but the message is clear. Nisha turns to me with an annoyed huff, head dipping. *"You must accept. He has chosen you, and you need a guardian for your journey. He's the strongest. Let him be yours."*

With a quick glance down, my pulse races at the golden stare that meets mine. I know just by looking at him that he's going to be a pain in my ass. He reaches my thigh, tall and confident, and waits for my answer. What the fuck am I going to do with a Howler?

"Is this what you want?" I ask the pup with an arched brow.

He gives me a slow, yet deliberate once over, as if assessing whether I'm up to his standards. A young voice enters my mind. *"Yes, I've made my decision."*

"It looks like I have a new guardian then," I say light-heartedly.

Ivy grips Ren's hand, disappearing for a few seconds, only to return. I'm next. I touch the pup between his ears, so he can make the journey with us, and Milena waves as we vanish in the Veil.

10

We arrive in another forest, and I turn just as Ren straightens and screws his eyes shut. Trees line the road, a blanket of snow covering every inch of it as if it hasn't been traveled on in years.

I hold back another chuckle, watching Ren adjust. One thing is certain: the Aetheri hate using the Veil.

"Where are we?" I ask Ivy, noting the faint sound of waves beating against rock in the distance. Still firmly planted in Elderheim, we must be close to Nymara. The pup takes off at a trot, darting down the terrain as if already familiar.

"Where are you going?" I call out, my words lost in the wind. I'm annoyed that I have responsibility over a living *thing*.

"We're not too far from Red Hollow. King Rydian will meet us there," Ivy says.

The small abandoned town is a few miles south of Nymara's streets, having crumbled into nothing roughly five years ago. Rumors had only grazed the ears of the castle at the time—that people had fled after a catastrophic rise of the sea, salty waves sweeping across the town and taking the residents with it.

Offerings to the Fates increased in the city squares after the town fell, as many feared punishment if their belief dwindled—like reverence alone might keep the same fate of destruction from finding them. But my favorite rumor was that the Fates had struck Red Hollow down for their arrogance.

Who knows, maybe they did.

Regardless of where we landed, we should be arriving in Aurelia soon, and that thought alone has my stomach twisting in knots. Rydian will be there.

Just as I sigh, Ren sucks in a sharp breath and glances around, his fingers curling into tight fists. He takes another deep breath through his nose, chest rising as if battling for control. The Veil isn't *that* terrible.

Confusion furrows between my brows, but as I go to ask, Ren says, "King Elion didn't open the border?"

Ivy strides forward, arms casually swaying, and says over her shoulder, "He did, but when we enter Aurelia, your power will be dulled. It can be… alarming. It's best to enter slowly at first."

We all begin to walk toward Red Hollow as a cold wind drifts by, carrying the scent of salt and pine. The pup continues ahead, circling his way back to us in a blur of shadow.

"Is there anything else we should expect?" I ask.

"Not really," Ivy replies. "King Rydian will be escorting you, so if there's anything else he wants you to know, he'll tell you."

"Howlers grow fast." The pup says casually, meeting me at my side once more. *"We're fully grown by spring. It's why I could leave because I can hunt and use my capabilities."*

My brows shoot up.

So that means he'll soon be near Grim's size or larger. I wonder if he'd been given a name. The Howler at my side shakes, ruffling the snow off his hackles.

"What do I call you?" I ask.

"Kalde," he replies.

Red Hollow sits isolated in the distance, still miles away.

Even from here, I can see the snow blanketing what remains of the town, its stone walls, roofs, and streets crumpled as if curling into itself. Small mountains rise behind it, their edges softened under the snow. To one side, the shadowed line of a lush, green forest presses in, while the other reflects a gray shimmer of the sea.

I pull my eyes from the destruction, sweeping them over our path. Trees line both sides of the road with the ocean on our right, salted air filling my senses.

So crisp it almost prickles my skin.

Ren quietly walks beside me as we follow Ivy toward the town. His boots thud against the packed ground, and the further we walk, the more the trees begin to thin. We're at the edge of the forest, near a rocky cliff, with waves crashing into it below. But squinting through the trees, I can almost see Aurelia from where we walk—verdant, rolling hills and cavernous peaks.

We're close.

"What are your capabilities, exactly?" I ask Kalde, distracting myself from the inevitable.

Instead of answering, he trots ahead with his nose to the ground. Then muffled growls pierce the air, forcing me to scan the area, a knot settling in my stomach. He sniffs, his hackles shooting up.

"Someone is near," Kalde growls.

"Ren," I say softly, fighting the urge to rub the inside of my wrist. I shoot him a wary glance.

A hawk flies above us, landing in one of the trees nearby—Ire. A nervousness snakes up my spine.

"I heard the pup." Ren scans the area.

The young Howler continues forward and halts at the edge of the road. He tucks his head, snarling at what appears to be nothing. Confusion settles over me.

Can he see through the Veil?

Ivy comes to a stop, hands on the hilts of her swords, just as a figure appears, clad in a black cloak with the hood lowered. Kalde growls again, and a deep, throaty hum escapes the figure, a familiar jaw peeking out.

"What do we have here?" Rydian drawls with a glance down.

Ren clenches his jaw, meeting my gaze before I drop my pack to the ground with a thud. My pulse climbs to my temples, skin too hot, breaths too shallow.

Everything from the last several days comes crashing down the moment he steps out of the Veil—the fury, the betrayal, the weight of those bargains he made. Or didn't make, considering he sent Ivy to sign them. The knowledge of it overwhelms me.

"I'll…" Ivy starts, looking over her shoulder at us. "I'll meet you at the castle. We can walk up together once you all arrive."

Rydian nods just as Ivy disappears into the Veil. He looks to Ren before landing on me. Although my pulse races, I meet Rydian in a few strides and take a deep breath. Ren follows closely behind.

Rydian tugs at the edge of his hood, the thick material falling to his snow-covered shoulders, and I take in his features. Dark circles shadow beneath his eyes, resembling someone who's been haunted over the last several days. Yet that does little to calm the simmering rage building in my chest.

He holds my gaze a moment longer before he releases a quiet, relieved-sounding exhale. Then I strike him hard across the face, so his head snaps to the side. He lets out a low, frustrated growl, jaw clenched, eyes burning as he faces me.

"A warm welcome, I see," he says icily.

Ren quietly chuckles behind me. "You deserved that."

"How fucking dare you," I hiss, getting in his face, my hands flaring with energy. Hair rises on my arms, blood simmering as magic pools in my palms in a flood of heat. I snarl, rage hot at my fingertips.

"You had no right!" I shout, the words scorching my throat— words so loud that birds flee from the trees above us, save for Ire.

Rydian's eyes narrow, a cold silence settling between us, before they slide over my shoulder.

"Don't look at me, you did this all on your own," Ren says.

Rydian turns to me again.

He rubs his jaw, frustration twisting his features. "Why don't we finish this when we get to the castle? If you're this angry now, I can't imagine how you'll be when we get there. Save your energy."

He pivots toward the trees behind him.

"What does that mean?" I say through gritted teeth.

Rydian whirls around, sharp and precise and inches from my face. "It means we will finish this conversation when we get there—*that's* what it means. We have a lot to discuss, and I won't do it out here. There's not enough time in the day to stand here and argue, or we'd be here all night."

Ren huffs an unamused laugh with a shake of his head, and watches Rydian angrily stride into the forest without another word. Tension hangs thick in the air.

Ren turns, his expression unreadable, and grabs our packs from the ground. Closing my eyes, I pinch the bridge of my nose and take in a long breath.

"I didn't mean to do that," I admit.

"I personally think he deserved it." Ren smirks, but it falters as he stares down at me. "He'll be fine. Let's get settled, and we'll figure it out when we get there."

I only nod, following Ren into the forest. Kalde silently trails behind us, and I find myself wondering what he thought of that exchange. Miles of ocean separate our realms.

Besides the Veil's Edge, the cliff is the only singular area where our lands overlap slightly. After a few minutes of walking, we stop yards from the cliff.

Rydian faces us. "This is where the realms meet. When you cross, you'll still be able to wield, just not as efficiently. I'll be able to Veil you all into Aurelia separately. I'll take you first," Rydian says, gesturing to me.

I shake my head. "You'll take Ren first, and then you come for me and the pup. He's coming too."

Rydian's brows lower, eyes landing on Kalde beside me, before he lets out a low, disbelieving chuckle. I believe Rydian will take me to Aurelia, but I'm still unsure of his trust in Ren, and I don't want to give him the opportunity to leave him behind.

From what Ren and I have had to endure over the last several days in Elderheim, I trust him with my life. But a small whisper at the back of my mind says that Rydian would leave him just to spite me. Especially with how this is going so far, I wouldn't put it past him.

Rydian huffs but nods anyway. "Very well. I'll arrive outside the castle so we can all walk up together."

Ren steps over first. A small twist of green light shudders around his shoulders and he nods, confirming that his magic has dulled when Kalde follows. Then it's my turn.

A faint shimmer hangs in the air, marking the difference in temperature—separating the realms from the harsh snowfall in Elderheim and the dense fog across the ocean. The air shimmers green, but there's no border or shield, just open space as Elion promised.

I step forward, but pain erupts behind my eyes, a searing agony so sharp that it forces me to clutch my head. Then I scream, the sound ripping from my throat and echoing across the sea. I press my palms against my temples, desperate for the pain to stop.

Make it stop, make it stop. Who's shouting? Why are they shouting? Can't they see I'm in pain? How do I make it stop?

My body seizes, muscles locking. And then my arms go rigid, my knees buckling and forcing me to the ground. But the pain in my knees is nothing compared to the pressure pushing against my skull.

A blur of movement, then shadows flood my body, cascading down my arms and onto the ground, as if swallowing me whole. I grit my teeth, willing the pain to fade. It only blinds me, leaving nothing but the echo of my screams as darkness consumes me.

11

Iron and dirt and mold sear my nostrils, my shoulders aching with every dragging minute. Strung up by my wrists, my shoulders are seconds from popping out entirely.

But finally, the ringing in my ears quiets, replaced by the clinking of chains. My eyes lift just as a sharp pain sears my cheek, the heated slap jerking my face to the right.

Blood slips down my chin, dripping to the floor when a wet, mocking laugh bubbles from me—the sound unfamiliar as I hold his hateful stare. We've been here for two days, but I've somehow managed to swallow my rising emotions.

No panic, no fear—only cold indifference.

"Tell me who they belong to," Ezra says in a tone that has the hair rising on my arms. If it weren't for the ache in my chest, the shock at his betrayal, I would have already killed him for it. It was only when I'd shown him my mate marks that I discovered his real role as King Elion's second-in-command.

He was supposed to be my friend, and yet he lied to me all these years. How could he?

His brown hair glows in the dungeon's dim light as he circles me, flipping a dagger with a menacing smirk, orange flickering from the sconces. He lets out a disgruntled hum, nodding even though frustration creeps through his features.

Two mate marks appeared on me four weeks ago at the age of twenty-one. Though I still haven't figured out how I'm marked to two mates—one from each realm. How is it even possible? The thought has been tumbling through my mind since then.

It just doesn't make sense.

But King Elion doesn't like distractions, and so I hid them for fear of repercussions. I'd made the mistake of trusting Ezra, revealing my marks, and watched him dissolve from a carefree training partner to someone I didn't recognize.

Within seconds, I was disarmed and on my knees, taken to King Elion shortly after discovering what marked my skin. What marked my hair.

Everyone knows he doesn't like the brethren to be tied to another, not when we've been trained to serve only him.

And now I'm tied to two more.

"I told you. I… don't… know," I grind out the words and then spit at him with a low snarl. Red splatters across his face in a fine mist—fitting for someone who's betrayed me. I grin.

His lip curls, and then another heated slap sears my cheek. With a grit to my teeth, I bury my emotions, refusing to give in to the interrogation. The fear. If only to keep him from feeling them.

A rattling laugh bubbles up my chest, and my head hangs low between my shoulders as I stare at the ground, blinking through silent blood-stained tears. He could torture me for eternity, and I wouldn't tell him who they belonged to, regardless of how brutal it became.

I'm determined to hang here and let Ezra do just that, as I'd never risk putting anyone in danger because of the marks we bear. We don't get to decide who we're marked to—the Fates do.

It's not their fault or mine, it just is.

All sense of time is lost, it could be days, weeks, for all I know. My blood continues to slowly drip… drip… drip—pooling beneath my dangling feet. Then I'm falling.

My knees land on the cold, wet ground when Ezra grabs a fistful of hair and snaps my head back. I cry out and blink, now gazing in the eyes of the cruelest second-in-command.

Despite it all, a dark smile spreads wide across my face, my teeth coated in blood that settles at the back of my throat.

"Fuck you," I get out with a mocking chuckle. "Kill me. Do what you have to—I don't care. I'll never tell you who they belong to, so you might as well just get it over with."

Another set of boots thud against the dungeon floor, slow and calculating, and my body stiffens at the familiarity. I know who they belong to.

"Take them." King Elion's voice echoes off the stone. "Take everything about the marks and whatever's tied to them. The knowledge. All of it."

Ezra smiles down at me, the kind of smile that chills my bones, my skin prickling with unease. I look at the King, his features hardening into something cruel while he stands in the entryway to my cell. He smirks, watching my body tremble with horror.

"Take what?" I manage to ask, and for the first time in several days, my chest tightens. Emotions crawl to the surface. Ezra chuckles, leaning down, inching closer to my face. I wish I had the strength to headbutt him, but the firm grip he has on my hair prevents me from doing that.

"Since you won't tell us who they belong to," Ezra sneers. "I'll be taking your memories tied to those marks. You'll be our loyal dog once again, serving King Elion like nothing happened."

"You're sure it will work?" Elion questions, doubt lacing his tone. Confusion enters my beaten face, breaths shallow as I listen. Unease creeps up my spine.

What do they mean, take my memories?

A yellow stone appears in Ezra's hand, swirling as if already occupied. My stomach sinks.

He's done this more than once.

"It'll work," Ezra chuckles, a throaty sound, his grip tightening a little, and I whimper. "Even if she's been claimed, her power will remain the same as it was before... once her essence is siphoned, that is. No chance for it to grow. She won't even feel the bond."

"Good. We can't have that," Elion says.

My eyes grow wide, my pulse racing at the thought of them taking what's mine. My essence...

No, no, no. Gods, please.

This is only a dream, right? It isn't real.

"Please," I finally beg and writhe in his hold, a sob tearing from my throat. Even as I kick and thrash, even as I scream in terror, he doesn't let go.

His grip tightens again. "Please, don't do this. I promise I won't leave. I'll— I'll do anything you want, just don't take them!"

My chest heaves, panic crashing over me in unrelenting waves. I beg and beg and beg, voice breaking, head shaking, desperate as I plead into the eyes of the one person I thought would never betray me. Why is he betraying me?

Yet all I can do is sob.

Then I feel it—at the base of my neck, threading through my thoughts— fear colliding with mine, even from hundreds of miles away. He feels me.

He feels my despair and panic and fear as I beg for mercy—beg for them to leave my memories alone. As I hold tightly to the one thing I never want to let go of. My heart shatters, crumbling into a million tiny pieces.

Still, begging does nothing.

Ezra's smirk only widens as he stares down at me. I release another sob when he settles his palm against my head, holding me steady while my tears fall to the cold, blood-spattered ground. A scream rips from me, guttural and unfamiliar, quaking the stone walls as the warmth of his touch settles in my hair.

"You won't feel a thing," Ezra says softly, digging into my memories, crawling through them like a spider weaving its web, yanking. And then darkness blankets my mind.

My temples throb, my pulse still racing from that dreadful memory. One that I know is very, very real. One I could have gone my entire life not remembering.

I hate them for what they've done.

With my eyes screwed shut, silent tears slip down my temples for what happened so long ago—for why I hadn't remembered where those marks came from or what they were. It was always them—King Elion and Witt.

But as the memory fades into a forgotten corner of my mind, my skin prickles at the sound of a frustrated argument to my left. I'm not alone.

As silently as I can muster, I take in a long, steady breath, my fingers twitching in the soft bedding beneath me. At least that blinding pain subsided—gods, the pain.

The border. Our argument. Where am I?

"You will tell her or I will," Ren says quietly—firmly, and in a way that has my adrenaline pumping. "I hope you're ready for what she's going to unleash when you do."

Tell me what exactly?

My brows furrow, but my eyes remain closed, and I slow my breaths. Jasmine, burning wood, and a hint of amber flood my senses. A comforting scent. Ancient.

Shadows stir beneath my skin, my blood icy and unfamiliar, similar to what Rydian feels like in my thoughts. The same shadows that consumed me earlier, but they're nothing like the warm buzz of energy in Elderheim. No, this is different—sharp and intense.

"She won't be as angry with me..." A low, frustrated grunt.

Ren grumbles. "Well, you need to do it before she gets word of it from someone in the castle. She needs to hear it from you, or she'll never forgive you for it. Not after what happened at that dinner, you'll only make it worse."

"I *know*," Rydian bites out.

Peeling my eyes open, I instinctively glance their way. Ren and Rydian stand near a long, darkwood table in a heated discussion.

Rydian stands with his back to me, rubbing his neck where his black mark would sit within his auburn hair. But Ren's face is pale. So pale my breath catches, leaving me to wonder if being in Aurelia is the reason for it. He crosses his arms, lips flattening to a thin line.

Tall doors tower over them both. The bathing chamber sits on one wall, and perhaps the room's entrance on the other. An exquisitely large wooden wardrobe sits nearby, carved to perfection save for the little scratches along the double doors.

Ren leans forward, resting his palms on the table, and draws in a long breath, holding Rydian's stare. Shaggy strands of onyx hair fall to his temples, but Rydian only shakes his head and sighs, as if at war with his thoughts.

"I—" Rydian halts and tilts his head, listening. "I'll be right back."

He whirls from the chamber, vanishing into the Veil. Ren straightens after a moment, sighing a long breath, and closes his eyes while wringing his hands. He remains like that a while longer, taking deep breaths, one after the other, until color slowly seeps back into his face.

His eyes open, and I squeeze mine shut, unwilling to be caught awake just yet. Only because nausea still curls in my stomach from that memory, as I'm unable to bury the rising emotions.

It doesn't take long before his boots thud closer to where I lie, and I hold my breath, remaining motionless with my arms at my sides. He stops beside me.

A silent minute goes by, and for a moment, I fight the urge to open my eyes, wondering if he quietly retreated without me noticing. Then his finger drags down my left hand, slow and unhurried, until it rests on my knuckle. Warmth seeps into my skin and my eyes open to catch the glow of his finger lighting up my skin. Confusion floods my mind.

I stiffen, my eyes flying up to find his locked on my face, also frozen—startled, actually. Judging by the flash of his eyes and his frightened expression, he definitely thought I was asleep.

My lips part and I shoot up, mumbling as my head spins with confusion and disorientation. "What was—"

A whoosh in the air halts my words, and my head swivels toward the door. Rydian stands there, eyes fixed on me when his jaw feathers. Ren slowly retreats, shooting Rydian a glance. He says nothing, just shakes his head and quietly exits the room.

Before I can question his odd behavior, I glance around the chamber, a room decorated as if it were created for someone important. The gilded mantel sits on the wall across from the foot of the oversized bed, accompanied by two embroidered settees and a long couch.

I blink and shift back to Rydian, though my head still spins from sitting up too quickly. He only stands there, hands in pockets, staring. An awkward silence settles, as if neither of us knows where to begin. Dread curls low in my gut, and I'm unable to form a single word.

My brows pinch, and I lean forward, swallowing the lump in my throat. "I—"

"How do you feel?" he asks, cutting off whatever words were about to frantically tumble out of me. "Before we get into the discussion that needs to happen, tell me how you feel."

I swallow again and palm my forehead, attempting to recall everything before my arrival, but all I remember is pain.

Blinding, agonizing pain. Until that memory took over.

I shudder. "Better."

Pulling my gaze away, my eyes land on the propped-open door near the mantel. A bed rests on the other side, clothes strung across the bedding, the adjacent chamber as grand as the one I'm in.

Directly to the right of my mantel are tall, intricate glass doors that reach the ceiling; beside them are two cream-colored drapes pinned out of the way. Doors that lead to a private balcony.

"We believe you experienced a surge of magic," Rydian says quietly. My heart stops.

"How?" I ask.

"I'm not sure." Rydian's brow knits, and concern etches into his face. "Since you've lived in Elderheim for most of your life, it could have dampened Aurelia's magic, preventing you from fully developing as you grew older. You haven't been here in twenty years, so we assume that when you began obtaining your magic as a child, Elderheim's was easier to adjust to since you were already in that realm... regardless of King Elion siphoning them."

"Is that possible?" My eyes widen when he nods.

"Yes, but with them siphoning you at a young age, I think Aurelia's magic was dulled even more. Now that you have some of your essence back, we believe planting your feet on the soil gave you a surge of your power—Aurelia's power."

That's probably why I feel more shadow beneath my skin than the warmth of Elderheim. Regardless of the gripping panic and the uncertainty of our future, I rise, planting my feet on the floor, and lean against the bed.

"You're in Aurelia," Rydian says, a seriousness coating his tone. "This is the queen's chamber. That door leads to mine." He points to the door near the mantel.

The queen's chambers.

"This is mine?" I look around in disbelief. "Why are your chambers right there?"

"They're the king's chambers. And yes, it will be yours until your reign ends," he says.

A thought surfaces, and my stomach drops.

"Was this my mother's room?" I manage to ask before my throat closes. Mainly at the question—at discovering who she was beyond a figment of my imagination. Because up until this point, up until Elion's vision and that tiny sliver of memory Rydian showed me weeks ago, I believed she didn't exist.

Still, she's felt out of reach, but now...

He nods. "I wasn't sure how you'd feel about taking her chamber, but I changed the quilts. The hand-maiden placed her items into a small chest for you. You can go through them later if you'd like. I did ask her to leave a few of her dresses; you're very close to her in size."

I nod and glance at my hands as I wring them together. The intricate, colorless mark on my wrist stares back at me, blazing into my mind like a secret I can't confess but desperately want to.

"I never meant for any of this to happen, you know," I murmur, unsure how to even begin. "When I went to Milena's, she told me everything. Told me how I carried both royal essences and that I needed to keep quiet, but... I knew you'd look at me differently." I shake my head, eyes lifting only to stare at the furious expression twisting his features.

He turns sharply and scoffs, walking around the long table to pace. A raging fury scorches my thoughts—*his* fury—pounding against my temples. How can I feel his emotions so easily when no one else in the Veil brushes my thoughts the way he does?

Perhaps it's intentional.

Perhaps he wants me to feel his anger.

Still, I hold back a wince. "I knew you were going to look at me as your enemy the moment I revealed who my father was."

"You made me your enemy!" he shouts, his composure cracking, and slams his hands onto the table. He leans forward on his palms.

His head drops into a disbelieving shake, auburn hair falling forward. Though his eyes remain fixed on the table below, refusing to look at me.

"Instead of talking to me, you handed over Aurelia on a silver platter as if everything we did together meant nothing. Even after he destroyed *our* realm. If I could guess, I'd imagine that was his plan all along, and you played right into his hands."

Anger crawls into my chest at that. "It wouldn't have made a difference if I told you or not—you would have always looked at me differently."

His head lifts, a wrinkle forming between his brows. "Do you think so poorly of me?"

Breaths halt in my throat, and a long, quiet moment passes between us. My lips part, though no words form. I can't even muster an explanation—I have none.

"I want to know at what point I led you to believe that you couldn't trust me? You never even gave me the chance, Isa. You'd made that decision before we even began working together. Being heir to both realms gave you leverage, and we could have found a way *together*."

"What was I supposed to do?" I ask breathlessly, rising off the edge of the bed to stumble forward. "I don't even know who to trust, or know what's real anymore. Everyone I know has betrayed me, or kept secrets, or has used me in some way. I feel like I'm forced to choose."

"That's not true." Rydian straightens and rounds the table to face me with a set jaw. "You trusted Ren," he says, and I blink. My mouth falls open, seconds from denying the accusation, but words fail me once more. "He stood on that dais and didn't move like he expected something to happen. The only reason he's alive right now is because he kept you safe, but don't think I didn't notice it. He knew more than I did, and you chose not to tell me. That was a conscious decision."

"The only reason he knew is because he found me shortly after Milena's—I had no plan. That is the truth."

"The truth." Rydian chuckles in disbelief, rubbing his jaw.

"Yes. You don't have to believe me, but it's the truth." My eyes drop to my hands as guilt tightens my chest. Guilt and shame and something else I can't quite name hold me hostage. I did trust Ren, for reasons I'm unable to explain.

"I don't want to be your enemy," I say finally.

Rydian has every right to be angry with me, the truth of his words tearing a hole in my heart. I had promised him in Elderheim that we would work as a team, and yet I broke every ounce of his trust. Truthfully, it's unforgivable, and I wouldn't blame him if he chose not to forgive my mistake.

And my *oath*. Gods.

"You gave up an entire realm," he says bluntly, crossing his arms. "You gave up my *home* to aid him. I was forced to bargain for you in the only way that made sense—"

"I would have given him anything," I confess, a huff of disbelief escaping my nose, and his brows pinch. Confusion enters his face, and despite myself, a tear falls to my cheek. I shake my head, unsure how else to explain it. "If he had asked me to give him the moon, I would have given him a thousand stars." My voice cracks, and for a brief moment, his expression falters before striding forward.

"Isa," he says so quietly, stopping just shy of my feet.

"I would have slit my own throat if it meant he'd never discover who you are or what you mean to me," I choke out. "That's why I did it. Aurelia means nothing to me. Elderheim means *nothing* to me. But you…"

"Say it," he whispers, and his finger gently lifts my chin. His eyes fall across my face. "I want to hear you say it."

I have no choice but to look into the eyes I often find myself lost in. The eyes that remind me of an ocean sunrise the day after a harsh storm, golden light reflecting off the vivid blue water. The eyes that promised me a future in Aurelia the night we stole that map together.

My heart shatters and fuses all at once, filling me with something like hope for the first time in my life. I study him—study the curve of his lips as his hand settles beneath my ear.

"I love you," I murmur, the confession lifting a weight off my shoulders. Off my chest. "And I should have told you that night. I should have told you everything. I'm sorry."

A small smirk rises on his lips, as if hearing it lit his entire world on fire. His thumb slowly wipes the tear sliding down my cheek, and he studies my face, the touch of him burning me.

"You're my mate, Isa."

12

"What?" I ask breathlessly, pulse pounding in my ears. Even though my heart races with excitement and fear and uncertainty, that's not...

Well, it doesn't make sense.

"You're my mate," he says again, and my stomach dips. A surge of fear pebbles my skin when another dreadful thought surfaces. If he's my mate and doesn't know about the other mark on my wrist... oh gods.

"Our marks don't match," I blurt, shaking my head, hoping this is only a dream. "You told me that you had someone waiting for you—"

"I didn't." He holds me steady by the back of my neck while my eyes grow wide. "I never told you anything about the marks; you made that assumption all on your own. I had planned on telling you when we argued at the loft, but I couldn't."

He lets the words hang in the air. Then I blink, images flashing across my mind as fragments of memory flood me. My chest heaves as I take it all in. Remembering.

I feel sick. Somewhere, in the darkest parts of my mind—my memories—I knew about the Shadovar marks. Knew that they were always opposites instead of matching in color. Elion used to send us to track them down, hunting them by their marks when he sealed the border. *I knew?*

Repulsion from those missions settles before frustration grips me. Why couldn't I have recalled this when we argued at the loft?

If I had remembered—if he had told me—I wouldn't have made him steal that map. I would've left with him that night, left my mother in Elderheim, as shameful as the thought is.

"How long have you known that I was your mate?" I grouse as the thought slides across my mind, recalling how he admitted to seeing my mate mark after our very first night together.

This must be what Ren meant earlier—something he knew I'd be angry about. Who else knows? A crawling fury shimmies up my spine; I know what his answer is going to be.

"I knew after our first time." A slow, menacing smirk rises on his lips. "Don't worry, you've already claimed me."

"That's not—" My lips part, shock settling once more, though I can't bring myself to deny it. Uncertainty tightens in my chest, and I release a rough breath.

I *did* claim him, and I felt it—that golden thread tethering me to him in my mind. At the time, I never suspected him to be my mate; I never even realized he had a mark.

Yet the only reason those little words had any effect was because he bore my mark. And I claimed him while we were fucking? My eyes flare with realization. That must be why I can sense his emotions.

Claiming a mate is not just a ritual—it's sacred.

An act of love and trust, as binding as any wedding save for the swapping of an oath. Our essences. And even though it's not required, it's typically done under a full moon—something you do together, outside, and in private.

Anger replaces my shock, and I growl, nothing short of a raging storm when I rear back to slap him. He catches my wrist, and yanks me to his chest with that maddening grin he wears so often.

He leans in. "I want to know at what point slapping became your weapon of choice. I miss the daggers."

"I claimed you while we were fucking?" I growl again, disbelief coating my tone. Emotions surface, unsure whether I should be ecstatic or angry that I'd done it without knowing.

"Whether you claimed me while you were wrapped around my cock or under the stars, you would've done it with a grin on your face," he chuckles. "At least you came."

A snarl curls my lips, and I attempt to tug my arm back, but his grip only tightens. "You owe me." I spit the words. "Mate claiming rituals are sacred, and we—"

"Fine, I owe you a ceremony and a ring," he says dramatically and releases my wrist only to tug me closer, his other hand sliding below my ear. "After I fuck you, of course. I still need to welcome you back. I suppose this means you accept?"

"A ceremony and a ring?" I exclaim, and my brows shoot up. "You could have at least—" I growl in frustration. "It better be a nice fucking ring."

He laughs, but before I can muster another argument, his mouth slams into mine. I instinctively groan, savoring the taste of him on my tongue, the realm fading entirely.

Every ounce of my anger dissolves into nothing, lost to the corners of my mind as he tangles himself around me. He tastes sharp and crisp, the faint scent of his arousal hitting my nostrils in a welcoming flood of heat.

He tastes like home—*my home.*

Every inch of my body is on fire now, humming with need, a heat settling right between my thighs.

The hurriedness with which he devours me has us stumbling, and we fall together. Rydian catches us by a hand on the lush rug, pinning me beneath him. He wraps an arm around my waist, rolling his hips so that I feel his hard length against me.

My lips part with a gasp, a whimper slipping out as his tongue sweeps inside my mouth as if he were starving. It's then that I realize just how much I need him inside of me.

I meet his tongue stroke for stroke, aching for him.

Aching for any sort of reprieve as heat rises from my core to the center of my chest. I arch into him when he tears his lips away, panting and fumbling with my tunic, fumbling with the laces on my pants. He hurriedly strips me bare, yanking them off.

I quickly pull at his tunic, tossing it aside when he leans down, raking his teeth down my neck. Dragging, licking, teasing. His hand dips between my thighs, a surge of wetness coating his fingertips, then he strokes me.

"Mm, already so wet for me." He parts me on a hungry groan, the sound of which prickles my skin. His fingers drag up and down in teasing strokes before driving them into me.

"Fuck," I moan, arching off the floor. He grins, his mouth hovering over mine before capturing it again.

"That sound would have anyone crawling to you," he grumbles. *"But louder next time—I need the others to hear who claims me in my own fucking castle."*

"Take them off," I breathe, my fingers clawing for his pants as the hard length of him strains against the fabric. They barely come undone before they're halfway down his hips, only low enough to free his cock. It juts out, hovering between us.

He grins again and then settles between my thighs, lining himself up, eyes blazing. "Welcome home."

He drives his hips forward.

My whimper turns to a breathy cry as he slides into me. Rydian lets out a low moan, the guttural, primal sound rumbling up his chest and setting my skin ablaze.

"Gods, I missed you," he pants, stretching me inch by inch, pushing until he fills me entirely.

The thick feel of him unravels my control and I tremble, aching for friction. He withdraws again, tauntingly slow, before driving to the hilt in a hard thrust. He groans, eyes fixed on me as I let out another small whimper, my nails clawing at his chest. Scratches trail down his body, and his grip tightens on my thighs to the point of pain.

"I missed those sounds." He thrusts into me with another hard slam, jolting me backward.

Gripping me by a shoulder, he moves without restraint,

pounding into me over and over and over until my breaths catch, gasping at the sheer size of him.

I let out another sound, mixed between a moan and a cry. Rydian echoes it above me. He watches himself, slick and gleaming in the dim light. I've never felt so wanted.

I meet every wild grind of his hips, arching my back for him to pound into me, and he drives himself deeper. His hand slides to the apex of my thigh, his thumb swirling over my clit.

I cry out again, my core clenching, the pressure of my release traveling to where his thumb sits. But just as my release builds, misted shadow floods from his shoulders, down his body, and onto mine, cool against my skin.

Full power I have yet to see entirely.

Then I realize it's not just his, but mine too, melding together in a thick wave of darkness. Entwining in a mesmerizing dance along my skin.

His mouth falls open on a breath, moaning as his hips continue to drive forward, unrelenting and hungry, his thick cock glistening between us. My eyes grow wide as his shadows reach out, circling a path around my throat in a welcoming, but painful, squeeze. His head falls back, eyes fluttering as he moans again—raw and wild— his control fracturing.

Fuck. My eyes squeeze shut at the tightness of his shadows. The tightness of my grip on his cock. I begin to crest the wave of my release.

"Come for me, Princess," he grunts, swiping his thumb again and again until I'm writhing, panting for any amount of air. "Tell them who you belong to."

With a sharp cry, my release explodes from me. I tighten around his cock, my entire body pulsing with desire, shuddering under the weight of him.

"Yes, that's it," he whimpers, thrusting once more before roaring his own release, spilling every aching drop of himself inside me.

His chest heaves a few seconds before he collapses, and for a long moment we just lie on the rug, breaths steadying, limbs tangled together. The familiarity of him beside me settles my racing heart, though the love I carry threatens to burst from my chest, pounding relentlessly.

"You are my undoing," he murmurs, propping onto an elbow to stare down at me. Auburn locks fall forward, dark and unruly. "You are breathtaking and wild," he says on a breath, a small smile tilting his mouth. "One day, in our future, you will bring everyone who walks our realms to their knees."

"I love you," I get out before my throat closes, tears sliding down my temples. He leans down, kissing them off my face before landing another soft one on my mouth.

"I hated being apart from you," he says softly. "I hated that I was angry, but my focus was getting you to Aurelia. I don't care about anything else. Nothing."

"Really?" He nods and then sighs when I reach for him, eyes fluttering, melting into my palm. Ren must have already filled him in.

I take a long breath and allow myself to enjoy how he feels wrapped around me. Enjoy the way his finger now trails a sweaty path from my breasts to my navel, sending another roaring heat between my legs.

But only for a moment.

Shame and guilt quickly follow as the faint gleam of my colorless mark shines in the light that spills across the room, as if beckoning me to confess. My brows furrow, hating the fact that I have to ruin our brief moment of peace, but it would kill me to keep it from him.

He needs to know.

Whether he sees where my eyes land or the expression I wear, he grips my wrist to stare at it, and my heart stops in my chest. My eyes grow wide, breaths stalling just as he takes my wrist and brings it to his mouth. He places a soft kiss along the inside of it.

"I know," he says, scanning my face as if studying my reaction. I jolt upright, leaning against my palms.

"Since when?" I breathe, my chest tightening with confusion. He knows?

With a lazy grin, he tugs my arm forward, and plants another kiss on my wrist.

"I didn't have any suspicions until after our confrontation with Elion—your confession of being heir." He pushes hair away from my face, but I'm shaking my head, staring at my wrist. "I'd seen it on you before and had initially thought it looked similar to Elderheim's mark. At the time, I believed you to be Shadovar, so I pushed it aside. It never occurred to me that you were..." He shrugs, his words trailing off, though I know what he fails to say. *Heir to two crowns.*

"What does it mean?" A wrinkle of confusion, concern perhaps, forms between my brow. "I shouldn't have two—there's never been two marks on anyone." Not that I know of, anyway.

"I don't know." He sighs. "But Varrin, our historian, is looking into it for me. We think it could be because you carry both royal essences, something that ties you to both realms. A balance, perhaps."

My breath quickens at that. At the idea of others knowing what I bear, and researching me like I'm an animal to be studied. At being bound to two mates. That feeling of being forced to choose resurfaces. Forced to pick a realm... forced to pick a mate. I swallow as unease pebbles my skin, but after a quiet moment, he lifts my chin, and I stare at him again.

"Are you angry?" I ask, completely dumbfounded.

"It wouldn't matter if I were." His jaw feathers slightly, and for a brief moment, a sliver of annoyance brushes my mind. "You're already mine, even if we haven't fully completed the claim yet. You could have a thousand marks," he murmurs, settling himself between my thighs again. He towers over me and pushes me back down. My blood heats, anticipation thrumming in my veins.

"You could have a thousand lovers if you wanted..." He grins, hunger forming in his eyes once more. "...and you'd still be mine."

"You'd never allow that." I chuckle, even though my stomach drops. I shake my head with disbelief and a hint of awe.

"You have no idea what I'd allow."

A menacing smirk lifts the corner of his mouth, and his tongue flicks over his bottom lip. His eyes drag over every inch of my body before he pushes my knees apart, lowers his head, and gazes up from beneath his lashes.

"Now, where did I leave off?"

13

We eventually find our way to the bed, remaining here for a few more hours as a fire roars in the hearth. It's hard to believe it's only been a day since arriving. Rydian rises, shrugging on his clothes, his hair in absolute disarray. Though a small, devious grin pulls at his mouth.

"Where are you going?" I ask.

I lean against the pillows before glancing at the lush fabric beneath me in awe and disbelief. Delicate. A mixture of ivory and sapphire embroidery on the soft fibers. Quilts made for a queen, apparently. My stomach growls, breaking the silence, and he chuckles, leaning forward to plant a kiss on my forehead. I only blink.

"I need to attend a meeting with the council," he says, handing me my clothes. I pull them on, frowning at the thought of him leaving me here, and wonder where Ren ended up. "I'll be back shortly. Why don't you eat something, and I'll have someone give you a tour?"

"A tour?" My stomach drops. People and courts and luxury run through my mind. "Why can't you do it?"

"I want to, but I think you'll like your tour guide." He grins as a soft knock sounds on the door. He turns and cracks it open, a gentle delicate voice mumbling beyond it. Rydian steps aside, pulling the door open.

"Hi, Princess," she says, her bright blue eyes going wide before she averts her gaze and bows. Her short auburn hair sways forward.

"Isa, this is my sister, Lettie," he says with a small smile. "She will be your hand maiden and your tour guide."

"You have a sister?" I say, though every ounce of shock was put into those words. He'd never said anything about her.

"Get acquainted, and I'll see you in a while." He disappears down the hall, leaving me to face her with wide eyes. A sliver of annoyance grates on my nerves over the fact that he just left me here.

That was hardly an introduction.

"Is he always like that?" I grit my teeth, and give her a subtle once-over. Lettie wears a simple blue linen dress, one with pockets on either side that barely brushes her ankles.

"Yes," she chuckles, though she remains in the hall.

Her hair stops at the shoulders, and she appears no older than twenty-four, but that could mean anything in the realms. The delicate points of her ears poke out from beneath the silky strands as she looks at me with curious eyes.

"A hand-maiden?" A personal one at that.

I scan the hallway, realizing just how enormous everything is. I haven't even looked around yet, but the castle is eerily quiet. Almost too quiet. Another set of exquisitely large doors rests across from mine, and I assume they're the ones leading to Rydian's chamber.

"Yes. Rydian said you were hungry and told me to prepare you a bath since you smell like that... other male." She winces a little, nose scrunching. "The one you arrived with."

Now I'm really confused. My brows shoot up since that's not true at all. I smell nothing like Ren. Perhaps his scent lingered from staying in my chambers all those days in Elderheim.

I only sigh, allowing her in, and she clicks the door shut with a silver tray in hand. The scent of freshly baked bread reaches me when she sets it down and lifts the lid. My stomach growls again.

Stewed venison sits in the middle, alongside fresh bread, various berries, sliced pears, cheese, and a baked berry tart.

"Does he think I'm dying of starvation?" My expression twists into a scowl, and she giggles.

"Considering the magic you attained by coming back, you'll need it to replenish your energy. I'll get the bath ready for you." She bows again, and I almost cringe, my skin prickling with dismay.

That is something I'll never get used to.

Sitting at the oversized table, I help myself to the food, scarfing it down like something feral. A few minutes go by when Lettie approaches from the bathing chamber, watching as I finish the last of the bread. Gods, I *was* starving.

"All prepared for you, Princess." She bows, delicate and practiced, though I can't help my rising curiosity.

"Where is everyone?"

She gives me a gentle smile. "Rydian asked everyone to remain near the front of the castle upon your arrival to give you privacy. You're in the private section of the castle, one floor above the back entrance in the royal wing. And as for the quietness, a lot of the guests and residents here prefer their conversations in the Veil, except for the humans."

My eyes barely graze hers before shifting back to the venison stew in front of me. "And what do they know?"

She steps forward, reaching the chair to my right. I catch a flicker of a wince before she gives me another smile.

"I wasn't supposed to mention it, but since you asked..." She trails off with a quiet sigh. "The castle knows of your mark and that it belongs to King Rydian. They believe it's a sign from the Fates that the missing princess bears the mark of their king."

I chew my lip, shooting her a wary glance as shame climbs up my chest. Little do they know it's not just their king.

"How exactly do they know that?"

A flat smile. "Eldric, on the council. He saw it when they attended that... dinner. He told the council, and rumors spread."

My teeth grind, recalling how Theron humiliated me at that dinner, and I force myself to push down the rising emotions. "Are you his only sibling, or should I prepare for more?"

"I'm the only one," she huffs a laugh. "We do have a cousin in Vyria, though. Zeeke lives in our family estate north of the city. After the royal essence was passed down to Rydian, he wanted me back in the castle, so I offered to serve as a maiden. I... didn't want responsibility beyond that."

"You look like him," I say, wondering how old she is. "Do you like him as a king?"

Lettie splits into a wide grin, beaming. So wide that it meets her eyes. She seems sweet.

"Very much," she says. "King Andre would have been proud of him. He's taken care of us since that battle and has even made a few changes in the realm. He usually keeps to himself, though. He was... frantic when he searched for you." She winces again, almost as if it's a sensitive subject. "He wouldn't give up, regardless of how many times the council urged him to let you both go. He swore you were still out there. It makes sense now, but he was reclusive and quiet. I had never seen him so..." Her head tilts.

"Obsessive?" I add, recalling the memories he shared with me.

She nods. "Yes, that's a good word for it. But since finding you, he's been less haunted, and even has a gleam to his eyes that I haven't seen in a while."

Silence lingers for a beat, leaving me to rise and awkwardly wipe my hands. "I guess I'll bathe now. Thank you, Lettie." As soon as I turn, she hesitates, lips parting.

"Would you... like a tour after?" she asks.

Right, a tour. I frown at the thought of walking around the castle, being studied and talked about. Eyes and ears on me wherever I go. I'm not sure I want to entertain that right now, not after just arriving.

My nose scrunches. "Can I say no?"

"You can, if you truly don't want one..." She trails off, but then her brows shoot up, and she blurts, "We could stay in the Veil. King

Rydian has declared no physical Veil use this week due to your arrival, but that doesn't apply to us."

Staring at her wide eyes and large grin, I find myself unable to say no and chuckle, giving her a nod.

"Sure," I say. "Give me a few minutes."

Standing in the Veil, the rich, welcoming scent of Castle Vyria floods me as soon as I step into the corridor. It's the complete opposite of what I experienced in Elderheim. Now it's leather, books, and spiced mead—old parchment with a hint of cloves. The walls are crafted of a light colored stone and the floors are made of a dark marble, reminding me of my time in Rydian's chamber in the Veil weeks ago.

I follow Lettie, turning left and heading toward our private stairwell, which leads to the first floor. Gilded chandeliers hang from the ceiling, bathing the spiral staircase in a soft, warm glow as we descend. Our feet quietly patter on the fine, marble steps, echoing in the silence. Depictions of our Fates decorate the walls.

House-maidens walk past without a second glance. We reach the first floor and go left, and I watch as they enter a door at the end.

"That's the side entrance to the kitchens," Lettie says quietly so as to not be overheard by those nearby. "If you turn left at that corner, it'll lead you to the front of the castle where the dining hall is. I'll show you."

I glance down as she takes the inside of my elbow with a friendly sideways grin. The castle is bustling with activity—more activity than I've ever seen. Elderheim was always so… stale.

No unique visitors or guests, no activity other than Elion's formal balls and festivals. No one was really allowed to freely roam, not like they do here.

"Is it always like this?" I ask, glancing around.

"Like what—busy?" She tilts her head, and I nod. "Yes, always.

After the battle, Rydian opened the castle to everyone, allowing them to use the archives, attend feasts, and enter the lounges as a way to encourage them to expand learning for the young. King Rydian finds our culture important to pass on—he has a thing for tradition."

"He publicly opened the royal castle?"

She chuckles softly. "Sounds crazy, I know, but he had a vision. Everyone thought him mad at first, but it has brought life back into the capitol. We have new visitors all the time, as well as volunteers offering to teach. It's been a welcome change. Everything is open except for the second floor—the royal floor," she adds, placing her hand on mine. "No one is allowed at the back of the castle either, which is where the council chamber sits, right up there."

She points as we walk past the grand staircase near the front of the castle, and I shift my gaze to the top of the stairs. Up the steps and to the right is a darkened corridor, but I can't see past it.

"There's a ward, so only council members and house-maidens can enter, and of course, you and whoever King Rydian allows," she says. "And straight ahead are the archives. You'll be introduced to Varrin at some point, as he'll be helping with research. He often helps King Rydian find anything he needs with his expertise."

We spend our time walking, chamber rooms passing by in a blur until I've already forgotten the layout. The castle is so large, it'd be easy to get lost in, but I find myself focused on Lettie's quiet voice as she explains everything in vivid detail. We twist through corridors and private chambers until we finally step outside. The frigid air hits my face, carrying jasmine and winter lilies on the salty, misted wind.

My thoughts briefly land on Kalde, and I wonder where he ended up. But as we stride through the gardens, I catch a blur of darkness weaving through the tall, pointed bushes. He lunges, lips curling as he snatches a piece of food from a nearby guard before darting out of reach. The guard curses, his hands rising before turning with a shake to his head.

"That doesn't look like you're staying out of trouble," I tell Kalde,

watching him skid to a halt down the path and swiftly turn toward us. He blinks.

"You are okay?"

"I'm fine."

He grunts, taking off at a trot once more. *"Good. I almost ate that king's face earlier. The Shadovar are odd… no one can speak to me,"* he says almost sarcastically, and I grin. Then I lift my gaze to the movement in the sky, a hawk soaring above Kalde—Ire. *"Except for the birds. And your other male."*

I chuckle just as he disappears, but concern and confusion crosses Lettie's face beside me at my quiet laughter. "I was speaking to Kalde… the Howler." I point ahead.

"Oh." She huffs a laugh. "What's that like?"

As I explain, we ascend the wide stone steps, entering the back of the castle through delicate paned doors and into my private corridor as the sun begins to set.

Our private staircase sits to the right of the hall. As soon as we enter, I spot Rydian casually standing at the end with his arms crossed and in a quiet discussion with Ivy. His eyes shoot to Lettie and me, as if he could see us through the Veil. One word enters my mind, tumbling around in my thoughts, warming my insides—*mate.*

He vanishes, and I let out a quiet sigh. Lettie says nothing else, walking beside me and up the steps, only stopping once we reach my door.

"Thank you for the tour," I say, reaching for the handle.

She bows. "Of course, Princess. I'll see you in the morning to dress you."

"Dress me?" Disbelief coats my tone.

No one in my entire life has dressed me, aside from Karina in Elderheim. She was a seamstress, though, not a personal maiden. I grit my teeth.

Lettie only smiles. "Yes. King Rydian has requested your presence at the council meeting tomorrow for a formal introduction. I'm to help you prepare for it."

"He failed to mention that." I groan and watch her descend the hall before entering my chambers. Clicking the door shut, I rest against the polished wood. My stomach sinks as dread washes over me in an unwelcoming shudder.

The council.

14

A faint knock sounds on my chamber door, stirring me from sleep. I blink, groaning slightly. The room comes into focus, and I'm reminded of where I am—*Aurelia.*

After Lettie escorted me back to my chambers, I crawled into bed and watched the fire blaze in the mantel until my eyes closed. I don't recall what time that was.

Rydian sleeps heavily beside me, and my heart stutters in my chest as I sit up and stare down at him. He must have crawled in at some point.

My stomach flutters, seeing him beside me. He rests an arm behind his head, tilted slightly to the left, breathing softly. I skim over his chest, carved to perfection, and focus on the ink swirling toward his shoulder and up his neck.

Though the knock wasn't the only thing that woke me—the mark on my wrist glows faintly, aching a little. I cover it with my hand, and glance through the large windows leading to the private adjoining, royal balcony. The moon sits high in the sky. It must be three in the morning.

Another soft knock raps at the door, and I shift my attention away from the moon and to the entrance. I quietly rise and inch closer to the door. Gripping a dagger and walking on silent feet, I creak it open to find Ren standing in the corridor wearing his cloak.

"What are you doing?" I whisper, peering into the hall.

I forgot to find him earlier as I settled into bed, and guilt claw at my chest. He must feel so out of place being in Aurelia and in an unfamiliar castle.

He eyes me and extends my cloak. "I couldn't sleep and it's quiet. Want to explore?" He arches a brow—an invitation. *Explore?*

A devious grin spreads across his face before I glance over my shoulder toward Rydian. Despite myself, I think about it.

Rydian wouldn't know if I decided to run around the castle tonight, not with how deeply he sleeps. Another moment goes by. I exhale, facing Ren, and he gently shakes my cloak. It rustles in the silence as he urges me to grab it, and I groan.

"No one will see us. We'll just have to be careful around the guards lingering around, but what's a little challenge?" he presses, encouraging me for a night of mischief.

He glances past my shoulder before his steely gaze meets mine again. But my eyes narrow as I recall the finger he trailed down my hand when he thought I was asleep. The glow of his fingertip.

"Are you going to tell me what that magic was earlier?"

Color seeps into his cheeks, caught in the dim light of the corridor. I smirk when he clenches his jaw and blinks at me.

"Elemental magic. You felt cold," he says.

Knowing he's most likely lying and embarrassed, a grin tugs at my lips. Whatever he's flustered about, I don't dwell on it. I stifle my smile, and glance over my shoulder one last time. It's just for a while, and since no one will be around, I could comfortably explore without worrying about anyone seeing me. Or me seeing them.

I throw him an annoyed smirk and a quick nod. "Fine, but if we get caught, I'm blaming you."

I take the cloak and meet him in the corridor, but I don't bother changing or getting shoes. Instead, I quietly shut the door behind me and fasten the cloak, pulling my hood up.

"Where are we going?" I whisper, and adrenaline courses through my veins with excitement.

"Anywhere you want, Princess."

"Ugh, don't call me that."

He chuckles but leads the way, pulling his own hood up just as we reach the private stairwell. On silent feet, we descend, sticking to the shadows as a faint crackle of a torch along the wall breaks the silence, the only noise in the otherwise quiet castle.

I trail behind until we hit the last step, only pausing long enough to peek around the corner. He looks over his shoulder, gesturing for me to follow him into the corridor, heading left. Toward the kitchens, I realize, and almost snort a laugh, knowing why he's most likely leading me there.

Ren's steps are precise and eerily silent as he makes his way down the hall, reminding me of the assassin I've come to know over the last few weeks. Then, unknown heavy boots thud from around the corner, and I halt, my eyes shifting to the back of Ren's hood.

Without warning, he whirls around to grip my arm, quietly shoving us into a large groove in the wall, deep enough for both of us. We hide in the shadows of the stone, but his hand remains firm on my arm as his finger rises to his lips. A smirk peers down at me, and my eyes narrow, my pulse racing.

The rough stone presses into my back as Ren pushes us further in, hiding me with his large frame. I hold my breath, not a sound to be heard in the cramped space. The lone guard finally rounds the corner and enters our corridor.

Even though Rydian allows others to roam freely, we don't know what the guards will do to those exploring late at night. Is it like Elderheim? Do they even care? At the moment, I'm not willing to risk finding out.

A light flickers closer, illuminating the edge of Ren's hood, and my body goes stiff. Soon, the light disappears, leaving us alone once again. Ren dips his head back far enough to peer into the hallway, ensuring it's clear. Then his eyes meets mine, his mouth curving into a devious grin, before he finally exhales.

"I'm surprised they didn't hear you," he teases, and I shove him out of the groove with a quiet grunt. He chuckles as we inch into the corridor, still hidden in the shadows, and continue down the length of it.

Stopping in front of a wooden door, he presses his ear against it. No voices. No footsteps. Nothing but the low thrum of the castle and the faint thud of my pulse.

"Come on," he says.

Pushing the door open, he allows me to enter first, and we stride into a large kitchen, vast and dark. Shadows pool across the floor, the moon spilling in from the enormous window directly in front of us.

"Is finding the kitchens on your to-do list for every castle you visit?" I throw him a sideways glance. "Coming to the kitchens isn't exploring."

"Sure it is," he says casually.

We walk past the wooden workstations, our footfalls barely a whisper against the stone floor, and take a left at the window. Following him, we halt near a large stone door just past the entryway.

"I'm hungry," Ren says almost to himself, creaking the door open to an assortment of cheeses, fruits, and meats inside a dark cellar.

"You brought me along to get food?" I ask in disbelief, doing my best to stifle my rising amusement. For a moment, I wonder if he plans on searching for tarts.

"Why else would we be here?"

I glance over my shoulder, eyeing the door, but when I turn back around, he hands me a crumble of fine cheese. My eyes widen, and I take a bite. I all but groan at the flavor—savory with smokey undertones. It's delicious.

He huffs out a laugh. "You'd think they would have given me more food considering my size. I'm starving."

"Grab that." I point to the carton he took it from.

He shoves items into my hands, passing me cheese and some kind of meat. On our way out, I catch him staring at a row of fine wines. He skids to a stop, reaching for one.

"There's whiskey in my chambers," I whisper, but he's already grabbed a luxurious crystal bottle, giving it a slight once-over.

"I'm taking it." He huffs, but his lips curve, eyes dancing.

We stride for the exit, heading straight for the door on quick, quiet feet. He presses his ear to it again, as the dim light catches the sharp line of his jaw. The scar on his brow twitches.

"How often do you do this?" I quipped.

Instead of answering, his gray eyes remain focused as he listens for the guard, and a slow smile tugs at my lips. It quickly falters, though, when a rush of familiarity washes over me.

I find myself studying his features, awareness prickling my skin, and I blink. My eyes flicker from the items in his hands to the smugness of his light-hearted grin as a whirl of images flashes across my vision. He looks down at me, catching my stare when he raises a curious brow.

"Ready?" he asks.

I nod, forcing myself to breathe as we slip through the door and back into the hall. We dart up the steps, reaching the top of the second floor in seconds, and I take a left.

"Where are you going?" Ren asks, and I turn, finding him still rooted in place near the stairs.

"To my chambers, come on." I nod to my door.

"Isa—"

"He's asleep, and you're invited. Let's go before someone catches us," I demand. It's not long before he quietly groans, and the near-silent thud of his footsteps reaches my ears.

Holding the items in one hand, I gently creak open the door. Rydian's sleeping form comes into focus, arm still propped behind his head. I almost chuckle, but on silent feet, we walk across the room and quietly open the door leading to the balcony.

When I inspected my chambers earlier, I noticed easy access to the roof—the perfect location to eat our contraband without disturbing anyone. Ren clicks the balcony door shut, but not before I catch him staring at Rydian through the glass. A flicker of irritation crosses his face in the reflection.

"Over here." I clear my throat, ignoring whatever just flitted across his face, and point to the stone railing leading to the roof.

He grabs a quilt off the nearby settee and hoists himself up, stepping as if it were a simple staircase. He grips my elbow, swiftly raising me to the railing, and I find my balance. With a quick turn, he steps onto the roof, throwing the quilt down with a flat smile. Something that appears he's trying to stifle.

An hour passes as we silently graze on the food we stole.

Ren opens the wine, pulling the cork out with his teeth. He wasn't lying when he said he was starving, having gone through almost everything we took. I lean against my palms, still in nothing but my cloak and night slip. My legs stretch out when he passes the crystal bottle to me having taken a large gulp. We sit in silence. The sweet wine hits my tongue as I drink, and it slides down my throat in a comforting warmth.

"Did you tell Rydian?" *About the oath,* I fail to add, hoping he catches on.

Ren looks at me, though he says nothing, just sits there and stares. I take it as a yes, knowing that what I asked of him in Elderheim means leaving me out of it entirely. That whatever I don't know, I can't relay back to King Elion. He stuffs a sliver of meat into his mouth.

"I assume you also know about my... mark," I say softly.

He levels his eyes with mine before averting them down. Then he sighs, nodding. "Were you angry?"

I huff a quiet laugh. "I was angrier that I had claimed him while we were..." The words hang in the air, as I'm unable to admit what happened. I cringe, my nose scrunching.

His brows draw together. "You claimed him?"

"Without knowing I did... initially. We still have to complete it since he hasn't done it yet. He owes me a ceremony and a ring." I shrug, eyes rolling.

His lips tilt up at that, and he faces forward with a throaty chuckle. "You've always liked pretty things."

My breath catches, and silence settles between us once more. Ren remains utterly frozen, shoulders taut, spine straight like he'd just revealed something—a sliver of those memories he keeps locked up so tightly—and curiosity blooms in my chest.

"I liked pretty things?" I dare ask, itching to know more, and wondering how much information I can squeeze out.

"Jewelry mostly. Rings, necklaces, perfumes." A small smile. "Expensive tastes. You'd spend every last gold at the markets."

"I did not." My face scrunches, and I sip the wine once more. Then I frown, recalling how I believed I'd never been to a market on our mission to Sylvanor a few months ago.

Was that… incorrect?

"You did." He grins. "You also hate ale."

A cool breeze brushes my skin, and the ocean crashes in the distance. I face forward, tucking a strand of hair behind my ear. My face warms, realizing he knows that about me. Something I've never shared before. His words in the loft after our mission with Theo momentarily brush my thoughts, leaving me to wonder how close we really were.

As close as you and Ezra, he'd said before.

But the thought of Witt sours my stomach.

Glancing at the cheese in my hands, my chest tightens, and I frown at the sudden familiarity of the moment. It's like living in a never-ending dream. Sometimes my memories are clear and vivid, other times they're not. Though one thing remains consistent— emotions flood me whenever they do.

Longing and fear and excitement.

"We used to do this—sneaking out," I say so quietly that my own words almost dissolve on the breeze.

But he catches it. His head turns, brows knitting once more.

I ask, "Real or a dream?"

He turns away, his knees drawn up, and looks over the expanse. For a moment, I think he won't answer until he mumbles under his breath. "Real."

I exhale as a weight lifts off my chest.

Watching him place his ear against the kitchen door reminded me of what I dreamt about in Eldherheim while I lay bruised and bloody in bed. Us at seventeen and twenty-three sneaking out of Castle Alvonia late at night so I could taste my first ale.

He would tell me that I needed to work on my infiltration and stealth, frequently sneaking into my chambers through my window late at night, claiming it was the best time to do it.

We'd often cause chaos throughout the castle. Whether it was gathering pebbles to throw at the guards off the roof or sneaking into the hidden tunnels beneath the kitchens, it was always something.

We're supposed to be training, I'd frequently tell him.

I focus on his hair as it catches the wind, but his gaze remains fixed on the ocean ahead, lost in thought. Lost in memories of a past I can't remember.

"I wish I had known sooner," I say finally, still annoyed that he refuses to share anything. "Why haven't you shown me your memories?"

"Because..." Annoyance of his own enters his face before he pauses, head shaking, as he calculates his answer. "I don't want to force my memories on you. We were just kids and we snuck out a lot." He huffs a quiet laugh, the breathy sound escaping his nose. "I know all of this is overwhelming, and I don't want to add to it by giving you memories of our childhood together. It'll only distract you." He shrugs, but his usual calm, composed mask slips, if only for a moment.

Even though annoyance runs through me, I quickly change the subject, unwilling to dwell on it much longer. Even if I beg, I know he won't show me anything.

"Lettie told me that we'll be meeting the council tomorrow. I want you there for introductions," I say.

"I'll be wherever you need me."

"Have you been in contact with Elion yet? I haven't felt any... tugs." I add, even though it's only been a day, wondering what it'll feel like when I finally get that yank through the blood oath.

He shakes his head. "Not yet. I wanted to wait a few more days. I'll send word to him soon, though, give him minor... updates on things. He believes I hate you."

I grin a little, pulling my cloak tighter around my chest, and glance at him. "Do you?"

He huffs a laugh, head shaking, and I know it's the only answer I'll be receiving. After a moment, he quietly pushes our leftovers forward, and my brows furrow when he grips the edge of my cloak. With a hard but gentle tug, he slides me to him until our shoulders meet.

The abruptness of it warms my cheeks, and I lift my eyes to see him staring. He studies me, and my stomach flips as his mouth tugs into a charming, yet devious smirk. One that would drive anyone insane if they stared too long. One that tells me there's something hidden beneath that calm exterior he wears every day.

Then he faces forward, not another word spoken.

My pulse threatens to betray me, but I say nothing as we sit beneath the stars, listening to the wind and the waves and the wildness of the forest groaning in the distance.

15

A grating silence hits the council chamber the moment we enter, doors swinging wide. The kind of silence that sends a shiver up my spine, and I begin to wonder if they had thought I wasn't real. If they believed I wouldn't arrive today. After twenty years, it's possible one of them had thought it.

I know I would have.

Rydian walks beside me, Ren at my back as we continue in silence, striding toward the long table in the center of the room. Where royalty sits. Even though Rydian prepared me as best he could, I fight the urge to swallow, lifting my chin as my gaze sweeps over unfamiliar faces.

My heart races, pounding relentlessly inside my chest as nervousness prickles my skin—I hate having their eyes solely on me. Each council member bows as we pass, eyes wide and glancing between each other—speaking in the Veil.

The council chamber is enormous—easily four times the size of Rydian's loft at the brothel. Windows adorn each wall, but the ones in the back are the largest, overlooking the courtyard with a small balcony as if meant for announcements.

To my surprise, the temperature is comfortably warm despite the cold air of conversation... or lack of any. The chamber's aesthetic similar to the rest of the castle with dark floors and light colored stone. Warmth spills from the windows, but most of the light comes from the series of chandeliers hanging above the table, flickering across the dark wood.

We reach the head of the table, near two exquisitely large chairs. Like thrones, but not quite as big. Rydian stands on my left, Ren to my right.

With a quick glance, Ren's steely gaze meets mine for a brief moment, his lips rising in a sly smirk as he clasps his hands behind his back.

Members of the council remain standing, and I finally recognize a few familiar faces including Ivy, Orin, and Eldric—the older gentleman from the king's dinner. But I also notice new faces, ones I've never met before.

I meet every one of their gazes.

We had agreed to come to this meeting as a team—as mates. Rydian's decisions are my decisions and everything after that, meaning that if the council has a problem with me, they can say it to my face.

Rydian clenches his jaw, his shoulders back, eyeing each present member. "Now is the time to air your grievances if you have any, council. If you can say them to me, you can say them to Princess Isa, *my mate* and your rightful queen, while she stands before you."

Silence continues to hang in the air, suffocating and dreadful.

"I'd prefer you speak them *aloud*," Rydian grumbles.

"How do we know we can trust her when she was raised by that mad king?" a male says with a sneer. Like Eldric, he appears older.

Rydian stiffens beside me, his fury pulsing through our bond, thrumming at the base of my skull. It feels like a headache, but I force down a wince and study the male who spoke standing to the left of the table.

Thanks to Rydian, I know every face here, as he had shown me his memories before our arrival. Rafe is the current Chief Diplomat, his responsibility is to negotiate treaties and manage alliances with other kingdoms. Like Elderheim.

I tilt my head, lips flattening into a tight smile.

"Are you accusing me of being a traitor so soon, Rafe?" I purr, letting the implication of my words linger. He pales, eyes widening as a cold sweat trickles down his temples. "I'd wait at least a few more weeks before doing that. I understand your concern, but I assure you, being a traitor is the last thing on my list at the moment."

Orin chuckles before quickly composing himself, giving Ivy a sideways glance on his right. The faint gleam of his golden matemark glimmers on the backside of his head, matching the amusement on his face. A slow smirk tugs at his mouth.

"I hope no one ever tries to save me from your wrath, I'm exactly where I want to be," Rydian purrs, and I have to fight the nervous flush rising up my neck. Fight the smile threatening to come out.

"Rafe has a point. There's no guarantee that she won't betray us, even if she bears your mark, Your Majesty," Eldric says on Orin's left, and my gaze swivels to him.

"You can speak to her directly, Eldric, she's right beside you," Rydian says quietly. "Were you not at King Elion's dinner when I suggested an alliance through a marriage bond? Were you not there when they struck her at that table, revealing her mark? Do you really believe she'd want to go back to that—to a castle where she was punished and used against her will?"

The soothing caress of his shadows gently graze my fingers, and I find myself relaxing despite their harsh words against me. But I don't blame them, not really.

"You've all known what we were doing over these last few weeks in trying to find Queen Elynor. You had no problem with us working with her then." Rydian points out.

Mikal scoffs next to Rafe with a shake of his head. "That was before we found out who her father really was, Your Majesty. She's a concern. Her loyalties will be divided."

The tall, pale-haired male appears to be in his forties and has been on the council the longest. Mikal's official title is High Mage, the one who counsels on magical threats, manages the schools, and advises on the use of magic within the realm.

"Unfortunately, my loyalties will always be divided due to my heritage, but my main focus is removing that king from his throne," I say with a small smile. "Even if it means aiding him now in order to have a better future for the realms. Elderheim has suffered enough, don't you think?"

Mikal nods after a moment.

"Aurelia has suffered enough, don't you think?" Rafe replies sharply with narrowed eyes, holding my gaze.

"Careful Rafe. I'd hate for you to lose a tongue over one of your outbursts," Orin warns quietly, though his lips curve up as if he'd enjoy cutting it out.

Rydian locks eyes with Rafe as he leans forward on his palms—a warning. The diplomat slinks back, face flushed. I have no doubt that Rydian just scolded him in the Veil.

Then Rydian straightens, placing a hand on my lower back. "I understand your concerns and appreciate those who have spoken up, but for right now, this is what we're doing. King Elion has something important of Isa's, and is using that as leverage. He believes we can find what he's looking for, but our focus is getting Queen Elynor back."

The members nod their heads in agreement. My eyes land on the female at the end of the table next to Mikal, who looks as if she has something to say.

"Do you have anything to add?" I ask.

With honeyed brown hair and warm skin, Anya stands with her chin high. She's the only other female on the council besides Ivy, and is the current Treasury Master. She manages and advises on taxation, trade agreements, and informs Rydian on what the realm needs.

"I do, actually," Anya says, and I arch a brow. "With your upcoming travels, I have prepared the funds for everyone on the journey."

"Upcoming travels?" I ask Rydian, shooting him a curious glance. *"When were you going to inform me of said travels?"*

"That was next on the discussion." He chuckles. *"After showing you the members, we didn't have time to discuss it until now."*

Then Anya sighs a dramatic, exhausted sound, and winces. "Also, Wayd and Kaeda have arrived."

A collective groan suddenly escapes the council members before they all take a seat, scraping their chairs back as they do. Some pinch the bridges of their noses; others sip their wine, as if those two names have already caused them a headache.

Rydian and I remain standing, but my brows furrow. *"Wayd and Kaeda? The same Wayd who visited Elderheim with you?"*

A chill snakes up my spine, recalling his activity at that dinner and how he accused me of being mute. How he lingered in the shadows when he and Rydian visited me in my chambers. He had a sharp tongue and a fiery glint to his eye, similar to my own, but I had yet to see him in the castle.

"You'll see." Rydian side-eyes me, nodding. *"Also, sorry in advance."*

His tone is light with amusement, and I almost groan, knowing exactly what that means. As if right on cue, the double wooden doors swing open with quick efficiency, practically blasting off the hinges.

Eldric rolls his eyes and our gazes swivel to the loud disruption. Wayd and Kaeda—two silver-haired Fae, clearly related—stride through.

Two pairs of emerald eyes hold mine, smirks on their faces as they reach the end of the table. Both of them are armed, wearing matching black outfits, with golden-hilted swords peering above their shoulders.

Gleaming silver-hair cascades down Kaeda's head, woven into a thick braid almost as long as mine. It swings forward when she bows with an arm across her waist. Kaeda smirks, dark and menacing, and tilts her head toward Wayd with an arched brow.

Wayd grins. "Hello, cousin."

16

"I have relatives?" I ask Rydian, eyes flaring as my shock settles. *"Were you ever planning on telling me?"*

That must be why they look so familiar.

They look like me except for their silver-hair and emerald eyes. Their lean frames are also quite similar to my own, only Kaeda has a menacing glint etched into her features like she enjoys causing trouble. And by the looks of them, I have no doubt that they do.

"Telling you in Elderheim would have been a mistake. If Elion had known you were related, he would have lashed out at the dinner. But we needed Wayd there—Kaeda too. I promised Wayd he could have his... entrance so he wouldn't ruin our plans at the dinner," Rydian explains.

"A dramatic entrance isn't needed every time you visit, Wayd. We can clearly see the resemblance," Eldric says flatly, head shaking in annoyance.

Wayd straightens, a wide grin spreading across his face when Kaeda lets out a breath of laughter beside him. His teeth are perfect —a smile that would sway many—but beneath that is pure mischief.

"I just wanted to remind you all of who I was related to," Wayd says with a huff. "Now that I'm here, what did I miss? And also..."

He pivots, turning to Anya with a sly grin and grasps her hand, placing a gentle kiss on it with a wink. "Anya, good to see you."

She flushes, cheeks turning a deep shade of red before quickly pulling her hand back. The rosiness contrasts her tawny brown eyes. Eyes that remind me of the walnuts found in the forest by Castle Alvonia. Wayd's grin only deepens.

"Wayd," she manages.

"Dear gods. I'm related to that?" I ask. Rydian chuckles beside me, shooting me another glance.

"You have no idea," he says, *"And there's two of them—twins."*

Kaeda strides toward us on quiet, nimble feet, aiming for Ren who stands a few steps beside me. Her scent lingers in the air— something wild, like the allure of a moonlit forest late at night. Amber with smoky undertones.

She plants herself in front of Ren, assessing.

His black hair brushes his brows, cut just this morning, as he watches her in a way that leads me to believe he's reading her too. He remains utterly silent, jaw set while she stands at the edges of his boots, giving him a calculated once over. He crosses his arms and suddenly, she looks as if she'd eat him. A sight to behold.

"Hello, Captain," she purrs, a voice made of pure silk. "I remember *you.*"

Ren holds her gaze as if she's the least of his concerns, certainly unamused. But I catch the faintest twitch of his brow. Is it curiosity? He doesn't so much as breathe a word, and she smirks—slow and wicked.

Shadovar are known for their strategic thinking and resilience, but most of all, for their manipulation. Possessing the ability to control situations and bend circumstances to their will with ease using what they have as leverage. And apparently, Kaeda's sultry, fierce appearance is her leverage.

A sudden wave of irritation washes over me when she flicks her tongue over her bottom lip, as if wanting a taste. Ren eyes the movement, and a few silent seconds go by before she turns sharply, braid swaying. Then she's back at Wayd's side.

"I'd love to know what she means by that," I grouse, turning to face Rydian with a glare. "Was she at the dinner?"

Rydian pulls out a rolled parchment, laying it on the middle of the table—the second half of Elion's map. I completely forgot.

"Well, now that grievances are set aside, I'd like to go over what we found," Rydian says, laying it flat and placing weights on the corners. He straightens as I lean forward. "You were right, by the way. There was more to his archives."

I glance up, lashes fluttering. *"Well then, you have a lot of apologizing to do."*

"Don't remind me."

"You're going to have to get creative," I sigh, and he groans a little.

Ren steps forward with a gentle touch to my elbow to inspect the map.

It's split into two separate plans, revealing an extensive layout of a hidden chamber behind King Elion's archives and the levels within it. A chamber that extends far beneath the floors of the castle, highlighting each one. My breath catches, the air feeling a little too thick.

Could my mother be there?

Orin points down. "Thanks to King Rydian and Princess Isa, we have this map. And because of the twins, we know that King Elion's shields are limited to his archives. It doesn't extend to his chamber or the corridor leading to the chamber beyond it. We don't know whether or not he was intentional with that decision, but we assume it's so that magic isn't dulled in the victims they siphon. It's only speculation at this point."

"You were at the castle during the king's dinner?" I ask Kaeda across the table, remembering the empty chair beside me that night. She gives me a firm nod, surprisingly respectful despite us not really knowing each other.

"I remained in the Veil and snuck into Elion's chambers to explore. Everyone was certainly too busy to notice me," she smirks. The dinner was a distraction.

A distraction for King Elion so he wouldn't notice what was going on within the castle's walls. And as annoying as it is not to be included in that, it was smart—but also dangerous. But I'm glad they took the opportunity while they could. Still, that does nothing to settle my stomach at the thought of them getting caught.

"That was incredibly risky, don't you think? What exactly was your plan if it had gone south?" I ask Rydian, my tone sharp.

He crosses his arms, staring down at me, and the room quiets. Their eyes shoot between Rydian and I, as if my tone with him was a risk.

"We knew that King Elion's guards would be focused on the dinner, so it was less likely that they'd even suspect her there. We needed to know how far those wards went and if he had anything specific about Elynor in his chamber. There was no risk of Kaeda's scent being traced back to us," he explains.

I hold his gaze a moment longer before giving him a nod, turning back to the group in silence. Finally, after an hour of hovering, planning and studying the map, we all turn to sit.

As soon as I reach for my enormous chair—my hands grazing the wooden arms—Rydian tugs me to him and forces me to sit on his lap.

My lips part, heart racing when he wraps an arm around my waist and leans forward, trapping me between him and the table. Ren remains standing beside us, a hand on his jaw while he speaks to Eldric on his right.

"What are you doing?" I ask breathlessly, hoping the council doesn't notice how flustered I am. How quick my breaths are. Their quiet discussions don't falter, though, as they ignore us entirely. Rydian's hands linger, a single finger moving in intricate circles along my thigh. Something that heats my blood.

"I just want you to sit with me," he says playfully, though his tone is clear. That and the fact that he's stiff beneath me, hardening against my ass. *"I want to play, and these meetings are quite boring."*

"Now?" I ask, but despite myself, excitement thrums in my veins. He ignores me—too focused on the discussions nearby and the finger trailing circles on my thigh.

Varrin quickly arrives and explains our upcoming travels to the northern part of the realm. He's an older male with rich warm skin, brown hair and bushy brows—one of the oldest historians in the castle.

He takes a few minutes, telling us about the rumor of Cassivene Strin, an artifact smuggler and thief who might have information regarding the Veilstone. About how she could have connections with various underground networks in the realm. If she doesn't have knowledge about where it is, she could point us to someone who might. We just have to find her.

"Her last known residency is unclear," Wayd says, casually spinning a gold coin on the table.

"We heard that she vanished shortly after being caught selling a stolen relic," Kaeda adds, leaning back with a crooked smile. "Meaning we'd have to scour the locations she was last seen."

"Which was?" Ivy asks, stifling a yawn next to Orin.

"Zelaryn. Halstra…" Wayd stares at the intricate ceiling. "Voltros maybe. Due to the large expanse of those cities, she'd flee there first. All perfect locations for a retired smuggler."

I mindlessly graze the room, noting where each member is as they continue talking. Excitement runs through me, a tiny flutter in my stomach at the thought of getting caught.

Would anyone even care?

Then Rydian's hand ghosts the edge of my pants, fingers dipping inside—touching, teasing—a lingering question as he tauntingly grazes my bare skin. My breath catches, my pulse climbing higher and higher until a roaring heat settles between my legs.

Fuck, he wasn't kidding.

"This would have been easier to do had you worn one of those dresses Lettie suggested," he complains, and I almost groan, but my breath speeds up in anticipation.

He goes lower, teasing near the apex, and I can't help but shift my hips, rubbing against the hard length of him. He groans in my head, leaving me to hide a grin, biting my cheek.

I watch as Wayd leans toward Anya, whispering something so she smiles. She hides it with a hand and waves him off. Kaeda sits near the end of the table, talking with Ivy, Orin, and Eldric. Mikal and Rafe are on the other side.

All too distracted to notice.

"I want you to ride me tonight," Rydian gets out, and then very slowly shifts his hips up, pushing into me in a way that has me stifling a small gasp. *"Dress or not, you're soaked."*

He slowly parts me, sliding his fingers inside before swirling over my clit. I bite my cheek again, squeezing my eyes shut in order to swallow the moan rising in my throat. I'm utterly speechless, too focused on managing my breaths as I lean into him.

"Interesting," Rydian mumbles, amusement lacing his tone. Then his other hand tightly grips the back of my neck.

Cheeks flushing and suddenly confused, I turn to look at him, though his eyes aren't locked on me. I swivel my gaze, and to my surprise, Ren stares at me—pupils dilated, chest heaving.

Quiet and watching.

My stomach flips, pulse pounding as an unexpected heat builds in my blood. I forgot he was standing there. Then Rydian traces his finger over me again, pressing, causing my hips to buck into his hand.

My eyes grow wide, my breaths quick. Still, no one pays us any attention as they scour over the map, their small bits of focused discussion brushing the air.

"I think he likes it," Rydian breathes, caressing my thoughts. *"Should we give him a show?"*

I can't decipher his tone—whether he's serious or not. Yet for some reason, I find myself wanting Ren to watch. The revelation so shocking, it almost fractures my control.

I would like that…

Ren's chest rises sharply, and he glances down just as I roll my hips again. My lips part on a quiet, yet sharp, gasp. Still, he says nothing, expression unreadable. Then I catch the faint scent of him lingering in the air—rich, wild and…

His cock pushes against the seam of his pants.

Gods, he likes it.

Rydian chuckles. *"I know a watcher when I see one."*

I blink, recalling the moment Rydian and I met in the brothel, about how he had wanted to watch Bess and me in one of those rooms.

"Is it because you're one yourself?"

"Precisely." No sooner does Rydian say the words, someone clears their throat, catching his attention down the table. If any of the council members notice our activity, they say nothing. Rydian only chuckles in my ear, and pulls away from me, leaving me heated and soaked and frustrated.

"We'd better finish this tonight," I growl, shooting him a glare before he gently forces me to rise. With a few deep breaths, I compose myself, flustered now that Ren stands beside me again, facing the members without a word.

"Don't worry, little fawn, we were just getting started," Rydian taunts, striding over to talk with Varrin and Mikal.

A few more minutes go by as they all finish up, when I suddenly feel out of place. It rolls over me like a violent storm, tangling in my thoughts. My eyes dart from member to member. They all know each other, having lived together for years, forming close bonds in a way that's similar to a family.

I've never had that, not really. And although there's quite a few people in this room, isolation grips me, whispering that I'll never earn my spot.

Regardless of how hard I may try.

In some form or another, I'll always be untrustworthy because of my heritage—because of my father and all the baggage that comes with him. I never realized how much that bothered me until now. I wonder if this was Elion's plan all along.

Did he know this would always be an issue?

Either way, the thought unsettles me as I soothingly rub the inside of my wrist with a thumb. Ren touches my elbow, as if sensing where my thoughts have gone. I glance up at his furrowed brows, and my spine straightens, remembering what happened just moments ago.

"You shouldn't have been watching," I whisper, but my breath falters slightly, a nervousness clawing at my insides. And despite myself, my cheeks warm. I didn't realize he liked that. "It's rude to stare."

Ren leans in, whispering so close to my ear that it has me holding back a shudder. "If you're going to do that in a public setting... I'm going to watch."

My neck flushes, and I blink.

Orin and Ivy depart in the Veil, and the remaining members quickly follow as Rydian strides toward me. Ren steps back with a small smirk, gray eyes holding mine before he turns on his heel and exits the council chamber. Yet something tells me that little smirk hopes for something more in the future...

And why doesn't that bother me?

"When do we leave?" I ask breathlessly, forcing a flat, humorless smile as I turn to face Rydian.

"Tomorrow morning."

I nod, remaining silent as we exit, though my thoughts still linger on Ren. I should be furious, embarrassed even.

Yet my pulse still stutters.

Still beats in a way that has me pulling in desperate breaths, eager to slow the racing of my heart. I tell myself that it's nothing, that I was too caught up in the moment as they both focused on me. But that doesn't explain why I wanted him to keep watching.

Or worse, why I liked it.

17

Two weeks pass by so quickly I blink in the dim light of our inn, if only to focus on the frustrated members of our group. Two weeks of following trails has led us nowhere, despite sifting through every faded rumor about this supposed Cassivene Strin.

We started with the smaller cities, where merchants hangout, eventually moving on to the homes at the edge of isolated towns where trades often happen. Places she was well known—speaking to people she knew. But after the eighth tavern, a slew of inns, and whispered rumors between drunken slurs, having no leads has begun to grate on everyone's nerves.

Including Wayd and Kaeda.

"We're splitting up today." Wayd all but growls as he stares at Ren who bites into what appears to be a sad excuse for breakfast.

Kaeda leans against one of the walls of our inn, a boot propped at the base of it, arms crossed and amused.

Morning light spills in from the cracked window beside her, a breath away from shattering entirely. The dirty walls creak, the bed sinks a little, and the floors look like they haven't been cleaned in ages.

I sigh, pinching the bridge of my nose.

We've been to so many inns that it's beginning to blur together. We haven't really cared about where we end up, just as long as there are beds and that we're close enough to where we need to be searching. The inns are dirtier than I'd prefer, but it's no different than the missions I've executed for Elion. I've stayed in far worse places.

"Too busy speaking with your dead friends to enjoy real conversation?" Ren arches a brow, leaning back in his chair, fighting a grin.

The Death Whisper Twins is what they call themselves—a Shadovar power that allows them to speak to those beyond the Veil. Only they explained it as speaking to essences—glowing beings in the shape of orbs—rather than Fae. The explanation did little to settle the unease curling in my stomach. If anything, it made it worse.

My cousins come from my mother's side apparently, sired by my uncle Torven close to two-hundred years ago. But when my mother and I went missing, they approached Rydian about joining his forces—being of use. Since then, Rydian has continued to use them as extra swords near the walls to help ensure it gets built along the edges of the cities.

Wayd suddenly kicks Ren's chair out from under him, causing Ren to lose balance and jolt upright. Ren bares his teeth like something feral, towering over him, getting in his face.

"Stop," Rydian orders, the sound exasperated as he storms into the room with lowered brows. He shoves a hand through his hair, but Wayd only grins, tilting his head slightly as Ren backs up a step. "Wayd is right, though. I think we all need… space. To cover more ground."

Rydian throws me a look, one that tells me that even he believes someone might die before this trip is over. After our meeting with the council, we had all decided that it was best that Wayd and Kaeda joined us while Ivy controls the army and castle. Orin is to remain working with Varrin, learning more about the ritual we believe King Elion has.

"Kalde and Ren can come with me," I say finally. "We'll search the southern market of Zelaryn and question a few merchants while you search north."

"You're sure?" Rydian slides into my head.

I nod even though it feels as if we're chasing a ghost.

Chasing nothing but false leads and cold trails, I'm starting to believe she doesn't exist. But the rumors remain the same: golden blonde hair, brown eyes, and knows how to talk her way out of any situation. Yet no one has seen or heard from her for years. Not even a glimpse.

"We'll all stay in touch through the Veil. If we're too far to speak to each other, we'll meet at the Fates fountain at dusk," Rydian says, then turns toward me, leaning in to kiss my temple. *"Shift your appearance if you need to get answers and come back to me."*

"Always," I murmur.

Over the last two weeks, Rydian has forced me to learn how to somewhat control my darkness. Forced me to learn how to shift my physical appearance in between stops and during our stays. It was hard to grasp at first, but after a few tries I've been able to catch on.

Though it's incredibly disorienting—a deep pulling sensation, coldness washing over me, my skin going taut across my body before rippling. My body unravels and yet puts itself back together after a simple thought of who I want to become. I can only hold it for a few minutes though.

Still, I choose to stay in my true form most of the time.

We all exit, dispersing in opposite directions as we stride toward the market. Dark cobbled streets line our path, shadowed spires of buildings climbing higher and higher the further we walk.

But like all the other days before now, looming gray clouds hover above us, lost behind the glowing yellow orbs of light lingering in the air. Though no storms rise, there's only a cold humidity as we weave through the crowds. Dew collects on our cloaks.

Ren walks beside me, boots beating against the puddles at our feet, hood drawn low over his brows. I don't need to see his face to know he's annoyed—I can practically feel it pouring off him.

But now, alone beside him, my thoughts drift back to the council chamber, and my skin warms at the memory of him watching us. Ren hasn't said a word since, carrying on as though it never happened. Then again, none of us has had the space to breathe or have private conversations—forced together, closer than anyone wants.

"Do we have a scent for Cassive?" Kalde asks, voice growing deeper as the days go on. *"If we did, perhaps I could attempt to track her."*

He trails behind us, paws padding against the stone, dark fur rippling in the cool breeze. Fae, humans, and halfling alike give him a wide berth when they see him, parting a path down the middle. Not many in Aurelia are familiar with Howlers, but at least they've kept to themselves.

Ren grumbles in annoyance, shooting him a sharp glare. "You waited two weeks to ask?"

Kalde growls, low and menacing, and I turn just as he snaps his jaws at someone passing by. They dart out of the way, a shocked curse quick to follow.

"I said attempt, Stone Shaper. There's no guarantee I can track her yet. I'm still growing. But if she has a magical signature, I'll be able to do it." Kalde's annoyance rumbles through his chest, and my brows rise a little. He's right about his growth, as he now reaches my hips in height.

"We've all been around each other too long," I say, head pounding, and annoyed after questioning the fifth vendor. I'm not even sure the stone exists. "How does Elion expect us to find something that hasn't been found in centuries?"

"I don't know," Ren says, glancing around as shops rise on every corner. "At least you have a private room. I have to share with Wayd and Kaeda."

I smirk as we turn right. "I'll have Rydian give you gold for your own room at the next inn. How does that sound?"

"Or I could just share yours." He says the words so casually, but for a moment, my stomach flips, heart thrumming in my chest.

Regardless, I snort a disbelieving laugh and shoot him a wary glance. It's not like we haven't shared one before. Perhaps he didn't mean anything by it, and he's just sleep deprived and annoyed that he has to share a room with them.

"I dare you to ask Rydian," I say back. I shouldn't like it, not one bit, yet I find myself intrigued at the underlying meaning of his tone. "I bet he'd be thrilled."

He chuckles. "Do you think he'd prefer me on your side or his?"

My lips flatten. "The floor, probably."

We finally come to a stop outside an enormous shop with shadowed framing, intricate stone detailing that shimmers slightly, and paned glass. Ren sighs and ascends the steps, the bell ringing above as he opens the door.

The next four hours of questioning vendors do nothing but frustrate us as no leads arise. I groan when my eyes land on the dark blur of movement at the end of the street, watching Kalde pace. I ordered him to remain out of sight, because one look at him sent a slew of merchants closing their shops.

The rest avoid our questions. Some answer a few, and those lead us into more circles.

Ren and Kalde now stride ahead a few paces when we take a left, shadowed in a darkened alley that cuts across the market toward the Fates fountain. Dusk looms closer and closer.

Then my skin prickles, jerking me to a halt and my eyes widen. Magic crawls forward, writhing and itching beneath my skin—pulling, tugging, yanking as I helplessly stand there.

"Ren," I murmur, voice shaking, hands trembling as I realize what it is. He turns, catching my expression, his eyes going wide as Kalde halts ahead. "He's calling for me."

"I'm going with you." He stumbles forward, reaching out a hand but I dart back and shake my head in refusal. His hands clench into tight fists and he hisses, "Take me with you."

"No," I snap, fighting the unnatural itch of my blood, still prickling until I answer that call. "You have to cover for me, please. I've never traveled that far with someone across the realms in the Veil."

My entire body trembles now, and I screw my eyes shut as the

Veil wraps itself around my body in an unwelcoming flood of darkness. The weightlessness pulls me in, urging me to enter.

Just as I'm about to vanish, disappear from Zelaryns' cobbled streets and darkened alleys, Ren grunts and lunges forward.

We're yanked into the Veil.

Whirled away from reality, we're thrust into darkness that swarms behind my eyelids in a blur. My attempt to focus on the castle fails, and my stomach lurches from carrying more than myself. Frustration tightens in me, and before I can pinpoint a single location, we land in a tangled heap that's not at the castle.

Vision blurring, my head spins. I grapple with my disorientation and blink, breaths quick in my chest.

Gods, why can't I breathe?

"I want to know which corner of your mind pulls you to brothels," Ren grumbles in annoyance, his warm breath brushing against my cheeks.

It's then that I feel the weight of him fully, pressing into my chest and snuffing out my ability to breathe.

My eyes fly open, lips parting at how he's practically laying on top of me with a leg pushed between my thighs. He hovers, resting on an elbow, the other hand braced beside me.

We've landed on a floor somewhere, the faint scent of incense and sweat and something musky hitting my nose. I stiffen slightly, feeling his body on mine, knowing exactly what that scent is. Is it the location or him? The thought tumbles through my mind.

"Where are we?" I manage to get out, trying desperately to inhale and blink again.

Perhaps if I blink enough times, the thought of Ren between my legs will fade, dissipating as fast as it floods my mind. The memory of the council chamber surfaces again. About how his eyes dilated with… something I'm currently too afraid to name.

"The Painted Bird," he grunts, pivoting slightly. "In the loft."

"Are you going to get off?"

"I would if you'd let go." He stares down at me, a tiny smirk tilting the corner of his mouth. His brow arches.

Heat floods me as I turn my eyes down to where I'm tightly

gripping his tunic. So tight that it bunches, exposing the skin of his chest. Gods.

My hands fly open, releasing the fabric and him. He chuckles and rises, hands smoothing out his tunic. I climb to my feet with a groan, smoothing my own clothes and glancing at the flooring to hide the embarrassment warming my neck.

To hide the shame and guilt jolting in my chest for gripping him so tightly—Rydian will be less than thrilled about that.

"You know, I missed how red you'd get for absolutely no reason," Ren says casually.

"I am not—" My fingers brush my cheeks—against the heat rising in my face—and my heart slams in my chest. Gods, I *am* red. "Whatever. Stay here. I'll be back as quickly as I can," I clip, wiping my damp palms.

"I will not be left here alone while you meet with Elion. I won't do that a—" He stops himself and winces, as if pained.

Do what again? What did he mean by that?

My eyes narrow as I catch the tension across his shoulders. Across his face. The quick rise of his chest has me questioning my decision, if only for a moment. I have no time to linger though, not with how my blood crawls.

"Well I can't have you burning the castle down if Witt's there. I won't be long," I say, and he opens his mouth as if to protest. "He won't kill me… or take my memories. I'm too important now."

His jaw feathers before he huffs, arms crossed. "Twenty minutes is all you'll get." His gray eyes hold mine. "If you aren't back by then, I'm coming to get you."

"Fine." I nod. "See you in twenty minutes."

I stifle the urge to shudder as King Elion's council doors swing open ahead, having been escorted by one of his new personal guards. Something he's increased since we left a little over two weeks ago. In fact, more activity flits through the halls, people and house-maidens weaving around us as I step inside.

The chamber is warmly lit from the series of gilded chandeliers dangling in the center, directly above a rounded table as dusk quickly approaches.

I stride forward and blink in the low light, stopping at the edge of the rounded table. Six chairs circle it, though only four are filled. Elion sits toward the back, flanked by Witt and...

Ekrin Highcrest greets me with a smirk, leaning back slightly with his arms folded. He sits carelessly and unbothered, wearing only the best fabric: a dark, smooth brocade embroidered in gold. Beside him is Caius Kleren, the other council member who attended that dinner.

But that's not what snags my attention and makes my chest grow hot with fury. Theo stands toward the back, hands clasped in front of him, eyes sunken in as if he's had very little sleep. The very Siphon I gave to Elion weeks ago.

What are they doing to him?

"Nice of you to finally arrive," Elion gripes, annoyance coating his tone as if I didn't just answer his call. "I need an update."

"So soon?" I ask cooly, practically shaking with rage. "It's only been a few weeks, and I don't have long before Rydian and his council notice my absence."

"Perhaps, but they shouldn't care about your absence. That king knows what I seek," Elion says. "He agreed to it. Now, what do you have for me?"

"They will care if they discover the oath I'm bound to—my requirement to answer your call at odd times," I say with a flat smile, and Elion huffs. I'm right, of course.

Theo lets out a whimper, his eyes growing wide at the sight and sound of me.

Caius snaps his fingers. "Hush boy. You're to stand there and observe like you were taught."

Hurt flickers across his face, tearing a hole through me at the betrayal. *My* betrayal when I handed him over when I knew I shouldn't. Just another mistake beneath a long list of all my other ones.

The trembling hands consume my focus, fingers curling into tight fists as a burning fury threads my veins. Elderheim's magic floods me momentarily, scorching my palms.

"Fix your face before they realize how angry you are," Ekrin's voice snakes through my thoughts, startling me, and my eyes fly to him. It's then that I see the tiniest gleam of a black Veil coin in his grasp. He smirks, but his attention is fixed on the council nearby, not me.

"How did you get that?" I ask, keeping my eyes focused on Elion. With a steady breath, I quickly smooth my expression, mold back into the trained weapon they created, and answer Elion. "What do you want to know?"

"Get it?" Ekrin hums, clearly amused. *"Do you forget what I am?"*

My breathing stalls momentarily.

An Herb Weaver—he made it.

"Army movements," Elion says finally, leaning forward on his elbows with a faint smirk, knowing I cannot lie to him. "Are they planning for war? Where are they stationed?"

Planning for war? Unease rolls through me. If *Rydian* signed an agreement, why would he be planning for war?

A pricking sensation crawls along my skin—my blood— preventing lies from forming on my tongue. I stifle a wince, as if my body knows what I saw just this morning. Papers spread across one of Rydian's desks at the inn. I'd glanced at the locations of the Aurelian camps spread across the realm. Though war had never been discussed, at least not in my presence.

"Aurelia has seven camps lining the perimeter of its borders," I say, my tone devoid of emotion. "Some flank south, others are centered around the larger cities. No one has mentioned a war."

"Do you know what's interesting about blood oaths to a king?" Ekrin purrs across my thoughts once more. *"There's only one thing powerful enough to break it…"*

Apprehension crawls up my spine, sending my heart thundering behind my ribs. *"What do you mean? Oaths cannot be broken."*

"Oaths to a mate can break blood oaths to a king, you know. Or if one already exists, the new one fades over time."

"How?" I ask.

The corner of Ekrin's mouth tilts into a smirk.

"When you claim a mate," he says, *"your blood and essence wholly bind to them. Your blood claims loyalty to only one person in your lifetime—your mate. Meaning, you would be able to mentally grasp your oath to Elion and magically sever it."*

I fight the trembling of my fingers. *"Does Elion know this?"*

"He does. It's a shame he doesn't know who he sent you off with." Blazing pale-green eyes stare back at me, laced with underlying meaning. Gods, he knows Rydian is my mate.

Could he have scented it at that dinner? He knew about my bloodline at the Aurorafest, so it's possible. My mind spins. An oath to a mate can break a blood oath? Meaning I'd have to complete my claim to Rydian. Perhaps, then, I could break free from Elion's grasp after all.

"Are you going to tell Elion?" I manage to ask.

"Where have you been searching, and where is Captain Demaris?" Elion continues his questioning. "I had requested that he be present during our meetings."

As the words form on my tongue, my blood prickles and then settles, over and over again, similar to an insect beneath my skin. I have to choose what I say carefully—spin my words in a way that allows me to get around Ren's true location.

"Ren is currently waiting for me." *Truth.* A tight smile lines my lips, though a cold sweat breaks across my forehead. "I told him he had to cover for me." *Also a truth.* "And we've been searching all over Aurelia. Tracking down someone who may have information regarding the stone. We haven't found anything yet."

I release a steady exhale, hoping that whatever I just said is enough for him to send me back to Aurelia. That it's enough to satisfy his need to know something.

Elion waves a careless hand, and the council members rise from their seats, as if being dismissed.

"*Do you have another one of those coins?*" I ask Ekrin when he stands, walking around the curve of the table to follow Caius out.

I'm sure Rydian would have another if I asked, considering I'd tossed him mine weeks ago. But he most likely didn't bring any with him, and the last he mentioned it, he said there were hardly any left between the realms. It would be useful on our journey if Ren could speak in the Veil, and the coin is the only way an Aetheri is able to.

Elion stands and looks at Witt for a moment, annoyed. "Very well. I'll call for you in a few weeks. I expect something more substantial by the time you return." *Dismissed.*

Elion turns, his voice dropping to speak to Witt as the other council members exit. Ekrin strides close enough to scent, a wide grin smeared across his face—dazzling enough to grate on my nerves.

It's the same smug grin he wore to the Aurorafest and for a moment, I can't tell if he's a trustworthy ally or not. I hold back an annoyed sigh. Add that to the list of my mistakes.

Ekrin says nothing though, ignoring my question about the coin, and exits the council chamber without a second glance toward me.

Gritting my teeth, the Veil consumes me, and I whirl away from the castle, landing back in the loft. Ren stares out the large windows three stories up and into the brothel below, hands clenched before letting out a quiet sigh. Then the faint sounds of pleasure fill my ears, forcing my nose to scrunch.

"Rydian lied. He said these windows were sound-proof," I complain, striding to Ren's side to gaze down at the couples. "Why exactly... are you watching?"

Rydian's words flit across my mind—how he said Ren liked to watch. Perhaps what he said was true, yet I'm stuck on not truly believing it. It's not something Ren would like.

He doesn't turn. "It's mesmerizing."

I scoff, head shaking as I focus on a female below, riding the male sitting on a settee. Hair spills down her back when her head falls back, and the male grips her hips, pushing himself into her.

"You don't like brothels," I say softly.

Ren slowly swivels his head toward me, brows drawn close together. An awkward beat of silence settles between us, and my chest grows hotter the longer he stares. I fight the urge to rub the inside of my wrist. His eyes shine with amusement.

"And how would you know that?" he asks.

My cheeks flush, because I'm not quite sure. Perhaps it was luck, knowing that about him. Regardless, I clench my jaw, breaking his stare with an annoyed huff.

"We have some things to discuss," I say finally, stepping away from the window. I focus on the fogged glass from heated bodies behind him, refusing to meet his stare.

For a fleeting moment, concern pulses at the base of my neck, though it's not mine. Can Rydian feel the emotions rising in my chest, feel my worry and rage so many miles away? He's probably worried.

"They have Theo." I sigh, glancing back at Ren with a tinge of regret. "And it looks like they're training him. He was in the council chamber."

Ren's jaw tightens, but he says nothing.

"We need to do something."

He squeezes his eyes shut—a flash of anger before it's gone, hidden behind a smooth expression. "We'll figure something out. I'll discuss it with—" He cuts himself off, inhaling once more, and then changes the subject. "What did Elion want to know?"

"About the progress of the stone and Aurelia's army movements."

"And you told them what you saw?"

I nod, knowing exactly what he's asking.

What I saw splayed across the desk this morning could have been true... or perhaps not. Or maybe the camps were intentionally placed there. I only relay what I see or hear; *that* was what we planned.

Ren nods, sighing a long breath as if relieved we'd somehow gotten away with it. But then, as a tiny thought enters my mind, my eyes flare.

"Do you know where his army is?" I ask.

Ren's eyes fly to me before he nods.

"You know, I haven't seen Ire in awhile. With you being the only other Aetheri among our group, you could... communicate with him. He's a good messenger and can soar above locations without being noticed," I add, hoping he catches onto what I'm suggesting.

He stifles a grin. "Good idea."

I scoff, insulted. "I have many of those, but we need to leave. Rydian's probably losing his mind. Kalde too."

He chuckles then grips my hand and we whirl from the loft. This time, I quickly focus on where I want to go—who I want to find—picturing the dark city of Zelaryn in my mind.

Within a moment, we're in Zelaryn again, but as soon as our feet touch the dark cobbled streets, we stumble right into the person I was searching for.

"Gods," I breathe, colliding with Rydian.

"About time," Kaeda grumbles with Wayd beside her. They stride toward the inn, not another glance toward us.

Cold, damp air hits my face, and my senses are infiltrated by a flood of pine and smoke and nearby rain. A fire roars in the center of the Fates fountain towering above, lit for the night as stars blaze down.

Offerings to the Fates lay bare at the base of the fountain—tokens of blood and spools of finely woven thread, damp with mist and clinging to the stone as water trickles from the statue's lips.

Asha, the Fate of Time and creator of the Veil.

"Where were you?" Rydian growls, and I give him a small, sheepish grin, smoothing out my clothes.

His brows lower a fraction as he eyes the both of us. Kalde paces angrily behind him, having been unable to communicate what happened with Rydian. Guilt claws at me, watching the Howler in distress.

"We were—" My words fall flat, lips sealing shut when magic surfaces beneath my skin. Gods, that's annoying. I quite literally cannot tell him. I throw Ren a look and his eyes graze mine for a beat before shooting back to Rydian.

Rydian sighs. Whether he reads my expression or realizes it on his own, he gives a curt nod, jaw feathering slightly. Then Rydian leans down, lips pressing into mine.

"I was worried."

"Sorry," I say breathlessly. *"Did you find anything?"*

"Yes," Rydian says aloud, wrapping an arm around my neck and pulling me close for a moment. "A merchant gave us a few names. We're going to Voltros."

Ren arches a brow, a knowing smirk lining his lips as Rydian pulls me closer. Though the way he stares leaves me to believe he's thinking of the Painted Bird and what we watched together. It leaves me wondering if he's thinking about us stumbling on the floor in a tangled heap—the way my cheeks heated in embarrassment.

Or perhaps that's just me.

I try to ignore it entirely, shocked that neither male hears the way my heart thunders loudly in my chest. But just as we begin to follow the twins, the heaviness of my pocket pulls my attention down. My fingers dip inside and graze the weighted material, warm against my skin. Familiar.

I withdraw to find a Veil coin resting in my palm, the diamond shaped sigil gleaming in the darkness as we stride down the cobblestone beneath the stars. The coin wasn't in my pocket before, but I have an idea on who might have put it there.

18

After Veiling into Voltros, we spent two days crawling through the cold streets, during which Rydian, Wayd, and Kaeda all shifted their physical appearances.

Primarily made of shadow stone, Voltros is built atop rolling hills connected by arched bridges and illuminated by the glimmering lights hovering in the clouds. Some buildings are built directly into the slopes, carved into the hillside; others tower like rising fortresses.

And although there are many open markets and courtyards, the buildings are crammed together, making the streets and alleys narrow to navigate.

During our first day, we ended up in Ebony's Alley, a hidden market that holds a variety of vendors—art dealers, rare artifact sellers, several thieves' guilds, and fighting rings—leading us further up into the hills. Luckily, our lead from Zelaryn pointed us to a few merchants in Voltros who might have known her.

So yesterday was spent questioning those merchants before finding one with actual information, the male claiming that her whereabouts aren't common knowledge. That if word spread about him passing off the information, they'd hunt him down for it.

Now, we aim to go beneath Ebony's Alley and into the hidden

city below Voltros—Umbra's Hold. The residence of Voltros's misfits. Dark dealings are whispered to be seen there... if you're brave enough to venture in from above to witness them.

"Do the networks worry you?" I ask Rydian as we walk the length of Ebony's Alley, eyeing the entrance toward the back. He raises a brow, striding beside me as we weave through the crowd. "Do you ever feel like you need to intervene or investigate the thieves' and fighting networks as the king?"

Our hoods are up, but Wayd, Kaeda, and Rydian remain shifted in different forms. Rydian's form looks similar to the king I'm familiar with but different.

And odd to look at.

Ren and Kalde trail a few feet behind, Ren's boots thudding as he keeps pace. Far enough behind us to survey the market, but close enough to hear our conversations.

"I never thought I'd see the day where you'd allow me inside your head. Strange, really—the Veil. Is it like this all the time?" Ren says quietly, amusement coating his tone. I know he speaks of the weightlessness we tether ourselves to. *"The only downside is not hearing your thoughts."*

The sound of his teasing voice across my mind forces me to shoot an annoyed glance behind me. My eyes narrow as he rolls the Veil coin from finger to finger with a smug smirk.

I'd given it to him a couple of days ago, and Rydian and I had taught Ren to search for us in the Veil. He's been in and out of my thoughts ever since, constantly interrupting mine and Rydian's conversations. Now it's beginning to grate on my nerves.

I face forward, but instead of ignoring him, I ask, *"Xane... from the Brotherhood. He's frightened of me because I almost killed him—beat his face into a pulp when I was sixteen. You pulled me off. Real or a dream?"* The faintest of chuckles brushes my mind.

"Real. We became friends after that."

A small grin pulls at my mouth. *"Leave it to you to want to be friends after I almost kill someone."*

"He deserved it."

Rydian gives me a lazy grin, unaware of Ren in my thoughts, and places a hand along my back.

"I've already investigated the networks. There are rules placed to ensure no innocent lives are ever targeted. They go after criminals," Rydian explains. "Regardless of how wealthy our realm is, someone's always stealing or fighting. If the Fates ever came down and asked me to step in more, I would." He shrugs. "But that hasn't happened yet. Plus, who am I to tell them what they can or cannot enjoy? I consider it a balance in a way—to let them do as they wish."

I stew over his words and wonder if that is something I'd change as queen. Perhaps Rydian is right—that it's a balance. Though I don't dwell on it long, and push it aside for now.

With only one way in, the uppermost level connects to Ebony's Alley through a stone ramp that leads down after exiting the market.

The city below looks as if it was carved out of a cave, spiraling stone and shadow and crystalized structures descending from the raw, uppermost parts of the ceiling.

Descending through tiered levels, each layer is a unique blend of shops and civilization, similar to the streets above but darker. Wet stone floods my nostrils as our boots tread the slick ground; the sour tang of something stale mingles in the air, moisture beading along the walls.

Golden light filters through the natural opening above, spilling pale streaks of light across the levels. The air is cool and damp, and droplets of water drip down, echoing in the chilling silence. The inhabitants speak primarily in the Veil here. A variety of winged creatures soar around us, shooting between stalactites—bats and messenger hawks.

I glance at the Dark Market at the bottom, where stalagmites rise like natural pillars between small pools of water varying in size. The market stalls below come into view, a maze of handmade trinkets to enchanted relics glimmering in the light.

Yet, the further we snake toward the lower level, shadows chill my fingertips. Unease settles in my stomach.

The twins walk ahead. Having lived on the outskirts of Voltros as children, they know the ins and outs of everything here. Wayd apparently has a fondness for the fighting rings and spent a lot of his younger years sneaking out to win bets. And wherever Wayd was, Kaeda wasn't too far behind.

Rydian's elbow brushes my arm, his hood lowered over his brow, and his oakmoss scent somehow overrides the dampness of the cavernous city. A single intake of breath has me wanting to tangle myself around him, breathing in the scent of my mate. Something I've come to really cherish as the days go on.

I've forced my thoughts not to linger on what awaits us when we arrive back at the castle though—at the formal claiming ceremony he says he owes me. At the approaching introduction to the entire court as their missing princess.

We keep our pace casual to not alarm the frequent passersby, but a few strides down the second level, a heavy feeling courses through me. My brows lift at the unexpected emotion, breaths catching in my throat. I squint to pinpoint the fleeting emotion— longing and... pain.

The dull, throbbing kind.

The kind that lasts and aches so long, it's almost ordinary. Familiar and present day to day. I wince as if the pain is my own. A crawling, lingering ache settles at the base of my neck, and I glance at Rydian.

"What is it?" he asks, curiosity pulsing at the edge of my mind when he catches my stare. Still, the aching pain remains, clawing and throbbing at the base of my hairline.

"Are you in pain?" I ask, a wrinkle forming between my brows. I'm unsure how to explain what I'm feeling when he shoots me another glance, confusion on his face. *"Like... mentally?"*

"No. I'm not in any mental pain," he says aloud, his head pivoting to me with a quiet, disbelieving chuckle. "Why do you ask?"

Ren halts, his gaze locked on the twins. My head swivels to them and I skid to a stop so as not to collide with Kaeda. We've paused right before the last level, peering into the Dark Market just feet away. But when Wayd faces us, a large male shoulders him with a grunt.

"Watch it," the male grumbles, heavy feet thundering on the wet ground as he strides past.

For a moment, Wayd's body stills before Kaeda snaps her fingers, gaining his attention like a well-trained hound.

"There's a ward," Wayd says, his voice laced with annoyance. He faces us once more, his expression hidden beneath the shadows of his hood. We all glance at the opening ahead—at the shimmering red ward rippling in the air.

"What's it for?" Ren asks quietly, stepping to my left.

"To dampen all magic," Kaeda says, tilting her head as if sniffing. "To protect the merchants. They use it to ensure no one uses the Veil to steal and to see their customers' true forms."

"Smart," I breathe, uncomfortably glancing around.

"They'll know who you are, so keep your hoods up," Wayd says to Rydian, who responds with a low grunt. We step through the ward a moment later.

In a millisecond, their forms faintly shudder, the only proof they shifted back into their normal bodies. My magic simmers down to a low thrum beneath my skin, as if quietly waiting in the shadows to come crawling back out. No access to the Veil.

We walk down the center of the market—tents, stalls, and shadowy stores rise on both sides as quiet, hushed chatter fills the air. It's crowded, as clusters of Fae stride in all directions. Our boots slap against the stone as we wind in and out, careful not to touch anyone. Finally, stepping around a large stalagmite on our left, we reach a shop.

The wooden-framed windows display innocuous trinkets, swirling bottles of red liquid, wares, and ingredients. Obviously a front, just based on the windows alone. I suppress a rising shudder, glancing at the hanging sign above.

The Vault—Wares, Artifacts, and More.

"I have a bad feeling about this," I say hesitantly, and look at Kalde before following Kaeda to the glass-paned wooden door. "Wait for us."

With no access to my magic, Kalde only growls as if in warning. His eyes lock on the shop and a shiver pebbles my skin.

The bell rings above us as the door swings open, alerting the merchant. Various items spill across tables, heavily covering all available surfaces—books, coins, jewelry, and relics reeking of dust and age. Not a surface left empty.

But a chill snakes down my spine, the air somehow thicker than it was on the upper levels. Wayd and Kaeda take the front, leaving Ren to stand behind us, silently guarding the door.

Soon after entering, a wiry male steps in from behind a curtained off doorway, his gray brows sitting low over his eyes, a heavy shadow cast across his weathered features. A tattered black cloak with patchwork pockets rests on his shoulders.

He shuffles, slow and hunched, to the wooden counter with papers sprawling across it. His inked fingers sweep them to the side. Sigil and script mark his skin, traveling up his hand until they're hidden beneath his cloak.

"Can I help you?" he asks, voice raspy and frail. The way his eyes glaze over, he appears as if he's lived countless lives.

"We're looking for the one called Silver Tongue," Kaeda purrs, giving the male a onceover, her hood drawn low. "Do you happen to know where we could find him?"

The male warily eyes her, narrowing his haunted, indigo eyes as he scans the rest of us in silence. "Depends on who's asking. I only deal with those who reveal themselves. Hoods off if you want answers."

A minute passes, a tense silence resting between us.

And then another. It's as if Rydian's deciding whether or not to follow the request. I know more than anyone how silence can be used in tense situations. But finally, Rydian pulls his hood down, the rest of us following as we settle into the cramped space.

The male behind the counter releases a sound—something in between a hum and a grunt—as he takes us all in, one by one. He leans on his elbows with a knowing grin, as if this moment has just gotten interesting. The hair rises on my arms, and my fingers twitch for my daggers.

"And what is it you seek from Silver Tongue? It must be important if the King of Aurelia is here." The old male chuckles.

I almost groan, shooting Rydian an annoyed glance, as a king with auburn hair and a scarred lip is quite easy to recognize. Especially with certain characteristics that force him to stand out, including his large frame. But between everyone here, it feels as if the walls are pressing in, the space too small.

Rydian only smirks, his cloak rippling out as his hands slide into his pockets, confident and carefree.

"And what is your true form, Death Whisperer? It seems the wards only apply to those who visit the depths of Umbra's Hold," Rydian asks calmly. "If our true forms are required, I'd expect the same from you."

The old male rasps a laugh, and an eerie ripple twists him into someone entirely opposite of who we'd spoken to seconds prior.

My skin crawls at the winding serpent inking the male's neck. With slicked-back brown hair, he appears to be in his mid-thirties. A long, pale scar slices from hairline to cheekbone—straight over his eye. His inked fingers, heavy with rings, clink as he moves them.

Alluring. Frightening.

Death Whisperer, I think, and a coldness seeps into my bones. He looks more haunted than the twins, and I wonder if their power has its repercussions. The male gives us a ghost of a smile as he bows low, his eyes glossed as though seeing beyond the flesh.

"Silver Tongue, at your service, Your Majesty," he says smoothly, almost serpentine—no hint of the old rasp we heard a moment ago. "How can I do you the honor?"

"We're searching for someone you may have dealt with in the past." Wayd says, slowly inching between Rydian and Silver Tongue. "Someone who goes by the name of Cassivene Strin."

"And what use would you have with Miss Cassivene?" he asks, leaning into his skull-topped cane as he steps around the counter. His eyes shoot to Ren behind me, assessing the blocked door before shifting his gaze back to Wayd.

"Do you know her or not?" Wayd clips. "We don't have time to play your games."

Kaeda smirks and casually places an elbow on the counter, nails clicking against it. "We're looking for something that she might know where to find... unless you could help us? I'd hate to insult your ability to track something down since you're so well known in Umbra's Hold."

He grins then studies Kaeda a moment longer before chuckling, low and throaty. "And what is it you're tracking?"

"The Veilstone," Rydian says.

"The King of Aurelia wants the Veilstone?" Silver Tongue's brows shoot up, his tone almost taunting. "And here I thought it was a myth all these years."

Although Rydian's frustration pulses behind my eyes, he reveals nothing, expression unreadable. Either Silver Tongue doesn't have it, or he's baiting for a reaction. It's even possible he's tried looking for it, especially if he believes it to be a myth. *If* he's telling the truth.

"So you don't have it," Kaeda says with a sigh, exaggerating the sound. "What a shame."

"And what if I did? What would be the reward for that?" He tilts his head and looks at Rydian.

The silence stretches.

Another moment passes when Silver Tongue's face pales, a cold warning forming in Rydian's eyes. "I don't have it, but perhaps Cassivene does—I can't be sure. Though, she's never mentioned anything about it to *me*."

"And where is Cassivene now?" Rydian asks.

Silver Tongue let's out a dry laugh. "I'd be happy to tell you her current location, but unfortunately, I still require payment even if you are a king. Payment I'm not sure you'd be able to... provide." He gives a tight smile. "Your Majesty."

Rydian huffs. "Name your price, Death Whisperer. Money is no issue."

"Oh, I don't want your money." Silver Tongue hums and glances around the room. "No offense, Your Majesty, but I have no use for it." He steps behind the counter again, stops, and faces us. "When it comes to wanting... information, I deal in secrets. My secret for yours, if you will. Secrets or truths that no one else knows."

My stomach drops, my pulse pounding in my ears at the thought of others hearing something so intimate. But I force the emotions down, wary of Rydian feeling my concern. Silver Tongue's attention shifts to me, as if sensing my dread.

"And how would you know these secrets are true? Who's to say we won't just lie to your face?" Kaeda chuckles when he grins.

"By blood, of course. A prick of your finger and a drop of blood onto my enchanted obsidian plate will tell me if you lie."

"Blood magic," Wayd growls. "Then we'll be leaving."

"It's not up to you, now is it? Let the king decide." Silver Tongue's tone drops, looking down his nose at us.

Rydian holds his gaze from across the room, and I know he's contemplating his decision. Contemplating how much he wants to find Cassivene—the Veilstone. If it's possible she has that information, I know he'd reveal a couple of secrets, no matter the cost. If it comes down to it, I'll do the same—anything to get my mother back.

Rydian nods after a moment, stepping forward when Silver Tongue wags his finger, shaking his head.

"I get to choose *who*; that is my rule," he says, and Rydian growls as Silver Tongue's eyes meet mine, and my stomach sinks.

Then his gaze slides behind me. "I'd like the quiet one to reveal something. The quiet ones always have the best to offer."

I almost heave a sigh of relief, my chest lighter when the realization hits me. He wants Ren to reveal something.

I pivot, searching his face, but Ren reveals nothing as he steps forward, as if the request were insignificant. Perhaps it is. Yet part of me wants to step forward, to offer myself if only to spare him from sharing the secrets of his past he guards so fiercely. The ones he keeps from everyone—from me.

His boots thud against the creaking wood, and he walks between us to meet Silver Tongue at the counter. The rich scent of him lingers in the air before he comes to a stop, shoulders back, spine straight.

Wayd and Kaeda take a large step back, creating space for us. Or perhaps they've seen enough blood magic in Voltros to not want to be near it. I glance at Ren, but his expression remains unreadable, with not even a flicker of emotion.

Silver Tongue smiles and flicks his wrist. A thin, black obsidian plate appears from the Veil with a clink, set right in front of Ren. "What is your name?"

"Ren."

"Well, Ren," Silver Tongue says and quickly pricks his finger.

The stench of iron hits the air, blood beading at the tip before Silver Tongue angles Ren's finger, dripping it onto the plate below. It bubbles, dancing on the flat surface as if sentient, and then shimmers a bright blue.

"That was your first test. Looks like you told the truth. You will give me three secrets, things no one else knows. Preferably something that may have caused you... pain."

My jaw tightens with frustration. He shouldn't be doing this.

"One," Ren clips, his biting tone leaving no room for argument. Silver Tongue hums and assesses our group before shifting his attention back to Ren.

"Three. Normally, I'd require payment from everyone here, but since the King is requesting... you alone will give me three," he says with squinted eyes.

"Two."

"Fine." Silver Tongue all but growls in annoyance before tilting his head, grinning, as if realizing that Ren holds many secrets. Secrets he's unwilling to share so easily.

Guilt and anger tighten my chest. Magic floods my palms in a tingling heat so fierce I'm forced to suck in a breath and clench my fists to control it. Rydian glances down at my hands, but I ignore his concern.

I'm the only reason Ren's in this position in the first place, yet he's willing to help without complaint. He knows as much as anyone how important it is to find Cassivene, especially if she might know how to find the Veilstone. It's a risk we're all willing to take.

Or perhaps it's out of sheer loyalty to me that makes Ren willing to confess his secrets. My chest constricts at the thought.

Ren takes a deep breath, but his posture remains rigid, hands flexing at his sides. If it weren't for his skilled composure, there's a chance I would have seen torment written across his face. My breathing stalls, the seconds dragging before he finally speaks.

"Fate marked me to a future I didn't want," he says softly.

Confusion grips me when I look between him and Silver Tongue —literally or figuratively? What does he mean by that? A ripple of frustration flickers across Silver Tongue's expression, but he squeezes the tip of Ren's finger, regardless. Blood beads, dripping onto the plate below, and shimmers blue.

"Now, one more," Silver Tongue says.

Ren stares at him, unblinking. "I failed to protect someone once."

"Details," Silver Tongue says with a low growl, his eyes narrowing. "That's not enough. *Who* did you fail to protect?"

Silence sunders the air, everyone rigid in the cramped space as we wait for Ren to answer. I glance at Rydian, and for the briefest of moments, his jaw feathers, a warning blazing past Ren toward Silver Tongue.

"The mate I had," Ren gets out.

Ren presses against his own finger—*drip, drip, drip*. Three drops, and it immediately shimmers blue, sparking. Silver Tongue's eyes gleam at the glow. *At the truth.*

Almost as if it's a delicacy.

My eyes widen, my breathing shallow. His revealed secret shocks even me, but then my eyes soften as the weight of his words settle in the shop. *He used to have a mate.*

Gods, how has madness not consumed him? His pain must be unbearable. Then a sense of understanding blooms in my chest, as his anguish isn't just grief but guilt, written all over his face. Something he can't quite hide fully, a wound so deep that even time refuses to heal it.

Realization sweeps through me, knowing it's why he keeps to himself, locking his memories away. Perhaps to hold others at arms length for fear of losing someone else, and I understand it.

Ren's body remains tense—shoulders back. Another lingering silence settles between everyone when Silver Tongue's eyes glaze over, cloudy and lost beyond the Veil, and then smirks after a moment.

"Had or have?" Silver Tongue asks quietly, humming in amusement as his eyes come into focus once more. "You do realize I speak to the dead."

Ren steps back, his eyes narrowing, face twisting into a disgusted sneer and says, "It's the truth and you agreed to two, Death Whisperer. Where is Cassivene Strin?"

19

It turns out Cassivene Strin goes by the name Professor Serin—a reclusive scholar who teaches at the Shadovar Institute in Halstra, one of the largest cities in Aurelia.

A smuggler turned professor—*talk about a switch.*

"Those who live in Aurelia can expand their magical or historical studies by attending the institute," Rydian explains as we walk beneath a tunnel of orange and red-leafed trees, the bricked streets flooding with students of every kind—halflings, Fae, and humans.

"Do they pay to attend?" I ask, but he shakes his head.

Ren strides on my right, Kalde trotting beside him though neither has spoken to me since rising this morning. I figure it has to do with those secrets he revealed—secrets that leave me curious.

"Do you want to talk about it?" I shoot a casual glance toward Ren, itching to learn more about his past. Though I don't want to press too hard, fearing he'd close himself off more and remain silent the rest of our journey. But I also hate that he's in pain.

"Not particularly," he replies, and I leave it at that.

"No, they don't have to pay, but everyone has a duty," Rydian continues our conversation. "Students pull their weight by maintaining an assigned job. The professors are paid a great deal for teaching, though. We set aside gold from the tribute each month."

Rydian had told me about the gold tribute collected from the Shadovar—money that goes toward rebuilding, education, and anything else they might need it for.

Admiration washes over me just as Wayd turns to flash us a wicked grin, the institute quickly coming into view beyond the trees. After Silver Tongue revealed her location, Wayd's smugness told me all I needed to know—that his suspicions about Cassivene residing in one of the larger cities had been right all along, and he'd be rubbing it in later.

Once Silver Tongue had told us where Cassivene was yesterday, we were gone, as we were unwilling to linger long enough for him to demand more secrets.

No one breathed a word though—not about Ren's secrets, and we certainly didn't ask anything else when Ren had turned on his heel and waited for us outside with Kalde. Both Rydian and Ren had remained silent the rest of the way up, as if the entire day had them tense. But as we strode up the cave, I finally worked up the courage to ask Kaeda about my mother.

"Have you ever tried to see if she was…" I trailed off, too afraid to mutter the word *dead,* but she seemed to catch on.

Kaeda's eyes softened a little, nodding. "I have actually, a few times. When someone enters the Veil, it's their essence and not a physical body as I explained before. But anyone I've spoken to about the queen who was a Seer hasn't come forward. Regardless of who I ask or where I look, it leaves me to believe she's still alive."

A wave of relief had washed over me at that, confirming what Elion had shown me, but then my brows pinched in confusion. "She was a Seer? I didn't know that."

"Yes. I'd often see her writing when we'd visit." Kaeda had smiled, as if it were a fond memory.

But yesterday's conversation quickly slips from my thoughts when we arrive outside the institute, stopping near the wrought iron gate. A stone wall separates us from the facility.

I turn, but before I can order Kalde to conceal himself in the trees behind us, he's already trotting away, blending into the shadows. Then Wayd and Kaeda's bodies ripple, shifting into students, grins lighting up their faces as they share the same knowing look.

"Do not speak to anyone." Rydian's eyes narrow before looking around. "We're here to talk to Strin, not cause a disruption. Stay focused."

"Fine," Kaeda grumbles, and the twins heave an annoyed sigh in unison as if Rydian had ruined their fun. I can't help but chuckle as they mirror each other's scowl and stride beyond the gates. I glance around as we inch our way inside.

The dark, shadow stone institute rises into the sky, the ancient spires lost in the clouds. Arched windows rise in graceful curves along the sides, the glass panes stained with hues of dark amber. Students stride down the covered walkway that encircles the building, its roof held up by stone pillars, each one carved to perfection.

Quiet chatter flits through the air, boots crunching as students mingle in and out of the walkway, wrapped tightly in their cloaks as a light snow begins to fall. A few quiet minutes go by when two forms finally approach us, shifting back into Wayd and Kaeda.

"We're ready—let's Veil into her office," Kaeda says. "We have roughly fifteen minutes before the next class."

"Stay here," I tell Kalde, and grip Kaeda's hand, reaching for Ren with my other.

"I'll be waiting, just like I've done for the last two weeks," Kalde groans, and then we disappear in the Veil, landing right in the middle of a grand office.

Wooden bookcases line both sides, a desk sitting near intricate arched windows in the back. A door behind us.

"Oh gods!" a female exclaims.

We swivel our heads to the young professor. Her brown eyes grow wide, her entire body freezing in place behind a wooden desk, hands splayed in front of her. Our hoods are up, so all she can see are our figures crowding her office.

Rydian steps forward. "Cassivene Strin?"

"Fuck." She takes off, attempting to reach the door on her left, but Wayd appears in front of it, stepping from the Veil with a devious grin. Fear shines in her eyes and she comes to a sudden halt, her long golden hair whipping around her face.

"I don't do that anymore, I swear. I have nothing you want, just let me go," she quips with a grin and then shrugs. "Old me, you know?"

Cassivene slowly backs up as Wayd steps forward, crowding her back toward the desk in a trap.

I stifle a smile. Her behavior is unusual for a supposed professor, sounding more like a troubled thief. Especially now if she's already trying to escape. She won't be doing that though.

Rydian tugs his hood, exposing his true form as King of Aurelia. Dark and menacing, his brows lower in annoyance.

"Oh Mother of all Fates," she whispers and then falls to her knees, her hands clasped as if in prayer. "Please don't kill me, please. Whatever it is, it wasn't me. I don't do that anymore."

She continues to murmur her pleas, remaining on her knees, and Ren actually chuckles as she begs us to spare her. Rydian all but groans as Kaeda snickers off to the side, Wayd's expression growing heated with... something I definitely don't want to name. Though my lips curve into an amused grin at her over-exaggerated pleas.

"Is that how you want me to behave?" I laugh softly, and Rydian throws me a heated glare, but something tells me he would love me on my knees.

"Rise, Cassivene. No need to beg for your life, we're not here to kill you." Rydian sighs. "We just have some questions."

The anxious, frightened professor rises, wiping her hands on her brown pants.

"What kind of questions?" she gets out, doe-eyes darting to each of us as we tug on our own hoods. She gasps when her gaze collides with mine.

Rydian strokes his jaw. "We heard a rumor that you may know how to track the Veilstone... or that you might have it. Is that true?"

Her spine straightens, tensing for a moment. "I... I'd rather not discuss it here—where I work—if that's okay. Is it possible for you to stay at my estate tonight? It's private and I'd be happy to host. I have plenty of rooms," she says quietly, voice trembling slightly.

"You won't run?" Ren asks, crossing his arms and giving her a look that reminds me of his role in the Brotherhood—the seriousness in his expression. The ruthlessness.

"I wouldn't dare. Especially not with the king and his mate present—our future queen," she says and I stiffen. "Whatever they want, I'll give them. Just give me until later this afternoon. My last class finishes around then, and I can escort you there."

Gods, news travels fast in this realm.

How the hell do they do that so quickly? I was hoping to have more time before the knowledge of Rydian and I got out. Then again, the castle knew long before I had even arrived.

Rydian's only response is a curt nod before we all Veil into the enormous courtyard and wait.

A few hours go by before Cassivene makes true on her promise, escorting us to her—quite enormous—estate, tucked away amongst the ancient trees near the height of the city.

Trees so tall, it's a shock that they don't graze the clouds. Kalde hangs back once more, settling himself on the outskirts of the overgrown gardens and plopping down. Then he rolls, scraping his back against the ground as if scratching an itch he can't reach.

Cassivene didn't even cower at Kalde, more intrigued about a Howler accompanying me to the realm than lingering in fear. She had gone into great detail about how the Howlers of Elderheim can sense magic from both realms, leaving curiosity to rise in my chest.

We quietly follow her inside the grand estate.

The air is cool, but warm enough that it wards off the chill from outside. We shrug off our cloaks, handing them to the waiting house maidens with outstretched hands.

The scent of roasted meat hangs in the air, melding with apples and spice and something savory, sending my stomach curling with hunger.

Then we all do a thorough scan of the foyer.

A study sits on our right: a rather large space, clad with hundreds of books from floor to ceiling. To our left is an enormous room enclosed by glass—a gallery of relics and collected items. It shimmers red—a ward.

I find myself smirking, wondering if any of those items happen to be stolen or smuggled in. My eyes instinctively meet Rydian's as he arches a brow, and I know he's thinking the same.

Cassivene turns, tugging her hood down. "One of our ladies will escort you all to your rooms. Fresh towels are already prepared for you. I'd love it if you all would join me for dinner in an hour to discuss... what we talked about," she says with a tight smile, clasping her hands together.

Wayd follows a house-maiden up the steps when Kaeda swivels to Ren. Her gaze drags over him in a deliberate once-over, then she smirks.

"Would you like to share a room, Captain? I certainly could use the company, and you look like you enjoy eating."

My brows shoot up at the double meaning. Then an unexpected anger floods my palms, swarming with shadows. My fingers twitch, my hands trembling with unrestrained magic, and I have a sudden urge to throw something sharp. Rydian furrows his brows—his eyes shooting to my hands—as if he's sensed the magic bubbling in my palms. But I say nothing.

Are the twins always like this? Does Kaeda not recall what he just revealed about himself? To my surprise, Ren lets out a quiet chuckle, staring down his nose.

"I have a feeling that not a lot of people tell you no," he says quietly.

She laughs, the sound taunting as she tilts her head, looking at him like he's something to consume. She purrs, "They don't."

"Well, allow me to be the first," he says, and shoves past her up the steps. Kaeda's mouth falls open before she throws me a grin over her shoulder.

"Oh, I like him," she says, ascending the steps, leaving me to stifle an annoyed curl of my lips.

Cassivene lets out an amused snort before pivoting to us. "You both will take the suite on the second floor. My maidens will prepare the table and fetch you in an hour."

She bows with a small smile and then walks down the corridor without another word. The shadow of a dark mate mark at the back of her head fades with her down the hallway, lost beneath blonde strands. Does she live here with her mate? Rydian's gaze meets mine. He fights a grin, like something in his mind just clicked.

"Did you see her mark?" he asks, and my brows pinch as we follow the maidens up the steps. *"Did it not look familiar?"*

My lips part, and I'm seconds from asking when it registers. I gasp, my eyes growing wide. *"Orin has the same."*

He chuckles, nodding.

"Are you going to tell him—or her?"

"No, definitely not," he states, hesitating a moment as he sifts through his thoughts. *"It's quite… frowned upon to involve yourself in those affairs, crossing that boundary between mates. That's something they need to discover on their own."*

"Seems unfair." I frown.

He only shrugs as we turn left, reaching our bed chamber door. The maiden steps aside for us to walk in. *"The only thing we can do is introduce them and hope they figure it out on their own. It's risky to mess with fate."*

The suite contains a large sitting room, bed chamber, and a bathing chamber, each connected by wide, arched doorways. The high ceilings showcase the detailed beams, the floors made of a creamy, glimmering marble.

The maiden quickly departs, leaving us fine clothing on the bed and in our correct sizes. My brows furrow in confusion, wondering how she could have possibly guessed our sizes.

The clothes are linen, soft and fine, but casual. Comfortable enough for a nice dinner, but not a fancy one. The bed is large enough to sleep three, with a thick quilt. Large, plush pillows fill the space by the headboard.

Glancing over my shoulder, Rydian stands near the arched doorway to the bathing chamber when he pulls his shirt over his head. I face him, watching muscle ripple in the warm light.

"Will you join me?" he asks, his hand reaching the laces of his pants. He pulls the seam apart. My breath hitches in anticipation, blood heating at the thought of sharing a bath with him. He reads my expression, turning for the bathing chamber, then throws me a devious grin over his shoulder.

"No foul play yet, we're saving that for later now that we have a room to ourselves," he gets out. "Or one that doesn't involve being connected to anyone beside us like those inns we frequented."

I follow him in and shut the door behind me, chuckling, wondering how long it will take before one of us cracks. Yet something tells me that saving it for later won't last very long.

20

____

It didn't last long.

In fact, I had barely sunk into the water before Rydian perched himself at the edge of the tub, eyes blazing down. It left me no choice but to get on my knees, lips tightening around him until he combusted, the taste of him sliding down my throat.

The memory still clings to me now, as I sit at the dining table. It sends another heat roaring through my veins at the thought, forcing me to squeeze my legs together, doing my best to focus on the food in front of me. I quickly stifle it, unwilling to have the others scent my _arousal_ at dinner. Though it's not really a dinner, but a feast, and if Wayd and Ren were to compete on who ate the most, they would have tied.

The maidens clean the table, pouring us more wine. Compared to the last two weeks of having to eat in taverns off the road—where the portions were questionable for the amount of money they required—it was nice eating a large meal. Rydian hadn't blinked at those paltry meals, paying without complaint, even as most of the proprietors begged the king not to pay their ridiculous prices.

The formal dining chamber is nothing short of exquisite, just like the rest of her estate.

"I live alone with my maidens since I have yet to meet my mate," Cassivene says down the table and sips, chuckling. "Hasn't stopped me from enjoying anyone though."

Clearly, if her house maidens were any indication. They continuously steal glances and watch her from a distance, serving us with warm cheeks and small grins. And she's reciprocated every one of those glances, even with the males walking around. Including Wayd, who currently has an enticing smirk on his face while he licks his fingers clean of food.

"Surely Wayd saw her mark," I mention to Rydian, shooting him a sideways glance. I arch my brow with a crystal chalice in my grasp. His hand grips my thigh beneath the table, squeezing.

"If he has, I'm not sure he'd care or has even connected the dots." He shrugs, as if Wayd's reaction is normal. *"It wouldn't matter anyway— some stick with only their mates but many in the realm have lovers they share."*

I almost spit out my wine, eyes flaring as I clear my throat. Concerned glances meet mine. Ren arches a brow before leaning back. He says nothing, though, only sits there and silently watches us, sipping his fourth glass of wine.

Something he doesn't typically drink as an ale lover. The thought tumbles through my mind, wondering why exactly that fact about him surfaced. I frown.

"Would they really share?" I ask in disbelief. Rydian only laughs and leans in, the breathy sound disturbing the hair at my temples.

My thoughts snag on Ren watching us at the castle again. How his eyes heated when he saw where Rydian's hand settled that day, and how Rydian didn't... mind. Would Rydian like that?

My chest grows hot, and I glance down the table, catching the tiniest of smirks lifting the corner of Ren's mouth, as if he knows exactly where my thoughts currently settle.

"Wayd would probably want to. Orin? Probably not." Rydian grins and then shifts his attention to Cassivene down the table, who's clearly speaking to Wayd in the Veil. A dark, taunting look races across his features, and I wonder if he'll be sleeping in his own chambers tonight.

If I were to guess, I'd say no.

Rydian grips the back of my neck with a gentle squeeze, and I almost purr at the pressure. "So, Miss Cassivene. You mentioned our... discussion. What can you tell us?"

She casually swivels her gaze to him with a grin.

"I was actually about to get to that, but I would rather talk in my study. There's a soundproof ward, so we wouldn't be overheard by... prying ears."

Even though her eyes shine bright, her smile wide and inviting, I know she's serious about taking extra precautions. She doesn't want others overhearing us, and my stomach recoils at the thought. Rydian nods, and we all stand, leaving our glasses as we follow her down the corridor.

Gilded, wooden-framed artwork lines the walls, expert paintings that practically reflect off the marble floors. She definitely has taste.

A phantom wind pushes the glass doors to the study open, and everyone files in before they shut. And then silence. The ward buzzes in the air, and we all pivot to face Cassivene.

Though the study is more of a library.

A wrap around mezzanine sits close to the fifty foot ceiling. Various settees and tables are scattered around as if specifically set up for different types of meetings.

She stands at a tall, glass-topped wooden island housing a variety of relics and places her hands on it, her expression grave and filled with what looks to be more fear than wariness.

"What can you tell us? Were you able to track the Veilstone down?" Rydian says now, more king than casual.

Her gaze locks with his. We take our places around the island, patiently waiting for her to speak.

She sighs. "Unfortunately, I have not been able to track it." Rydian growls at that, pacing as her voice brushes the air again. "I'm wary to discuss the Veilstone, only because I was forced to stop searching for it."

Rydian halts his pacing, coming to my side once again. "What do you mean?"

"I was one of the best smugglers and thieves in Aurelia." She chuckles with a small shake of her head, as if in disbelief. "But what made me the best was my studies. I used to bury my nose in the histories of this realm—Elderheim too—learning everything about relics and art. It gave me leverage."

"That made you want to search for the stone?" Kaeda asks.

"Well, when the battle happened, I had a wild thought that if King Elion was still searching for it, that maybe the stone existed. So yes, I began looking for it." She sighs again and then paces, mumbling as if sifting through her thoughts. "At first it was to challenge myself, you know, but I realized that a king had started an entire war over this stone—this *myth*. And then I got to thinking: well, maybe it wasn't a myth at all. I searched up until a few years ago."

"What happened?" Ren asks, stepping to my left, his elbow brushing against my shoulder. Even though I glance up at him, his gaze remains fixed on Cassivene.

She shakes her head. "I found a really old tome at The Sanctum of the Veil."

"The ancient Shadovar archives?" Rydian asks, and she nods.

"I assume I got really close to finding *something*, because I started being followed. I will say that some of the rumors about me are true—like getting caught selling a stolen relic, but that's not why I vanished. They got so close to capturing me, I had no choice but to flee. Silver Tongue was the one who helped me at the time because they tracked me to his shop in Umbra's Hold. His only rule was that if the king of Aurelia came knocking, he'd aid you. I'm assuming he was the one that gave you my specific location."

With my mind buzzing, an unexpected flash of Umbra's Hold flits across my vision—glancing over my shoulder in panic, weaving between stalls, relics and merchants and artifacts blurring when Silver Tongue's shop comes into view.

I blink a few times and take in a breath, shaking my head to rid me of my thoughts—of suddenly being thrust back into that cave.

That was... odd.

Rydian peers down at me, his brows furrowing before turning back to the group.

"Who followed you?" Kaeda asks.

Ren crosses his arms, grumbling, "I'm willing to bet it was King Elion's men. Wouldn't shock me if he sent a few from the Brotherhood."

Cassivene only nods, confirming our suspicions when she shoots me a glance and winces—no doubt over the fact that I'm his daughter. Another rumor that has made it to her estate, apparently. She tugs on a hidden drawer beneath the table then pulls out a very large, weathered tome and places it on the island with a thud.

"This is *The Aethevar Tome*," she says with a sigh. "Created before the realms were separated and written by the Fates themselves, it's the only one of its kind. It will have some answers for you, but unfortunately, not the specific location of the Veilstone. It does say that you can use an Herb Weaver and a Seer to track it. They just have to be used together. I never got past that part."

"You stole the tome?" Rydian practically growls. Disbelief and mild annoyance thud against my temples. "You're lucky the Fates didn't strike you down for it."

Cassivene gives a sheepish smile and a small shrug.

"Are the Fates even real?" I ask, staring at the tome, though an awkward silence settles at my question. Rydian swivels his head toward me, his expression twisting with confusion.

Cassivene's eyes grow wide. "Oh, they're very real. Otherwise, you wouldn't have your power. Our realms wouldn't have the magic that makes them unique."

"So… why would you need both magic users when we could just use a Seer?" I ask, holding back a grimace for questioning my belief of the Fates so boldly.

She laughs softly. "Balance. Elderheim and Aurelia have to have balance in order for them to exist, because the Veilstone is meant for both realms. You can't have one without the other. I assume it has something to do with the Herb Weaver's origin of magic alongside the Seers in order for it to work." Rydian shoots me a glance, leaning forward to look at the tome.

"A balance in magic? What does that mean exactly?" I ask.

She opens the tome, flipping through the pages before landing on a specific one, worn with wrinkles and various marks.

She slides it over. "The realms are all about balance. It's why capabilities for each realm vary slightly, but a lot of them are the same in their own way. Like the Shadow Shapers and Stone Shapers. They have the same capabilities, do they not? Seers and Scrys, Healers and Shadow Menders—all similar in their own ways. But Herb Weavers have the ability to work with almost anyone through the magic they wield. They were responsible for making all those Veil coins for Aurelia, but since the warded border, now the coins are hard to find," she says, pointing to the descriptions.

Confusion settles over me as I mull over her words when a thought crosses my mind about my own Vision Walking capabilities. I know for a fact that I'm Shadovar. But I'm also Aetheri.

Is balance meant for everything? Would balance mean that I'm still waiting to wield a specific magic besides what I gained from Elion since I can Vision Walk?

"What would that mean for me since I can Vision Walk, and carry both royal essences?" I ask.

She hums, brows drawing close together. "I'm actually not sure. I assume that if you have the power of Aurelia coursing through you like Vision Walking, you would have the ability to do something from Elderheim as well. Especially royalty. If you weren't royalty but from both realms, you would most likely be able to wield both kinds of magic but exhibit stronger capabilities in one."

Rydian sighs. "We'll take this with us back to the castle to have one of our historians look it over. Then it's going to be *returned*." He stresses the word.

She smiles, the kind that tells me she's brewing a thought. "Of course. But would it be possible to visit and study alongside your historian? I've yet to visit the castle, even after you opened it up." She shuts the tome with a soft thud before locking it back into the drawer it came from. "I'll need to find someone to cover my classes, but I bet I could make it work."

"Yes, I'm sure Varrin would love that." Rydian chuckles,

throwing me a knowing grin. *"I'm sure someone else would love that, too."*

I stifle the urge to laugh behind my hand when her eyes shoot to the right, settling on the twins behind us. Wayd and Kaeda have inched themselves away from the island and to her bookshelves, casually sifting through them as if searching for something interesting to read. My lips curve up, knowing they're being nosy.

"Perfect, I can't wait to visit," Cassivene says.

I sigh—at least we have some answers. Now all we have to do is find a Seer and an Herb Weaver. Perhaps we can have Varrin go through the tome to find what we need in order to track it down.

"Let's see if Bess can help," I offer, my hand on Rydian's arm. His eyes meet mine before he nods. "And then maybe we can convince an Herb Weaver to help."

Cassivene shuffles, clearly uncomfortable, and scratches her head. "Actually... The only Herb Weaver's that qualifies come from a line of dukes and duchesses—nobles. But I heard a few years ago that King Elion slaughtered them in front of their son."

My head snaps to her, eyes flaring as a wave of unease settles in my stomach. I know exactly who she speaks of.

"Does that mean we can't track the Veilstone after all?" Ren's brows furrow.

"Well, the magic in that specific noble bloodline is the only one strong enough to create what you need... in order to track it," she explains. "Centuries ago, the noble families were divided into the strongest familial lines, their power passed down through blood. Surprisingly enough, King Elion's line didn't always hold the throne. Eighty years ago, the previous king and queen forfeited their lives to pass the royal essence to the Scrys. I hear there's still royal essence from the previous rulers simmering in Elderheim, even now. Royal essence doesn't disappear just because a crown changes hands. The noble lines are listed in the tome, but there's one remaining Herb Weaver in that family. Last I heard, he works for King Elion."

I squeeze my eyes shut, the knowledge of it sitting on my chest like a weight, forcing me to take a deep breath. A nauseating coil has my fingers curling into fists. I'd seen him just days ago, unable to decipher if he was friend or foe.

Ren's eyes find mine, a flicker of annoyance across his features as he begins to piece it together. Head shaking, he releases a heavy sigh. Then Rydian's gaze sharpens on me, a question forming when he pivots to Cassivene, certainly realizing who exactly works for King Elion.

The only reason King Elion would be unaware of who works beside him is because he doesn't have this tome for his own research. If he had known who it was, he would have already used him. I'm certain of it. Which is also why he was tracking Cassivene.

"What's the familial line?" Rydian asks carefully.

"The Highcrest line."

21

"Before we leave tomorrow, I have something for you," Rydian says, settling himself on the long settee near the hearth in our suite, wearing only the soft linen pants from earlier. Chest rippling, he rests his elbows along the back, and he smiles when my eyes suspiciously narrow.

He holds two items, both wrapped in cloth.

"What is it?" A grin pulls at my mouth. After locking the door, I stride over, unable to stifle my rising curiosity.

A fire roars across from us, crackling here and there as evening settles over Cassivene's estate. After two weeks of travel, the quiet space feels like taking a fresh breath.

Tomorrow, we'll deliver both the tome and Cassivene to the castle before leaving for Ekrin's estate. Something I'm dreading. And if he has the answers we seek, I may claw his eyes out for keeping them from us.

Rydian laughs now, gesturing to his lap and I straddle him, my silk robe pooling on his legs. A second later, he lifts the fabric on the first item, gently pulling out an inky black dagger with silver sigils etched onto the blade. Crisp and sharp. A soft gasp slips from me, followed by an eager but menacing grin. It's exquisite.

The black metal is cool and smooth, absorbing the light rather than reflecting it—an aura of power. The sigils catch the faint glow of dim light, their delicate lines shimmering like stars in a blackened sky. The blade is similar to what I saw in Arcan, but more intricate. Yet all I can do is hold my hands out to accept the heavy blade.

"That's mine?" I ask quietly, my eyes flicking to his grin. Excitement coats my veins when he nods, but a wrinkle of confusion forms between my brows. "Why are you giving me this?"

His eyes narrow for a moment, studying my features as if he doesn't believe my confusion. Then he says *"Happy birthday,"* and I stiffen in his lap, silent and still.

He quickly reminds me of what I shoved into the back of my mind—my twenty-sixth birthday. Too distracted to even remember the damn thing. I almost groan.

His fingers graze my collarbone, sweeping the loose tendril of hair over my shoulder. I look back to the metal in my hands, its weight anchoring me as words dissipate right off my tongue.

Utterly speechless.

I forgot my own birthday, but he somehow remembered it.

Then I clear my throat, embarrassed. "I love it, thank you. Is this why you wanted to wait tonight?" I tease.

Before I can say anything else, memories of previous birthdays flood me, and I stop breathing, my chest tightening. I blink, staring at my hands as images whirl across my mind, leaving my skin flushed, my mind dizzy.

"Maybe," he says, lifting my chin and searching my face for a sign that I understand. I quickly shake the memories. "Do you remember when we met?"

"Which time?" I breathe a laugh, looking at him in awe and a little disbelief. The heat of his chest sears my knuckles as I balance the blade between us.

"Hmm." His hands settle on my hips. "You threw many daggers at me. I felt that if you were going to throw one at my face, it should be one I made for you. Made of shadow and a hint of frustration since I had a hard time forming it the way I wanted." He offers a lopsided, sheepish grin.

"You made this for me?" I ask in disbelief. "And how exactly did you make it?"

"Shadow Shapers craft weapons sometimes." He shrugs, and his hands tighten on my hips. "That one... I made for you."

Shadow Shapers are a strange blend between Siphons and Stone Shapers. But instead of pulling essence or stone from a realm, they draw darkness from their surroundings, shaping it into weapons as hard and enduring as anything fired in our metal forges.

An embarrassing flush rises in my cheeks, realizing that I'd never asked him what his power was as a king. Something that most lovers or mates would have at least discussed by now, yet... I'd never bothered.

Guilt unravels in my chest.

Perhaps I never truly believed I'd end up in Aurelia. I surely didn't believe he was my mate at the time—believing what we had was fleeting.

Rydian plants a soft, delicate kiss onto my mouth, pulling me from my thoughts. But despite it being soft and delicate, his touch sends a heat down my body before he pulls back, and I'm now eager to finish what we started earlier. He sets the blade on the table beside us.

"Would you like to see the other one?" he asks.

I nod eagerly, my eyes now fixed on the fabric in his grasp, anticipation flooding my veins.

"I had originally planned on giving you a ring, but I want to wait because I want you to wear this first."

Heart racing, my lips part. "You were going to get me a ring?"

He stiffens, hands stalling on the fabric of my gift as he winces, as if he didn't mean to spoil my surprise. "I've already gotten you one. But you can't have it until we complete the claiming ritual, so this will have to do."

My heart skips.

The ritual where our essences meld together—the one that might be able to shatter my oath to Elion. I've yet to share that information with anyone though. Considering I don't have my full essence back from Elion's crystals, I'm unsure the binding would even work. Plus, there's no way of knowing if what Ekrin said is true, and I'd hate for hope to rise where none even exists. But...

What would happen if I was able to break the blood oath? What would happen to my mother or Theo? A risk I'm not sure I want to take.

Rydian unfurls the second gift, and my breath stalls at the sight of an intricate, glittering black crown with an assortment of rubies along every point. The flames in the hearth reflect off the surface, and the sight is so beautiful, I remain speechless.

Beautifully fit for a queen. Fit for *me*.

Rydian holds my gaze and quietly places it on my head, even as his eyes heat with something more. Something I'm eager to give him.

I stare at him for a moment, studying the king I don't deserve but desperately want for my own selfish reasons. A future with the male who spent twenty years of his life searching for me. A king that, even now with all my secrets and broken past, still wants me.

I don't deserve him.

Wearing my new crown, I lean forward, capturing his mouth as a ferocious hunger claws at my spine, my heart aching and bleeding for him. Squeezing so tight that breath leaves my lungs.

My tongue slips inside his mouth as he opens for me, and he groans, settling further into the settee with an arm secured around my waist. He tugs me closer, our bodies melding together and becoming something not of this realm.

And, for a moment, it's only the two of us that exists as my worries fade away with his lips on mine.

"I take it you like the gifts?"

His chest heaves, his hands roaming up to delicately slide the robe off my shoulders until I'm bare. A hungry growl tears from his throat when he pulls back, his teeth dragging along the inside of my neck, grazing and biting. His fingers thread through my hair before tightening into a wonderfully painful grip, forcing my head back on a delicate cry.

"Fuck yes I do," I admit as his cock stiffens beneath me, hardening against the arousal pooling between my legs in a flood of warmth.

Slick with need, I roll my hips. His hand dips between us, swirling and rubbing and teasing my arousal.

He tears away from my neck, every breath labored and shallow. Then he works his pants down. I hover, studying him as he inhales, slow and steady, doing his best to reign in his control.

But it's then that I see it begin to unravel.

Without breaking our gaze, he grips my hips and slowly eases me onto his cock. I gasp, welcoming the pressure of him stretching me.

"Gods," he groans, breathy and raw, tension taut across his skin like glass under too much pressure. "So fucking tight."

His brows lower, features darkening as his lips part on the softest exhale. My breath hitches, my own control fracturing in the wake of his need—his eagerness to please me.

And just like that, something snaps.

I sit up, tauntingly slow, withdrawing him from me and begin to seat myself over and over. His eyes glaze over, lips parting, desperate for air as I slam into him. With his hands on my waist, his hips match my wild pace, pushing up and up. My core tightens, clamping down until I feel his release build.

"Fuck, Isa," he gets out, head dropping to the settee behind him as pleasure consumes him.

Then he devours me again, his tongue tangling with mine, fingers swirling over my clit. I nuzzle his neck, my release building, seconds from climaxing when his body stiffens. A fleeting brush of annoyance and frustration enters my thoughts momentarily, pulling me from my climax.

"Don't look now, but we have a visitor," he growls, chest heaving with exertion, beading with sweat. My eyes fly open, snapping to the door. Rydian's chest rumbles with another annoyed growl.

Ren is propped against it by a shoulder, smirking and watching us. My heart races for a reason I can't quite explain. Adrenaline floods me, heat building as our eyes meet.

Staring with the same hunger he had in the council chamber. Primal. And something that sends my arousal into overdrive, apparently.

My eyes snap to Rydian. *"Are you going to tell him to leave?"*

"Do you want him to leave?" he asks with a hint of curiosity. And a question I wished he hadn't asked because now I'm not so sure. Despite myself, I hesitate, saying nothing. I only stare at him with flaring realization, frozen in his grasp.

Do I want Ren to stay? What does it mean if I say yes? And if he stays… what happens exactly?

Then Rydian lifts me with a small smirk, easing me back onto his cock, and I release an uncontrollable breathy moan. My eyes squeeze shut. I shouldn't like it. I shouldn't want Ren's gaze while Rydian pours himself into me. Yet I do.

Shame should course through me right now, but even as I search for it, reach for it… it doesn't surface. It only heightens my arousal.

My heart races—am I betraying Rydian for liking it?

"Let him stay," Rydian demands quietly, his eyes fixed on Ren, though his jaw feathers. *"Show him how pretty you sound when you come around my cock. He clearly wants to watch."*

Rydian's thumb swipes over my clit, hard and intentional, and my voice breaks with a cry. My walls clench around him, and I buck into his hand, gasping as pleasure builds in my core once more. We begin to move. Like a tidal wave, desire floods my entire body. He thrusts up, pushing himself deeper, fingers tight in an almost painful grip.

Guiding me, owning me.

"Do you like when I watch?" Ren carelessly slides into my thoughts, his voice cutting through the haze of my need for Rydian. Words that have my entire body heating in a way I never expected.

Heating as Rydian's hands travel to my breasts. Heating as his cock stretches me, bare and open for Ren to view from the doorway.

"The crown is a nice touch," Ren murmurs, heated and low, near inaudible. *"I told you that you liked pretty things."*

Unable to reply, my breath hitches, my lips parting as I tear my mouth from Rydian to focus and to squeeze my eyes shut, head falling back. My release builds once more and I writhe against him with frenzied speed, unable to push Ren from my thoughts. They consume me.

"You like it, don't you?" Rydian breathes, nibbling my breast as his cock drives deeper and deeper. All I can do is moan, unable to form words. "Maybe he should join us."

My eyes fly open as his breathy grunts fill the air.

Despite my shock, I don't slow—seating myself over and over, and his eyes haze once more. Every inch of him pushes deeper, and his fingers swirl over my clit. Rydian growls when I don't answer, and I moan, our movements frantic and hungry and wild as we chase our release together.

My mind thrashes between the two of them, the tension unbearable as my entire body tenses, breaths quick. Would they fight over me? Would they—

I shatter, crying out as I spiral into my climax, trembling against Rydian in a wave of tremors. Release barrels into him when I slide down once more, rolling my hips, and he shudders beneath me.

Finally, we slow our movement, our breaths heavy, and crawl back to reality. Sweat beads on his chest, dripping from his brow and neck. A devious grin tugs at his mouth before he leans in to kiss me.

"*Remind me to get you more gifts,*" Rydian teases, and then reaches for my robe, sliding it over my shoulders. He sets me beside him and pulls on his linen pants before shifting his attention to Ren with lowered brows. Anger coats his tone. "Is there a reason you interrupted?"

Ren huffs a dry laugh then says, "I have..." His eyes shoot to me. "News."

"Give me a minute." Rydian stands, sighing as he disappears into the bathing chamber. My cheeks warm when Ren's gaze collides with mine, leaving me to stand, now flustered as I stare at him. Silence settles between us. Unsure of what to do with my hands, I pull my robe tight and stride toward him, stopping near the table by the door.

"No need to be awkward about it, I've seen you naked already." He smiles, but it doesn't reach his eyes. The memory of him dressing me in a fresh set of clothes after Theron's beating runs through me. I'd forgotten about it—pushing it to a corner of my mind, unable to fully process it at the time.

"I thought you said you'd only watch in a public setting," I say finally, clearing my throat.

Ren still leans against his shoulder, his eyes on my crown. "The door was open."

"It was not," I scoff, head shaking in disbelief because I locked it, I'm sure of it.

He smirks at that, eyes sliding to the opening of my robe. "It was after I picked the lock."

My stomach dips, heart racing. He picked the lock and let himself inside? What does *that* mean? His grin widens.

Before I can muster a simple reply, Rydian steps out from the bathing chamber and motions for Ren to follow, disappearing beyond the wide entryway and into the sitting area. A chamber with a door, a lock, and a sound proof-ward. Understanding sweeps through me—the reason—why Ren's here and why Ire was flying around Kalde earlier.

Ren leans down and whispers, "Happy Birthday, Wench."

I blink when he walks past me, staring after him in shock.

"Ren," I murmur, and he swivels toward me, hand on the doorframe with an arch to his scarred brow. "You used to knock on my window with your knife to bring me pie for my birthday... Real or a dream?"

He drops his eyes to the table near the door, rolling the Veil coin from finger to finger before mumbling, *"Real."*

The door clicks shut.

A lump rises in my throat when my gaze drifts to the table beside me. Waiting on the smooth surface is a single slice of pie and a bottle of enchanted wine—Verellan Gold.

22

───────

The moans brushing the air nearby have my brows furrowing in bed. My eyes flutter open, and I quickly glance around the chamber, confused.

The sun leaks through the windows; it's barely sunrise, and a faint chill envelopes the room. I flick my wrist, lighting the hearth as it's too cold to leave the bed just yet. Rydian's arm is slung across my waist, breaths steady against my neck, and I snuggle deeper into the warmth.

Then sharp, loud moans echo again, the air sundering with wild pleasure. My brows lift at the intensity.

It's coming from down the hall.

"Wayd," Rydian groans, his voice raspy from sleep and utterly unamused as he pulls me closer. "He can't seem to help himself, but I think Miss Cassivene is enjoying it, yes?"

"Are you sure they're related to me?" I gripe.

My mind goes back to Kaeda and Ren in the corridor yesterday, and a flurry of annoyance washes over me. They *do* act like no one ever tells them no, but then I grin at the memory of when Ren denied her. Grin at the fact that he would've rather watched Rydian and me instead of joining her in bed. An unexpected smugness grows at that, warming my face.

"Yes." Rydian chuckles. "They're a rare breed, those two."

"I thought he and Anya were... together. They seemed friendly with each other at the council meeting." She had blushed when he flirted, but perhaps I misread the relationship. Or perhaps that's just who she is.

"Anya won't give him anything. And even though she's infatuated, she denies his advances. I think she fears she can't give him everything he wants because they're not mated."

"That'll be quite interesting when Cassivene visits," I say.

"He'll be thrilled by that, don't worry. Just the thought of him stirring up whispers in the castle probably turns him on."

I bark a laugh, pivoting. "Keeps things interesting, I bet."

"You have no idea," he says, his scarred lip rising into a grin before he leans in for a quick kiss. "We should get dressed. After we drop them off, we'll leave for Elderheim. It shouldn't take longer than a few hours, but I want to talk to Varrin while I'm there."

He rises, shrugging on his tunic, and I slam my head back into my pillow, gritting my teeth at the thought of working with Ekrin. Just thinking about that arrogant male makes me want to throw something sharp. Preferably at his face.

But if he's who we're going to be stuck with to find the Veilstone, I'll have to get over it. That's if he agrees to aid us. I'm willing to bet he declines, because if he truly wanted Elion to find the Veilstone, I'm sure he would have offered. Or perhaps he doesn't know about his ability to track the stone with a Seer.

Knowing Ekrin, I wonder if he *does* know and just doesn't care. I'm thinking it's the latter. Given the history of how his parents died by Elion's hands, he probably hasn't said anything for that very reason.

Maybe bridging somewhat of an alliance at the Aurorafest will soon pay off, and the Fates are on my side for once. My thoughts flicker back to the king's dinner though, wondering if Ekrin wanted to marry me or only offered to irritate Rydian.

Just thinking about it has my blood boiling.

Rydian tosses me my clothes, bending to lace up his boots when I finally rise and reach for them. He finishes tying the second then stands with lowered brows, eyes fixed on me. I finish the laces on my tunic as a growing sensual hunger floods my thoughts—not mine, but his.

I'm not sure I'll ever get used to feeling his emotions through our connection, but now I'm suddenly hyper aware of where his eyes have truly gone.

"My eyes are up here, King." I smirk, pushing my hair back over my shoulder. "In case you forgot."

"I didn't forget; I know where they are." He strides to my side of the bed, leaving nothing but a step between us. "Finish getting dressed and then meet me downstairs so we can all discuss what we'll be doing over the next few hours."

I incline my head, eyes squinting. "And what if I don't want to do that?"

A challenge sparks my blood, but his hand slides to the back of my neck before gently gripping a fistful of hair, tugging my head further back. Not enough to cause me pain, but enough to leave my lips parting with a flood of heat.

"Then it sounds like you want to be punished."

"Sounds exciting." I grin. "How would I be punished exactly?"

He chuckles, leaning down so that our lips are a breath apart. "Disobey me and find out, little fawn."

My blood heats at the nickname.

If he weren't gripping my hair, I'd fall to my knees and beg for whatever punishment is brewing in his head. His brow lifts, as if reading exactly where my thoughts have gone.

"You'd like that wouldn't you?" he asks like it's a shock, and then releases me, leaving me aching for him, but his expression remains unreadable. "Then I guess we have something to look forward to, now don't we?" And then he steps out, shutting the chamber door behind him.

With a shake of my head, I wipe away all remaining thoughts of said pleasurable punishment and finish getting ready, debating whether or not I should even leave this room. It's better not to crawl towards punishment, no matter how enticing it is.

Choosing to weave a thick braid at the top of my head, I leave half of it down to show off the auburn mark behind my ear. I secure my daggers—including my new one—at my waist and thighs before finally clasping my cloak and exiting.

The creamy marble estate is brightly lit as the early morning sun shines through the windows, birds chirping through the delicate paned glass. But I only get a few light, thudding footsteps down the hall before Ren exits his chamber, clasping his cloak at his neck and looking as if he got very little rest. My cheeks flush—well, that makes two of us.

"Did you at least try to sleep?" I ask, forcing my tone to remain casual, even as last night runs across my mind.

"Did you?" he asks, hardly making eye contact, and my brows draw close together—maybe he regretted it. "Seems like no one in this estate got any rest."

Wayd traipses down the corridor with a smirk on his face, walking between us to descend the stairs.

"You could have joined us, Captain. There was room for one more and I bet Miss Cassivene would have liked that," Wayd calls out with a breathy chuckle. He quickly reaches the bottom floor and turns right. I shake my head, sighing as he disappears below us. Though Ren seems to have been extra annoyed by the suggestion with the way his eyes narrow at Wayd's back.

"Thank you for my... gifts. The pie and wine were good," I say, stifling a smile. "Did you steal that too?"

Ren looks at me momentarily, a breath of silence settling between us as if he's waiting for me to add something else. Yet, I have nothing else to say. He just... stares.

"What?" I ask a little too sharply, unable to take the staring— the awkward stretch of silence as I wait for his reply.

All he does is huff before darting down the steps without another word. A sharp turn toward the dining hall and he's gone from sight, his footsteps quietly echoing behind him.

Though frustration rises hot in my blood, magic pebbling along my skin, jaw screaming as my teeth grind. I've never wanted to throttle someone into speaking before.

I hurry down the steps and trail behind him, my steps light as I catch up, even though I'm fuming at his deliberate silence. Then the door to the dining hall swings open, and Rydian steps out with a worried glare. He eyes Ren before looking at me.

He must have felt my anger through the bond—gods, how often does that happen? I'm going to have to work on managing my emotions if I'm as easily felt as this.

"What's wrong?" Rydian asks.

I shake my head as Ren shoulders through the doorway, ignoring him altogether.

"Is there something I need to take care of?"

I only huff, watching Ren settle himself in front of a large assortment of food. "No. Ren's just being... Ren."

The group hovers nearby, but no one has taken a seat as they all gather around to discuss our travels. Not a single-house maiden is in the room, and I wonder if Cassivene sent them away for the morning as a way to give us all privacy.

"What have we decided the plan will be?" I inquire before my lips tilt in a small, teasing smirk. "And unfortunately for you, I obeyed your orders." *No punishment for me*—I fail to add.

"Don't worry, little fawn, I'll find a reason to give you one," he says quietly. Heat blooms up my neck as he rests his hand along my back, and we stride toward the center of the group.

"Wayd and Kaeda will be checking in with Ivy to see how the army is doing. Orin mentioned reaching out to a few informants in Elderheim before we left. Now that we have a little more information on the Veilstone, we need to update the council while we're there. Varrin will be with Cassivene while we visit Ekrin at his estate in the next few days."

"What about King Elion? We'll need to send... something," I say, my eyes landing on Ren before averting my gaze.

"I'll send him a leaf when we get back. I assume you'd like to read what I send again?" Ren casually asks Rydian, but his tone is laced with mild annoyance.

Wayd's brows rise at the presumed challenge, and he shuffles forward with a grin, as if it were reason enough to start a fight. His fingers twitch and I can't help but grit my teeth, because who would I defend in this situation?

My cousin who's loyal to my mate? Or Ren, the only other Aetheri besides me who probably feels isolated in his own right?

"I love it when things get interesting," Kaeda mumbles. "Though I do get quite bored when it's just a bunch of males in a measuring contest. We get it, you're big," she says sarcastically, flaring her hands out as if measuring before casually popping a grape into her mouth.

Cassivene's eyes widen, and she takes a small step back, like they might destroy her expensive estate with all her fancy artifacts. I wonder what she would protect first?

"Should I have a reason to read it again?" Rydian tilts his head. His tone is light, but his anger builds to a throb between my ears, suffocating me and forcing me to catch my breath.

"Please don't start fighting in the middle of this estate." I push the thought out and look between them. Ren throws me a long sideways glance, and Rydian's hand grips me at the base of my neck. He gives a gentle squeeze as his lips curve into a faint smile.

Finally, after taking the time to eat a quick meal, we all follow Cassivene down the corridor toward the estate entrance. Back to Vyria. Though I can't help the sudden relief I feel at the thought of returning to the castle after being gone for almost three weeks.

As soon as the doors open to outside, we all come to a screeching halt before almost stepping on Kalde, who rests right in front of the doors. Gods, I forget how big he is.

"I almost forgot you were here," Cassivene says, sweeping her golden hair over her shoulder. Kalde rises and gives a quick shake of his fur, dusting off the snow from last night. His yellow eyes meet mine.

"We're leaving?" he asks.

"Yes. Back to the castle in Vyria."

"That's so fascinating how you can hear them," Cassivene says under her breath, stepping to the side to let us pass through.

"About time." The Howler huffs his annoyance.

Ren crosses the threshold, thudding down the steps and onto

the path as Kalde follows behind. With how Kalde trails Ren wherever he goes, I wonder if the Howler likes him more than me.

And why am I suddenly jealous of that?

Wayd and Kaeda attempt to step out when Cassivene halts them with a hand, a wry grin tugging at her mouth. "Did you think fucking me made me forget about you stealing from my study last night? Quite bold of you to assume that I wouldn't notice—in my own home, might I add." Her gaze sweeps over them. "And if that was a true example of your thieving capabilities, you have some work to do."

She holds out her palm, waiting for the artifacts.

"Wayd," Rydian growls, the emotion flooding our bond is laced with annoyance and the predictability of their behavior, expecting nothing less from them. They're definitely... something.

"Mm," Wayd hums, his eyes narrowing. And then his perfect teeth gleam in the morning light, as a wide grin spreads across his face. "So, you weren't lying about being the best thief in Aurelia? I'm impressed."

"It wasn't hard to notice, considering how obvious you two were." Cassivene huffs, her hand still extended.

"That definitely makes my cock hard." Wayd laughs with a shake of his head, digging into the pocket of his cloak.

"Oh my gods, Wayd." I groan. *Do they not have manners?*

"No," Rydian laments, sounding utterly exasperated.

"I'd love for you to teach me sometime, Miss Cassivene, preferably in the sheets." Wayd winks and drops a shimmering crystal pendant into her palm.

Kaeda only sighs, dropping her own stolen artifact. "I told you she saw us. You were obvious *and* loud."

"Now *that* must run in the family." Rydian chuckles and then groans when I throw out an elbow, catching him in the ribs. "I told you they're related to you."

23

Ren circles me with his stone daggers in the castle's training facility, brows lowered as he assesses my weaknesses. I meet his persistence with an icy smile.

He studies me a little too hard, and I lunge, quick and precise, my blade slicing through the air with a hiss.

He quickly sidesteps, bringing his daggers up to deflect my blow, metal clanking against stone. Sparks fly as they grind together, and I kick out a boot, connecting with his hip. He grunts in frustration, lip curling as he jolts back.

Spinning to face me once more, his hands twirl his blades in a menacing blur of movement.

We had arrived at the castle yesterday morning, landing right in the council chamber when Rydian called for a meeting to postpone our trip to Ekrin's estate, claiming they had more to discuss and that he wanted Varrin to study the tome we'd delivered.

Instead, we'll leave for Elderheim after we talk to Varrin today. Ren and I will scout the area before I Veil everyone into the estate tonight, meaning we're thrown back into our training in the Brotherhood.

In the meantime, Rydian ordered me to train. I didn't argue.

And right now, a shortsword is my weapon of choice. Regardless of how much I want to pull my magic forward, I can't rely on it all the time.

I study Ren's movements, catching the little quirks he does before striking, the way his brows lower in concentration when he thinks he's bested me. Or the way his eyes dart to my feet before sweeping a leg out, an attempt to flatten me. Unfortunately, he's becoming easier to read the longer we train together.

"You're getting predictable," I tease, my breath heavy with exertion.

He grunts, lunging toward me and swiping his blades down, forcing me to dart back. I sidestep once, going into a roll and popping back up to face him.

Panting, I wipe the sweat off my brow, though hair plasters my forehead. Although it's an hour before sunrise, we've been training for two hours, reminding me of how incredibly ruthless he is with a weapon. It leaves me no choice but to keep up—improve my speed and focus.

"I'm not predictable," he fires back, and I huff a laugh just as he throws himself forward.

I spin to the side, aiming an elbow toward his ribs. He predicts my move, throwing his weight into my shoulder with enough force that I stumble forward with a growl, my braid whipping around my face as I plant my feet to keep from falling.

Exhaling and frustrated, I whirl back around. Ren's forehead drips with sweat, mirroring my own as he takes a long breath a few feet away. It drips down his nose and onto the curve of his lip before it falls off his menacing grin.

He takes the small reprieve to peel off his soaked tunic, pivoting to toss it to the side before swapping his daggers for a shortsword. His chest ripples, sculpted and thick, but lean—the only evidence of our harsh training over the years. And with him being an entire foot taller than me, it makes it hard to calculate where he might throw his weight...

But that's not why my brows furrow in confusion.

Two four-inch scars mirror each other on the back of his left shoulder through the other side just below his collarbone. As if something had impaled him. A simmer of curiosity rises in my chest as I study him. I've never truly seen him without a tunic. And that necklace he wears with a—

He swivels it to the back of his neck, hiding it from my line of sight and my eyes narrow.

"What happened to your shoulder?" I ask.

He stiffens but ignores my question with a quick twirl of his short sword. He presses forward, his expression unreadable. Sweat glistens on his skin, and his hair falls forward right before he bulldozes, forcing me to duck from the swing. My frustration rises, and I grind my teeth, knowing he won't be replying.

He's hardly said a word since we arrived back at the castle, leaving me to believe he regretted watching Rydian and me at Cassivene's estate. I've pushed it aside though—pushed it to the corner of my mind where that little flutter of heat rises anytime I think about it. A flutter of excitement, something that begs me for more.

A distraction is what it is.

Still, I force it down, unwilling to dive into that feeling as shame and guilt continue to claw at my chest—ashamed I even feel it in the first place.

I pop back up with a grunt and kick out, connecting with the back of his leg, and force him to his knees. Tossing my sword with a clang, I wrap an arm around his neck with a growl. If there's anything I know about Ren, it's that he's stubborn and won't give up unless forced to.

Even though he's difficult to train with, I like that he doesn't go easy. It's what's kept me alive all these years—him and his ruthless training.

A hiss of frustration escapes him, and my arm tightens right before he throws me over his shoulder. The wind gets knocked from me as my back connects with the floor in a hard thud. My vision blurs.

"Fates!" I cry out.

He yanks me by an ankle, spinning me to face him. A sweaty screech cuts the air when I slide across the floor, but he quickly gets on top of me, pinning me there. I writhe to free myself, but to no avail.

"Give it up. You lost," he says breathlessly, capturing my wrists in a single hand and pinning them above me. "Again. You know, I was hoping you'd win this time."

My lip curls in frustration, and I aim a knee at his groin—failing. He holds me there as if I'm nothing but an inconvenience. An annoying insect.

He grins, chuckling. "Come on, Isa, getting you on your back will always be your weakness." His sword now rests at my throat, a clear indication of my failure, as he arches his brow.

I know he's right, though. I've been thrown on my back every single time I've lost to him, but that's not why my face sears red. Lips parting, I stop struggling and stare at his lips.

Fuck.

His face is so close to mine—close enough to feel his panting breaths against my cheeks. Close enough to feel the heat of his bare chest as he pins me there. Sweat drips from his nose onto my throat.

It trickles down my neck, and his eyes track it all the way to the floor. His eyes flick back up, holding my gaze, and for a moment I wonder if he's going to lean in. My blood heats.

He wouldn't dare... would he?

Before my shame can rise for enjoying the full weight of him on top of me, I smirk. Without breaking his stare, I roll my hips, pressing into him in a way that has him feeling all of me.

"Don't do that," he growls, tightening his grip around my wrists, hard enough to bruise.

Heat shimmies down my body.

"If I moan a little, will you let me go?" I tease, unable to prevent the words from spilling out.

"I fucking dare you," he murmurs.

A warning or a challenge or perhaps something... more. I blink, caught off guard by the sudden seriousness in his tone, and feeling as if he has more to add to that, but refrains.

I release a breath and snap back to reality when a fluttering leaf lands right next to us on the floor, appearing out of nowhere. My eyes widen as he gets off to read it, knowing exactly who it came from. He swiftly stands and scratches the back of his head.

"What does it say?" I ask and blink away that little moment between us, slowing my racing heart. I remain sitting, but movement out of the corner of my eye catches my attention. Rydian stands in the doorway, auburn hair grazing his brows. He crosses his arms, expression unreadable as he leans against the frame with a hard stare aimed right at me.

My stomach flutters, and I tug on that thread between us—a fleeting spark of anger before it's gone. He's locked his emotions up, preventing me from gauging the rest of his mood. My eyes narrow.

I'll have to ask him how he does that, so I can learn. Ren extends a hand to help me off the floor when I scowl and swat it away. He only chuckles, shaking his head and then returns his attention to the message in his hands.

"He wants us to meet at the castle in a few weeks," Ren says. "For an update on the stone and our progress."

Even though I already knew he'd summon us both, my stomach drops, dread crawling up my spine. It's hardly been a month since we arrived in Aurelia. Perhaps he wants to lay eyes on Ren, get word from him directly even if I'm blood sworn by an oath.

Still, the thought sours my stomach.

I smooth my clothes and pick up my shortsword as Rydian walks up and stops a foot from me. I meet his gaze, feeling everything from Cassivene's estate resurface in his presence. I nearly quiver in delight at the sight of him.

"I was looking for you," he says quietly and a small grin tugs at his mouth before he leans in to graze mine. "How was training?"

"Frustrating," I huff.

Court members from the castle begin to file in, and with that group come Wayd, Kaeda, and Ivy, who meet Ren near the weapons.

Orin trails behind them, the heavy thud of his boots and the sway of his shoulders stealing everyone's attention as he strides toward us. He extends a message to Rydian, who then tucks it away with a nod.

"Varrin is ready to meet." Orin's voice bellows off the stone. "We've discovered the ritual King Elion has. Head to the archives when you're ready." He leaves and we follow him out, entering the corridor as the others trail behind us.

"What was that?" I ask, realizing that it was a message on parchment, and not something spoken through the Veil.

"A…" He glances at me, calculating his words. *"friend from Elderheim has been keeping me updated within Elion's council."*

Our steps halt in the corridor as Ekrin flits through my mind, but so does the informant Ivy had mentioned weeks ago when we searched the halls in castle Alvonia. Curiosity blooms in my chest as I piece together the information, wondering who it could be.

"Is it Ekrin?" I ask, but he shakes his head.

The groups walk past, taking a left down the corridor, but not before Ren glances over his shoulder. Rydian places a hand on my back, urging me to follow them to the archives.

"As much as I want to, I can't tell you yet."

Frustration tightens my chest, though I know he can't tell me in case it gets relayed back to Elion. After all those years of having no memories, I'm still somehow left not knowing anything regardless of how desperate I am for information.

"Also, we're staying another few days," he says and I face him with drawn brows. "We need to introduce you to the court."

I grind my teeth, sighing in frustration. "Now? Can't it wait until after we find the stone? That's more important."

He shakes his head. "Normally, I'd say yes. But they're becoming quite restless, and it needs to be done. You've been missing for twenty years, Isa. They need to see you."

"What's another few days?" My brows lift but he doesn't budge, forcing me to bite my cheek.

Despite myself, a whirl of unease settles taut across my shoulders as my mind whirls with all the possibilities of rumors spreading. Rumors of being a traitor—daughter to the enemy. And I hate that I'm put in this position, that tug to choose.

"A small celebration, that's it." His lips curve into a light smile the same time he tugs my elbow, urging me forward. Even though his grin has my stomach flipping, I groan and follow him down the corridor.

24

____

After a few minutes of weaving through the halls with quite a few Shadovar stealing glances at us, two guards swing the archive doors open, and we step inside. It's nothing short of overwhelming, and I pause as soon as my boots touch the aged, wooden floors.

Lips parting, I stare at the enormous space, mesmerized by the size. I hadn't been inside the archives yet, just walked past the arched doors when Lettie gave me a quick tour.

Parchment and oak and something ancient greets me upon entering. Something that warms the inside of my chest, enveloping me with something I can't quite name.

My eyes lift.

Stretching up all three stories is the largest archive I've ever seen, easily holding millions of copies of history. Orbs of light float and twirl above us, slowly weaving through each shelf. Rows and rows and rows of them stretch down the length of it, large and long enough to get lost in. Whispers graze my ears—whispers of court members while they casually browse—and I quickly realize we aren't alone. I glance around, noticing the carved, pale columns that line the walls near the windows—figures of our Fates in each one.

Warm and inviting, I exhale a long breath.

"Queen's don't drool." Rydian chuckles, and I snap my jaw shut, narrowing my eyes as he walks past me with a wide smile.

He extends his hand for me, and I hurry to his side, letting him lead us through winding rows of text. Lettie wasn't lying—anyone is allowed at the castle and in the archives should they choose to expand their studies.

Down the center and near the back is a domed window, stretching down every side. Couches, tables, and settees settle around a mantlepiece that overlooks the gardens outside. A perfect environment for cozying up with a quilt or staying up late. But off to the side of that cozy space is a private chamber, which is where Rydian leads us.

"So far," Varrin says as soon as we step in, "we believe that this is the ritual King Elion has in his grasp." He points to a large board hanging on the wall at the back.

Orin leans against his chair at the center while Ivy and Cassivene press themselves forward, heads bent to read the text before him. Ren, Wayd, and Kaeda linger near the door, watchful and listening. The cluttered table with weathered texts catches my attention, the air thick with leather and old parchment—pages as ancient as the castle itself, perhaps older.

"What have you found?" I ask finally.

Varrin slides the opened book to me—leather bound with unreadable text inside—and points to the worn pages. "This is in the language of Old Aurelish. I've been translating the text over the last few years, but we've been looking for any mention of the Veil-stone. Orin is reading what I've translated so far, which is a third of the book. We believe that the ritual we found is the one that King Elion is using for his… ascension." Varrin winces.

I frown, glancing at the notes hanging on the wall and everything that's needed; a list of items. Nothing but cryptic words.

"He would need the essence of a king or queen—doesn't specify who," Ivy says with a sigh, straightening.

"And blood of two, whatever that means," Orin mumbles. He looks at Rydian, who then nods as if answering a silent question.

Varrin grunts his agreement. "And lastly, that specific blood needs to be spilled on the both realm blades and then driven into the Veilstone."

"Did the Fates create the ritual?" I ask. "Why would we need an ascension ritual if the realms were separated for balance? Wouldn't ascending throw off that balance with the Fates?"

"That's a great question," Cassivene says as she finds a chair across from Orin. Her golden hair shimmers in a small wave over her shoulder, fixing her attention on the historian.

Varrin nods, a small grunt leaving him. "I'm not sure how familiar you are with historical texts about the realms, but rumor has it that there *used* to be four Fates instead of three. This specific text—*The Book of the Fates*—was written by a king many centuries ago. It's possible the ascension was created by one of the Fates in order to eventually restore the balance."

"There used to be four Fates?" Rydian asks, his brows drawing close together. "I didn't know that."

"Me neither," Cassivene says quietly, her scholarly wheels turning as she bites her lip. Orin glances up, studying Cassivene, and I catch the way his eyes linger before he glances back at the translated text in front of him. Knowing what's buried in her hair, I stifle the grin threatening to surface.

"Restore balance for what, exactly? The realms are already separated," Kaeda says, and I pivot back to Varrin.

Varrin nods. "It's been over a millennium since the Fates created the two realms. We've had four kings and queens since then, but it's said that when the Pillar was created, the Fate of Balance sacrificed himself to separate the realms due to strife between the noble houses. The Fates believed that if they separated them—creating the Shadovar and Aethralis bloodline—they could create balance between the two. I assume they have this ritual to eventually recombine the realms once more due to a power imbalance of the noble bloodlines." Varrin scratches his head then waves his hand. "How many pure Aetheri Fae are dwindling in Elderheim? The Siphons are as they've become scarce until recently. And if you aren't aware, so are the Herb Weavers."

Ekrin brushes my thoughts as I recall him being the last noble in his bloodline.

"Why was the Pillar created, and what is it?" I glance at the unfamiliar text with a scowl, eyeing the illustration of two ancient blades. Familiar blades.

"Our three Fates are Asha—the Fate of time who created the Veil; Lyora is the Fate of life and magic; and then there's Faelar, the Fate of boundaries and death. Each one served a purpose in separating the realms, securing their magic to the Pillar. But the one that sacrificed himself was Vaelith, the Fate of Unity, binding himself to the Pillar in order to successfully separate them. It's rumored that the Pillar is where it all started and is what gives our realms their magic, acting as a conduit. It's an extension of their will and is what gives our land life, but the only way to do that was to bind him to it."

Cassivene leans forward, elbows resting on the table. "If Vaelith was bound to the Pillar, does that mean he can be freed?" Our gazes collectively swivel to Varrin, but he shakes his head.

"No. Once he bound himself to that Pillar, his life was forfeit, which is why our realms continue to mirror each other."

"Do you think the ascension ritual is a way of becoming something higher than the Fates?" I ask, remembering what King Elion said about becoming a god. I'm worried that he plans on destroying the realms if he gets his hands on the Veilstone.

Varrin sighs, stroking his jaw. "I'm not sure, but it's possible it could disrupt the balance of the noble houses if he were to gain what he needed to complete it. Like I said, it's possible the Fates created this ascension in order to eventually rejoin the realms, but if King Elion goes through with it..." He trails off. No need to exaggerate his concerns—we all feel it. "The right person would need to ascend in order to restore that harmony."

My brows furrow, a flicker of doubt and unease settling in my chest. In all the history of both realms, there's never been someone who carried the strength to bridge that divide between them. There's *always* been strife, regardless of who sits on the thrones.

None of the rulers between the two have been wise enough to

maintain that peace—King Elion sure wasn't, though King Andre could have been. Still, they were never enough to mend what was already broken.

Orin reaches our side of the table and bends to read the text, squinting. Then Cassivene stiffens beside me, small enough not to alarm anyone else but enough for me to notice. Her face pales, wide eyes fixed on the back of Orin's head, before she reaches up to uncomfortably scratch hers.

"I think Cassivene figured it out," I say to Rydian, elbowing him and biting my lip to swallow a laugh.

Rydian peers down at me and then glances at Cassivene before throwing me a devious, knowing grin. *"Told you."*

I look at Wayd almost instinctively, but his attention is fixed on Cassivene as realization settles on her face. And yet... a wide, knowing smirk tugs at his mouth, as if he were trying to stifle it.

"You knew," I say, pushing the thought to Wayd.

His eyes flick to me, and a devious grin grows on his face.

"Of course I did." He shrugs. *"Makes for an interesting visit, don't you think?"*

I stifle a laugh and shake my head in disbelief.

Orin hums quietly, his eyes fixed on the old book. "We think the Veilstone is an artifact created by the Fates that helps the realms maintain their balance—maybe acting as a key of sorts. There have been rumors of it being pure energy, or even something that holds dark power. We still aren't sure. I do think we should be the ones to find it first so that Elion doesn't get his hands on it," he says.

I almost wince. That's something I probably shouldn't know. Rydian catches it, glaring at Orin beside us.

"I say we just kill King Elion to avoid all of this," Wayd scoffs, leaning against the wall with his arms crossed near Ren.

Rydian shakes his head. "Although Isa is technically his heir, who's to say Witt wouldn't go through with the coronation after he died? Witt is his second-in-command, and by the decree of the Fates, he's allowed to take the throne. We can't risk that. As much as we all dislike Elion, I think Witt would be worse if given the opportunity—which he would take. We don't even have the Lumen Sword."

Ice freezes my bones, my hands curling into fists at the mere thought of Witt rising to power. It would be catastrophic.

A ruler with no mercy or restraint—someone capable of flipping a switch in a moment—and something Witt is really good at. Blood would spill before the essence settled in his body, before Elion had a chance to crumple to the ground. That thought alone turns my stomach, a cold dread raising the hair at the back of my neck.

And then I realize, the feeling isn't just my own but someone else's as well. I glance at Rydian clenching his jaw while he looks down at the illustration of the two blades.

I peek around his shoulder, studying the weapons. The illustration shows two blades beside each other. One made of a dark stone no longer than a dagger, the other a deep golden shortsword.

"What is that?" I ask, pointing to the smaller, darker blade.

"That's the Veilblade," Rydian says quietly.

My body goes rigid as I quickly understand why it looks so familiar—I've seen it. "And the other one?"

"The Lumen sword, the Veilblade's opposite," he says, brushing the page. "Balance. It does what the Veilblade does and can kill any ruler on the throne of Elderheim, only we haven't seen that one in ages either." I lean in for a closer look at the darker blade, recognizing the sigil scribbled on the hilt.

Rydian brushes the edge of my mind with curiosity. *What is it?*

"I've seen that." I point. "The blade and the sigil."

"Where?" Rydian straightens, his eyes narrowing. Then an anger so relentless pounds against my temples—*his anger*—melding with mine.

I nod. "I've seen King Elion fumble with it on his throne. He'd hold it during formations or mission updates, acting like he wasn't listening."

"You're sure?" he asks, his anger slowly bubbling.

Then Ren steps to my left, crowding me and I slide the text over for him to see. Now squashed between the two largest males in the room besides Orin, my cheeks warm.

Ren nods. "King Elion definitely has that blade."

Anger barrels through me—sharp and fierce—my eyes burning with rage at Ren's confirmation. Magic sparks at my fingertips. But before I can clench my fists and stifle my magic, books shudder on the surface of the table and crash to the floor.

25

"Where are we going?" I ask Rydian as we descend the back of the castle and into the cool wind coming off the ocean.

The two guards positioned outside quietly close the doors behind us as we step into the gardens, sealing us within the crisp mid-morning air. The scent of winter florals, frost-kissed jasmine and lilies with the faintest hint of pine, flood my senses.

Even though it's still morning, there aren't a lot of courtiers in the gardens, but instead of going left toward the ocean, we veer right. The soft crunch of the gravel beneath my boots mingles with the chilled air as I raise my hood.

"Wait for me," Kalde says, somehow sensing my presence.

I glance over my shoulder, finding him trotting in our direction from the trees near the vale as Ire flies above. The two have become inseparable. His coat of darkness rustles as he picks up pace and I rush to catch up to Rydian.

"To the training grounds. Even though there's a small facility in the castle, this one is bigger. I want you to work on your control."

"I don't need to work on control," I object, but he throws me a questioning glance.

"I know you're mastering your ability to shift and use the Veil, but you're practically buzzing with power," he says. "Have you tried using it beyond that?"

I sigh. "Not really."

He laughs. "Well, you need to let off some steam before you unintentionally redecorate your chambers or chop my head off. A little control would do you some good. It'd make you lethal."

"I'm already lethal," I huff as we walk past the dark fortress and into the trees waiting beyond it.

Kalde finally reaches us, and we take a well used path to the left toward a vast expanse of trees. The walk is uphill, leading us further along the cliffside and toward a clearing ahead. With Kalde at my side, I remember what Cassivene mentioned at her estate.

"Howlers can sense magic? What does that mean?" I ask.

Kalde huffs beside me. *"Howlers can detect magic, but also see those in the Veil. We have the Sight, the same as a king or queen of Aurelia."*

"The Sight?" I question, glancing at Rydian, who's throwing me a wicked grin. "You saw me that day I toured the castle, didn't you?" He made direct eye contact with me as Lettie and I walked in the Veil before disappearing himself.

"Yes," Rydian says. "Once the royal coronation is complete, you will also have the Sight. It will enable you to see those who travel in the Veil and prevent others from sneaking around without you noticing."

"What else can Howlers do?" I ask.

"We're excellent at tracking—people, creatures, or any object that leaves a magical signature," Kalde explains.

A thought blooms.

"Would you be able to track the Veilstone?"

He puffs a breath. *"Not unless I have a scent for it."*

Then he shakes his coat, dusting off intricate flakes of snow before trotting off and quickly disappearing beyond the trees.

Finally, we reach the edge of the path, revealing the expanse of what appears to be enormous training grounds clearly meant for warriors, and partially enclosed by rock.

Four magical stone pillars rise into the sky, a makeshift domed ward protecting it from the elements. It glimmers above, rippling in the air. The only way to know it's working is how the snowflakes drift down and away, sheltering the arena below. It's bordered by low stone walls, serving to enclose the green, rocky terrain for sparring, archery, and hand-to-hand combat.

And plenty of space to blow things up.

My brows rise, a menacing grin spreading across my face as my magic thrums in anticipation. Rydian chuckles beside me, sensing my thrill.

"Come on. I want to see what you can do," Rydian calls out.

He steps into the arena, striding past the stone walls and settles in the center, feet planted. I follow him into the dome, which is surprisingly warmer despite us being at the edge of the cliffside.

"Your essence continues to grow," he says as I stop in front of him. "And in order for you not to lash out and destroy everything in sight while angry—which is often—you need to learn how to control it. You'll want to take off your cloak for these exercises." He smirks while shrugging off his own.

I narrow my eyes at him and clench my jaw as he rests his cloak upon the wall. He carefully rolls his sleeves as he walks toward me with a wide smile.

He chuckles, head shaking. "See, that's why I said that. You're already fuming and we haven't even started. You need to release it before it begins to hurt."

"Hurt?" I arch a brow.

He nods and steps behind me, wrapping his hands around my forearms. My breath catches, the scent of him overwhelming my senses, and I can't help but appreciate the steady warmth at my back. He leans in, his voice dropping to a low murmur as he guides my arms forward, palms up. His jaw grazes my temple.

"Yes. It can put a strain on you if you don't release the growing power. That being said, we also have a limit. If you don't learn to control how much you use, you risk draining too fast and end up without power during a battle. So it's a good thing you're already trained in combat. Now, I want to see what you can do."

It doesn't take long for me to become incredibly tired and dripping with sweat. And unfortunately, he's right. After only ten minutes, I'd discarded my cloak from the strain.

It tickles my temple as it drips down, and my body quivers while trying to maintain control. My hands are extended as he circles me, watching the small tendril of shadow wrap itself around my forearm like a whip.

For the next few hours, we focus on shaping the darkness into small forms, hovering and controlling them in my palms without letting them dissipate or grow wild. Only when the darkness comes out and I get even a little distracted, they disappear.

Rydian assesses my form and my capability to hold the darkness writhing down my arms, letting out a quiet hum of approval. The sound of it sends my stomach dipping, a jolt of warmth rippling down my body in a welcoming shudder.

"Now hit that target over there. Use it like a whip and aim for it." He gestures to the target roughly fifty feet away from us.

"What?" I get out, and the darkness trembles at the distraction. "That's too far; I won't be able to hit that."

"You can. You're doing well. Now hit the target," he orders then stops on my left, waiting with an arch to his brow.

I shoot him a glance, distracted as the breeze catches his hair, the unruly strands fluttering over his brows. Strong, unwavering, and with his arms folded, his mouth tilts into an amused grin at my struggle.

I groan, shifting my focus back to the target. I summon the last of my strength, willing the shadows to extend from me. A shudder runs down my body, tensing while my arms tremble with the effort, and force my thoughts to shape it into a whip.

Gripping the energy, I mold it until the shadows obey and move forward. They instantly lash out, completely missing the target by twenty feet. Rock and dirt fly into the air and I gasp, covering my head as debris rains down.

"Good," he says with a nod, completely unfazed as he watches the destruction settle ahead.

"Good? I missed the target. That wasn't good," I snap, whirling toward him and dropping my hands. Only now that I'm drained from built-up power, my shoulders are less tense, my body lighter than hours before.

He eyes me. "It *was* good. You're not going to get it right the first time, but you're a natural. Most of those who come into their power don't even know how to use it or shape it, though they have been training since they were as young as three. For someone who's had little magic training their entire life, I say it's good. It just needs to be refined."

I groan, wiping my forehead. "Are we done yet?"

"Not quite, but we're done with the shadows for now," he says, leaning against one of the stone pillars. "The reason you didn't hit that target is because you haven't been able to ground your power yet. Grounding will help you control it."

"And how do I ground it?" I sigh, pushing the sweaty strands off my face.

"By focusing on where it's coming from…" he says, tapping a finger against his temple. "In here. You're blocking it instead of letting it flow naturally. Are you frightened by it?"

I scowl. "No. Why would I be frightened?"

He pushes himself off the pillar, boots crunching before stopping just shy of my feet. "Well, you've gone your whole life barely being able to form an orb. Now, all of a sudden, you're overflowing with power. It can be… alarming. Unsettling even."

"I'm not…" I trail off, brows furrowing.

He's right. Every time I've summoned my shadows, I've either writhed in pain from consuming all my power at once or dissipated it as soon as magic formed on my fingertips. The only control I had was when I was focused on confronting King Elion in his throne room.

When I held Witt by my power.

I was grounded—felt in control. My focus was razor sharp then, but anger had also consumed me.

"Let me show you. Since our powers are very similar, I can show you what it feels like to be grounded." He raises his hand, gently pushing my auburn mark over my shoulder as his eyes lock with mine. "You know, being king heightens my ability—gives me a few more perks. If I show you how to master it, maybe we can have a little... fun later."

The insinuation in his words has my heart thrumming, excitement coating my veins as I recall his shadows... reaching for me. "Okay, fine. Show me."

With a grin and a small laugh, his hands settle on my face. My power rises, sensing his presence and I tug on the familiar feel of Vision Walking. Then his memories flood my thoughts.

He shares his mind with me—how magic balances between control and surrender. A steady connection between reality and a sudden stillness washes over me—a deep anchoring sensation— tethering me to my power.

My eyes roll behind my eyelids, soaking in the knowledge and how it feels to be grounded. Yet for some reason, my body yanks on the connection, jolting me.

It quickly takes over and before I can pull back, I fall into him—a memory he had no intention of showing me. Like it was second nature for me to go sprawling into someone else's mind and take it.

What the fuck?

A rush of ecstasy—pleasure and heat—washes over me, my chest tightening as the memory unfolds like an inescapable dream. His face and hers swarm my vision, along with something I definitely don't want to be in the middle of.

Oh, dear gods. I've unwillingly pulled an intimate memory.

A memory I could have gone my entire lifetime not seeing. With a gasp, I force myself free. My body lurches back as if burned by his touch, and his eyes flare with realization, knowing exactly what I just saw.

The breath caught in my throat releases on a rough exhale, my pulse pounding against my temples. Then a low, furious growl escapes me.

If I wasn't drained of my power, this arena would be destroyed by the fury rising beneath my skin like an unrecognizable beast. The look on his face tells me he's in absolute shock over what I just saw swirling around in that strikingly beautiful head of his.

"Tell me that wasn't real and that it was just a figment of your imagination." I grind out even though I already know the answer. Now it's his turn to be rendered speechless, his mouth falling open as if searching for the right words.

His eyes settle on me. "I can explain."

"Your *mistress* lives in the castle?" I snap.

A menacing laugh, dark and sinister, leaves my lips on another exhale. The kind that promises pain in the near future. The kind that warns him of my wrath and growing fury.

"Not *current*, mind you. I parted ways with her after my mark appeared five years ago. My love for you has never wavered, even before I knew it was you it belonged to."

He lunges forward with a grin, gripping my waist, yanking me to his chest. He forces my face up with hand curling around jaw, his gaze locked with mine. "The only reason she lives here is because of her work in the castle and the fact that she's Rafe's daughter."

"You wouldn't have even told me if I hadn't snatched it from that head of yours," I grouse.

He breathes chuckle.

"Only because it was fleeting—there was no need to tell you about it. What I had with her was nothing more than just me passing the time. She was a distraction, and it didn't matter; but *you* do. Can't you feel how obsessed and aroused I am by that reaction?" He groans, but I do feel him through the bond— arousal and a hint of amusement. "I'm quite turned on right now."

My eyes narrow. "Can't you read the room?"

"What room? We're clearly outside," he says, rolling my head to the side and leaning down to press a soft kiss to my neck. "You're all I want for the rest of my days. Until the very end, I can promise you that."

Before I can stop it, I'm melting into his arms, fully embracing the way he firmly holds me. His hands slide up, pulling me in tighter as he trails soft kisses beneath my mark. Then I'm wrapping my arms around his neck, accepting it with an exasperated groan.

Damn him. My eyes flutter closed.

"Are you saying there are no feelings toward her?" I ask, and he grumbles against the column of my neck.

"There were no feelings there to begin with, but yes."

I find myself grinning.

He nibbles and a gasp leaves me as he whirls me around, pressing my back into the cool stone of the pillar. The contrast between the chilled stone and the searing heat of his touch sends a shiver down my spine.

My panted breaths hit the air, heart hammering against my ribs as I grip a fistful of his hair, anchoring myself against the sensations fluttering my stomach. A shudder ripples down my body when his lips trail lower, grazing a molten path to the curve of my collarbone.

My mind blurs, and I fight the burning need to have him right in this godsforsaken arena. Without stopping, his fingers graze the ties of my tunic, idly working the laces.

Then a frustrated growl escapes him, and he pulls back, lips curling as he glances over his shoulder toward the entrance. "I'm starting to believe we'll have zero privacy."

I peer around him, catching Ren's smug smile as he strides into the arena, Ivy and the remainder of the group in tow. Despite myself, my stomach dips, watching as they all discard their cloaks. Ren's sleeves are already rolled from our training this morning, his tunic wrinkled and worn.

"Are we training?" Kaeda asks, flicking her wrist out to shoot a tiny flame toward us, so we have to jolt to the side.

Rydian growls again and faces me with an arched brow. *"We can leave."*

"Or we can stay." I shrug, smirking and nodding to Orin as a grin spreads across the warrior's face. "I want to see you fight."

"Maybe letting off some steam would do me some good."

Rydian laughs and plants a quick kiss to my lips before pulling his shirt off. A sword of darkness graces his hand a moment later. Orin immediately draws his sword, twirling it as they center themselves in the arena. The clanking of metal cuts the air, both males dancing around each other with practiced ease. Kaeda and Ivy begin training. Wayd hangs back though, perching himself on the low stone wall with an apple and a wide smile.

"I'm next," he calls out, biting into the fruit.

I glance over just as Ren steps up my right, arms folded as he watches them in the arena. He says nothing, just stands there, yet I find myself riddled with awkward tension. Even though we trained just this morning, I can't help but feel that the line of our friendship seems to be fraying. Slow and uncertain. Rydian makes me more than happy, but Ren is... well, I can't quite put him into words.

"Are you going to give me another show later?" he teases.

"Would you like another show?" I ask hesitantly, but he only shrugs. Still, my stomach flutters at the carefree movement.

"I wouldn't say no to watching."

A burning heat crawls up my neck, face warming in... anticipation or shame or arousal? I fight the urge to fidget, unable to wrap my head around what he just shared. He's not typically one for sharing at all.

Would he only watch or want to join? I suddenly fear what his answer would be if I ask.

"Why now?" I blurt, wondering why he wasn't interested... before. Not to mention I have a mate, and encroaching on someone else's mating bond is quite insulting, if not dangerous. Though Rydian hasn't truly cared about his interest, not really—secure in our claim. I suppose it doesn't really matter.

"Why not?" Ren counters, jaw feathering a little—the only indication that he's either annoyed or hating the fact that I asked. "Do you not enjoy it?"

"I don't know," I say on a breath, facing forward and ignoring how my pulse just electrified my blood, pounding relentlessly against my eyes. I did enjoy it.

I enjoyed the way his eyes lingered while I gave Rydian every inch of myself. It felt like I was being worshipped, cared for and cherished by two completely different individuals at the same time. I'd never truly experienced real relationships—nothing outside of the Brotherhood or the brothel, anyway. And for once in my life, it was nice to bask in the blaze of their stares—two males that clearly enjoy *me*.

He hums. "Liar. You like it, you just won't admit it."

My eyes narrow, and I fold my arms, facing him once more—if only to study his expression, something that's entirely devoid of anything. My frustration rises at his lack of emotion as he blankly stares at the arena before casually skimming my face.

I know that look—he's reading me.

Studying my expression.

"There were… restrictions before—in the Brotherhood," he says under his breath. "With Elion. Is it so bad that I enjoy watching? Your king doesn't seem to mind, why would I?"

My lips part, pulse racing, flustered that he even admitted that.

But the memories of the Brotherhood that have surfaced the last few weeks remind me of our hidden friendship and how I had been frightened of the repercussions that would rain down had someone discovered it. Even when we'd sneak out and venture into Alvonia, we kept our hoods up, too worried about the others finding us together outside of a mission. Specifically Ezra, Luke and Malrik.

Though at the time, we'd believed Ezra to be an orphan like us, instead of Witt. Taverns and markets and old missions rise in my thoughts—years worth of memories. I'd lost my childhood, the years I crawled into adulthood. Even though confusion tightens in my chest, so does frustration.

"And our friendship—does that not mean anything to you?" I ask finally, brows drawing close together as I aim to understand.

I've never had *friends*, but if something were to fracture that line between us now, I'm afraid we'd never get it back. I never thought I'd say this, definitely not a few weeks ago but… I think I want to be his friend.

He leans in, voice dipping to a low murmur, "Were we ever really friends before?"

I blink in confusion, pivoting to hold his gaze as he stares down at me. *Yes, we were friends,* the very fibers of my being scream at me.

But he was also my instructor, a ruthless assassin.

The one male who forged me into a weapon, forced into training me—a child much like myself at the time. He'd helped me master my skills and pushed me to perfection, something he'll always have my gratitude for.

Yet as I hold his gaze—study the hard lines of his face—I know without hesitation that I'd lay my life down for the one male who spent his childhood protecting mine.

Yes, I think, *we were friends.*

26
___

A glimmer of my reflection stares back at me in the soft light of my dressing chamber—a reflection that looks like me but not. Someone unfamiliar, dressed to perfection as the delicate silk cinches my waist, cascading off my hips into a puddle of crimson at my feet. I'm prepared for my introduction to the court.

Long slits expose the edges of my thighs, and my new dagger absorbs the light as it comes into view with a half turn. I release a small sigh, and my fingers brush the shiny golden pendant at my throat. The dress swoops down, exposing my shoulders with low-cut sleeves that drip to my wrists.

My second mate mark is hidden from sight.

Lettie gathered my hair into an elegant twist, leaving only a few dark sections loose around my face, having pulled my auburn mark down from the rest. The waves cascade down my back in soft, loose tendrils, knowing it's what Rydian will prefer.

A message for the court—that I'm *his*.

"Is this really necessary?" I question, even though I could probably sleep in this dress, admiring the way it feels along my skin. Smooth and intricate and something that looks like it shouldn't belong to me.

Yet the black, sparkling crown of rubies that shimmer atop my head says it does. A crown beckoning a future destined for more than killing. Something I'd dreamed of long ago.

And here I am, as if all my dreams came crashing down at once, stripping me of the life of a trained assassin. Only now I'm set to rule a realm I hardly know. The coronation—my claim to Rydian and Aurelia—hasn't even taken place yet, but would lives be lost in my reign?

Unease prickles my skin at the thought, knowing that other people's lives will be in the palm of my hands. I suppose it's no different from my life before, except now I wouldn't be holding the knife—I'd be passing it to someone else. Barking orders at them to take care of something I'd rather not do myself.

Just like Elion.

My stomach sours, knowing that my reflection is that of my father, and all those years of training led me to this day. The day he can use me for his benefit from an entirely different realm, calling me to him whenever he wants. The mark of my oath.

Rydian was right; I played right into his hands.

Lettie chuckles beside me, though her blue eyes glaze over as she studies my reflection, gleaming with admiration. Her knees practically quake, hands trembling against her chest before fumbling into a flustered bow.

"Gods, Lettie," I gripe, reaching for her elbow. "No need for that."

"Sorry," she says with a wince, auburn hair swaying back as she rises. "You just look so beautiful."

"Yes, you do," Rydian says from the doorway, a single hand placed on his stomach like the sight of me stole the breath from him.

He wears an intricate, long-sleeved black brocade that slightly opens at the chest, his muscled arms stretching the fabric. His own crown rests on his head, the twin to mine, only larger. We hold each other's gazes for a few breaths, silent, too afraid to say anything as we admire one another.

He clears his throat. "Lettie, I'd like you to leave so I can..." His heated eyes flick to her, brows lowering a fraction. "...touch my mate."

She scrunches her nose at that, then quickly darts out of the room. I grin. As soon as the door clicks shut, he reaches for me.

In two strides, he yanks me to him, devouring me like a delicacy he'd been deprived of. He groans, his tongue sweeping across mine. Despite ourselves we break apart, panting and breathless, yet eager for more.

He glances toward the chest near the tall gilded mirror—at something that's been gnawing at me since I stepped foot in here. "Have you gone through her items yet?"

"No," I say a little too quickly, too harshly, stepping back to wring my hands together. I soothe the inside of my wrist, my eyes locked on that chest. Only because going through them feels as if I'm accepting her absence. Accepting the fact that she's not here, serving Aurelia as their queen like she should be. Not me.

"I will eventually, just... not right now," I say softly.

He nods, kisses my temple and then says lightheartedly, "Let's go. Don't want to be late to your own event."

The introduction was short and to the point, having spent all of five minutes standing atop the small raised platform while court members warily sank to their knees in the ballroom. Hesitation ran across each face, a lingering, grating silence quick to follow. Certainly voicing their opinions about me in the Veil.

Knowing that only makes the tension across my shoulders more unbearable, my stomach twisting as their whispers disturb the air. Some are kind, while others are... clearly uncertain of my position. I can't bring myself to be upset though, as a missing princess of twenty years is now set to hold their throne. I'd be wary too.

Yet, I can't help the rise of disappointment, or the lingering flush of not truly belonging in this realm. An annoying emotion.

Still, the pounding of my pulse hasn't ceased since I stepped in, my palms sweating profusely while everyone steals glances across the room. I'm too frightened to wipe them though, afraid I'd ruin my dress, so I suffer in silence.

Rydian sits beside me, casually leaning back, a hand grazing his jaw and close enough that his other arm brushes mine. Our fingers tangle together—the only thing grounding me and keeping my eyes from glazing over entirely.

"They don't want me here," I tell him finally, hating how out of place I feel. I glance to my left just as Rydian orders a maiden to get me another glass of wine, and the female scurries off to find me something. I've had three in a single hour.

"Give them some time," he says, gently squeezing my hand. *"They are mostly curious and want to speak to you—a lot of them are in awe."*

"Awe?" My brow arches.

He hums, nodding. *"You resemble Elynor in a lot of ways."*

And here I thought I looked like Elion, but regardless, my stomach flips at the sentiment.

"You're certainly not helping my ego," I retort, leaving him to chuckle quietly.

Either way, I rub my temples just as another glass of wine arrives and take it with a sigh. Sipping, I survey the room, grazing over those in the dancing crowd and those who linger near the towering glasses of imported wine. The music swells and dips, my mind too tangled with the intricate sounds to form a single thought.

Wayd dances with a beautiful female in a pale violet gown, having already danced with several. Council members walk with partners, each one having already greeted us, and make their way across the polished marble. Ivy and Orin remain at the edge of the platform, hands clasped behind them and only allowing guests up one by one to greet us.

A nervous shiver runs down my back. Crowds make me uncomfortable, especially the ones that are here for only me. I'm too used to hiding in the shadows, apparently.

Though I have yet to see one person in particular—a brooding assassin who typically avoids large crowds unless he's on a mission.

I only assume he's avoided the event altogether, choosing to remain in his chamber for the duration of the night as the only other Aetheri here besides me. I can't fault him for it, as I'd rather be doing the same, but I haven't seen him since yesterday morning in the outdoor arena.

Despite my urge to bolt down a corridor and disappear, the ballroom is nothing but ethereal magic.

The high ceiling is a masterful illusion, bathing the room in twilight and glittering orbs, ranging from indigo to amber to violet. A colonnade lines the perimeter, supported by intricately carved pillars that form a walkway around the ballroom.

Stars shimmer above, as if the vaulted ceiling completely disappeared for the night. And the golden chandeliers look as if they're floating, snow fluttering softly around them. They steal my attention, and I'm now captivated by each flake that catches the warm glow around us. Yet none of it touches the ground—stopping just shy of guests shoulders.

The effect is quite mesmerizing. An enchantment made to feel as though you stood under an endless winter sky, only warmer. Though lazy, drifting orbs hover over a variety of guests, illuminating faces, jewels, and intricate gowns as they weave with their partners.

"No more," Rydian says to Ivy, pulling my attention, though I stifle a relieved sigh. *Thank the gods.* He arches his brow. *"Will you dance with me?"*

"As long as it's no more than one," I tease, and he laughs.

Reaching for my hand, he tugs me up and carefully leads me down and toward the center of the ballroom, pulling me into a graceful spin as guests wordlessly part. The silk of my dress flares softly, and I quickly find myself drawn back into his embrace. Rydian's hand rests on my lower back, the other gripping mine close to his chest.

As music rises—soft melodies brushing the air as we gracefully sway—guests slowly join us once more. His jaw rests against my temple as we find our rhythm.

"Are you enjoying yourself?" he asks finally.

"So formal, Your Majesty." I pull back just enough so that our eyes meet. "You know, I didn't think that I would but you've made the night bearable."

He grins. "That's insulting. I'll have to try harder to make your night more than bearable." Then his expression turns serious as he stares down at me. "I know we haven't discussed our claiming ceremony yet, but I want to do it soon."

My heart skips, stomach flipping as I ask, "How soon? I thought you told me Varrin was looking into my..." *Second mark,* I fail to add.

He sighs, features drawn taut. "He told me it shouldn't be an issue since we're technically already halfway there. We just need to formally complete our mate claim and exchange our essences. We need to crown you."

"Okay," I breathe, taking in a steady breath as the weight of it all settles—the weight of being a queen of Aurelia. But with it comes my knowledge of what Ekrin had told me—that a bond to a mate could potentially break my oath to Elion. The confession rests on my tongue.

Then Rydian's fingers tighten around my wrist, as if feeling how my pulse thrums with uncertainty, and he pulls back before I can say a word.

"Do you not want to do it?" he asks quietly—carefully—and my breath hitches at the unexpected question.

"Of course I want to. I love you." I blink, though my eyes snap up, brows drawing together because I don't know how else to explain it. "I just wasn't sure if it would be possible since we discovered—" I stop myself, unable to say the words out loud. My voice dips. "I'm not sure I'm made out to be a queen."

Concern etches his features. "You know, I'd never push you into something without teaching you how to do it. You'll make an excellent queen, Isa, do not worry about that." His head tilts slightly. "But... you want to, right?" *Finish the claim,* he means.

A small smile. "Of course, I want to."

"Good." He exhales, fighting a small smile and leans in. "I'd hate to tell Lettie she couldn't plan the celebration since that's what she's been secretly doing the last few weeks. She's quite excited and doesn't know that I know."

My cheeks warm at the thought, but I mindlessly nod against him. When the music fades, ending our dance together, I smooth my expression, unsure of what else to say.

Rydian plants a slow, devouring kiss on my mouth, my head dizzy before he leads us toward the tables of food near the right side of the room. Toward a lifetime of fruit and cheese and delicacies from all over the realm.

"Try this," he says, the corners of his mouth tilting as he hands me a sliver of cheese. Flavor explodes in my mouth, the tang of it forcing my brows to rise when Kaeda and Cassivene stride toward us, chuckling and giddy.

Both wear only the finest gowns: Kaeda in smooth emerald silk, similar to my own, while Cassivene wears a golden two toned gown.

"Turns out, the scholar isn't too bad for company." Kaeda shrugs, throwing Cassivene a teasing smile.

"I imagine that anyone who has five glasses of enchanted wine can tolerate almost anything." Cassivene snorts a giggle, sipping from the glass of wine in her hand. They both continue laughing as they gossip about the nearby guests when Rydian leans down.

"I need to speak with Mikal and Orin for a moment," he says, and my brows pinch. He hesitates and then says, "They've reported a minor... interruption. Nothing to be concerned about. Stay here and I'll be right back. Can you manage that?" He smirks and I shove an elbow against his side with a laugh. "Stay away from the dark wine, not unless you want to get filthy tonight."

"I guess I'll grab a large glass then," I muse as he walks off.

A small plate of the cheeses rests in my hand when I sense someone on my right. With a quick glance, I scan the person who stands beside me, a glass in her hand and a tight, knowing smile raising the corners of her mouth. The sight of her sultry features causes my breath to hitch.

Golden hair spills over her noble shoulders, back straight, as she studies me with distaste.

Alina, Rydian's former mistress.

Rafe's daughter and the one responsible for keeping the castle running smoothly. The same one that ensures all the house maidens have a job. And too pretty not to mean something to *my* king.

Despite myself, my blood simmers, the edges of my eyes darkening as if on a mission for Elion. I smooth my expression, though, a mask of indifference sliding into place so she doesn't see how furious I am at her bold approach.

Alina wears a dark, shimmering gown of chiffon and starlace—as if crafted from the threads of darkness itself—that hugs every luscious dip and curve. Even though she's alluring and quite stunning, malice clings to her.

"Quite the spectacle tonight, isn't it?" she asks casually.

Her smile isn't warm, but her voice—gods. Sultry and smooth and something that causes my brow to arch. I could kick myself right now, but damn, I can't even be mad at Rydian for being with her.

"You do look…" She scans me, a cold smirk lining her hardened features. "Charming. Though I suppose charm can only go so far when trying to fit into a role that wasn't meant for you."

Ah, there it is. I stifle the laugh bubbling up my throat.

She feels the need to corner me while Rydian is preoccupied, taking her chance to pick apart my heritage without so much as saying my name. I push a grape into my mouth, unbothered, and skim my eyes over her.

"I appreciate the compliment, Lady Alina. I'm actually surprised you had the time to spare from your other… duties," I say, and clasp my hands together.

Hatred flashes in Alina's eyes, narrowing at the sound of her name on my lips, like she assumed I didn't know who she was. I know plenty, thanks to the memory I unwillingly snatched from Rydian. Kaeda's wild grin shines out of the corner of my eye, her gaze shooting between the two of us as if eager for things to escalate. Cassivene quickly averts her eyes, awkwardly staring at the wine in her grasp.

Alina scoffs, stepping closer. "I just thought I'd come and see how you're settling in. It must be hard to fill shoes you barely fit into since you were raised in an entirely different realm. You know, I heard you don't even have Vaelborne blood in you. You'd be a traitor for a Queen." A chuckle.

Rydian doesn't have Vaelborne blood either, so what does that matter at this point?

There's no doubt she heard that from her weasel of a father. Even though her words send a searing heat of rage through my veins, I return her jab with a small smile. Little does she know, her hateful comments only encourage me.

A light, breathy laugh slips free when I step forward, invading her space, and her eyes widen. She shuffles back, her confidence wavering as a sinister thought creeps into my mind.

"You know, *Alina*, envy is a rather unbecoming shade on you. It makes you look weak and frail, but you know what shade would look good?" I purr, and grasp a lock of her silky, golden hair. I rub it between my fingers. "A deep shade of red searing your face after a good fuck."

She remains silent but her flush deepens, lips parting in surprise. Kaeda barks a laugh, quickly hiding her smile behind her hand as Cassivene snickers. The filthy words left me before I could stop them, but the look on Alina's face tells me it was worth it.

So fucking worth it.

"Do you know where King Rydian met me?" I ask finally.

"What?" Alina chokes out an uncomfortable laugh, glancing at Kaeda and Cassivene beside us.

"He met me in a brothel. I wasn't there for him, though, he just happened to be there. *Actually*, now that I recall the night, I was there for a female and you..." I chuckle again, leaning closer, and whisper, "Well, you look like my type."

As if I can sense him, I look over her shoulder. Rydian leans against a pillar with a smirk, arms folded and watching the spectacle in amusement.

My eyes slide back to Alina, assessing.

She's so flustered that she stumbles back in surprise, wiping her hands on her gown, the nervous scent of her sweat permeating the air.

"I... I—" she begins, mouth gaping.

I tilt my head, amusement shining in my eyes as she trips over her words. "Don't bother apologizing. You're more than welcome to beg, though."

Kaeda laughs again, causing Alina to burn bright with embarrassment all the way to her pointed, noble ears. Someone tugs on my elbow. I remain fixed on Alina with unwavering confidence, now itching for my dagger, but I know how that would end.

My breath quickens, as I'm eager to make it happen, but then she storms off in the opposite direction, completely flustered.

Kaeda's smile grows wide before meeting me at my side. "Looks like the apple didn't fall too far from the family tree, cousin. Don't worry, I have a special dislike for that one too." She winks. "I must admit, I've been waiting to watch someone put her in her place. That was quite entertaining."

A low, unamused growl escapes me when Alina storms straight to where Rydian perches against the pillar, an amused grin on his face. His smile falters, and he straightens, brows lowering, a snarl curling at his lips as he begins to argue. He grips her elbow, forcing her into a private corridor off to the side.

What a fucking—

"Isa." Ren's voice cuts through my thoughts. He tugs one last time, dragging me from the table as my anger rises. "Dance with me... now."

With a hard yank, I'm pulled into his chest, the need to obliterate Alina quickly dissolving as he towers over me, pressing his body against mine.

"I thought you were going to kill her," he muses.

Refusing to meet his stare, I imagine what he saw as I fixed on Alina—an assassin, assessing her target. I huff out a small, unamused laugh.

"I thought about it, but I don't think Rydian would appreciate me destroying the castle toy," I say, then glance down, realizing that we're dancing. "Since when do you know how to dance?"

Finally, I lift my gaze, my heart stopping the moment I do. He stares down at me, a teasing smirk on his lips and wearing something he wouldn't typically wear and yet... it fits him. I'd never seen him so put together, not even at the Aurorafest—the face of a ruthless assassin never truly relaxing. Though what he wore then wasn't exactly his preferred attire—too extravagant for him.

But here... he's quite beautiful.

He wears a simple dark satin tunic, open at the chest. I blink, and avert my gaze. Push the thought from my mind while his scent infiltrates my nose. I know how much he hates this type of event, how he avoids them unless he's forced to go.

He says nothing, though, ignoring my question as he stares down at me. I glance up just as a hint of mischief shines through.

"Do you want to leave?" he asks quietly—so quiet I almost miss it among the music and conversation. I peer over my shoulder, following his line of sight to Rydian who's now in a deep discussion with Ivy and Orin, everyone's faces drawn taut.

I face Ren. "Where are we going?"

"Wherever you want."

My stomach dips at the thought of escaping the stares and whispers, the invitation too sweet to deny.

I glance around the court, at the too foreign throne, at the gowns and crystal and delicacies—all too nice for me to cherish fully. Who abandons their own event? Rydian will come looking for me, but what's a few minutes of peace?

"Like old times." A smile tugs at my lips. "Real or a dream?"

"Real."

27

Seconds after agreeing, Ren tugs me by my hand, quickly weaving us through the crowd with expert precision. Right toward the exits. No doubt something he scoured hours prior.

I stifle a grin, my skin prickling with excitement despite feeling as if everyone's eyes remain on me. Perhaps it's my own anxiousness surfacing—that little twist in my stomach as my thoughts settle on my unknown future here.

One that Aurelia clearly doesn't want me to be a part of. If I focus hard enough, I can almost hear their doubts clinging to the Veil.

Instead, I focus on my steps, the wine now coursing ferociously in my blood as we bolt for the back. We reach the colonnade lining the perimeter of the ballroom, hidden in the dim glow as we veer right.

Leading us further in, Ren urges me forward with another quick glance over his shoulder, and I release a sigh as the weight of everyone's gazes begins to fade—the weight of my responsibility as heir and future queen that I feel like I can't bear.

As we duck into one of the many shadowed corridors on our left, I halt and pinch my nose, slowing my breaths.

"Gods, that was stifling," I say under my breath, then peer

around the corner. No one has seemed to notice my absence, dancing, swaying and eating like earlier.

I sigh, facing Ren once more while floating a glowing yellow orb between us. Light ripples across his face, and I realize now that his eyes are locked on me. His jaw feathers, his chest hardly moving as his eyes slowly drift from my face to the floor and back.

"What?" I ask, swallowing and fighting the urge to soothe my aching wrist when his gaze lingers a little too long.

"I didn't quite see what you were wearing…" He pauses for a moment, taking another long breath before turning on his heel with a quiet huff. "Red is your color."

The orb dies, and despite the flush of my skin, I chuckle a little, shaking my head as I rush to his side. The padding of our shoes echo in the empty corridor, still quiet enough not to be noticed. We aim for the doors to the gardens, the moon's pale streaks of light filtering through the glass. We're halfway there when a tease twists my tongue, likely from all the wine, and I smirk.

"Careful, Ren. If you keep throwing out compliments, someone might think you want me," I say lightheartedly and snicker.

He whirls so fast the air shifts, and clamps his hand around my jaw before I can muster a single breath. My lips part in surprise as he backs me into the stone wall with a hard thud, our mouths now inches apart.

"*You want me.*" I blurt, my tone laced with disbelief as realization sweeps through me. I thought he only liked watching, but perhaps I was wrong. Good gods, was I wrong?

He holds my gaze, though heat sears my skin, burning where his hand firmly grips my jaw. Warm, heavy breaths brush my cheeks, his chest rising sharply against mine.

Still, shock settles in my core—at how easily his composure cracked. His composure never cracks, and here he is, crumbling at my feet over a simple tease. Is he going to kiss me?

Surely he's not that… foolish.

Yet we both pant, and tension coils along my shoulders, our bodies strung tight like bows ready to snap in unison. We don't kiss, just stand there. Only I realize now how much I want him to. Realize how much *he* wants to.

"Do it," I say, my breath ragged.

"You have a mate." He hisses the words, baring his teeth.

I hold his gaze, breathing heavily as my skin grows hotter and hotter. He tightens his grip, my jaw screaming beneath his hand. I welcome the pain, if only to distract me from the conflicting emotions whirling in my chest. The impulsivity shouting at me to do it—to close that distance.

"At this point, I'm not sure he'd mind," I breathe.

Though my humor falls flat and silence permeates the air once more. Silence so stifling it makes me want to lean in just to rid the simmering tension, but his grip holds me in place.

Then his brows draw together, lips still parted as he leans closer, head dipping down like he wants to. So close that we share the same breath and our noses graze each other. So close that his body presses against mine—pushing, feeling, testing.

Fabric spreads thin across his muscled chest, and his heart thunders, beating so relentlessly against my palm that I fear it may burst. I squeeze my eyes shut, unsure of what to do as his control slowly, slowly frays.

I've never seen him so... unhinged.

Feral, needy, and dare I say wild.

It sends a shiver of need coiling at the base of my spine, my skin now prickling with electric intensity as his touch lingers. If I were to raise on my toes even the slightest, our mouths would meet.

"Do you love him?" he asks softly.

I blink twice, my heart skipping in my chest, because I love Rydian more than anything—would die for him if it ever came to it. I was willing to do just that had Elion discovered who he was in that throne room. Ready to slit my own throat to protect him.

"Yes," I declare.

He releases a rough breath, eyes squeezing shut. His forehead dips to mine, and his grip on my face loosens a fraction. My pulse skitters, fearing he'll let me go when I don't want him to.

Whether it's to tease him or because of that crawling fear of mine, I shift a little. My back arches off the wall, breasts brushing against him, and he stiffens. He stops breathing entirely.

Then, with agonizing slowness, he pushes his hips forward and presses into me with a low grumble. Slow enough to torment. Slow enough that it sends a raging heat shooting down my body in anticipation and a flood of warmth pooling between my legs.

I'm aroused by this—by *him?*

He groans, low and guttural, further pressing the hard length of his cock against my stomach. Gods. Every inhale tangles in my throat, my heart racing at his unexpected arousal.

Still, he doesn't close the distance between our mouths, only hovers with his hand curled around my jaw, tightening once more as if struggling with a decision.

My knee drifts upward, moving of its own accord, and the fabric of my gown falls away, exposing the bare skin of my thigh as it grazes his hip—a lingering, voiceless question.

A low growl rumbles through his chest, primal and hungry, and his hand seizes my knee. With a hard squeeze, his rough palm slides up my thigh, higher and higher until it grazes the underside of my leg. His fingers dig in, hard enough to bruise, and a broken sound slips from me—a soft, aching whimper.

The touch of him burns, a fire electrifying my blood, and for the first time in a long while, I feel clear headed. I want him to kiss me —want him to shatter that fine line between us.

Repercussions be damned, I want him to utterly ruin me.

Were we ever really friends? His words from yesterday run through my mind. At this point, I don't want him to be, not right now. Not as his stare sets my soul on fire.

Ren's composure fractures even more, as the very stone behind me trembles in tune with his hand on my face. The floor at our feet quakes.

He drags that hand down my neck, grazing my breast and the peak of my nipple until his palm settles where it wants. Against my erratically racing heart.

"Kiss me," I breathe, unable to take it any longer—the tension between us that's been simmering for weeks.

He growls again, only this time it's frustrated and angry, and his fist cracks into the stone beside my head. Pieces crumble to the floor, debris falling at our feet. I gasp, and my lips part in surprise when he quickly pushes himself away, hands clenched tight, eyes blazing.

Confusion races over me. Then he's gone, at the end of the hall within a single breath and shoving the door open, before he disappears beyond the gardens.

But the imprint of his hand still burns my skin, and shame scorches the very piece of me he touched. Despite my love for Rydian, my body screamed for Ren's control to fracture entirely, aching and craving for him to touch me more.

Gods, I wanted him to kiss me.

I shouldn't want Ren to kiss me, not when I need to complete my claim to Rydian. But I wasn't thinking about that.

What kind of queen craves another male when her mate is only yards away, offering her a life she's only ever dreamed of? One who can't seem to make the right decision, that's who.

I stand there for ten minutes, eyes squeezed shut, head resting against the stone as I slow my breaths. As I swallow the rising guilt clawing at my chest now that the wine has settled.

Surely, it was only the wine.

I need to find Rydian and hope he doesn't rain his wrath on me or Ren. Unfortunately, I feel as if he'd be angrier with Ren than me, and I hate that. But I'm desperate to leave and talk to him— desperate to explain whatever the fuck that was, even though I can't form a single explanation.

"Where are you?" I push the thought out, stepping around the corner, but he's nowhere to be seen.

Ignoring the bustling activity in the ballroom, I weave through the columns, sticking to the shadows of the colonnade.

Lettie and a few dressed-up house-maidens come into view, laughing and clinking their glasses. Some I recognize, others I don't. But just as one of them swivels their gaze toward me, I step into the Veil. I sigh, straightening to peer around a column, my eyes resting on the swaying crowd as music swells and dips.

No sign of Rydian and no response.

I grit my teeth, annoyed that he's suddenly chosen to ignore me and close my eyes, tugging on our bond. Sharp and crisp, I cling to him, holding tight to the familiarity of his presence like the cool mist of a dense fog.

Annoyance and anger and jealousy jolt across my mind like ice, emotions so heavy and cold it twists in my stomach. But I sense his location, and he's not too far from where I stand. In fact, he's two corridors down.

I weave through the lingering groups nearby, making sure not to touch anyone as I round the corner before slowing my approach in the shadows. I tuck myself further into the wall, knowing that Rydian can see me in the Veil if he turns, and steady my breaths.

He stands with his spine straight, shoulders rigid. I can't see his expression, though, as he's silhouetted by the windows near the back. Clearly in a heated argument.

"Do you forget whose halls you walk, Captain?" Rydian bites out. "You will abide by my rules."

My breathing grinds to a halt, stomach flipping at the severity in his tone. That's not my mate at the moment, but the King of Aurelia. And I know exactly who he's talking to before a reply brushes the air. Are they discussing what just happened between Ren and me a few minutes ago?

Surely not; that would be...

Realization runs through me. Rydian can feel my heightened emotions, meaning he definitely already knows. *Shit*. Ren's humorless chuckle follows, and he shoves his hair back as he paces near the wall, saying nothing.

Despite Ren's silence, Rydian growls, "*That's* what I said."

My confusion whirls, sharp and dizzying as I try to decipher their meaning. The very walls tilt around me.

What are they talking about?

Questions slip through me like water in my palm, their words too vague to understand. I know I shouldn't be listening, not if there's a chance Elion will ask for details about anything significant.

Ren laughs again, shaking his head in disbelief.

Then the walls and floors tremble, a dim glow flooding Ren's palms, and my eyes flare. Fear prickles my skin, and I worry they may begin fighting in the middle of the ballroom.

"What exactly are you discussing?" I force myself to ask, stepping out of the Veil.

Their attention snaps to me. Rydian curses and strides toward me, Ren on his heels. Their faces come into view, just barely in the low lit hall, when Rydian growls and whirls around.

"No, you're not doing that," Rydian snaps, inches from Ren's face, who then stifles a snarl. Gods, they were talking in the Veil.

I grind my teeth and sharply turn toward the ballroom, as I've clearly not had enough to drink. The crowd blurs as I stride across the floor, hands trembling with anger and frustration. The hard thuds of Rydian and Ren echo behind me, and one of them calls my name. I ignore it.

"Princess, I'd like to speak to you!" a female calls out, and I angrily look to my left.

She's no one I recognize, petite and dark-haired as she inches closer, wearing something that doesn't look suitable for a celebration—comfortable and easy to move in.

"Maybe later." I brush her off, heart hammering with fury, and the crowd parts as I storm through.

Frantic whispers and gossip pierce the air, forcing me to focus even though I cut straight down the middle of the festivities. I have no interest in hearing what they have to say.

Then I hear it—the faint scraping of a blade being pulled right before the hiss of it whizzes toward my back.

The depth of my training surges and I jolt to the right on instinct, catching it by the handle right before it can pierce skin. It clanks against the marble, and for a moment, the room narrows to only the perpetrator and the sound of my blood pounding in my ears.

I'm in no mood to deal with this.

Despite the shocked cries, I focus on the dark-haired female— my eyes darkening at the edges, my skills snapping to attention.

All-consuming rage blankets my expression and I stalk forward with a low growl.

Her eyes grow with fear, and she attempts to bolt into a run. But the magic in my veins flares to life. I thrust out a hand, fingers curling, and the air around her throat weaves into a twist of shadow and light.

She freezes, her feet lifting off the floor, and she claws at her neck—choking and gasping and kicking. Her lips seep purple from lack of air.

"Isa," Rydian growls behind me, close enough that the heat of his anger sears my back. His rage buzzes across my temples, pulsing against my thoughts. Then fury throbs at my neck.

I hear nothing else, just a sharp ringing in my ears. I step forward, palm out. Whips of my dark and glowing magic mingle along my forearm in a mesmerizing dance. Time seems to stop entirely as every attending guest holds their breath, waiting.

"What is your name?" I purr, low and unfamiliar, and loosen my hold a fraction for her reply.

"Mari," she rasps, nails biting at her neck.

"Tell me why I shouldn't kill you, Mari."

"I... I thought you were a fraud," she chokes out. "An abomination. Someone like you shouldn't exist—shouldn't be ruling our realm. You weren't here when we all bled... for our realm at the hands of your *father*." My grip tightens a little and she gasps, wincing. "You're not chosen; you're cursed."

I chuckle, short and bitter, despite the urge to stiffen at her cruel, yet truthful words. "That's not a very convincing argument."

My magic rages, and the dagger she threw floats toward her, suspended by nothing but my focused will, its delicate point balanced beneath her chin.

"I'm... I'm clearly wrong."

"And what makes you say that?" I tilt my head, eyes narrowing as a cold smirk lifts the corners of my mouth. "The fact that you're currently suspended by your neck?" Another low chuckle. "Or perhaps it's the dagger settling at your throat by my power alone?"

I will the blade forward, nicking her soft flesh until tiny droplets of blood fall to the trembling floor. The very stone quakes beneath my feet. Iron singes the air, flooding my nostrils, and something wild inside me stirs. Something hungry and eager, enough to set my skin aflame, my pupils dilating with the primal urge to end her on the polished marble.

"Isa," Rydian murmurs.

My skin pricks at his tone—at the hint of fear skittering across my mind like something sour before I shut it out. I ignore him entirely, too focused on the girl in my grasp.

Then images of her flash across my mind—her memories. I haven't even touched her, yet they run over my eyelids like a living thing, my eyes wide open. Like I'm *her*. And I know that she speaks the truth, having come here alone in her attempt to kill me.

I blink them away, focusing on her once more.

"All of it," she gets out. Her fear and sweat permeates the air, hitting my nose with putrid force before her eyes squeeze shut. "To die by your hands would be an honor, but if I live I'll serve you dutifully."

My brow arches, lips twitching into a cruel smile.

Interesting.

Still, the urge to end her scorches my veins, hair rising on my arms—power itching to be set free. The itch to snuff her from the realm as a message to everyone in this court.

Primal, fucking rage and duty bellow inside me all at once.

With a simple thought and pure will, I could snap her neck. Or I could press the knife into her throat and watch her bleed until nothing remained, crumpling to the ground like all my other targets.

It would only take a few seconds.

But as those thoughts enter my mind, so does Elion. He would have already killed her. Would have ended her life for attempting to end him without so much as a flicker of hesitation. Knowing that sits heavy on my chest, and if I did that...

Well, I'd be no better than him.

I'd dreamt of a life without killing, yet here I am debating on ending hers because she was wary of my role. If I kill her now, respect from the court would go with her.

I inhale a long breath, and the fury rippling through my body slowly dissipates. The whips around Mari slacken as I reel my magic back. Shadow and light uncoil until my magic is only a low simmer beneath my skin. A thrum in my veins.

"I'll have someone find a job for you," I say, dropping her to the ground. She falls to her knees—into a kneel—trembling, eyes fixed to the floor. "Don't make me regret it. There won't be a next time."

As my vision clears, the scene around me sharpens and the ballroom comes back into focus. The music has died, but so have the whispers.

An eerie silence lingers in the air. My heart skips when I glance around. Every single guest has fallen to their knees—some trembling, others whispering prayers. Bits and pieces of glass sprinkle throughout the room, mixing with wine and ale. Confusion settles over me though, brows drawing close together as I glance around the chamber.

Heart racing and looking for answers, I turn to find both Rydian and Ren kneeling behind me: heads bowed, hands on their thighs, and utterly silent.

Bowing to their future queen.

28

The crowd—and Ren—quickly departed after what happened with Mari. A young Shadovar who Rydian had taken to the dungeon for questioning. Yet I couldn't bring myself to admit that I had accidentally pulled her truth—pulled her memories without touching her. Maybe the power that wrapped around her throat had allowed me to do that?

I suppress a shudder.

Now, the door slams shut as we enter my chamber in absolute silence. Grinding my teeth, my frustration rises once more, and I whirl around to face Rydian.

He leans against the door, jaw tight with barely-managed fury. Then, he flicks his wrist, lighting a fire before dimming the chandeliers. Soft crackles and the scent of burning wood fill the air, drowning out the dreadful silence between us.

"What?" I ask when he takes another long breath, as if he's still attempting to manage his emotions. I tug on our connection, fear and confusion running through me. "Are you frightened of me?"

"No." His brows lower before he smooths his expression and sighs. "I just don't think you realize how much power you carry. Everyone in that ballroom saw your wrath and your forgiveness at once. She should have been executed on that floor, but then you gave her mercy. They willingly knelt for you."

"I don't understand." Unease pebbles my skin, sending a shiver down my spine.

"The court only kneels for me. I know you carry the essence, but technically, you aren't supposed to have that much power. Not until we complete the ritual, and the fact that—" He exhales again, head shaking. "The full royal essence only gets passed down after the ritual is complete."

A beat passes between us, but I say nothing as the weight of his words settles in my chest. I'm not quite sure what it means, having all that power. But I'm also not sure how to feel about people kneeling for me. I certainly don't feel like a queen, just the weapon I was created to be. An assassin.

Perhaps, in one form or another, I'll always feel that way.

Rydian's expression changes, twisting for the briefest of moments, and I tug on our connection once more. Anger. It pounds against my temples, and I force back a wince. His conversation with Ren brushes my thoughts, pulling me back.

"Are you going to tell me what you were discussing with Ren?" I dare ask, and then quickly regret it as anger marks his face.

He inhales, chest rising sharply. "Are you going to tell me what *you* were doing with Ren?"

I swallow, cheeks burning, and turn my gaze to the flames in the hearth. Even as I search for an explanation, nothing rises, because I have no reason for it. It shouldn't have escalated, and guilt tightens in my chest at betraying Rydian. Something that should have never happened in the first place.

Then my eyes snap to him when the angry beat of his steps hit the marble. Rydian stalks forward and in two strides, snaps out a hand. His fingers curl around the back of my neck, yanking me to him, and I stumble forward with a gasp.

"What were you going to do with him, hm?" His voice dips low, and the hair rises on my arms. "Sink to your knees and take his cock down your throat?"

My cheeks warm with shame or... perhaps arousal. A menacing

smirk curls his mouth, dark and heated. His scar glimmers in the light, stretched thin along his lip. My chest grows hot, and for a moment, I itch to provoke him.

Itch to see how far I can push.

"Did it cross your mind? Or do you like me jealous, little fawn?" His fingers sweep a tendril of hair off my face before he leans closer. "Do I need to remind you that you're mine?"

"No," I say breathlessly, panting in his grasp. Perhaps he should, though. Maybe it would squash whatever I feel for Ren.

"Good." A beat of silence as he skims my face. "If you want to play... then you'll play by my rules."

"Rules?" *What fucking rules?*

Before I can react, he backs me against the edge of the bed, a deep growl rumbling up his chest. His grip tightens, and I whimper, the sound sending his pupils to dilate with hunger. Pressing into me, the scent of his arousal cuts the air.

He kicks my feet apart, spreading my legs.

"I either get to watch," he breathes the words, "or get to join. But none of it will be without my approval."

He grips my knee and props the heel of my shoe against the bed, spreading me wider.

The heat of him burns me when his hand rises higher and higher, reaching the apex of my thigh. He groans and grazes his thumb over my center, swirling in taunting strokes. Stroking right over my silk undergarments, warmth pools between my legs. My entire body trembles in his grasp, my legs quivering, and my mouth falls open on the faintest of exhales.

"It's all fucking mine, do you hear me?" he whispers, and I manage a weak nod, my eyes fluttering as he pulls the silk aside.

Another whimper.

Desire shoots through my veins and I push my hips forward, eager for his touch. I moan when he drives his fingers in with a low growl, his palm rubbing against me over and over. I grind against him, riding his hand as his fingers work inside me. *Fuck.*

He peers down his nose, a devious smile pulling at his lips. "Say 'Yes, Your Majesty, I'll follow your rules.'"

"Ye—yes, Your Majesty—gods." I moan when he presses down, pleasure barreling through me. "I'll follow your rules."

He hums, low and throaty. "You looked so beautiful with all that power. Did you see how they knelt for you—so eager to drop to their knees?" Another moan slips from me, and I nod as he says, "A little louder. I want to hear how sorry you are."

Against my better judgement, I oblige, and sharp moans leave my lips. Tight pressure coils deep, heat building, my clit swelling with release.

His speed picks up, and desire electrifies my blood. So wild that the coldness of my own shadows skim my knuckles, spilling across his chest as my control fractures. My hands grapple his tunic, bunching as I chase my release. I want more and more and—

The movement abruptly stops.

My eyes snap open when he steps away from me.

"Good. We have a long day tomorrow, and I don't want to argue." A menacing smile grows when he sticks his fingers in his mouth, tasting me. "So, so sweet. But consider that your warning, and if you touch yourself... Well, the punishment for that will not be pleasant."

Shock marks my face for the briefest of moments, then my eyes narrow at the realization—that he's punishing me for what I did with Ren. My lip curls into a frustrated snarl, and I straighten, my dress brushing the floor again. My fingers tighten into fists.

His eyes skim over me, expressionless. "You can fight me all you want, but you won't get what you desperately crave. You'll have to deal with that *ache* all night. Now get in bed before I make it worse."

He slowly works the buttons on his brocade until his chest gleams in the light. Then, without a word, he turns toward the bathing chamber, leaving me standing there, panting and flushed.

Yet, as I watch him disappear beyond the doors—arousal and annoyance flooding my veins—I fear that I liked my punishment a little too much.

29

The sharp stench of iron floods my senses, and I lift my hands to find them drenched. It runs down my fingers in dark streaks of crimson—blood.

So much of it drips from my fingers and onto the freshly polished wood beneath our feet. Darkness blankets every inch of the room save for the small flicker of candles melting on the desk. The floors creak under the weight of my boots. Floors of a half-blooded Aetheri in Arcan, now lying in the mess I created with his eyes wide open.

Half Shadovar, actually.

Nausea and fear and dread curl in my stomach, a panic so unrelenting that it steals my breath. A dizzying certainty that I've made a dire mistake sends my pulse skyrocketing, my vision blurring.

I took a life. I took my very first life.

There were times in the Brotherhood when I thought I'd be able to do it with ease, jumping into the fray without a second thought for the lives I'd be taking. And here I am, riddled with guilt and regret on my very first mission.

I'm not made for this.

Air desperately drags through my lips, scorching my throat as panic consumes me, the weight of my decision settling. I can't go back now, not anymore.

The next thing I know, I'm whirled around by my shoulders to face my new captain. I'm unable to breathe, sucking in more breaths when he gets low, bending to stare into my frightened eyes.

Young just like me, though his gray eyes remain hardened despite the concern etching his face, even at eighteen. Like he's witnessed years worth of atrocities working for King Elion.

Atrocities we were never meant to endure, yet here we are, carrying out missions as if those very lives mean nothing. We're too fucking young to be playing with fate, that's for certain. And here I thought training all those years in combat would have hardened my heart, hollowing out my chest until nothing remained.

I was wrong.

"Take a breath," he says, his tone slightly sharp with an undercurrent of annoyance as a mess lays at our feet. It pools, collecting at our boots.

Mine, shiny and new. His, dull and worn.

He was ordered to come with me, sent to monitor my first mission, as we all are in the Brotherhood. My Captain, not my friend, I remind myself. Not right now at least, not that I ever thought he could be.

He sighs, hands still gripping my shoulders. "The firsts are always messy, but you need to breathe."

"I thought I could do it," I say, my voice small and trembling, head shaking as moisture pricks my eyes. "I can't... I can't do this."

He takes a slow, steady breath, holding my gaze. "You can. You have to, or we're sent back to the orphanage. Is that what you want?" I shake my head again. "Then you'll need to get over it—you have no choice. I'll help you, okay?"

My head drops, and I use the back of my hand to wipe the tears sliding down my cheeks and sniffle, so as to not get blood all over my face. Another one of my small cries brushes the air, and I somehow manage to slow my breathing. Guilt quickly follows.

He straightens, eyes fixed on the male I decimated minutes prior. "The next thing we'll be working on is swallowing those emotions. If King Elion sees you even remotely caring about our targets, he'll send you to Theron and I won't allow that. You'll be the best he has, I'll make sure of it."

He rubs his jaw and sighs, a flicker of something unreadable passing over his features in the shadows before it's gone.

"Ren," I murmur. His gaze flicks to me, the edges of his eyes softening slightly. "Thank you."

All he does is nod.

With my head back, my hands curl around the rim of the tub, knuckles white against the porcelain in my bathing chamber. I force my breaths to slow. Force myself to loosen the tightness in my chest and drag in another inhale.

Yet my skin pebbles, the water near freezing by the time my head slows the blur of fragmented images across my mind. The trembling of my fingers shifts my attention down; the entirety of my body practically shakes the walls of the tub as I rise. Water sloshes, dripping onto the marble as I step out and sway.

I stand there, leaning against the rim with my eyes shut.

After training with Kaeda this morning, Rydian urged me to prepare for Alvonia tonight while he held a quick meeting with the council this afternoon. When I arrived in my chambers, food had been waiting, an early lunch delivered by Lettie even though I told her I wasn't hungry.

With a deep breath, I straighten and immediately regret my decision. My stomach twists once more, bile rising in my throat. I bolt for the basin, curling over the counter as I retch into the bowl.

That unrelenting panic consumes me; I'm unable to halt the flood of emotions rising in my chest, feeling every moment of that day—my first kill.

The one I didn't want to make.

I was too young, and although I was confident in my ability to complete the mission, it came with repercussions. It was as if I were in that very room all over again, forced to relive the kill as my memories continue to return.

Many that contain Ren.

Another thought pricks my skin—he was captain before? All

this time, I'd believed he'd only been promoted recently. If that isn't true, then what happened?

A shudder ripples down my back as fear and nausea and disgust wash over me again. Twelve years old—I was a child.

Lifting my gaze, I glance at my reflection, my face clammy and pale. I can hardly believe I wanted them back, since all they seem to be doing is giving me a fucking headache. Tormenting my body with sickness. Yet anytime I master my control, another memory floods me.

My hands tremble, and wisps of shadow collect at the bottom of the basin. I clench my fists, snuffing them out. The returning memories pull my essence to the surface, but ever since my rage with Mari last night, they've been writhing beneath my skin.

Or perhaps it's my lingering arousal from Rydian's punishment that's fracturing my control.

Regardless, my control is fraying the more time passes, only it's not just shadows that surface, but the warmth from Elderheim too.

I rinse my mouth when the creak of my chamber door cuts the air, forcing me to straighten. Lettie must be here to collect the tray, but since I've retched up breakfast, I should probably have her leave it.

Tugging my silk robe secure as my fingers fumble with the sash, I rush to the door on wet feet, hoping to stop her before she takes it. I call out as water slips down my legs.

The door swings open, and I come to a screeching halt, slipping on the water pooling at my feet. I fling my arms out and lose my grip on my robe. It falls open, and I quickly tug it closed, eyes wide as I glance at the towering figure in my chamber. *Gods.*

Ren hums quietly, peering down his nose, almost amused while his hands grip my shoulders. Heat rises in my face at him seeing me wet and partially naked.

Not like he hasn't before, but...

I crane my neck and scan the room—Rydian isn't here. We're alone. After last night, I'm not quite sure where we stand in the midst of whatever sits between us.

And it's definitely not friendship.

Not as Ren scans me from the floor to my face in a slow, deliberate once-over. Inspecting.

"What are you doing here?" I attempt to bite out the words, but they come out flustered and shaky. Nervous.

Of all people, *Ren* makes me nervous. Perhaps it's the deliberate silence and the way I can't decipher what he's thinking.

"I heard you getting sick, so I came to check on you," he says, releasing my shoulders. He takes the tiniest of steps back, and his hands curl into fists.

"You heard me across the castle?" A crease forms between my brows, nausea curling again as my mind continues to spin. Those memories are nothing but a nuisance.

Ren ignores my question.

Then he inhales, slow and steady, as if struggling—for control, perhaps. Yet his gaze burns a hole through me, hands unfurling once he's finally mastered his emotions. Another breath.

My cheeks burn hotter, hating the way he just stares at me in silence, like he's waiting for something. We stand like that a moment longer, not a single word spoken as the rift between friendship and something else begins to fracture in the blaze of his stare.

Fracturing ever since we arrived in Aurelia, that is. Especially after our shift last night—a shift I don't quite understand. But it's like something snapped when we entered this realm. Like he dared explore a fantasy I wasn't aware of.

But I know that look, the same hungry gaze from yesterday—he wants me.

Still, I can't help the confusion tightening in my chest. Was it always there? Is this a new feeling for him, or am I just naïve? I would have noticed.

"If you want to see me naked, just ask," I tease to mask the nervousness, breaking that dreadful silence lingering in the air.

My breath hitches, lips parting when he slowly steps toward me. His brows lower, sure in his decision—the only sign of something brewing in his mind. Something I shouldn't like, but do.

Without a word, he carefully reaches out and brushes his fingers across my collarbone, a path of heat branding all the way to my shoulder until my robe falls to the side. His touch lingers, and I tighten my grip on the fabric. Still, the peak of my breast is suddenly exposed and my nipple tightens in the air.

He hums in approval, and I squeeze my eyes shut at the sound, my breath catching in my throat. Only because that little hum of approval sent a raging fire through my veins, my blood buzzing with something I'm too afraid to name. Yet for some reason, I can't bring myself to cover up.

Can't bring myself to tell him to leave as heat builds in my core, wiping every dreadful emotion I'd felt a moment ago. What is happening? Why don't I want him to leave?

"What are you doing?" I murmur, voice trembling slightly as I open my eyes. His jaw clenches.

Rydian hasn't been gone that long, but I know there's a chance he'll step in and discover us. After last night and my... punishment, I think he would be furious.

Unless he watched or joined. Gods.

Still, I can't help but think of the wrath that would rain down should he come in. I'd hate to be the reason blood was spilled on my lush rugs, and I'm not interested in staring at the stains for the duration of my rule after scrubbing it out.

"You feel like you could use a distraction." The words are casual, though his eyes blaze down at me. A beat passes when my brows pinch in confusion, pulse climbing to my temples.

Did he say, *you feel*? Surely he misspoke—

My heart skips, stopping entirely in my chest when a *whoosh* breaks the air. I stumble back, and pull my robe up my shoulder. *Fuck.*

Rydian appears from the Veil, leaning against my bed post, though his annoyance pulses at my temples. My cheeks burn in embarrassment and shame, the room stifling as I stand motionless in front of Ren—someone who doesn't move away like he should. Why isn't he moving?

"Please, don't stop on my account," Rydian says, and then whispers in the Veil. *"Did you not learn anything last night?"*

"Will you watch?" The question slips out before I can stop it, and

I blink, chest heaving at my impulsive tongue. I've hardly even thought it through.

What the fuck am I doing?

My uncertainty rises as Rydian straightens, his jaw feathering as he eyes the both of us. Uncertainty races over his features. I can't read his expression—can't feel his emotions when I reach out and tug at our bond. A blank slate.

"Are you asking for my approval?" He asks in a tone I can't quite decipher, though my stomach dips.

Am I asking for his approval? Why would I even consider it? Would indulging with Ren fracture my connection with Rydian? Would he still want to complete our claim as mates—something that could sever my oath to Elion? I glance at Ren, studying him, as my thoughts bounce around in my head.

Ren is... distractingly handsome.

Hardened by the years of our training, yes, but even then, that does little to hide how attractive he is. Even though I admire his features, it definitely doesn't explain why I feel anything other than mild indifference towards him. Not when I had hated him just weeks ago.

Not when Rydian stands feet away.

Though I must admit, I think I'm beginning to... like them both. Fuck. I'm in quite a dilemma.

Warmth pools in my core as I stare up at Ren, but still, he hasn't moved. In fact, he's hardly breathed since Rydian stepped in, eyes fixed on me, shoulders taut... hands faintly trembling. Like he's seconds from his control splintering at my feet.

"And if I was?"

Rydian blinks and then exhales, slow and steady. "If that's what you want, I won't stop it," he says aloud, the words slicing through the tense air.

Then the tiniest of smirks lifts the corner of Ren's mouth, and a prickle of awareness runs through me—the sense of being excluded from an understanding I'm clearly not aware of. Is this what they were talking about last night? My eyes narrow.

The Rydian I know would never allow another male to touch

me, not if we're mates. He'd even threatened to kill Ren at the thought of him touching me in that clearing. Said that the only reason he was alive now was because he kept me safe in Elderheim, but... is that true?

What changed in the last two weeks, and what did I miss? Perhaps these were the rules Rydian spoke to Ren about last night. *Our rules.*

Confusion ripples through me. *"Why aren't you angry?"*

"Who says that I'm not?" Rydian chuckles, low and throaty, a deviousness flickering across his expression. "But as I told you before, you already have me, so what do I have to be worried about? Plus I'd hate to be the reason you couldn't have a lover as our new queen. Consider it another *claiming* gift." Sarcasm and a hint of venom laces his tone, but it's not aimed at me, but at Ren.

My pulse skyrockets when Ren snaps his head to Rydian, unspoken words settling between them. Ren's lip curls into a snarl.

Rydian ignores him though, casually placing his hands in his pockets and says, "Do you want him?"

A cold sweat breaks across my brow, breath stalling at the uncertainty crawling across my skin. Do I want him? For the first time in a long while, I fear my own answer.

I want to say no. I want to tell him that the feeling is only fleeting, something to get out of my system... but is it?

Because I know, deep in the very pits of my soul, that I shouldn't want him with Rydian nearby. I know that I should tell Ren to leave and let Rydian have his way with me... but something in my chest is forcing me to hesitate. It doesn't make sense.

"You need to say it, or it's not happening," Rydian warns quietly. Ren slowly faces me, waiting for my reply.

"Yes," I say.

"Why?" Rydian questions, and his eyes shoot between us.

I only shake my head, lips parting as I try to come up with an excuse. A reason for why I want him the way I do. Yet nothing surfaces. My heart thunders so loudly in my chest, so loud that it pounds between my ears. Is this really happening?

Perhaps I've grown attached to Ren after what we experienced in Elderheim together. Perhaps it's the way he stares at me when he thinks I'm not looking. Or perhaps I like that his control fractures when he's around me.

"I don't know," I say on a breath.

Another beat of silence passes between us when Rydian sighs.

"Very well," he says, low and sharp, like he'd rather snarl than force it down. He slides his hands from his pockets, eyes lingering on me before fixing on Ren. "Make her beg for it."

He turns for the door, and my heart stops.

"You're not going to watch?" I blurt, unable to slow the racing of my heart—the confusion—as he reaches for the handle.

He pivots, a smile lining his mouth. "I will, just not right now." The door clicks shut.

Heat floods my face, and I blink. But with hardly any time to process, to say even a simple word, Ren stalks forward and captures my mouth with his.

30

The shame and uncertainty I felt moments ago fades as Ren devours me, gathering me into his arms by the backs of my thighs. Like all that worry was for nothing—a complete and utter waste of time.

Instead, I crave his touch, melting and surrendering as he hauls me closer on a hungry groan. I fight for breath, lungs burning, heart racing with excitement. Within moments, I seize his tunic, tearing it off and tossing it aside. Hard muscle flexes beneath my hands like something dangerous and forbidden.

Though I can hardly process anything as the chamber compresses and time disappears entirely. My lips part, granting him deeper access; and the taste of him…

Gods, he tastes like rain. Not the crisp chill of autumn showers, but that of summer. Warm and inviting and wild.

Heat of desire surges through me, tangling with the magic roiling beneath my skin, humming and dancing as he sets me on the table.

His arm sweeps out, sending my lunch clattering to the floor, but my legs stay locked around his waist. One hand threads through my hair; the other pries my thighs loose. I shouldn't want this—shouldn't crave the way his touch burns me.

Yet I arch into him, gasping as he eases the robe from my shoulders, letting it pool on the table. Then I'm bare, trembling with want.

Our mouths break apart, only for him to sear a path down my throat, devouring my breast before dragging back up again. My head spins, dizzy from the reckless hunger of his mouth, as if he's starving and can't decide where to begin.

What the fuck is happening?

"We shouldn't do this," I say between breaths.

Perhaps we should stop... whatever this is. If I open this door with Ren, I fear I'll only want it to continue. Nothing but a mess of confusion clouds my thoughts.

"Yes... we should," he growls then pulls back. "The king has been too gentle with you."

His mouth clamps the crook of my neck, teeth sinking hard enough to draw blood. A flare of pain ignites behind my eyes as I fist his hair and wrench him back.

"That fucking hurt," I hiss.

He only chuckles, low and devious, then yanks me to the edge of the table by my knees and forcefully pushes them apart. My legs fly open as he seizes a fistful of my hair, jerking my head back.

"Good." A small smile. "Pain and pleasure are practically the same thing. You'll be begging me for more in a minute."

His mouth claims mine in a brutal kiss, sharp and forceful. His teeth catch my lip, and I gasp when iron and heat coat my tongue before taking me deeper.

Then a roaring, primal, unrelenting need tears through me—so fierce it feels as if I've been overtaken by someone else entirely. Unrecognizable. Raw and wild.

I claw for more, my nails raking down his chest, and his groan vibrates against me, guttural and utterly desperate. The intensity burns, sparking a need that spreads far beyond my mouth.

My desire engulfs me like wild flames searching the forest, destroying everything in their wake. His hands trace up my thighs, and I roll into his touch, desperate to soothe the ache he's stirred.

Knowing that if he grazed me there, he'd find the slickness pooling between my legs.

He brushes over my center—feather-light, agonizingly fleeting—then withdraws, continuing the movement over and over. Teeth rake down my neck, and it's only when I'm bucking into him, a growl tearing from my throat, that he finally presses where I need him the most.

He chuckles again and his thumb swirls, pressing, and then repeats—once, twice, three times. I moan and stars shoot across my vision, pleasure consuming me, coiling low with a sudden quickness.

Then he drops to his knees.

A breathy hum rumbles up his throat and he pins me with an arm, holding my hips as his head settles between my thighs. He hooks my leg, the heel of my other foot bracing against his shoulder. Gray eyes find mine from beneath his brows, and then he grins.

"Already trembling?" He drags his tongue up my center and then swirls it over my clit. "I've hardly even touched you." My chest heaves and I release a very loud, quite embarrassing sound.

Fuck, fuck, fuck.

Another whimper escapes me as his tongue drags up again. Even as my thighs tremble, even as his tongue swirls, I can't look away—mesmerized by the way his head works between my legs. I'm utterly trapped in his snare, writhing for more. *Damn him.*

He spreads me wider, his mouth consuming me—swirling, licking, nibbling. Breathy moans escape in tattered bursts as my hips grind against him, moving on their own, riding and rolling and chasing the edge of my release.

"Make the king jealous and come for me." Ren slides into my thoughts and my brows pinch.

Without warning, two of his fingers slowly push inside me, stretching my opening, curling before picking up speed. He withdraws then pounds into me, repeating twice more. Tingling heat barrels down my center, my clit already swelling—way too fast. Way too fucking fast. He flicks his tongue again.

Forceful.

Intentional.

A shocked cry tears from my throat, unable to process the quickness of my climax. A menacing smirk lifts the corner of his mouth.

"What the fuck," I breathe.

"If you're good for me, I'll give you a little more," Ren grumbles and stands, towering as he works the laces on his pants, his cock straining against it.

My pulse skyrockets, core tightening for more as I watch him pull the last lace. Watch the muscle shift beneath his skin, veins and corded tendons glimmering with sweat in the light of my chamber. Blood pounds in my ears, my chest heaving as I stare at him.

Gods, he's beautiful.

Yet for a moment, I want that shame and guilt to rise because I know I shouldn't want this. But they aren't there, and I don't quite understand why.

Ren's brows lower, but I loosen a breath and tug him to me, my hands roaming across his skin. His eyes flutter for a moment, chest heaving when my mouth travels along his stomach, nibbling and licking, tasting the salt on his skin. He draws in a long breath, muscle flexing as if the mere feel of me is his undoing.

Then, he locks his eyes on me, staring down his nose. But I avert my eyes, forcing myself to stare at the wall. I'm too afraid to decipher what blazes down—something primal and hungry. He reaches out and forces me to look at him, his mouth hovering over mine.

"Once I sink myself into you, I won't be able to stop..." The words come out in a heady rasp, but a war plays out on his face—emotions he doesn't typically reveal. "I need you to tell me that's what you want."

He skims my face when I release a heavy breath. Still, I can't find a reason to say no. I only grin, saying nothing, and work his pants down, reaching between us to grip his cock when it juts out.

My gods, he's huge.

He groans, pushing against my hand as I squeeze, stroking the length of him. His abs work, his breaths ragged and heavy, and I run my thumb over him.

"Fuck," he says, and then smirks. "Do you think of me when you're with him?"

"When he's inside me?" I ask with a tight squeeze and he groans with pleasure. My own teasing smile tilts my lips. "No."

He snatches a fistful of my hair, yanking my head back with a grin. "Wrong answer."

Pleasure builds in the pain of his grip, my body tightening with something wild as I hold his gaze. His eyes narrow.

"Join us next time," I say with a breathless chuckle. "Maybe I'll say your name."

"I'm about to make you scream my fucking name." He releases my hair, grips my jaw, and then lines himself up. His cock brushes my entrance, his other hand hooking my leg high on his waist. "Look at me when I bury myself. I want to watch the breath leave your lungs."

Then he pushes his hips forward, unhurried and intentional. I let out a small, gasping cry at the feel of him slowly stretching me, and a smirk curls his lips. "Bet he doesn't feel like that does he?"

Words fail me when he begins to move, forcing me to take in a shuddering, panting breath. Two painful strokes and my sharp gasps hit the air, my chest frantically rising against him. Then he rams into me, and I have to claw at him to remain steady.

"Fuck... oh, gods."

"Who's name will you be screaming again?" he pants, his eyes momentarily squeezing shut.

"Yours," I say on an exhale. Another ram.

The table shudders beneath us, scraping against the floor, drowning out the crackle of wood burning in the hearth. Drowning out my cries that tangle with his wild groans, the air thick with our sweat.

I want to push him away, but each thrust drags a breathy cry from my lips. Whimpered, desperate cries that don't sound like mine as my pleasure builds. As he drives deeper and deeper.

My body arches for more when he withdraws, almost entirely, before slamming back in.

His forehead drops to mine, breaths ragged and feral when he snaps into motion, hips driving into me with brutal force. Something so delicious it has my body tensing, nerves burning as he buries every inch of his cock inside me.

Then he lifts my leg by my knee and sinks himself deeper. His hand wraps around my throat, holding me steady.

"You look so beautiful when you cry," he grunts then drags his tongue up the side of my face.

It's then that I realize the moisture running down my cheek, my shock now mingling with the heat of my pleasure. He teases my clit with his thumb, barely touching until I'm writhing and crying out again, my hips bucking off the table.

"That's it," he breathes. "How badly do you want to come?"

"I... I want to come." Another cry.

"Beg for it," he says, pounding into me. "Use that pretty mouth for something useful other than teasing me when you know you shouldn't." His thumb halts its movement.

"I want it... please... Please, I want to come."

"Again," he murmurs, and his teeth scrape my jaw, the sharpness sending a shiver of heat barreling through me. My murmured, desperate pleas brush the air when his thumb begins moving once more—swirling, pressing, teasing until it's unbearable.

"Please, Ren..." Pressure builds, my release winding tight and low, my body trembling in his grasp when he chuckles.

"So greedy." Then he presses his thumb down, and I explode, climaxing so hard that stars fill my vision.

So hard that another shocked cry escapes, his name on my lips as he drives into me with a hard thrust. I clamp down, my core tightening around him.

He seizes my mouth, wild and needy, groaning against me the moment his release takes over. He spills himself, his body shuddering with pleasure, and slowly eases his pace.

Even as the high of our climax settles, even as we slow our breaths, he kisses me. Unwilling to let go. He deepens our kiss and his hand settles below my ear, the other wrapped tightly around my waist. I relax into him, exhaling as if what we did was the most normal thing. *Familiar*.

The word echoes in my thoughts, and the feeling of this…

My brows pinch in confusion when his tongue lazily sweeps over mine—tender and sweet and drawn out. The way a lover would give someone they missed.

It makes my breath catch, and I pull back, blinking up at him. The heat of him still clings to me, but it curdles as a jolt of adrenaline floods my veins, heart racing with realization so hard that I nearly choke.

A fleeting flash of memory. His eyes meet mine for a breath, a look of knowing written across his face.

A flicker of raw guilt.

I glance down, my eyes focusing on the arms trapping me between him and the table, unable to decipher if it's only my imagination. Confused between what is real, and what is not.

His mouth still hovers over mine when I lift my eyes again, studying his features. Studying the gray eyes I'm all too familiar with. He exhales, slow and steady—stifling his emotions.

He's stifling his fucking emotions.

"We used to be more than friends," I blurt, the whispered words slipping from me before I can stop them. My heart races. "Real or a dream?"

He steps back, pulling himself from me when his jaw tightens. He says nothing. I jolt upright, reach for my robe and pull it on, hurriedly tying it at the waist. Still, my eyes never leave him as shock shoots through me, and I'm unable to breathe.

Yet a thousand words play across his face.

A thousand wordless thoughts that make the air die in my lungs. Fear and worry course through me, my pulse climbing higher and higher as I register at what he refuses to say. Disbelief floods me.

We used to do this, we used to—

"Real or a dream?" I repeat, more urgently this time. He quickly pulls his clothes back on, the silence between us stretching, thick and unbearable.

"Ren," I clip—one last plea as he turns for the door. His hand freezes on the handle, hesitating. He half turns, lips parting as if he were going to explain. Then the air shifts, and a familiar presence enters the chamber.

"We need to leave soon," Rydian says.

My eyes snap to the edge of the bed, catching the tightness of Rydian's jaw even though he appears steady and unshaken. As if he can't feel the uncertainty rippling through me—can't feel the whirl of confusion and anger tumbling around in my thoughts.

Within a moment, I swallow the rising emotions, too worried Rydian might question me for answers I can't give him. I face Ren once more, waiting for *something*. Anything. But not even a whisper grazes my thoughts.

Ren exhales a long breath, shoulders rigid, and slips from the chamber without another word. Even if he didn't reply to the question I was too afraid to ask outright, I fear I already know the answer.

But why didn't he tell me?

31

A dull throb beats beneath my skin, my ears ringing with nothing but frustration. I recline in Ekrin's chair, hands behind my head, boots propped on his disgustingly organized desk in his study.

Only waiting for him isn't the only reason fury tightens my chest, as hurt and confusion and questions sit beside it. Many, many questions.

Ones I desperately need the answers to.

My teeth grind, knowing we need to finish this task before I can demand answers from Ren, which I'll be doing as soon as we leave. We haven't spoken since we left Aurelia, leaving me more annoyed. So I swallow my emotions and focus on what we came here to do.

Yet waiting for Ekrin is like watching a candle burn down to nothing but wick—slow and a waste of time. But finally, after thirty minutes, the sound of his shoes crunching on gravel brushes the air through the cracked window.

"Took him long enough," Wayd gripes.

The group waits in the shadows across from the door, hidden in the Veil, while I sit in plain sight. Flames flicker in the fireplace on the right, only bright enough to allow a view of our surroundings.

His study is not as big as Cassivene's library, but still large. The fire reflects off the polished wooden floors, warm and earthy. Or perhaps that's just from the abundance of greenery—vines drape from beams and potted plants grace every ledge, including the hanging plants above the arched window behind us.

An Herb Weavers' wet dream.

His study is the first place he'll go because I left a nice message at the door ensuring he would.

I grin when the estate door slams shut, practically shaking the walls. A slew of curses echo up the stairs, followed by the unmistakable scrape of fingernails against the floor.

Most likely, Ekrin gathering the carefully dispersed documents of the eligible ladies within the realm that I left carefully spread across the floor. Or perhaps it was because of the single word I took the time to scrawl across each one, damning them altogether: *denied.*

No need for those if he never marries.

A dark, menacing laugh floats up the stairs, his shoes angrily pounding against the steps. My smile widens when the door swings open, and with a quick flick of my wrist, my new dagger slices through the air—right toward his face.

The blade hisses before it connects with the door frame, imbedding into the wood with a loud thud mere inches from his face.

He stills in the doorway, glances at the dagger, and then slides his eyes to me. He shakes his head with a low chuckle, his neat black hair rustling with the movement.

"I'd love to say I'm surprised," Ekrin drawls as he neatly puts his hair back into place. "But I'm not."

After stepping into Elderheim, my shadows have dulled, replaced by the heat of my first home. I almost forgot how it felt to have warmth seeping into my fingers, thrumming beneath my skin.

With sharpened focus, I use Rydian's training to yank the blade free, light pouring from me like extra hands. I snatch it from the air as it hovers and secure it to my thigh.

"Hello Sensa," Ekrin says quietly, his pale green eyes dialing in on my boots crossed atop his desk. "Or should I say, Isayara. Heir of both realms."

I grin. "Did you miss me?"

"Did I miss you?" He lets out a dry laugh and walks to the center before stopping and tilting his head to the side. He squints. "I knew you'd come crawling back sooner or later."

Rydian's fury rises at the edge of my temples, forcing me to hold back a wince.

Ekrin scans the room before looking at me again, his hands sliding into his pockets. "Where are they, Isa? I know you're not alone."

"And how would you know that?"

"Because I know you wouldn't leave without your... shadows. Or at least, they'd never let you go alone. Not after what happened at that dinner." As if I could forget.

A smirk rises on my lips as they all step out of the Veil. I rise, walking around the desk, and lean against it, arms folding.

"Ekrin," Rydian says, low and smooth, settling on my right while Ren stands on my left. I clench my fists at Ren's approach, unable to stifle the shiver of awareness down my back.

Wayd and Kaeda remain casually propped against the bookshelves near the mantel—Wayd with a boot on the bottom shelf. Ekrin eyes his boot, awfully close to what appears to be old books, and scowls. His gaze pans to Rydian.

"Nice to see you again, Your Majesty," Ekrin says almost mockingly, and a slow grin raises the corners of his mouth.

Rydian only smirks, cold and unfriendly. Ekrin pours himself a glass of wine near the far left wall. The glass cork clinks against the neck as he seals it shut.

Ekrin's gaze meets mine.

"Just think of all we could have created together." He sighs dramatically, and I almost roll my eyes. "I'm quite disappointed you accepted his proposal, if that was a proposal at all... not that you had a choice, per se. But I bet you would have chosen me if you had. It would have been the wiser choice, don't you think?" He sips his wine, a gleam of amusement shining in his eyes.

A genuine laugh slips from me. Not because he's right, but because of how wrong he is. His brows lower a fraction, either mesmerized or annoyed. Likely both.

My voice dips. "Why would I choose a duke when I can marry a king?"

Rydian's approval pulses through, a soft caress in my thoughts. I can't help the straightening of my spine, or the flicker of warmth pebbling my skin from his wordless praise.

Ekrin chuckles. "You could have made me your king."

"That's the last thing the realm needs, another male with a power trip. I think I'll pass," I say.

"Your loss, but I can understand why you'd want them..." He shrugs, an underlying meaning in his tone, and my eyes narrow. He sets the glass down and assesses everyone in the room. "Why are you here, Isa?"

"I think you already know why we're here," I say. "Why haven't you helped Elion?"

"You know why and I won't help him." His head shakes. "*That* is something I will never do."

Wayd and Kaeda inch toward the door, blocking the exit. They separate from each other only to crowd forward on either side of Ekrin—far enough away, but close enough to ensure he doesn't run.

"You could help *us*," I say. "What if I told you we have no intention of ever giving him the Veilstone? We need to find it before he does. We both know the destruction he'd cause."

"And what's in it for me? I'm already risking my life talking to you, and if he were to track this back to me, I'd be hanged from the nearest post."

"How about not dying, *right now*?" Rydian asks cooly. "Considering I've already allowed you to extend your marriage proposal to my *mate*. You and I both know how we males can get... territorial. Especially with a fresh claim."

My heart stops but Ekrin just grins—the kind of grin that tells me he really enjoys stirring trouble. He glances at me for a heartbeat before subtly scanning the room once more. He steps to the side, backing up so that Wayd and Kaeda remain in his view.

At this moment, I'm thoroughly impressed at how Rydian hasn't lashed out and strangled him. Unfortunately, we really need this to work, and I fear Ekrin will continue to refuse us.

"I wouldn't be able to do it without a Seer," he says finally, "considering what I know."

"Don't worry, we have one," Kaeda purrs, tilting her head as she inches forward. "We made sure to get one before even coming here."

Which is true. Rydian found Bess when we Veiled in earlier, asking if she'd be willing to help. She, of course, was not happy about it, but her loyalty to Aurelia trumped whatever grievance she had towards working with a duke. Though Bess told Rydian that as long as it didn't take her away from the brothel too much, she'd do it.

His eyes narrow. "If King Elion finds out—"

"He won't," Wayd interrupts, crowding him, but I hold up a hand to halt his steps.

Ekrin sighs. "There's no guarantee that this *stone* even exists, or that any of my experiments would work. I'm the last Herb Weaver who would be able to track it—*technically*." He holds up a finger. "But I have no experience other than what little information I received from my parents before they died."

"And King Elion has no knowledge of your parents' abilities or your lineage?" Ren asks, eyes narrowing.

"He knows of my lineage, not of our ability to track the stone," Ekrin explains. "If he did, I'm sure he would have spared them, regardless of being Shadovar sympathizers. His waging a battle against Aurelia was the very reason they didn't offer. They had high hopes after the treaty was set in place, but Elion ruined that pretty quick."

"But you could do it?" Ren asks.

"I'm saying I could *try*; there's no guarantee it'll work."

His response is enough for me to send Wayd for Bess with a nod. He vanishes into the Veil.

Both of them appear half a second later. As if instinctual, Bess's eyes find mine and I give her a small, knowing smile. I haven't seen her since we left for Aurelia.

Her straight brown hair falls in curtains around her face, down to her breasts, and she wears an emerald tunic that compliments her eyes. It's tucked into loose, baggy pants, but the way she holds herself is still so mesmerizing.

Ekrin gives Bess a slow once-over, practically drooling. If someone like him was capable of that. His eyes crinkle with admiration, lips slowly tilting into a menacing curve.

"And who are you?" Ekrin asks, eyeing her as if they were alone. I have half a mind to smack him, but Bess remains utterly unamused.

"Don't bother, I like females," she says coldly, then crosses her arms. But I know she's not exclusive to females, she just prefers them… like I once did.

Ekrin's brows rise. "Do you?"

"That's Bess, your Seer," I say. "She owns The Painted Bird. And I can assure you, she likes females. Don't waste your time."

Ekrin's breathy laugh is somewhere between utter amusement and pure mischief. He strokes his jaw, glancing between Bess and me. His gaze finds Rydian.

"Have you ever thought about a threesome, King?" Ekrin asks. Rydian growls, hands clenching but then Ekrin's eyes shoot to mine. "Or in your case, four?"

My stomach sinks, dread coursing through me for a heartbeat at what he's implying, but I force myself to control it—I don't want Rydian sensing my unease.

Does Ekrin know about both of my marks?

Rydian's fury slams into me so hard I almost choke and clamp my jaw shut. Fury prickles my skin, and I throw Ekrin a warning glare. I might end up killing the Herb Weaver before we can use him.

"Not interested in sharing, Your Majesty?" Ekrin chuckles. "It's not uncommon. In fact, lots of mates are shared. Especially in rites and brothels. I'm sure Bess could tell you all about it."

A jolt of awareness crawls up my spine, as if I can feel Rydian's shadows rising beneath his own skin. His anger pounds against my temples. But then I feel it—ice.

Ice cold fury.

It's the sudden tranquility you feel right before snapping, shattering whatever control you had just minutes ago. He's quiet, his expression made of lethal composure.

The twins haven't cracked a single remark, eyeing each other warily. They return their focus to Ekrin, tense and unmoving, but Wayd subtly shifts—his hand pressing against Bess, guiding her behind him. A quiet, instinctual move, as if shielding her from whatever is about to unfold.

Well that's not good—not if Wayd is pushing her aside.

"Not unless you want your head rolling on the floor," Rydian says with a calmness that has the hair rising on my arms.

Ekrin huffs in disbelief, as if he can't read a room. "Then you'll be disappointed to know that she's—"

I spring forward, and Ren's boots thud angrily behind me, but Rydian meets Ekrin in two strides. His hand snaps out and grips Ekrin by his tunic, bringing him to his face with a low snarl. Ekrin's feet come off the ground, his eyes wide with fear.

"I know who she's been with and all you're doing right now is pissing me off. The only reason you're still breathing is because you're the last damned Herb Weaver who can help," Rydian snaps. "Now are you going to help us or not? It would be wise to agree."

At this point, I'm not quite sure Ekrin could make this any worse than he already has. Still, I wouldn't put it past him to try. With his life in Rydian's hands—quite literally—I know he'll say yes if he has any sort of self-preservation left in his body.

Ekrin pales, and I glance over my shoulder to find Ren stifling a grin. Anger and confusion flood me when he meets my gaze, and a small smile tilts his lips.

I face forward, releasing a slow breath.

Though Rydian didn't seem to notice in his fury. Ekrin dangles like a helpless puppet in his grasp before giving a shaky, frightened nod.

Rydian drops him to the ground with a hard thud and he stumbles back. Ekrin huffs and flattens his tunic with both hands, pretending as if his life wasn't in danger just now.

"Yes, fine. I'll help," Ekrin gets out, though his hands tremble slightly. "Follow me and I can show you where I work."

We quickly file out, following him across the second floor as he leads us to the back of the estate. Unlike his study, the rest of the manor is made of fine, black marble floors with textured walls.

Plants and vines hang from the ceiling, inching their way toward the enormous skylight above, as if searching for the sun. Potted plants rest on tables and shelves, hardly leaving room for anything else. The faint scent of crushed herbs and a hint of sage mingles in the air.

But directly in the middle of his estate is an enormous tree climbing up each floor—three in total—and through the roof, as if the estate was built around it. Leaves brush my arm as we walk past, condensation clinging to many of them.

"He talks too much." Ren slides into my mind, and I throw him an annoyed glance. I'm not in the mood to talk, even if my heart slams against my ribs at the sound of his voice.

I ignore him as Ekrin leads us through two arched glass doors and onto an enclosed bridge. It's separated from the rest of his estate, entering what looks to be a grand Herb Weaver's greenhouse.

Definitely a greenhouse for a duke in Alvonia.

It rises higher than the estate itself, held together by an intricate domed glass ceiling with walls made of windows in every shape and size. But those windows are just as fine and intricate as everything else here, including the dark floors and gold detailing.

Even though the greenhouse is filled with plants, trees, potions, salves and vines, it's organized. As if he knows where each item is according to how he's arranged the wooden shelves and tables throughout the room. A fountain trickles in the air near the back.

We all halt at a long table, the surface covered in ingredients. I can almost taste the bitterness of the crushed herbs that fill a series of neatly stacked bowls at the end of the table.

"In order for me to begin my research and test theories, I need as much knowledge about the stone as possible," Ekrin explains then looks at Bess. "Once I gather everything and begin creating elixirs, I should be able to create something for Bess that enhances her vision capabilities. They will help narrow down its location. But like I said before, it's possible that this might not even work."

"Tell us what you need and we'll make it happen," Rydian clips, likely still annoyed from earlier. Though his hand gently grips the base of my neck—a small gesture but a claiming one—sending a shiver down my spine.

"I need whatever information you have regarding the stone," Ekrin says. "I have Herb Weaver tomes, but none about the ancient artifact. If I can discover where it originated, then maybe I can dial in on the herbs I'll need. The herbs themselves will be next—from both Aurelia and Elderheim. Some of the tracking herbs I might need to use are usually found in the north."

Rydian nods, his eyes fixed on the ceiling, as if calculating. He strokes his jaw.

"*What?*" I ask, glancing up.

"*Do you think he'll offer information about what Elion's planning?*" Rydian asks. "*The informant I have isn't that close to the council. He's... quite a ways away actually.*"

I shrug. "*Couldn't hurt to ask. He's already helping, how much worse could it get for him?*"

Rydian's warm amusement brushes against my mind before his gaze shifts back to Ekrin.

"What can you tell us about Elion?" Rydian asks. The air shifts as a heavy silence settles between us, thick and unyielding. Ekrin narrows his eyes.

"You're already helping us; what's a little more?" Rydian taunts, and it takes every ounce of my control not to laugh.

Ekrin sighs, his shoulders drooping. "I do have some information. We were told that they tracked down more Siphons. I'm not sure how many, but Elion needed more of them to create his... weapons."

"What?" I breathe, unease washing over me.

"Gods," Bess says in disbelief.

More Siphons? How is that possible? Unless there are more popping up in the realm. If they're as young as Theo, it worries me. Guilt tightens my chest at the thought, knowing we're the reason he's there. I swallow as Theo's flash of hurt and betrayal in the council chamber enters my mind.

"We're working on it." Rydian gives me a gentle squeeze, as if sensing where my thoughts have led me. *"That's about as much as I can tell you."*

I release a quiet sigh. Still, I think about Elion's plans—something I'm clueless about. Why would he need more weapons when I'm already scouring Aurelia to find this stone? It sours my stomach, but I'm curious to know what type of legion King Elion wields.

"If they're tracking more Siphons, we need to warn Milena." Bess wrings her hands together, worry etched into her features.

I pivot toward Rydian. "I agree. We need to send someone—get her from the Whispering Woods before they find her, or at the very least, give her a warning. Could she stay at the castle?"

Her ward should protect her from Elion, but still, I worry if she's out there with only Grim and Nisha. Rydian nods, his gaze softening before he turns back to the group.

"Wayd, go get the tome Cassivene gave us. While you're there, I want you to inform Ivy and Orin of what we learned. Kaeda, go with Bess to warn Milena, and if she wants, bring her to the castle."

Within a moment, they all vanish into the Veil, leaving me with Ekrin, Rydian, and Ren. An awkward tension hangs between us, the kind that has my hair rising and my fingers twitching for a blade.

Habit, perhaps.

Only the faint hum of the chandeliers and the faint trickle of water dripping off the fountain near the back break the silence. Ekrin crosses his arms and smirks as he leans against his work table. Smug and written with mischief.

His eyes slide to me as Ren steps to my left.

Ren's arm grazes mine, something that sends warm heat up my shoulder. I stiffen, fighting the urge to release a strained exhale. Ekrin sees it though—our closeness—and narrows in on that tiny little touch between us.

"You know, none of this will matter if she's still sworn to Elion," Ekrin says casually. "If you don't truly plan on giving him the stone, perhaps you need to figure out how to break that oath first. Now that you've gotten so close to finding it, he's bound to ask questions."

My stomach drops, dread crawling up my spine at the truth in his words. Elion will ask those questions the moment he calls for me. I only assume Ekrin is mentioning it now because he's caught in the middle—an attempt to save his own ass.

But hearing the oath on Ekrin's tongue has me holding back a snarl, my lip curling in annoyance at him spewing what he'd told me over two weeks ago. It's not that I didn't want to tell Rydian, I just hadn't found a way to, and now it looks like I've been intentionally hiding it.

A lingering, painful silence settles. A silence so long that it has me rubbing the inside of my wrist.

"What do you mean?" Rydian asks finally, as if he couldn't help his own curiosity.

My breathing stalls and my lips part as I fear what his answer is going to be. The air grows warmer, and a hint of something electric hangs in the air as we wait for his reply.

Ekrin only shrugs. "As I told Isa before, an existing blood oath to a mate can break that *blood* oath to Elion."

Adrenaline and fury flood my veins all at once as Rydian swivels his gaze toward me. For a brief moment, his own hurt and anger brush my mind before he stifles it.

An explanation forms on my tongue, but my blood crawls, twisting and spreading from my chest to my arms. I fight the urge to wince as Elion's oath prickles my blood at the mere thought of discussing it with Rydian. And so I face Ekrin with a tight jaw, as if I'm talking to him and not Rydian.

"We don't even know if that would work or not," I bite out with malice. I'd hate for Rydian to think I withheld the information because I don't want to complete the claiming, which isn't the case. "I thought you were lying, that's why I didn't say anything."

Ekrin smiles wide, huffing out a laugh, and for a moment I consider killing him. Consider ripping his head off his squared shoulders to place it in one of those potted plants hanging from the ceiling. If we didn't need him, I would have already done it.

Rydian faces Ekrin again, his jaw tight. He lets out a strained sigh. "We'll complete the ceremony when we get back to Aurelia."

"Tell me why we need him again?" Ren growls, posture rigid beside me. Our eyes lock momentarily before he turns back to Ekrin. His hands curl into fists, trembling slightly.

"You misheard me," Ekrin mumbles, and blood pounds in my ears. "An *existing* blood oath. Why complete the ritual when she's already mated and claimed?"

"To me," Rydian clips in annoyance, though his stare blazes a warning.

Ekrin tilts his head, as if listening to Rydian in the Veil, and then laughs, rubbing a hand over his jaw.

His eyes bounce between all three of us.

"Trust me, she knows who she's mated to, and it's not you, Your Majesty," Ekrin says.

Rydian stiffens beside me, his own breaths halting. He remains utterly motionless.

"She even smells like him," Ekrin says. "I can only assume it's because of the essence she got back. Now that it's growing, her claim to him has only been getting stronger. Quite amazing what a claim can do to someone's power, even when it's been stifled for years, apparently."

"What?" I exhale, my eyes widening.

Rydian's head snaps to me before he glances at Ren, his teeth baring as his composure frays. "What the fuck is he talking about?"

"Interesting that you don't know," Ekrin says on a dramatic sigh, casually pacing the long table of herbs. "Her claim to you hasn't been completed by a blood oath *yet*... but his has." He looks at Ren. "Hasn't it, Isa? Which means you can break that oath to Elion whenever you want."

Ekrin's words slam into me, sharp and painful, stealing the breath from my lungs. It's not possible. Ren wouldn't keep that—

He stiffens, his jaw clenching as if those very words were spoken in truth. My mind whirls so fast, I'm left dizzy, stumbling as if I'd been slapped.

Disbelief mixes with the memory of him kissing me in my chamber—the familiarity of it. Only I thought we had just been tangled in something a little more than friendship, not that he was my second mate. Not that we were *mated*.

He knew for years, and he kept it from me? How many years exactly? How long have I been missing my memories?

"You lied to me," Rydian growls—not at me, but at Ren.

Heat burns my skin, and I snap my eyes to Rydian, fury and disbelief tangling with the ache in my chest. At the terrifying sense that I've been betrayed by not one, but by both of them.

Rydian knew who my second mate was? How long has *he* known? They had the time to discuss it and they said nothing?

"Did you know?" I breathe.

Ren widens his stance, eyeing Rydian across the room, and tilts his head to the side. Then he smirks.

Rydian ignores me, growling. His face twists with anger as he stalks toward Ren. His raging fury pounds behind my eyes so fiercely, my breath stalls, lungs constricting, chest tightening. I suddenly find it hard to breathe.

Ekrin's grin widens, his eyes fixed on me as if this were another day for him.

"Has she claimed you?" Rydian snarls, shadows pooling in his palms, power unrestrained. "You lied to me—you told me the claim was never made, which was the only reason I let it happen."

"It was the only way it was going to work," Ren says finally, a menacing smirk pulling at his mouth. "I suppose that makes *you* her lover instead of me."

The only way *it* was going to work? What does he mean?

I exhale sharply, eyes wide and frozen with shock. Everything comes tumbling down at once, and Rydian's control fractures entirely. He throws his shadows, aiming for Ren's neck.

Only Ren anticipates the move and jolts to the side. Then the floor cracks beneath our feet, and I stumble back. *What the fuck?*

I glance at the trembling walls, the rattling windows, plants toppling over and shattering around us. Stone Shaper power. The very power I wielded in that ballroom, only it's... heightened.

A rift splits right down the middle of Ekrin's greenhouse with an ear piercing crack. Windows shatter, and shards of glass rain down on the floor. Ekrin groans, catching himself on the table, his narrowed eyes aimed at me as if he didn't just cause this.

In seconds, Ren twirls two black short swords, ripped straight from the estate's marble floor. Swords that glow with the golden power consuming his entire body, flooding down his arms and engulfing his blades.

Power that Stone Shapers do not wield.

My power.

32

The air cracks, raising the hair on my arms as Rydian lashes, shadows thrusting from his palms with a darkness so consuming, it swallows the light.

Only, Ren dodges every blow, effortlessly avoiding Rydian's darkness with the whirl of his blades. A blur of movement, even I can't track.

I've never seen him move so fast, as if he were an entirely different being. Otherworldly. Certainly not the same male who was trapped in Rydian's grasp all those weeks ago in Nymara.

Ren is powerful.

I blink, and what knowledge I have of melded essences and mate claimings tumbles through my thoughts—along with the memory of Witt and Elion siphoning my essence in the dungeon.

Of our power combining. Growing.

A completed claiming, Ekrin had said. *We* had already claimed each other, Ren and I. When had that happened?

Disbelief whirls in my stomach, but before it can consume me, my fury rises. Blood pounds in my ears so loudly that the noise around me muffles. My face grows hot, my narrowed eyes now focused on Ekrin whose lips flatten in annoyance.

Annoyance at the destruction *he* had caused.

And in that moment, everything comes crashing down, clawing at my chest like a beast eager to tear out the throat of its enemy.

The secrets. The betrayals. Theo. My mother. My anger and heartache and pain and the time I lost. All of it. But most of all, it was the way my mating to Ren had been exposed—by Ekrin of all people—that sent my anger over the edge.

It just... consumes me.

Before I can comprehend the power surging through my blood, I lash out with whips of golden light and yank Ekrin to me. His throat collides with my hand, jolting us back, and I squeeze until the veins in his neck bulge from the pressure. I snarl in his face.

He gasps, clawing at his neck with bulging eyes. His lips turn purple. My eyes glaze over, darkness creeping in at the edges as my chest constricts.

"You need me," Ekrin croaks, thrashing in my hold. "It needed to happen. It was bound to come out, anyway. It's the only way, trust me."

His words only fuel my rage, and I throw my fist into his nose with a sickening crack—breaking. He crumples, landing on his back. Blood drenches his tunic as he frantically crawls away.

In seconds, I'm straddling him, my fist raining down over and over and over. A scream tears from my throat, my fist hot with rage. I punch—once, twice... I lose count as my bloodied knuckles scream in defiance, my teeth baring in feral urgency.

I continue until someone's arm wraps tightly around my middle and drags me away, my feet kicking to be let down. I'm unable to stifle it any longer—like something unknown and wild took over my body.

But I lose my grip on Ekrin.

He lies on his back, blood marking every inch of his face, his chest heaving with quick, panted breaths. He groans, and lifts a shaky hand to his face—to his split lip, swollen eyes and broken nose.

Kaeda peers over him, a smile on her lips.

"As satisfying as this is, cousin, you can't kill him." Wayd chuckles in my ear.

I thrash wildly, realizing now that it's Wayd who holds me. With a growl, my blood-lust takes over, and my head connects with his nose. He grunts in pain, but his grip only tightens.

Then Ren is in front of me, his brow set in sheer determination. Unharmed from fighting. His hand fiercely grips my jaw, forcing my gaze up. I pant in his grasp and angrily skim over his features.

"Let her go," Ren demands softly, his eyes fixed on me.

Wayd carefully releases me from his hold.

"Breathe, Isa."

It's then that I feel the tangle of his thoughts in mine. The caress of affection he holds so deeply for me, reaching out in a gentle graze to calm the fury in my chest.

For a brief, flickering moment, it works.

Then I see—*feel*—the thick wall of stone he's crafted in his mind. The same wall that kept me from feeling his emotions for the last few weeks as our essences grew together. But there's a crack in it, right down the middle.

Like the ache he endures is so painful that sometimes, despite his effort, those emotions spill from that fractured center. The very emotions I feel along the base of my neck.

The ones I often confuse with Rydian's.

Rage burns through me at the realization, and I create a wall of my own, slamming it down in my mind as I tear my face from his grasp.

"You fucking lied to me. Both of you," I snarl, and look at Rydian off to the side.

Rydian winces as if I had physically struck him, and shoves a hand through his mussed locks.

I scan the room—the destruction caused by utter chaos and the people in it. Or the people not in it. Bess sniffles off to the side, Kaeda squeezing her shoulder. Ekrin manages to sit, bracing his back against the broken work table behind him and heaves a breath. Rydian's jaw is set, still furious apparently, but at least they aren't fighting.

"Where's Milena?" I ask.

"She wasn't there," Kaeda says, and my stomach drops. "There wasn't any sign of a fight, but her home was destroyed, like they were searching for something. We think she fled."

The entire ground shakes, interrupting my reply, when a loud boom sunders the air. I stumble forward and extend my arms for balance.

"What was that?" Rydian demands, the question aimed at Ren who only scans the room in confusion.

It came from outside.

"We have more important things to worry about than your *mate claims*," Ekrin says with a ragged breath, and we all swivel our gazes to the bloody Herb Weaver on the floor.

"What do you mean?" Rydian asks, stalking toward him.

"I fear Elion has already begun," Ekrin sighs and then pinches his bloodied nose. "Those crystals he's used to siphon essences... He's created explosions of sorts. You need to leave."

Another boom.

"Is he destroying Alvonia?" I ask.

"I told you." Ekrin glances up. "He's looking for Siphons. It's their... new interrogation tactic."

A breath of disbelief leaves me.

Instead of demanding more answers, I throw myself into the Veil, away from the estate and onto the steps outside overlooking the city. From the swell of Mount Ravenrock, Alvonia comes into light below, fires glowing on the western side.

A cold wind bites at my eyes, with such a force it whips my cloak back. Screams pierce the air, muffled and drowned out by the wind, mingling with the sparks rising in the sky.

"We have to do something," I say the moment Rydian steps out of the Veil, appearing on my left. No one else seemed to follow. "We're going down there."

"No," he clips.

Clenching my fists, I snap toward him. "I don't think you're in the position to tell me no right now. We're going down there, and we're going to help the people of Alvonia."

"While I agree..." He exhales slowly. "*You* can't go down there.

If you do, Elion's legion or whoever is there will see you. I'll take the others with me to investigate."

"I can shift."

"No," he bites out.

I laugh, shaking my head in disbelief.

The wind howls, whipping my braid around as I lift my gaze to the moon—shining down on me like a silent witness. Almost mocking, as if warning me of an impending storm. Everything feels like it's seconds from unraveling, crashing down on me in a way I wouldn't be able to stop, regardless of how hard I might try.

"How long have you known about Ren?" I ask finally, my anger surfacing like a ravenous beast. "Weeks? Months? Anything else you want to add while we're here, because I seem to be the only one who didn't know about *that*."

"Since you arrived in Aurelia," he admits.

"And you didn't think to tell me?"

"Technically, I did tell you. I said I knew about it," he says quietly. "But as I told you before, it's risky to mess with fate. The most I could do was hope you'd be able to figure it out. And a few other reasons, but you'll have to talk to Ren about that."

"That's not enough," I hiss, storming over to him. "You're using that as an excuse. You knew, Rydian, and you said nothing."

Another wave of realization swoops over me, knowing now why he never seemed to be truly angry about Ren watching us. Understanding why he suggested that Ren join at one point. It was because he was my other mate. My stomach sours.

"Neither did he," Rydian mumbles, staring down his nose.

The words settle between us, and at this moment, I'm not quite sure what to feel. What to believe as I stare into the eyes of my mate while Alvonia burns below us.

His quiet fury rises, and that's when I feel his emotions stirring like a storm beneath the surface. The amount of pain I feel pounding against my temples takes my breath away, but it's not just pain; it's agony and devastation and torment.

"You hate this, don't you?" I get out, recalling how many times he'd mentioned that he already had me. That he had no worries because of the claim we had on each other.

But... we never completed it.

A short, breathless laugh escapes him, edged with disbelief as he inhales sharply. His hands curl into fists, his expression hardening when he faces the city below, lips pressing into a thin line.

Silence hangs heavy between us, with only the wild wind filling the space. And then his gaze skims the city below, like he's searching for something—anything—to explain how this is possible.

"It doesn't matter how I feel," he says with his back to me, heaving a long sigh. "Fate has already marked you."

My stomach drops, fearing what our future holds when the others finally join us. I turn as Wayd, Kaeda, and Ren stride forward, their boots crunching against the gravel. Darkness shadows their features. Ren ties a black scarf at his neck before slipping it over his nose, as if preparing to step into Alvonia's flames, and eyes the destruction. An orange glow sparkles in his eyes; a reflection of the chaos.

"Am I supposed to just wait for all of you then?" I growl and face Rydian, grinding my teeth.

"Yes. We'll meet you at the castle," Rydian says with finality. He walks past me, head shaking, and then says, "Ren, you're with me."

I narrow my eyes. "If Ren goes, *I'm* going. I won't be left behind like some *princess*."

Rydian whirls to face me. "That's what you are. Do you forget why you're here? I've already lost you *twice* over my failure—I will not have a repeat of that battle. And if *Witt* is there—"

"That wasn't your fault—"

"Yes," His lip curls, and he takes a single step toward me, "it was, and I take full responsibility for not protecting my king and queen—their *princess* when I should have."

I blink, caught off guard by his words. His guilt. His fear of losing me. Raw and unrestrained as if a thin layer of fabric had lifted from his kingly control. Before I can manage a reply, Ren's boots thud behind me. Rydian's eyes shift to Ren behind me and the air plummets. I stiffen, my breath faltering.

"She goes," Ren says. "You may know her as the missing princess, but she's a trained weapon. It would be wise to bring the strongest one you have in case of an ambush."

For a moment, I think they might start fighting again as Rydian's gaze locks behind me and a hardness settles over his features. A look of pure authority. Then his eyes shoot to me, his expression unreadable.

"Fine," he clips. "Wayd, get Ivy and Orin. Tell them to prepare the Menders should we bring any injured people back."

Clearly frustrated, Rydian walks off. I go to follow when my elbow is tugged back. Fury tightens my chest, and I spin around, snarling inches from Ren. The crackle of Alvonia's burning embers mingles with my rage.

"You owe me answers," I growl, my hands shaking. "And I expect you to answer them all."

"I know," he says gruffly and releases me.

He extends a black scarf, similar to the one he has slipped over his nose. I snatch it and turn away, sharp and angry, to follow Rydian toward destruction as everyone arrives.

We Veil to the western edge.

Alvonia's outskirts—shops and homes mostly—are already consumed by flames. Like Elion's warriors were burning the places they had finished questioning. The ones who didn't give them the answers they wanted.

I adjust my mask as people scramble through the streets, screaming and reaching for their children. Even as darkness looms over us, the flames paint the sky in shades of orange and crimson and destruction.

Screams split the air, and buildings crumble. Some Elderheim Fae attempt to put out the fires, channeling water from the nearby fountains through their palms. Though it's not enough as the buildings burn—stone and glass shattering to the ground.

Ivy and Orin come with five extras, the group small enough not to be noticed but large enough to help where it's needed.

"We'll go east," Ivy says. "Take the injured to Vyria."

Everyone nods and takes off into the burning city.

"Follow me," Rydian says, disappearing in the wave of black smoke swallowing the street ahead.

I palm my daggers, and Ren follows close behind as we make our way down the street, our cloaks billowing in the harsh wind. Adrenaline floods me, and my heart pounds as we sprint toward nearby screams.

A warrior chases down a mother with her child secured to her hip. She trips, stumbling toward the ground. The warrior raises his weapons, and Rydian's shadows whip out, flinging the warrior's swords in the opposite direction.

Ren draws both his swords mid-run, twirling them before cutting down a warrior on his right. He swipes, dancing with deadly rhythm as more warriors rise from the nearby smoke. A single swipe cuts one down—another rises on his left, aiming for Ren's shoulder.

My stomach sinks.

The dagger in my palm flies before his sword falls. The warrior's head snaps back just as Ren glances at me. I know just from his eyes that he's grinning beneath his mask. Grinning through the chaos. I reach the downed warrior and yank the dagger free as Ren takes down another warrior with a low, breathless laugh.

Then we're sprinting toward Rydian, taking out the warriors trailing behind us. Rydian's distracted with another attack as I help the frightened mother, grabbing the child from her. They're both covered in soot with burn wounds marring their flesh.

"Can you walk?" I shout and she nods. I get her to the end of the street, where others wait to be taken back to Vyria with Ivy and Orin. All burned, dirty, and broken.

I glance behind me to check for more, but no one shows. My spine straightens, breaths speeding up. I've lost sight of both Rydian and Ren in the chaos.

A sudden tug pulls me toward the edge of the city and I push my way down the cobblestone street. Buildings crack, the heat of the flames splintering the stone as if it were nothing more than brittle parchment.

My heart falters as a small group of children tumble out of a falling building. They stumble, covering their faces with frightened cries as they prepare for debris to crush them.

A shocked cry burns the walls of my throat, and instinct takes over as my magic lashes out. My palms fly forward, a flash of golden light breaking the air. I hold the crumbling walls up with nothing but the light pouring from me. Sweat trickles down my temples, my arms trembling with strain, teeth grinding as the seconds tick by.

Smoke thickens the air, smothering the street and leaving me gasping for air as my control slips. When the last child makes it out, I let go, and the stone crashes to the ground. Children, Fae and humans, yell their thanks and run past.

Smoke billows out, choking the narrow streets as the flames lick the sky. Coughing and gasping, I squint in an attempt to see through the haze and stride down the street in search of others. I peer through broken windows when Rydian and Ren force their way through the debris.

"Get the kids to the castle," Rydian shouts as they approach.

"Ivy and Kaeda can do it," I reply, but the sound of the buildings collapsing around us drowns me out.

I glance at Ren, but he only nods.

"Rydian's right. There are thirty more headed this way." Ren glances over his shoulder, his words muffled behind his mask. "We won't be much longer."

Another explosion sounds ahead of us. The ground quakes, and a few more buildings lose their walls, tumbling onto the path ahead. I turn and hold Rydian's gaze a moment longer, his eyes blurred by the lingering smoke. Against my better judgement and instinct to stay, I nod.

"Wait for me at the castle walls," Rydian demands, and moves past with Ren. But before I can stop myself, my hand shoots out. Despite our earlier argument, worry consumes me.

"Come back to me," I say.

Rydian smiles and steps toward me, tugging my mask down to capture my mouth with his. "They can't kill me, remember?"

He disappears beyond the smoke a second later.

Then Ren's eyes meet mine, something unspoken gleaming beneath his mask before he turns to follow Rydian into the destruction.

"You too," I blurt, and he halts with his back to me. Silence lingers for a moment, but I don't move, not even as the flames dance toward us. I wait.

"I'll see what I can do," he says gruffly, and follows Rydian into the fray without another word.

I huff but turn for the end of the street, dodging the falling debris. I jump over fallen stone, bolting toward the children at the end. Fire spreads, the heat unbearable as I hold back a cough, my lungs aching. A soot-stained wall fractures beside me, and I jump sideways as it crashes to the ground, missing my shoulder by inches.

Kaeda, Wayd, and Ivy come into view, gathering women and children to take to the castle. I break through the smoke and yank off my mask, welcoming the cool breeze from the mountain with a sharp inhale. I follow Kaeda's lead and nestle a few children in my arms as we whirl into the Veil, arriving in Aurelia within seconds. Shadow Menders swarm us outside the castle walls, some dropping to their knees to tend to the children.

"Did we get enough out?" I cough, as Kaeda sets a few children down and urges them toward the back entrance.

"Yes, we saved who we could. I'm going back, wait here. They'll come to you," Kaeda says and vanishes.

Another Mender rushes to our side, though that does little to settle the unease swirling in my chest—at the thought of leaving my mates in Elderheim.

"You'll want the smoke cleared from your lungs," a Mender says and I glance at her. With warm brown hair and amber eyes much like my own, she gives me a soft smile.

I nod even though my chest heaves, everything from the last

hour settling like a heavy weight. Like I've lost all sensibility to breathe.

Or perhaps that's the black smoke coating my lungs.

Regardless, I search the castle grounds for Rydian and Ren as the minutes go by. Without a word, the Mender grasps my hands, her shadows caressing my arms in a cool embrace, settling beneath my skin.

"This might hurt a little," she warns, her voice calm yet firm.

The Healers from Elderheim use light magic instead of darkness like the Shadow Menders. They typically cause pain as their shadows heal from the inside out.

I nod at her and a beat later, fire erupts in my lungs—a searing, white-hot burn that claws at my chest, scraping the smoke out. A sharp inhale forces its way past my lips, and my breath stalls, my vision blurring.

The pain quickly recedes, unraveling like a loosened knot. My chest expands, and my lungs feel as if I never inhaled smoke at all. Energy is pushed back into my body, revitalizing me in seconds.

The Mender shifts her attention to the whimpering children nearby, and I turn away. My spine straightens as I scan my surroundings once more, but they're not here.

After a few minutes, Rydian and Ren finally step through the Veil. I sigh in relief and break into a run just as Ren drops what appears to be a captured warrior with a thud to the ground.

Then something shifts in his steps, and he stumbles.

I skid to a stop, my braid whipping around, my lips parting on an rough exhale. He pivots toward me, and the blade lodged deep in his ribs come into view.

Ren's eyes lock on me as he sways, and he releases a muffled groan, wincing when his hand instinctively flies to the wound. As if he could somehow stop the blood flowing beneath his fingers.

My heart slams against my ribs when he struggles to keep his eyes open, a flicker of something unspoken crossing his features.

An apology perhaps.

Then Rydian lunges to catch Ren as he falls to his knees.

33

The air in my lungs burns as I sprint, gravel spraying as I catch Ren beneath his shoulder. The weight of him is almost too much to bear, and my knees scream in pain. But I steady myself, my chest heaving when he presses his hand against the wound.

He groans, panted breaths grazing my ear as iron infiltrates my senses. Blood soaks my tunic—*his* blood.

"Don't touch it," I clip, swatting his hand from the blade.

"I'm okay," he pants. "A flesh wound."

Rydian pivots, barking orders to a few nearby guards. Something about taking the captive down to the dungeon, though his words are nothing but muffled whispers to me. Blood pounds in my ears.

"Where do we take him?" I glance at Rydian.

Without a word, Rydian touches both of us and we land inside a darkened infirmary lined with beds. Warm light cascades from golden sconces, glimmering on stone walls. Menders rush for linens, their feet pattering against the shiny marble.

We set Ren on the nearest bed, his face paling with each passing second. Covered in soot, a dark line runs across his face where his mask sat on his nose.

"What happened?" I clip, guiding him to lie on his back.

He continues to pale, his face draining entirely of color. His breath rattles, his chest struggling to rise as he forces another inhale. I glance at the saturating bed, a dark crimson seeping into the fibers before dripping to the floor in unrestrained splatters.

Ren's lips part, his breaths now slowing.

"Look at me." I grip his face, forcing his gray eyes up. They meet mine in a stubborn hold, a clench to his jaw. "Don't fucking die—do you hear me, brute?"

He gives a feeble smirk; the only indication he heard me before going unconscious. The Menders rush to the bed, and Rydian tugs on my arm, forcing me to take slow, deliberate steps back.

They remove his weapons, cutting his tunic down the front and around the embedded blade, revealing the wound on his right side. The rush of his blood isn't slowing.

Shadows cascade from the Menders' arms before they yank the blade buried deep in his ribs. Blood spurts, pouring in ribbons as he helplessly lies there. Then shadows dart forward, shooting beneath the skin, writhing and twisting as they mend from the inside out.

Ren's eyes fly open and he bellows, teeth bared, the sound feral as darkness invades his wound. His back arches as he thrashes in their hold, hard enough that the ground shudders beneath us. His head lolls.

Unconscious again.

Nausea twists in my stomach, bile burning the back of my throat as I clamp my hand over it, but I can't look away. My chest presses in until my lungs stall with a suffocating weight that squeezes so tightly, it feels as if my ribs might crack.

If he dies, it's over. All of it.

None of this matters.

A searing fury washes over me, so hot it steals my air. So hot that I lose sense of my reality, and my vision blurs.

The thought of losing him burns hotter than any amount of grief, and all I see is fire behind my eyes. Flames of a future where the realms are torn apart. The skies split open until I drown them in crimson, raining down on every living being.

I'd drown them in their own fucking blood.

And they would burn until nothing remained but ruin and petrified screams. Flames upon flames. They would beg me for mercy, beg for their lives, and I would give them *none*.

Heat ignites my palms, sudden and violent at the thought, and I flex my fingers. Molten warmth prickles my skin, threatening to explode. Power writhes there, clawing to be unleashed while I stand frozen, watching Ren lie broken and lifeless. Staring at the life that's tethered to mine.

"Isa," Rydian says behind me. "He'll be okay. They will not let him die, I promise."

When I don't reply, he steps in front of me, blocking my view of the bed. Everything is blurry and black swarms my vision. I blink, attempting to slow my breaths, but my chest tightens with an ache I can't stop.

It's unbearable—the pain.

Like my soul is splitting, my skin burning and peeling, my bones shattering—cleaving me from this realm as I watch a piece of me die on a bed. And I can't fucking fix it.

I sob and a gasp slips free as I search for air. It tangles in my throat. My hands claw at my chest as if I'm being pulled under water, unable to staunch the flow of heartache pouring from me.

I can't—

I can't breathe.

I can't—

My face snaps up. Rydian tightly grips my chin, forcing me to look at him.

"Isa," he says calmly. So calm that, for a moment, it pulls me from my panic. My anger. The ache in my chest. "Ren will be fine, do you hear me?"

"Ye—yes," I choke out, and tears roll down my cheeks. He holds my gaze for a moment, searching my eyes when another sob escapes me.

Rydian pinches his brows, his chest heaving as if trying to block out the intensity of my emotions. His eyes squeeze shut, then he exhales, his fingers tightening on my face.

Finally, he opens his eyes. "Breathe. I need you to take a deep breath and listen to me. They will not let him die, but I need you to ground yourself. Find your control. Do it now."

I choke before I'm able to successfully drag one in. Then another. Closing my eyes, I focus on finding the bottom—grounding myself to the power that floods my veins. Another minute goes by before I'm able to speak.

"What happened?" I rasp, hands trembling.

"We were fighting a few warriors when they swarmed us. One of them lunged with a dagger. Unfortunately, it hit him just right. They were doing anything they could to prevent us from capturing that male we brought back," he says.

I glance at Ren again, unconscious but breathing. At least he's breathing.

"I need to check on the victims in Vyria to ensure the council is getting them set up properly. Why don't you come with me?"

"I need to stay," I say quietly, my voice hollow with terror. He gently tugs my face up again, holding my gaze.

"Will you be okay by yourself? I need to know you won't level the castle if I leave."

I nod.

"Then why don't you sit. They'll mend the wound, but he'll be sleeping for a while. I'll make sure Lettie checks in and brings food." He hesitates a moment, then murmurs, "I love you."

I echo the words back and he leans down, kissing my forehead before vanishing in the Veil.

At some point, Lettie brings me food and a change of clothes even though I'm not hungry. But her blue eyes fill with worry, and she tells me to bathe, urging me to use the chamber in the infirmary. I assume it's because of how I look and smell from the fires as dirt and soot paints my features.

Now, my knees nervously bounce beneath me, my lip caught between my teeth as I wait for them to finish.

They've managed to seal his wound and strip his clothes along with the sheets. The menders walk off and I watch him sleep from where I sit, minutes passing. There's no sign of blood or soot across his face, but the wound on his ribs is a dark pink.

The chair scrapes back as I rise, and I walk to the edge of the bed. His chest rises and falls in deep, steady breaths, his head tilted slightly. He looks peaceful in sleep, like the torment of his life is nothing but a dream.

They've stripped him bare, save for the thin sheet pulled to his hips. I graze the scar on his shoulder before settling on his chest, his heart thrumming at my fingertips. I exhale and flatten my hand to feel the steady beat of it pounding against my palm—strong and stable—but my eyes snap down, fixed on his bare wrists.

They removed the linen he wore. The linen he used to hide his mate mark, apparently. I grip his left hand and tilt his wrist toward me, revealing the mark he's kept hidden for so long that his skin is paler where the fabric sat.

Tears prick my eyes at the sight of it—the faint, colorless mark shaped into a vine with an intricate center. Its location is distinct on the inside of his wrist, an inch away from the base of his thumb and mirrors my own. A perfect match.

For a brief moment, anger tightens my chest. It was a choice, him not telling me. But beneath the confusion and hurt and anger, I can't help the rising emotions that have been surfacing recently—a raw, deep sense of longing.

A clawing ache surfaces at the thought of Witt torturing me for answers. Then everything in that dungeon comes flooding back, stealing the air from my lungs.

I never told Witt who my mark belonged to.

Yet, the chance of life I gave Ren that day—by not telling Witt—must have caused him an unbearable amount of pain, if what I just experienced is any indication. He had to live with half of himself missing.

After a few long minutes, I finally crawl onto the bed, tuck myself into his side, and listen to the quiet rhythm of his heartbeat. The sound of it pulls me in, my eyes heavy with exhaustion, before sleep blankets my mind.

34

—————

Warmth consumes me, and for a moment, I forget where I am. I blink and fix my gaze on the pale streaks of dawn filtering through the slender windows in the infirmary.

They glimmer off the floors, dancing in rhythm to the swaying trees outside. I inhale the familiar scent of Ren beneath me, and wrap my arm more tightly around his waist.

His own arm sits securely across my back, his hand threading through my hair, holding me in place while his steady breaths stir the loose strands at my temple. I can't find an ounce of embarrassment, not as his chest rises against my cheek. Not as his warmth seeps into me, the only indication of the life he still has.

I close my eyes on an inhale and breathe him in.

Deep and steady, the rhythm of his heartbeat pounds against my ear. I lift my gaze, only to find him staring down at me.

Calm and quiet, Ren's expression is nothing but practiced composure. It's his eyes that tell me more though, and I can't help but wonder what he's thinking.

Silence settles between us. A silence so long, I think he won't say anything as his eyes skim my face.

Then I clench my jaw, a coldness washing over me as I recall him keeping this little piece of information to himself. I know he senses it, because his worry crawls up my neck. Still, he says nothing.

As if waiting for me to snap.

He holds my gaze a moment longer then moves a strand of hair from my face, tucking it behind my ear. I'd find the gesture sweet if it weren't for the heat surging beneath my skin, my heart thrumming with restrained fury.

"Where is everyone?" I ask and glance around. The infirmary is quiet—no one here but the two of us.

"A lot of the victims had severe burns, so they left to tend to the wounded in Vyria. Rydian stopped by earlier with an update. He's in the city," Ren says. "We can meet them there later."

I stiffen against him, my face warming at the thought of Rydian finding me curled up next to Ren. I can't imagine how he felt—can only imagine the fury on his face at the sight of me. Then, that same familiar shame runs down my spine, and my stomach drops as guilt presses in. Guilty for even lying down.

But Rydian knows—he fucking knows what Ren is. My other *mate*. Has known for weeks apparently.

"It's fine," Ren says finally. "He didn't care."

"I find that hard to believe. He definitely fucking cares," I snap, recalling the torrent of emotions I felt from him just last night. I drive my elbow into the mattress in an attempt to rise but his arm tightens, firmly holding me in place.

Before I can growl in protest, he loosens his grip and shifts, turning on his side so that his face lines up with mine. I lie wedged between him and the bed, but I refuse to look at him.

Refuse to stare into the eyes of someone who'd kept this from me, and despite myself, moisture pricks my eyes. Now that everything has settled, I don't even know where to start.

I don't know what to say.

"I'm sorry." His voice comes out rough, leaving me no choice but to meet his gaze. A wrinkle forms between his brows. I let out a rough exhale, shaking my head with anger or disbelief or confusion?

Regardless, my heart cracks as I stare at the pain so clearly etched onto his face. Not the pain from his wound, but from the ache he's buried. The ache he spent years hiding from *me*, apparently. To my surprise, a tear slips down my temple.

I hate that I care. I hate that I can't control it.

"Give me answers," I whisper finally, though my voice cracks. His eyes squeeze shut at the hurt of betrayal in my voice. Then he nods, heaving a breath.

"Ask me."

Thoughts and memories and emotions weave through my mind like a tangled web, leaving me unable to decide on where to start. I know we were friends, but it all remains so... fragmented. Pieces I can't put together fully—flickers of images from one memory, flashes from another. Time melding together.

"How long were we friends?" I ask.

He's quiet for a long moment before saying, "Five years."

Another piece of me fractures a little, and I wonder how often we snuck out. I wonder how often we were together, and what we did during those late-night visits to my chamber. Those nights we'd climb the castle rise to visit Alvonia.

"And our friendship..." I hold his steely gaze. "They never knew we were friends, did they?" He shakes his head, and I swallow. He'd trained me—made me the best—but even then, we'd kept our friendship hidden. It's why my memories are mostly of him sneaking in at night. No one knew.

"Our marks? How old were we?"

He shoves his hair back, eyes dazed. "You were twenty-one. I was twenty-seven."

"How long were we together?"

He hesitates, his lips parting as if he doesn't want to confess, then says, "A month."

A month. The words echo like a returning nightmare in my mind, turning over and over until nothing but tears slide down my temples. We only had a month? Five years of friendship, and we spent only a month of that as mates.

I squeeze my eyes shut, unable to wrap my head around those years we lost. The bitter tang of the truth sours my stomach, twisting with something I can't quite name because I don't recall any of it. Yet one question surfaces—the one I truly don't understand.

"Why did you keep this from me? Why didn't you *tell* me?"

His head dips between us, slowly shaking as if he can't come up with a good enough reason. As if all those years of suffering were enough for him. Then his confession to Silver Tongue runs across my mind—that he failed to protect someone once. What happened on the day Witt took my memories?

His voice drops. "Which answer do you want?"

"The truth, Ren. I want the truth."

"What would I have said to you? You would never have believed me. You hated me that much and this..." Ren trails off, scanning my face, and exhales once more. "Please know that I had no choice."

"No choice?" I bite out.

"You looked at him the same way you looked at me, Isa." His hand brushes my cheek. "I wanted to give you more time before I ruined it. But I also needed to know if you still wanted me, even if you couldn't remember. I needed to know it wasn't something I had imagined."

My eyes squeeze shut again, my chest constricting as my world crumbles and falls together in the span of a heartbeat. I did want him, even when I couldn't understand it.

"We were almost there," he says softly. "We were going to leave together—we were going to slip out without telling anyone."

My body stills, heart racing as his words settle. We were going to leave the Brotherhood? A beat passes between us, my breaths heavy, our silence drawn out in a way that even the realm needs to breathe.

The dungeon enters my mind.

"I didn't know they'd take my memories," I confess. "I didn't know what it would lead to until it was too late." Torment enters his face. "What happened that night? Will you show me? Please, I have to know."

He quickly rises with a huff, and the movement forces me to

follow. A rush of confusion enters my mind at his sudden frustration. I scramble to my feet and stand behind him. Then he faces me with a clenched jaw, gripping the sheet in one hand, using the other to shove his hair back.

"I can't show you."

Rage burns my eyes, my vision blurring as I fight the darkness creeping in. My fingers curl into fists. "Why not?"

Warm streaks of light continue to race along the floors in contrast to the storm brewing beneath my skin at his refusal to show me his memories, even after all this time.

"Because it's not something I want to relive, that's why," he bites out. "Do you think I want to relive the worst day of my life? The most that I can do is tell you what I can about *us*, nothing more. Showing you anything would risk exposing you to things you shouldn't see."

A line he won't cross.

I narrow my eyes and sharply inhale at being left out of more secrets. More things that he refuses to share with me. When will it end?

"What do you mean?" I say slowly, stressing the words.

He growls, as if at war with himself. "You haven't gotten your memories back yet, and you haven't broken that oath to Elion. I can't tell you until then, or it risks Elion knowing things he shouldn't. And I'm telling you now, he doesn't need to know what I know. You're going to have to trust me."

What exactly does he know?

His words only pull my anger to the surface, and I snarl as all of it comes crashing down. The secrets, the lies, him not *telling* me anything for five years.

I close the distance, and before I can hesitate—stop myself from impulsivity—I strike him across the face. His eyes slide to me, and his brows lower. My palm burns from where it struck his cheek.

"After all this time you couldn't tell me? Almost five years, Ren," I hiss, my chest tightening with frustration and hurt and anger. "We lost five fucking years, and you can't show me?"

His hand tightens around the sheet again, and quiet fury crawls up my neck—*his* fury. He says nothing, just stands there and blinks, stifling his rising emotions.

Gods, he's really good at that.

But a frustrated growl leaves me because he's pushing it down. Desperate for a reaction, I hit him again, harder this time, so his face jerks sideways.

A dark, disbelieving chuckle brushes the air, and he steps toward me, grazing my body. My lip curls and I pull my hand back for a third, but he catches my wrist.

"Hit me once and you have my attention," Ren growls, teeth bared. "Hit me twice and you're flirting with me." He leans in, inches from me before he releases my wrist and grips my face, forcing me to look at him.

I stumble, air dying in my lungs as his hungry, blazing stare sears a hole through me.

"Hit me three times and we're fucking."

I stand there, panting in his grasp as I struggle with a decision—push him over the edge or storm out. Despite my anger, a roaring heat courses through my veins as I stare into the eyes of my other mate.

The one I lost so much time with.

The one I had before Rydian stepped into my life. All those feelings I had for Ren years ago flood me, tied to those memories as if they had never left. Even after all this time, I still want him, like my soul refuses to let him go.

But then I yank myself out of his grasp, putting distance between us as fury and pain and a shattered heart consume me. I'm unwilling to let go of what he's kept from me for so long.

After all these years, he just let it happen. Let the history of us fade into nothing while we went on about our lives. While I lived my life without my memories.

If Rydian hadn't stepped into my life, would Ren have said something? Would he have tried again—tried to refresh my memories? A part of me hopes the answer would have been yes, but the other thinks he wouldn't have. I don't know what to believe anymore.

I heave a long breath, smoothing my face into practiced composure. The wall in my mind builds, and slowly, it becomes nothing but a blank slate.

"Do you think fucking me will make this all go away?" I say, iciness coating my tone, and I back away until another bed halts my steps.

His nostrils flare as he holds my gaze. Annoyance and something else flicker across his face—the only evidence that I've struck a nerve.

"I'm only doing what I promised you," he says quietly.

Heart thundering, my world tilts. What does *that* mean?

He sighs and steps forward, face drawn with a wrinkle of sadness. "I made a promise to you, and I swore on that oath—*our* oath. Break your oath with Elion, and you can have every fucking piece of me. My life was always yours, anyway."

"I don't know what that means," I say, my mind drowning in more and more questions. "Did I know—did *you* know—any of this would happen?"

"No, but this was the only way it would work."

Again, that term. "The way *what* would work?"

"*Us.* It was the only way we'd get our chance at freedom." He gives me a small smile, either pained or knowing... so much in that gaze of his. "Will you trust me?"

Trust. The very question I'd asked him weeks ago in my chamber. Such a fickle thing for my heart, yet despite the secrets he keeps, I desperately want to say yes. That even after all this time and the loss of my memory, I still trust him.

Because the fragments from the dungeon and all the others in between only prove how much I cared. That years ago, I sacrificed my memories for his life—something I know I'd do again if it came down to it.

Only now, I fear that whatever happened between us is far bigger than I think. Especially if he's doing his best to keep it from Elion. My stomach sours at the thought.

"I don't know how to break that oath," I admit, swallowing the bile rising in my throat. The uncertainty. "What about my mother and Theo? I can't just... break the oath and not have repercussions."

"I know," he says. "We'll figure it out together."

35

I'm not quite sure how much time has passed, but ravaged by hunger and the excessive use of my power the previous night, I eat what Lettie left for me at the break of dawn.

By the time I finish dressing, strapping my daggers and weaving my hair into a thick braid, Rydian enters with a quiet *whoosh*.

I turn, expecting to find his expression drawn taut, riddled with frustration, but all I see is exhaustion. Dark circles line his eyes, auburn hair strung in all directions, as he gives me a weary smile. One I enjoy and cherish, despite his tiredness.

Regardless, anger crawls into my chest, causing my teeth to grind because of what he's kept from me these last few weeks.

"I know we need to talk, and we will," he says, brows drawing close together. "But I'm not sure I have the energy to argue right now."

"So you want me to just forgive you, is that it? Forget about what you kept from me? Is Varrin even looking into anything?"

His jaw clenches. "He is."

"And what is he looking for exactly?"

"If it's possible to be mated to both of us." He sighs and shakes his head. "But it doesn't matter at this point, because you can, considering you're already mated to him. I'm sorry for not saying something, truly, but it was *his* decision to make, not mine. I know we're mates too, but that's not something I want to encroach on, regardless of how much I hated it."

I scoff, turning away.

Letting go of my anger feels like accepting my current situation —like I'm supposed to just go on knowing I'm mated to both of them. Did they fight over it?

I'm left wondering how Rydian reacted to Ren telling him that— left wondering whether or not he was angry. If they had fought, surely I would have noticed it. Though, when Rydian admitted to knowing about my mark, his emotions had been locked tight.

After a few long minutes, I release a breath and face him. My shoulders droop at the sight. At the desperation in his eyes to shelve our disagreements for now.

"Fine," I admit. "We can argue more later."

He strides closer. "Can I kiss you?"

I nod, and he meets me in the center of the room. His scent envelopes me as he leans in, and his mouth gently caresses mine. For a moment, I get lost in the taste of him.

He pulls back, so his forehead rests against mine. The slow, exhausted sigh he lets out tells me more about what he's feeling than if he were to speak the words out loud.

What do we do now? An answer I wish I had.

I wrap my arms around him, settling my cheek against his chest for a few more minutes. Like we're both unable to let go, trapped in the incessant blur of neverending chaos.

"I came to bring you to Vyria," he says after a moment, pulling back to look at me.

"To help with the infirmary?"

"I was wondering if I could show you the capitol. The council is taking care of the refugees, so they'll be occupied." He gives a sheepish smile. "I have some places I want to show you. I think we need... a breather, after all this."

I blink, caught off guard by the sincerity in his tone. I think that's exactly what we both need, especially after what happened at Ekrin's estate. So much of what's going on has stolen our focus—our time together. We haven't had a single day to ourselves.

Come to think of it... I don't think we've ever had a day that didn't involve a mission or a goal. I'm unsure if the prickle along my skin is because I'm uncomfortably aware of how much leisure I lacked in Elderheim, or the fact that I'm eager to spend time with him.

"All day?" I smile, my pulse racing with excitement.

He leans down, his lips brushing mine in a feather-light kiss, and says, "Yes."

We stand high on a hill overlooking the city below as dawn shimmies across the sea. We gaze down into Vyria. A warm dew collects on the tall grass at our feet, the scent of yesterday's fresh snow coating the air, though most of it has already melted.

From this vantage point, the marketplace comes alive in the distance, a number of people walking around as merchants set out their trinkets beneath tarped stalls. The buildings vary in shape and size, rising in clusters, some low enough for us to view rooftop gardens with winter vines and flowers spilling over the sides.

Distant conversation mingles in the air, a blend of the merchants' calls, laughter, and music. Like every minute, even early morning, is reason enough for celebration. Though the buzz of the lively city gets drowned out by the waves of the ocean crashing against the nearby rocks. Many Fae kneel at the base of Lyora and Faelar's fountain statues in the square, their offerings spread across the stone beside them.

"Is that the wall?" I ask, pointing to where a few Shadow Shapers work near the market ahead. He leans against one of the many trees surrounding us, some as large as the buildings below. The wall lines the perimeter of the city, fifty feet high, half a mile from the shore.

Rydian eyes me before answering.

"Yes. Do you see where they're working currently?" he asks, pointing near the front and I nod. "That's where they're building the portcullis. It will protect the city and keep unwanted guests out."

He then points to the large vertical gate they're shaping for an entrance. Surrounding it are stone walls, tall and thick, built to withstand any threat. Towering battlements line the top but leave space for the guards.

"During the day, the portcullis will be raised to welcome travelers and citizens of Aurelia," he explains. "But in the possibility of a threat, we'll be able to lower it quickly."

"Why is it being built now?"

Rydian steps beside me. "Because King Andre was convinced we would all live peacefully after the war and found no reason to put it up. But now that he's gone…"

"Now we need it," I say quietly, and he nods. "Who will be guarding it?"

"Archers and guards are scheduled to work the wall on alternating shifts, but ultimately, we'll let them choose what works best for them and their families."

I can see why Lettie has such wonderful things to say about her brother—he puts his people first, keeping those inside the walls safe from harm, or should I say, Elderheim. After the destruction of Vyria, I can understand his reasoning for taking extra precautions. After all, a repeat of the destruction caused twenty years ago is the last thing we need.

Rydian pivots, peering down at me with a delicate smile curving the edges of his mouth, much softer than I'm used to, sending his scarred lip shining in the light.

"I would like to show you something," he says quietly.

"Like what?" I ask, my face warming under his gaze. He stays quiet, though, smiling a little wider as we enter the Veil together, vanishing from our moment of peace on the hill.

What was lush, dewy grass and hilltops before is now a cobbled path leading to an enormous shadow-stone estate. Delicate. Pristine. And clearly hundreds of years old.

The dark stone rises high enough to assume that at least two floors are inside, a number of windows rising with it. A porch made of warm, red brick lines the perimeter.

I release a shocked breath. He steps away and grips my hand, pulling me forward. Our boots graze the cobblestones, icy scuffs breaking the air.

"Where are we?" I ask finally, and for some reason, nervousness runs through me.

Lining the path are many pointed bushes, dripping melted snow onto the finely trimmed grass beneath them. It's warmer today. Much warmer than all the other days before it as the sun rises higher and higher.

"My family's estate," he says casually, and I skid to a stop, my face paling. He turns toward me. "What?"

"Family…" I say breathlessly, my entire chest hot with embarrassment. "You want me to meet your family?"

His brows furrow before quickly smoothing out, and a smile spreads on his face. "What's left of them, anyway. You've already met Lettie, what's the difference?"

"I—I…" My eyes narrow.

Now that I'm flustered and annoyed for being so caught off guard, a frustrated growl escapes me. I've never met someone's family before—unless you count the married couples eager to share with me at the brothels. Then Lettie's words surface, her mention of a cousin in Vyria—Zeeke.

"Your cousin lives here," I say, and he nods, reaching for my hand to tug me forward. I reluctantly obey, despite wanting to flee in the opposite direction.

"Yes, he does. He lives here with his wife, Mia. They're both halflings. Zeeke is from my mother's side." He gives me a light squeeze. "They've been pestering me about meeting you since your arrival. They couldn't make it to your celebration, so I told them we'd drop by."

No amount of words can explain how uncomfortable I am, the

feeling wholly unfamiliar. I spent the last twenty years of my life believing I didn't have a home—a family. Forced into isolation. Forced to swallow my emotions. Only now, those emotions seem to be surfacing the longer I'm around Rydian and Ren, and the more I retrieve my memories.

Gods. I hate to admit that it was much easier when I didn't remember anything.

We reach the wide doors with frosted glass, clear enough to view the person striding toward us. As if Rydian had already announced our presence.

The door swings open, and a male appears on the other side. His hand remains on the knob, and a smile warms his face—his features so similar to Rydian that I could have mistaken them for brothers. Only his hair is shades lighter, appearing more blonde than auburn.

"Cousin," Zeeke says lightheartedly, though his eyes shoot to me. Then a female appears beside him, small and petite. Her hair cascades down in smooth, tawny waves.

She bows, her face splitting into a wide grin. "King Rydian, you didn't tell us how beautiful your mate is. I'm Mia."

"That," Rydian says casually, placing his hand along my back, "was something you had to see for yourself. Can't spoil everything."

"Isa," I say in greeting, unable to stifle my own smile as they both step aside, allowing us entrance.

We step into the grand estate, a mix of dark stone and wood lining the floors. Spiced apples and something heady mingles in the air, sending a jolt of excitement across my skin. A feeling I didn't quite expect.

Portraits of Zeeke and Mia holding two young children decorate the walls, and near those are delicate oil paintings of Rydian, Lettie, and two individuals I've never seen. His parents, perhaps, given that they all look very similar.

"We are so excited to have you," Mia says with a rush of enthusiasm, her hazel eyes bright and eager. "Please, follow us."

Mia takes Zeeke's arm as they walk down the corridor, leading us to a large circular sitting area. Long, dark settees rest in the center, a grand piano on one end, shelves of imported wines and whiskeys on the other. Above all that is a glorious mezzanine, lining the upper half of the room, with a set of stairs to our left.

"Would you like anything to drink?" Zeeke asks, gesturing to the settees as a maiden drifts in, bows, then clasps her hands behind her back.

"Tea," I reply, sitting beside Rydian.

Just as the maiden leaves, an older male walks in and skids to a stop, eyeing the both of us. Blonde and appearing in his fifties, the male clenches his jaw and grumbles something under his breath, clearly unhappy. Still, he remains frozen in the wide entryway, eyes locked on Rydian in a fierce glare. Zeeke groans a little, eyes flashing.

"Are you going to bow, Uncle?" Rydian says, his tone a mixture of cold sarcasm and kingly authority as he leans back. He rests his elbows on the back of the settee, his legs spread wide and his lips melting into a menacing grin.

Mia sighs, entering my thoughts as she sits across from me. *"Zeeke's father, Aran. We told him you were both coming today. Not sure why he has to make a spectacle of it."*

Aran's eyes narrow before he hastily bows. He grumbles once more as he exits. Rydian huffs, tilting his head when Zeeke meets his gaze—speaking in the Veil.

"They don't get along?" I ask, and she shakes her head.

"Rydian's mother, Alora, died because of what Rydian's father did many years ago—something Aran still hasn't gotten over. He was very close with his sister," Mia explains. *"Even though Rydian was a young child at the time, Aran places blame on him."*

Questions surface on the tip of my tongue, but before I can muster a single one, Rydian fixes his attention on us once more. Tea arrives and we spend the better part of the morning talking.

After a while, both of their children come sprinting in, running to Mia first and then Zeeke. Perhaps seven and eight summers old, both with hair similar to Mia's.

"Cece, Moira," Zeeke says, leaning forward with his arms

wrapped around their middles. "This is Isa, King Rydian's mate and our future queen. They are here to visit."

My stomach dips at the title, and my face flushes. Regardless, they both smile, bending into small bows as they collectively mumble their greetings before darting down the corridor.

"Cute, aren't they?" Rydian slides into my head, shooting me a grin. *"They just started their studies not too long ago. I try to ensure they get the best from our scholars."*

"That's important to you?" I ask and he nods.

I'm not sure why it surprises me, but it does. I know Lettie mentioned his fondness for tradition—opening the castle to those in Aurelia to further their studies—but I hadn't expected him to be so centered around his family. Or kids for that matter.

Perhaps there's more to him than I thought.

As morning bleeds to afternoon, the space between my temples pounds relentlessly when we all finally stand. I force myself to steadily inhale, taking everything in.

"I'd love to show you around," Mia suggests, her arm looping Zeeke's.

Rydian shakes his head.

"Thank you, Mia, but I'll give her a tour myself," Rydian says.

She smiles and bows. "Of course. Thank you for visiting."

After they depart, I exhale in relief, and we quietly weave through the halls. I finally glance at the various paintings, large and wide, set with gilded frames. Most are more portraits of Mia and Zeeke, but others are depictions of the realm with a few of Rydian and his family sprinkled in. If his father was responsible for his mother's death, why do they keep the portraits?

I turn to him, my brows furrowing when we round another corner, unable to stifle my rising curiosity. "How did your mother die?"

Rydian hums. "Did Mia mention my father?"

"Maybe," I say.

"She died when Lettie and I were children. But from what I know, she was caught in the middle of my father's... betrayal of

King Malvain. I know nothing beyond that, other than what I was told by Queen Jhessa."

My heart aches. Rydian carries his own haunted past, living in the shadows of his father's mistakes, so much like my own.

"And you weren't raised here after she died?"

He shakes his head. "Aran wouldn't allow it. Thankfully, Queen Jhessa fought on our behalf and allowed us to be raised at the castle. Lettie left when she could; I stayed behind for Andre and joined their legion."

"And your father?..."

"Executed."

"Yet, you keep the paintings." I glance at the walls once more, fixed on the delicate strokes of oil on canvas. Rydian looks like his father with the same dark auburn hair and blue eyes.

We round another corner, our shoes echoing in the empty hall when Rydian opens a door leading outside. Wide steps descend into a vast courtyard, gravel paths webbing toward different areas. Though the one we take opens toward an expanse of trees, some drooping lazily near a lake toward the back of the estate.

He grips my hand, squeezing. "Just because he made mistakes, doesn't mean we can't cherish the life he lived. The preservation of my mother's memory shouldn't be destroyed because of them. I know he loved her though."

I find myself nodding, and we walk in silence, knowing the upcoming conversation we need to have is inevitable. My marks. Ren. And everything that comes with that.

Nervousness coats my insides, fearing what lies ahead as we come to a stop beneath a drooping willow tree, the branches swaying in the breeze. The water ripples in tiny little waves, the air coated in a thick humidity. Tall grass dances at our feet, the gentle breeze hitting my cheeks as we take in the expanse.

Though peaceful, an unnerving sense of realization washes over me—the reasoning behind why Rydian insisted on our quiet, lazy day in Vyria and meeting his family. Something we probably won't be able to do again for a while.

"Why did you bring me here?" I ask finally. "What's the real reason for today?"

He only sighs, head shaking, before rubbing his jaw. The wind catches his hair, blowing it back. "I know you can't talk to me about it, but I can talk to you."

Elion and the oath. My skin prickles at the thought—the seriousness of his tone.

"A war is coming."

My stomach plummets. "What do you mean?"

"What Ire has reported... it's not good." He faces me, jaw tight, but a flutter of his fear throbs in my temples. "His legion is a mix between trained warriors and those... things he's created. Like the Grokees, but also what appears to be Fae—the ones he stole essence from. That's how he's getting those explosives, I think. They're being controlled by slivers of crystal embedded into their flesh."

My mind flashes to our time in the Whispering Woods, when we were attacked by those creatures and injured by their claws. When we were stranded in that cave for a night. Has Elion figured out a way to control them? Nausea curls low in my stomach.

"How soon?" I manage.

"I don't know, but soon, which is why we need to figure out how to break that oath." He hesitates a moment. "...and why I want to complete our claim to each other."

"Is it even possible to complete it?" I sputter, my face warming.

His eyes flash, anger marking his features for a brief second before he smooths his expression. After what we just discovered about Ren and me, I'm not even sure we could do it.

"We've already completed half of it," Rydian says slowly, stressing the words. "We should be able to do it; otherwise, Fate wouldn't have marked you with two."

I swallow, nodding as my chest tightens with uncertainty. A choice I fear I have to make—keep my oath with Elion and save my mother? Or sever it and potentially lose her? Would fully claiming Rydian undo my claim with Ren? Would I have to choose between them?

"What do we do, Rydian? What should I do?" My voice cracks with the weight. "You don't want to—"

"It doesn't matter what I want," he clips. "Fate has marked you, and we can't avoid that."

"What does it matter if Fate has marked me?" I say breathlessly and blink.

"It matters, trust me." He holds my gaze, his lips flattening into a thin line. "Do you not want to complete our claim?"

"I—of course I do, otherwise I wouldn't be here."

He exhales, shoving a hand through his hair.

"Why do you keep asking me that," I ask, "and why are you allowing this? You're angry and clearly want nothing to do with—" I cut myself off, the words dying in my throat as another wave of realization floods me. "Ren told you… didn't he? You know, which is why you aren't stopping it."

He looks at me, his jaw clenching, but remains silent. His silence is answer enough, though. I cross my arms as warmth settles in my palms, my anger rising to a simmering heat. How much does he know?

"Was it worth it? Were the secrets he kept from me all those years necessary? Because I can't find a good enough reason," I snap, though my words are carried away on the breeze.

It's the one question that's been bothering me since I found out about Ren—about why he didn't tell me.

"Yes," is all Rydian says.

I exhale. "And you trust him?"

"As much as I don't want to, yes." He chuckles, the sound dry and unamused. "He's also your mate, Isa. He's *tied* to you in every aspect—do you know what that means?"

I clamp my jaw shut and face the water as I'm unable to reply. Unable to accept the truth of his words. Yes, I know *exactly* what that means, but what can I say? I don't remember any of our time as mates, and the memories I do get back are all so broken.

A rush of confusion enters my chest, my face, my entire being as I stand there. Still, no answer surfaces for why I'm mated to both of them. But apparently, Rydian knows. At least, that's what I believe.

"And because of this *tradition* that you're so fond of..." I say slowly, refusing to look at him as I stare at the delicate reflection along the water. "You won't be stepping in to prevent it."

"I couldn't even if I wanted to." He crowds me, turning me by my shoulders so that I face him. Then he forces my gaze up, his brows pinching—a mirror to the love and pain and confusion creasing my own. "As much as I'd love to have you all for myself, this is not something I can prevent. You care for him—" I open my mouth to reply, but he silences me. "You cannot deny it, because I feel it."

Every inch of my body flushes in an uncomfortable heat, and I'm now acutely aware of the truth in his words... I just don't know what it means for us. What it means for our future.

"I don't understand why I'm feeling it now," I say, my vision blurring as tears prick my eyes. "I don't understand why you won't stop it, even when you hate it."

He only sighs. "Your lack of essence stifled your bond to him— prevented it from growing—so when you got your memories back..." Rydian trails off, the silence stretching, as if he's thinking of the correct thing to say.

Is there a correct thing to say?

Regardless, a breath leaves me. That must have been why Ren was in my chamber after I left Milena's all those weeks ago. He must have felt it, our essences re-joining after I retrieved my memories. His power has been growing since then? *Our power.*

I had silently hoped I was tethered to some unknown person left in Elderheim. I never expected this, not really. I never expected Ren to be that person, and that complicates things.

Rydian looks off for a moment before sliding his eyes back to me, his expression soft. His lips part and then close, as if stumbling over his words, and he releases a heavy exhale.

"In the infirmary, when you thought he was dying? I felt you. I felt how you did towards Ren in that moment, and it was..." He trails off, eyes glazing over as if haunted before squeezing them shut. His voice dips to a whisper. "It almost dropped me to my knees."

Tears collect in my eyes as I relive those moments and how I felt like my entire world was shifting right before my eyes. It was like Rydian wasn't even there and everything I felt for Ren came rushing back, and I couldn't stop it. It was like watching my soul shatter into a million pieces, my breaths stolen from me.

But now I'm really fucking confused about how to navigate my feelings for both of them, and I have no idea what I should do. I don't want them to think I'm choosing one or the other and, at this moment, that's what it feels like.

It feels like I have to choose—Aurelia or Elderheim.

Rydian or Ren.

His voice softens. "I felt your pain, Isa, and it felt like I was losing you—or half of you, anyway."

Tears slip down my cheeks as he watches me.

"I understand it, even though I don't want to. And that pain is not something I'd wish on anyone, and it's not something you can avoid forever. You've already lost too much time."

My brows knit, and I let out a disbelieving laugh with a shake of my head. "You don't want to share, though."

"I never want to share." He offers me a grim smile. "But what I *felt* changed my soul. I don't know how else to describe it—it altered me. I don't want to feel that again, even if that means sharing. It might take a little time, but I know you'll give me all of you, and I just want to say…" He hesitates, and a quiet sob escapes me when he runs a thumb over my cheek. "It's okay, and you're *enough* for me. None of this was ever your fault. You will always have me—*always*. What you have with him is different. I can't give you what Ren does, and he'll never be able to give you what I can. Maybe that's the balance, I don't know." He shrugs, and his eyes skim over me, and I realize he means everything he says.

I attempt to pull away, but he grips my chin, forcing me to look at him. My breath catches when he leans in, hovering over my mouth before devouring me as if it were the first time. He kisses me, cupping the back of my neck, deeply and irrevocably. I grip his tunic, not wanting to let him go, savoring the moment.

"I love you," he declares, his forehead dipping to mine.

"I love you," I say back, even though my thoughts tangle as I try to mentally prepare for everything ahead.

He wraps his arms around me, and together we stand in silence. Listening to the breeze and the lake rustling at our feet, knowing our peace is about to be disrupted in the upcoming months.

Knowing that sooner or later, I will have to break my oath with Elion if it means a better future for our realms. And accepting that I may never get my mother back.

36

"What does it feel like?" Cassivene asks across from me as she curls herself over the table, scribbling notes on parchment. Appearing more scholar than smuggler at the moment. Her golden hair is tied into a loose bun on the top of her head, shiny pieces escaping and falling forward.

Aside from my magical training with Rydian, I've met with Varrin and Cassivene in the archives pretty frequently over the last two weeks for research.

So far, we've learned about the different types of oaths between realms, but today, we're dissecting the one I swore to Elion—something I'm not supposed to be able to talk to outsiders about.

He still hasn't called for me since the last time, and a shiver runs down my spine at the thought. Yet, the prickling sensation has begun to fade, like my claim to Ren is overriding my bond to Elion.

I suppress a shudder, releasing a sigh instead. "Like the magic is crawling. An unpleasant, tingling sensation. And when he tugs on it, I can't... deny the call."

"Compulsion," Cassivene says, and looks at me. "Have you tried grasping it—the bond?"

"No. I'm not even sure how I'd do that." A partial truth, as I've tried to graze it with my magic, if only to stifle that uncomfortable feeling in the morning when I rise. But no luck.

She leans back, bouncing the quill off her chin as she thinks, studying the intricate ceiling in the private back room of the archives. Her eyes drop back to mine.

"It would feel similar to your... mate claims," she says. "Even though Elion has a tie to your essence, he can't feel your emotions and his power can't grow. He's only able to bend you and your magic to his will, *but*—" She stresses the word, leaning forward. "It should feel similar to your mate's claims—like a thread. Could you feel for it?"

"Would he feel it if I did?" I ask warily.

"I'm not sure, actually," she says. "You could graze it for now— test it and see what happens."

My eyes close, and I focus on my tether to Elion with a deafening ring between my ears. A weightlessness consumes me after a moment, similar to how I attach to the Veil, only I sense the oath's presence. That... darkness.

After a few minutes of concentrating on that specific itch beneath my skin, I brush my mind against it. It jolts and slithers back, avoiding my touch entirely. Over and over again, like fingers grasping water, it dissolves, slipping from my hands.

My eyes flutter open at my failure, sweat sliding down my temples, my hands clenched in my lap. I didn't realize I was doing that.

Bess, Ekrin, and Orin walk through the doors just as I unfurl my fingers and wipe my brow. Ekrin halts, his eyes landing on me, before he continues forward with an exhale.

"Your face healed nicely," I say with a cold grin, noticing how smooth and perfect his skin looks. "Can't even tell I broke your nose. Were you able to find a Healer from Elderheim?"

Being a Shadovar sympathizer, it's no surprise that he's here. But Ekrin has avoided me entirely these last few weeks, so this is my first time seeing him since our fight at his estate. Can't say I blame him though; I almost killed him that night. And I would have if Wayd hadn't pulled me off.

Cassivene stifles a smirk, but remains silent. But I catch the way her cheeks warm as Orin's gaze lingers on her. Does he know about their marks yet?

"No success," I say to Cassivene. "The oath—the magic—feels sentient though, like it knows I'm reaching for it."

"It may feel that way," Ekrin says cooly, standing near the doorway. "But he won't be able to realize you're grasping it."

"That's the magic responding to your touch," Orin says.

"No one asked you, duke," I say icily, hating the way he tracks Bess as she rounds the table and bends to greet me with a kiss on the cheek.

"*I wish I had been there for your little tiff,*" Orin stifles a grin, crossing his arms in delight. "*I would have paid a lot of money to see it. I'm thinking me and Wayd should take you to the fighting rings.*"

I roll my eyes. "*I'm sure Rydian would love that.*"

"*Don't be fooled; he'd place a bet.*" Orin chuckles.

"Either way." Cassivene clears her throat, the scratch of her quill breaking the unbearable tension. "It's good information."

Ekrin smiles, smug and unbothered, sliding his hands into his pockets as he leans against the door frame. Gods, he's infuriating.

"*Ekrin's here.*" I push the thought to Rydian, annoyance coating my tone. "*Figured I'd warn you.*"

"*Thanks. I'll do my best not to kill him today. I can't promise anything, though. Actually, I should have just let you kill him that night,*" he says with heavy sarcasm, but the words are strained.

He's been working with the warrior they took from Alvonia in the dungeon for weeks, unable to get any information out of him. I've offered my vision capabilities multiple times, but he's held off, saying I'm a last resort. Regardless, I force back a grin over his humorous words despite what he's currently doing.

Unfortunately for us, we need Ekrin.

Turns out, hardly anyone can tolerate him, save for Bess. She's surprisingly been able to work with him without complaint. Almost like she... enjoys his company. She hasn't said it outright, but I also haven't prodded.

"We're done for the day." Cassivene stacks her notes, placing that quill behind her ear before rising. "I want you to continue grazing the oath until you can successfully hold onto it. That way, when it's time to sever it, you can do so without strain."

My stomach sours at the thought, but I nod to Cassivene then look at Bess. "Any sign of Milena?"

"No." Her brows pinch, sadness creeping into her features. I know she feels guilty for her disappearance. "Wayd and Kaeda are still looking."

"While they find what I need, of course," Ekrin says with a sigh.

"Is there a reason you're here?" I clip, rising from my chair with narrowed eyes.

If Ekrin has left his precious estate with Bess, that means he has something for Rydian—most likely the sleeping tonic Rydian had requested a week ago.

We plan to enter the Veil in our sleep tonight and scout Castle Alvonia while Elion visits his legion—information we have thanks to Ekrin earlier this week.

We're going to look for them; my mother and Theo. I probably shouldn't be going, but my oath to Elion continues to fray. If I can speak to others about it, surely I can weave a few lies the next time I see him, which will be soon.

Knowing that we'll be entering Elderheim tonight has my stomach twisting, but my hatred for Ekrin outweighs the nervousness.

Ekrin eyes my strapped weapons—my daggers in particular.

"You know, normally I'd tell you, but I'm not sure I should," he says with another smug grin. "Given you're still tied to your father."

Does he not learn anything?

My head tilts, a coldness washing over me that chills my very blood. Stabbing Ekrin is beginning to look quite enticing, and my fingers twitch at my sides. Whether he senses my hostility or not is hard to tell, but he slowly inches away from the door and closer to Cassivene.

"*Don't kill Ekrin,*" Rydian says casually, as if sensing my thoughts. "*Ren is headed to you.*"

Heart racing, my pulse effortlessly climbs to my temples, and I quickly forget about Ekrin, bolting for the exit instead. Just because I trust Ren, doesn't mean I need to see him.

Thankfully, he's been spending his time with the legion as Kalde follows him around.

But I've done my best to avoid him for the last few weeks, unable to confront whatever sits between us as more and more memories continue to flood me—in sleep, during my meals, in training. Memories and memories and memories, all of him. All tied to past feelings I can't evade much longer.

They quite literally haunt me.

But just as I reach the wide archive doors, guards open them to reveal Ren striding down the hall, right toward me. I skid to a halt, my pulse beating against my skin, hair flying forward with the movement.

His gaze snaps to me, narrowing the moment I enter the Veil. I linger long enough to catch the tightening of his jaw—the flash of anger marking his face—before I force myself back into my chamber without a word. Cowardly, perhaps, but I can't bring myself to face him just yet. I know too well that once I do, I'll shatter. So for now, the Veil will have to be enough.

"Really?" Ren slides into my head, his tone laced with annoyance. *"Can't avoid me forever, Princess. Or do you prefer wench? Does the name bring back any memories yet?"*

I grind my teeth, knowing he's only doing it to irritate me. It does irritate me, actually. It gets right under my skin and crawls up my neck in an embarrassing flush.

Unfortunately, it brings back quite a few memories of him calling me that name in the Brotherhood. Especially when we were supposed to be hating each other all those years of friendship. Our only shield against Elion.

He'd call me wench, and I'd call him brute.

Looks like some things don't fade entirely when your memories are siphoned, given I still called him that.

I flick out an angry hand to light the hearth across my chamber as the sky bleeds into evening. Dinner rests on my table thanks to

Lettie, the scent of soup and cheese lingering in the air. I'm not hungry. Instead, I pour myself a heavy glass of whiskey, downing it in a single gulp. The glass thuds against the table, my eyes momentarily squeezing shut as warmth settles in my stomach. As my thoughts begin to slow.

A steady breath.

Rydian will be here soon, but either way, I inch toward his chamber and push our adjoining door open. I let out a huff. It's a ridiculous door, if you ask me.

A mirror of my own, his bed rests against the wall across from the door. Yet on that same wall is another doorway—one that leads to his own private archive. Not as big as Elion's, but large enough to hold centuries' worth of information. The same one I saw in his memories so many weeks ago when Ivy confronted him about being king.

I stride toward the door and pause, eyeing the desk near the windows and flick my wrist. Light dances off the sconces, warmth spilling across his desk. His windows peer down into the vale.

Even through the thick, paned glass, waves crash in the distance, pounding against black rock and a shallow shore. With hardly a sound, I walk to his desk, spotting castle plans for expansion resting on the top. My fingers slowly spread the papers, and my face warms. Plans for more chambers along the second floor. Royal chambers, that is.

Then my eyes snag on something beside it, a little wooden box that looks as if it were made for envelopes and seals. Despite myself, I creak it open to find a smaller one inside—a delicate, crimson velvet box the size of my palm. My heart thunders, breath catching in my throat as I reach for it.

"Don't you dare open that," Rydian says, and my hand halts, though his tone is light. Playful. I peer over my shoulder to find him leaning against the doorway with a smug grin.

"Is this what I think it is?"

He strides closer. "Yes. I should have hidden it better. I didn't realize you'd go snooping and immediately find it."

I grin as he settles against my back, his arms wrapping around me before he buries his face in my hair. I stare at my hands, still holding that velvet box, knowing what sits inside—*a ring*. The one he said he'd gotten me weeks ago.

He reaches around, attempting to open it, but my grip tightens and I squeeze it shut.

"Don't," I say breathlessly, turning in his grasp to face him, even though my pulse threatens to betray my calm facade. "I want to be surprised."

He grins and then backs me against the desk, pinning me. "Are you sure? I don't mind showing you. I think it's quite beautiful."

"Yes, I'm sure." Without looking behind me, I place it back inside the wooden box and shut it. My eyes flick down to the papers beside me. "Are you expanding?"

Silence lingers, as if he's gauging my reaction, before a small smile tilts his lips. "Perhaps."

"Then I have a request."

"Is that so?" He arches a brow, his curiosity pulsing at my temples. I push myself onto the desk, and he leans in, his mouth coasting over mine—so close we share the same breaths. Warmth spreads, sending a delicious shiver down my spine.

"Tear down that damn wall separating our chambers," I say, huffing in annoyance. "Who needs two rooms when you're in mine anyway?"

A loud laugh escapes him, but he nods. "Done. Anything else, little fawn?" My heart skips at the name, my entire body melting as he hovers over me.

"Add another chamber," I demand, and he stills, unblinking.

Then something like hope shines in his eyes. I narrow mine, unsure if I like what glimmers in his stare. Regardless, a slow, teasing grin lines my mouth. "Don't get any ideas, King, that's not what I mean. I've drunk every ounce of that contraceptive tea Lettie's given me." I smile, my shoulders rising in a shrug. "But you can't be too prepared. Another chamber would be good."

He exhales, chuckling. "Done. I'll give you seven more rooms if it pleases you."

"Gods, seven? Too many."

My lips curve up, and I lean forward, grazing his mouth in a feather-light kiss. He pushes himself forward to devour me, his lips parting fully, with a low grumble that bubbles up his chest and vibrates against me.

I'll never get over the taste of him—his scent—as oakmoss floods my nostrils, enveloping me in a dizzying caress. He steps forward, and I wrap my legs around his hips. Heat floods me, running down my body when his hands settle on my thighs. But before it can escalate the way I want, he pulls back.

I groan, my eyes flashing in annoyance.

"As much as I want to bend you over this desk and fuck you until your lungs give out…" He laughs light-heartedly and nibbles the inside of my neck.

My eyes flutter, arousal now coating my veins.

"We don't have time for that tonight," he says, and pulls back to peer down at me then scrapes his teeth along my jaw. "We have to leave soon, which is why I brought that sleeping tonic with me."

Another groan. "I know."

Nervousness runs through me at the thought of entering Castle Alvonia again, and I wonder what we'll find. This is the closest we've gotten to discovering where my mother and Theo are being kept. And if they're there, I'm not sure what I'll do.

Will my oath feel stronger once I enter Elderheim and step inside the castle? Will it be easier to grasp onto even if I'm in the Veil? Whatever nerves burn in the pit of my stomach, I hide and let out a breath. I suppose I'll face the issues once as they arise.

"After we take care of that, I'll take you however you want," Rydian says with a slow, devious smirk. "I'd be more than happy to re-decorate my archive just to hear my name on your lips. Are you ready?"

"Let's get it over with, then." I hop off his desk with as much elegance as I can muster, smooth my clothes, and follow him out.

It's going to be a long night.

37

For what feels like the thousandth time, I stand in darkness, staring at Elion's archives from across the moonlit courtyard.

Only now, I remain in the Veil and am unable to open doors or touch things like I normally can, so entering in different sections of the castle is done with intention.

My body hums, tingles spreading across my skin as my head spins. It's been a while since the Veil has enveloped me in sleep, and the sensation feels more chaotic than normal.

Rydian stands beside me while Ivy inspects the guest corridors, looking for Theo.

It's eerily quiet save for the wind howling against the domed ceiling, and the rising conversation of the guards stationed outside the doors—different ones than the last time we'd snuck into the archives to steal the map. I only assume Witt has taken care of the lazy ones since then. He probably slit their throats and replaced them by dawn.

After silently monitoring the guards for a few more minutes, Rydian gives me a firm nod. We whirl from the courtyard and slip into Elion's chamber. Stagnant air hits me, and my nose scrunches in distaste.

Even his chamber is stifling.

Just like last time, his workspace table remains in organized disarray, as if only he knows where each item is among the slew of papers.

And since our bodies remain asleep in a realm across the ocean instead of physically in Elderheim, Elion's ward does not sense us. This time, the door to the archive corridor—the very thing we need access to—is cracked open.

Our eyes meet, and we stride forward, peering into the hall. Dark and empty, we both glance at the center, deciding where we want to go. Another moment, and we Veil right to the spot we focused on. I release a relieved breath even though adrenaline floods my veins.

"From what we saw on the map, once we get to the archive doors, another corridor veers right," Rydian explains. *"We'll enter and inspect it there."*

We had poured ourselves into that stolen map, studying the levels and the entrances before deciding to enter the Veil tonight. A hidden corridor surrounds the perimeter of his archives, looping toward the back. One that's only accessible through his chambers or the archives, apparently. We figured, since there was no chance to re-enter his archives, we could try his chambers instead. Partial success.

"I've inspected the dungeon as well as the remaining corridors," Ivy says, though the sound is made of utter defeat. *"Theo isn't here."*

My chest tightens with guilt. Wherever they're keeping him... it's against his will. Our assumption is that Elion is keeping him somewhere beyond the archives, sealed in one of those hidden chambers. Where my mother could be.

We're so, so close. So close that my skin prickles with unease and excitement all at once. I'm not even sure what I'd say to her if we got her out.

We come to the end of the corridor, and my eyes focus on the single archive door. Somewhere beyond that, two more guards stand posted near the entrance. Rydian peers into the private hall and around the corner. He shakes his head—no guards, just as Kaeda said.

Another exhale.

We turn the corner, quietly walking until we get to an enormous steel door, one that faintly shimmers. Locking runes mark the frame—one, two... at least seven. Intricate designs, meant to keep even the most skilled out. Even me, despite it being my own specialty.

I clench my jaw, holding back an annoyed huff. *"Even if we had the time, I'm not sure I'd be able to get in."*

I know just by looking at them, I'd have to memorize each one and bring them to Ren. Perhaps even Cassivene, if she's familiar. Rydian's gaze meets mine, and a dark fury marks his face. The kind that would have sent me running weeks ago, though his expression still has the hair rising on my arms.

"They're in there," he says with an eerie calm. *"I can feel it."*

Their gazes fall to me, all the council members clad in a variety of flowy yet casual attire. All disrupted from their lazy mornings only for them to gather around this damn council table once more. Gather around this map.

They all stare at me in what appears to be disgust? Uncertainty? Mistrust? Perhaps it doesn't matter, because once Rydian steps beside me, their gazes fall to the table.

A flicker of warm light spills from the arched windows near the back, shimmering across the floor, barely bright enough to be considered morning. I'd rather be asleep right now, too.

"And your plan is to what?" Eldric grumbles, his eyes drooping with exhaustion as he casually waves hand. "Waltz in there and pry open those steel doors?"

I almost scoff. If only they knew.

Yes, it would be quite insane to stroll through those halls and break the runes without some sort of issue. Perhaps we could formulate something more substantial than the last plan we had, or lack of one. *If* I can break that oath.

"That's suicide," Anya says, her words barely above a whisper and laced with a hint of fear. "We've already lost one king and queen, we don't need to lose more."

Mumbled agreements pierce the air, nods quick to follow.

Yet for a brief moment, I focus on Anya and the pain in her voice. Focus on her honeyed brown hair, warm skin, and the haunted grief in her eyes. The space between my brows tingles, warm and inviting. Curious.

I blink, my breath stalling as images flicker across my eyes like something wild. Fleeting and barely there. Still, I catch them... Intentionally or unintentionally?

Memories of my mother through the eyes of Anya caress my thoughts. Lazy afternoons and tea and casual walks around the market when the sun shone the brightest. Flowing dresses and shared experiences. My mother's smile grows wide in a fit of laughter, bright and almost an exact mirror of my own. Dark hair cascades in waves around her face, a glimmer of her blonde Varethin mark shining in the morning light.

A breath tangles in my throat. *Friend*. The term jolts across my mind, and my chest tightens. They were friends.

How long, though? How close were they? Was Anya around when I was born? I release a slow, careful breath and smooth my expression, fighting the sudden tears pricking my eyes.

Within those private thoughts, I felt the grief of her missing friend. Harsh and unpredictable. Like a beloved sister, almost. Anya swallows, eyes fixed on her hands and completely unaware of my mental presence.

Realization sweeps over me at that.

Those were her treasured memories, and I accidentally pulled them without permission. Worry and shame prickles my skin. I skim my eyes over each council member, knowing that I somehow did that. This has happened more than once. How did I do that?

Silence continues to hover, though, and I don't need to glance beside me to know that Rydian remains frustrated with the council. His annoyance gradually rises to a soft thud between my ears, pulling me back to reality.

Granted, they're asking reasonable questions. Ones that need to be asked, because... How exactly are we supposed to waltz in there and pry open those doors? The runes are intricate, more complicated than we imagined they would be.

"I understand your concerns, but we will not be *waltzing* anywhere," Rydian says with an air of authority, his shoulders back. "We will conduct a strategic plan for when Elion calls on Isa."

"So soon?" Rafe scoffs down the table, and my stomach sinks. "And you don't fear she's already been compromised?"

"Our camps have already reported spotting the Aetheri hawks scouting above them." Eldric scratches his long, gray beard, his eyes shooting to me. "They have our locations. That can't be a coincidence."

"We know what they're reporting Eldric," Orin's jaw feathers, arms folded as he stares him down. "And Isa isn't compromised. We've already discussed this."

Regardless of Orin's defense of me, I hold my breath, knowing the accusations are closer to the truth than I care to acknowledge. They might have kneeled for me weeks ago, but it doesn't mean they trust me. Rightly so, I suppose.

Yet they speak as if I'm not even here. Invisible.

"If she's not compromised, that other male surely is." Mikal huffs, his head shaking. "We can't trust him. He shouldn't even be near our legion—not if he remains a captain for Elion. We should have killed him the moment he arrived, or at least placed him in the dungeon."

Despite my current silence with Ren, my lip curls into a sneer as I press my palms into the table before me. If anyone has reason to turn on King Elion and aid our mission, it would be Ren. Elion took everything from him—from me—and they all know that. They know what marks I bear, and what Ren and I endured in Elderheim. Still, they have the audacity to throw around accusations as if we haven't all been working diligently for weeks and *weeks*.

Exhausted doesn't even come close to how I feel, my patience wearing thin the longer I remain tied to that fucking king. And staring at their distaste all morning isn't helping.

"What exactly are you accusing him of?" I growl, so furious that heat floods my palms instead of the coolness of my shadows.

Mikal's spine immediately stiffens, a hint of his fear permeating the air—acrid and stale. The kind of scent that has my nose scrunching, fueling my anger. It's then that I feel Rydian's calming hand on my back, grounding me, forcing me to straighten.

A touch that tells me he understands my frustrations, but also, to calm my fury before it consumes me.

It's then that my eyes collide with Ren who stands frozen in the doorway, as if he'd just witnessed my outburst. Embarrassment seeps into my face and my stomach dips as he quietly strolls through without a word and props himself against one of those intricate black-marbled pillars.

Expressionless, he crosses his arms before shifting his gaze to the council, meeting Mikal's stare with a lifted brow. A quiet challenge.

I didn't realize he was coming today.

"Whether we tear down those doors or patiently wait it out," Ivy says firmly. "A war is coming—it's unavoidable. It's better to have the upper-hand than to be ambushed. We all know that."

"We are not prepared enough," Mikal says, jaw tight with frustration as he leans forward. "Our legion may be large, but with the amount of—" His words grind to a halt and he glares at me. "We need aid. Especially if Elion's legion continues to grow. We cannot fight that and win."

"Don't worry about that right now," Rydian says, rubbing his jaw in thought.

My brows furrow.

Don't worry about it? Another wave of anger rolls through me. Is he really going to force me to agree with Mikal? Last I checked, a well-developed legion is something we desperately need. Especially if we're to plan and win a war.

Either way, I swallow my emotions and remain silent for the duration of the meeting, listening and watching as their bickering rises to a level that sends my head pounding. By mid-morning, everyone is dismissed, and a weary sigh escapes Rydian as he turns to me.

"I'm meeting Ivy and Orin in the dungeon again. We might… need you soon," he says carefully, knowing exactly what he's asking of me. "If he doesn't give us anything today, we'll do it tomorrow. I'll head straight to you after."

I nod, forcing a smile, eager to crawl back into bed as my exhaustion mirrors his. Even though we had slept for the duration of our scouting in Elderheim, it's my mind that's tired. Spinning with what seems to be never-ending planning and uncertainty, tangling with my recovering memories.

As everyone enters the Veil and leaves, Anya remains standing at the end of the table. Her gaze fixes on me.

My heart thunders, recalling everything I'd seen in her memories moments ago and for a brief second, I wonder if she felt me in her thoughts.

I shoot a glance toward Ren who's still perched where he was earlier, arms folded across his chest. He studies me, silent and waiting.

I say nothing, unsure of where to begin even if I wanted to. Even if my heart beats wildly at the sight of him. At the voiceless question in his gaze.

For a moment, I think he's going to approach, but then Anya strides toward me. Another stretched out stare between us, and then he turns, exiting without so much as brushing my thoughts. Unlike yesterday.

Despite myself, a pang of disappointment rolls through me, knowing that sooner or later, I'll have to speak to him. I *should* speak to him. But the thought of breaking our silence has my stomach in knots.

Anya smiles warmly, her eyes crinkling, when she approaches and clasps her hands in front of her petite figure. Her smile is genuine. I never realized how pretty she was until now.

"We're all… frightened," she explains quietly. "It has nothing to do with you, truly. We're just wary of the outcome."

"As I suspected," I say, then decide to ask what I'm truly curious about. "How close were you to my mother?" She stiffens, eyes leaping to mine, as if caught off guard by the question.

"We were pretty close." She sighs, gazing toward the balcony as the wind beats against the glass. "I wasn't... at the castle when it was overrun. I had been sent to Halstra that week. When I arrived a few days later, you and Elynor were already missing."

A beat of silence settles between us, like we both need a moment to breathe. Losing a friend and being unaware of what happened to them, is not something I have experience with. But I know that look she gives me, the underlying emotion there—I've felt it. Longing and grief and raw pain. I felt it in that dungeon.

"Do you miss her?" I ask finally. Her eyes go distant, then soften as she looks back at me.

"Yes. Very, very much." Then her lips part, as if wary, before smiling once more. "She used to take you to the northern plains in the spring, near Zalaryn."

"Really?" I manage, my chest tightening with a familiarity I'm desperate to grasp, even if I can't remember.

Perhaps my soul does, and for some reason, knowing that settles something in me. But there's something about that shared little detail that makes my mother feel... real. Not like a figment of my imagination.

"The wildflowers up north tend to overgrow along the hills—it was her favorite place to visit. I can show you sometime. If you wish."

I swallow the lump rising in my throat, at the sincerity in her tone. Like she'd enjoy showing me. "I'd love that."

38

Later that night, I find myself digging through my mothers items, one thing after another.

Even though Rydian's awake too, I told him it was something I wanted to do by myself and in private. He gave no argument, only kissed my forehead and said he'd see me later.

So now, I sit alone in the archives while the rest of the castle sleeps. An arch of windows extends on every side of me, a fire crackling in the hearth as my fingers reach into the small, compact chest.

Small enough to carry.

As if her entire life was small enough to put into a box.

Journal after journal, it's an endless amount of memories and thoughts. Experiences. Her writing is fluid and delicate, carefully scripted words all laid out in perfect lines across the smooth parchment.

And yet, the more I read, the more I want to talk to her. Discover who she was beyond being a queen and what it was like serving in King Andre's legion before she married. Was it like the Brotherhood, or did she have a particular freedom here?

Freedom. The word beats over and over in my mind.

Did she feel free, or was she always bound by duty similarly to me—to a life where choices were stripped from you, forced into servitude? Or in her case, forced into royal games she didn't want to play? She wasn't noble, but she bore Andre's Varethin.

My fingers brush against something colder than the rest. It scrapes against the parchment, snagging pieces as it sits on the bottom, and I pull out an intricate golden pendant.

I exhale and lean against the settee, staring at the item. Firelight reflects off the surface.

The spherical charm rests in my palm, though it has a shimmering middle wrapped in golden filigree and swirls around as if shards of life consume the center. Yet, one tiny sliver remains untouched by the gold.

I have the urge to press my eye against it, peering in similar to a looking glass. Perhaps it's a matter of instinct, but I bring it up to my face.

Lips parting, I gasp as images run across my eye. I wretch it away and blink a few times, shock flooding me.

Were those... memories? Her memories? It's clearly magical, capable of holding precious moving images in the charm.

I sit staring at my palm for a long moment, shocked and confused, contemplating whether or not I should continue to look inside. Despite my fear and something else I can't quite name, I bring it up to my eye once more and hold my breath.

A flicker of fragmented images race past my vision, clearing into vivid, vibrant pictures, like I'm right there with her. So vivid that sound even brushes my ears. A perfectly encapsulated memory.

My mother peers down at me—perhaps four or five years old— as we walk the bright market of Vyria hand in hand. Merchant chatter and distant waves cut through the air.

Afternoon light spills across the shadow stone, dancing around the merchant tents lining both sides of the street. Contentment fills my mother's chest as she gazes down at me. Genuine joy. A basket filled with fruit and treats hangs heavily off my other shoulder, so I wobble on tiny feet.

"That one!" I squeal, pointing to a large tent.

"I told you, Princess," my mother says, exasperated, "one item and we're leaving, so make your choice count."

"Four." I argue in a small voice, peering up with a ridiculous pout to my lip. A wrinkle forms between my brows.

"One, and I'll take you to see the flowers." Her voice is stern, yet lighthearted, like she knows I'll muster another argument.

I tilt my head, amber eyes squinting in defiance. "Two?"

"Fine, two." She chuckles and lets out a sigh. "We don't have much time until we meet with your father."

"From the other realm?"

Shock barrels through my mother, forcing her to crouch and lean in close. She casts a nervous glance around the busy market before focusing on me with an exhale.

"You cannot say those things here," she whispers, hands lightly gripping my arms. "Others will hear you."

My young brows pinch, dark hair falling in tiny waves over my shoulder. I huff. "But... Why? I seen pictures in your head like that pretty rock. Trees and flowers and...and—"

"Because it's..." Hesitation and nervousness tightens her chest. She sweeps a strand of hair off my face. "People of Aurelia wouldn't understand, darling. And you're not supposed to take memories without permission; it's rude."

Moisture pricks my eyes. "It was accident. I didn't mean—"

"I know. No need to be upset." She grins, her features softening. "Your heart is so big, but I fear it'll get you in trouble in more ways than one. Now let's find something pretty before we leave."

"How pretty?" My face lights up, a grin splitting my face. I quickly forget about my tears.

"Very. I have a feeling you'll like those beautiful pendants over there." She points to a nearby tent, and dangling from the canvas are a slew of sparkling jewels and necklaces. I giggle and take off in an uneven run, my hair whipping in the wind.

Then the memory fades into another one, trees and flowers coming into view. I quickly pull the charm from my face with a racing heart, unable to bring myself to watch another one.

With trembling fingers, I settle my hands in my lap. Isolation and heartache consume me, knowing that this might be the only way to get to know my mother. The fire crackles, and I take a moment to slow my breath, inhaling the soothing scent of burning embers and old parchment.

Then the soft scuff of boots has my head snapping left, and I jolt upright. The pendant falls, landing on the floor with a quiet thud at my feet. My heart races, my eyes wide as I stare at Ren near the corner of the settee. His eyes soften as he steps forward and picks up the pendant. He extends it to me, but says nothing.

"I told him not to bother you," Rydian says from afar, his words soft in my thoughts like he knows exactly what I just sifted through.

I only stare and inhale a long breath, unsure whether or not I should break my two week silence. But staring at Ren only fuels my anger.

"What are you doing here?" I bite out, annoyed that he caught me so off guard. It's late, perhaps two in the morning as the moon shines beyond the glass.

"I just came to check on you," he says. "And I wanted to talk."

"Talk," I clip. "Like all those years before now?"

He actually winces, like my words cut him deeper than any of my blades could. And for a moment, I feel the guilt he carries pounding in my chest, so hard that my breath catches. What he said in the infirmary enters my mind—that he's doing what he promised me. What did he promise, and why?

Why, why, why? None of this makes any fucking sense.

"I want to be angry with you—I *am* angry with you." I clarify, but I'm more confused than anything.

"Because anger is easier to hold onto?"

Yes, I want to say.

It's so much easier to hold that anger in my chest than it is to let my other emotions roam free. To let them consume me, because once they do, I'm afraid of what may happen. And I fear I may not want just one of my mates, but both. Something Rydian doesn't want to do, despite what he continues to tell me.

I glance out the windows and listen to the wind—listen to Ren's deep breaths as he stands silently beside me. I find myself wondering what would have happened if I'd never lost my memories. If I'd never told Witt what marked me.

"You lied to me in that clearing." I wring my hands together. "You told me that I had lost my memories when Rydian came for me at the orphanage. Yet we were mated five years ago."

Meaning Witt had taken my memories twice—at ten when they'd killed Ezra, his brother, and at twenty-one after I'd received my marks. Twice they'd ripped my past from me.

"I know." He sighs, scratching the back of his head. "It wasn't my intention, but imagine my surprise that night when I found out your memories had been stolen. All those questions I had were answered in a single conversation."

Another beat of awkward silence passes as I stand there, blinking and waiting for him to continue.

"I didn't know what Elion was doing, truly, but I did remember Rydian from that day. I'd brought it up to you a few times over the years, but you..." His brows pinch. "I thought you either chose to forget about it, or just didn't want to talk, so I let it go."

His words sink into me, each one heavier than the last. I'd even been able to wield magic in my younger years with ease. Meaning Ren and I had more than enough time to get acquainted.

From captain to close friend and then...

"Did you love me?" The impulsive question slips out. My chest heaves, my pulse racing as I wait—a different kind of fear singeing my blood at the answer he might give me.

He holds my gaze. "Don't ask questions you don't want the answers to."

"You hated me," I scoff. "All those years, and you treated me with such... distaste. With such hatred. You could hardly stand to be around me—"

"I never hated you." He takes a single step toward me, his head shaking like he hates that I think that. His voice dips to a low murmur. "I hated how much I ached for you, knowing that you didn't remember me. I hated how everything we'd done together was gone without a single explanation, and how all I was left with was confusion and anger. I hated how you consumed my thoughts like a recurring nightmare—a dream I longed for but could never have." A disbelieving breath leaves him before his jaw tightens. "Regardless of how hard I tried in that fucking castle, I could never find the answer. I *never* hated you." He stresses the words as if desperate for me to believe them.

My breath grinds to a halt, yet my heart thunders so loudly between my ears, the vein at my neck beats against my skin. What do I even say to that?

Despite the growing crack in my chest, I manage a scoff. "And yet, you couldn't even remind me."

"I did remind you," he says. "Or tried to anyway. I don't know why, but you don't remember that either. I think Elion and Witt had just finished with you when I—" His words cut, as if he's having difficulty expressing his thoughts. "You were bruised and delirious—confused. But when I approached you at night like I usually did, you nearly took my eye."

My stomach sours, and a cold realization shivers down my spine. The scar across his brow...

"Did I give you that scar?" I breathe.

"You slept for two days. I'd left to find answers, and when I came back, you had already woken up." He releases a long, drawn-out breath. "I could never explain it, and I felt insane. Like what we had wasn't real." His voice dips, his eyes fixed on me. "I don't know what you've gotten back—your memories—but if they have me in them... It was real, Isa. All of it."

The way he says my name catches my breath, the walls of my chest caving in. Tender and sweet, filled with longing. I hate that it's filled with such longing and yet, I can't help but love the way he says my name. Like a whispered, pleading prayer, only meant for the night sky.

My resolve wavers.

"Where were we going to go?" I whisper.

He exhales. "North, but we had a few places in mind. You convinced me to build us a cabin, hidden from everyone."

I heave a deep breath, exhaling sharply, as the reality of everything settles like a weight on my shoulders. That sounds like something I'd request—somewhere quiet and free of the king's obligations. Even now, I still wanted it—cherished the thought of disappearing somewhere.

Gods, we were going to leave.

We were going to abandon our duty to Elion. What would have happened if we had? Would I even be here right now? Would I have met Rydian?

Even as those thoughts enter my mind, I can't help the ache in my chest over what happened in that dungeon. My head frantically shakes as I fight the urge to scream.

"They—they took it from us. Everything. We lost—we lost it all and—" My words come out tangled, my composure cracking as it all becomes too much. Anger flashes in Ren's eyes, and he steps forward, hands curling into fists.

"Five years is nothing, Isa. *Nothing*," he says firmly, stressing the word as if he could shout understanding into me. "It's nothing compared to the rest of our ridiculously long lives, and I'd happily do it again if it meant that you came back to me. Do you hear me? I would have waited a thousand fucking years if it meant I got some piece of you back."

Came back to him? Confusion races over me as another question surfaces. Did he... did he wait for me? For five years he'd waited, hoping or knowing I'd somehow regain what I'd lost? His gaze sears a hole through me, as if he knows what type of uncertainty prickles my skin.

"And look where we are," I say breathlessly. "Now we're in Aurelia fighting a war nobody wants."

"It was always bound to follow us." He sighs, pain forming between his brows. "Peace was never our path, was it? But I'm willing to fight for it... if you are."

I blink, my head shaking with annoyance. "I don't want to fight at all—I don't want to be here conflicted about... *this*." I gesture around us. "Feeling like I have to choose."

"No one's making you choose anything."

"Well, that's what it feels like."

He only chuckles, the sound disbelieving as he shoves his hair back. The onyx strands catch the firelight in a way that it looks more chocolate than black.

"You're still keeping things from me," I say finally. "And you won't tell me anything else because of my oath."

"Among a few other things."

"Like what, exactly?"

He exhales sharply through his nose. "Like how despite your effort to bury your emotions, the disappointment and ache you feel toward Elion still surfaces. Your doubts aren't about your feelings for me or Rydian; it's your loyalty to *him*."

"Excuse me?" I manage, holding back my rising fury, my palms heating, fingers curling into fists. "That's not true."

"I feel everything, Isa. You think Rydian feels a lot now; imagine what I feel being fully claimed to you. Ever since you got your essence back, every emotion of yours is heightened. Pain, love, heartache... sex," he gets out. "All of it. And that disappointment only surfaces when Elion is being discussed or when you're at one of his meetings. So no, I can't tell you anything. Not until you shatter that oath."

His jaw works, and for a moment, it looks like he might say more—like he's fighting the words back on the brink of a confession. Like he might spill the truth anyway. Then he exhales and takes a single step back, like the distance itself keeps him from breaking.

Embarrassment warms my cheeks, my lips parting as I try to wrangle my thoughts. My breath falters, and a whirlwind of confusion washes through me like a violent wave.

"You haven't picked your path," he says softly. "The one that gives you the future you want. All I can tell you is that what's coming is far bigger than either of us, and if I tell you too soon—" His words catch and he swallows. "I can't risk—I can't do it again."

My jaw tightens, anger flooding my veins. *Of course I've picked my path.* I've wanted nothing more than to escape the version of myself Elion created.

But perhaps...

Perhaps a tiny part of me still craves Elion's approval. The connection to a father I never truly had.

I just want to know who I am. That's it.

Or maybe, more truthfully, I'm asking the wrong question—*who do I want to be?* Even as it surfaces, frustration coils tight in my chest.

Ren waits, silent and expectant, frozen in place. His stare burns the side of my face. I ignore him and, without another word, gather my things and step into the Veil.

Yet, for some reason, I can't quite shake the way he looked at me—haunted, guilty, and desperate.

39

A warning—that's what it is.

The leaf in my pocket burns a hole through the fabric of my cloak, written in Elion's elegantly scripted words. I fight the tremor of rage and force the carefully-built wall in my mind back into place.

I keep my expression neutral, even as Ivy and I descend the dungeon's corridor beneath a floating orb. We walk side by side, the brush of our cloaks stirring the air around us.

I received the letter earlier this morning, a day before we leave to search for the herbs Ekrin requests. Even though it was written as if Elion were merely informing me of my upcoming meeting, I know what was written between the lines.

Give me something by the time I call on you.

When, though? When will that be? A shiver runs down my spine, fearing it will be sooner than I want.

Granted, Elion has given me more time than I expected; it's been almost five weeks since my last summons. He hasn't called on me or Ren in that time, but he has other ways of reminding me. By sending warnings through my oath.

That same prickle in my blood that has me wanting to shed my own skin like a serpent.

"I'll give it to that Elderheim warrior," Ivy says on an exhale. "He's lasted longer than I thought."

We remain levels below the castle, stopping right outside two steel doors. Ones that seal us off from the warrior they captured three weeks ago.

A nervousness crawls up my spine, adrenaline pumping now that they plan to use me to pull his memories. I should care, yet I can't bring myself to find that emotion. After all, Elion's warriors destroyed Alvonia in search of a few Siphons.

Ivy turns for the doors, and my eyes land on the silver mark in her hair once more. If she has a mate, why did she offer herself in place of Rydian for the bargain? A question she's avoided answering since I arrived in the realm.

"Do you have a mate?" I ask finally.

Her hand freezes on the door then she half turns, and pain flickers across her face. She sighs. "I did."

My stomach drops. "I'm sorry. I didn't mean—"

"It's okay. It happened a long time ago," she says.

Only now I wonder how she survived the loss. Curiosity pulls the words from me. "How have you not gone sick with madness?"

Her eyes soften, hands now resting on the hilts of her swords. "Before Andre died, he had put a lot of his focus into creating a tonic for those who'd lost mates. It was a way to aid those who suffered from the intense heartbreak. He found a few Herb Weavers in Nymara to create that tonic before he died. Because of that, I've been able to manage."

Her gaze shifts to the wall behind me as if remembering that painful part of her life.

A wrinkle forms between my brows as I'm unable to say anything. What can I say? She'd lost a mate, forced to live without the other piece of her. The ache I felt when Ren's life was fading brushes my thoughts—the emotions I couldn't control. Not until Rydian stepped in.

Either way, my own guilt surfaces at what she was willing to do for Aurelia. For Rydian and me.

"I'm sorry," I tell her. "For what I did; I never wanted you to sign—"

"I would do anything for this realm," she interrupts. Not harshly, just firm. "I know you would too, but in our hearts, our mates come first. I understand why you did it. Plus, King Rydian won't allow Elion to live long enough to call on that agreement."

Reassuring words I didn't know I needed to hear at this moment. I only nod and quietly follow her inside the dungeon cell.

To my surprise, Rydian, Ren, and Orin stand on one side of the chamber, walls made of stone and steel. It almost looks like a makeshift workspace with a weathered stone table set up beside them. On it are a number of tools—weapons. It's colder here, and a damp musk clings to the air.

Wheezing breaths sound from the other side of the cell.

I turn my gaze to the shirtless, barely conscious warrior strung up by his wrists, blood streaming down his body in violent streaks. It drips onto the floor, splattering into a puddle at his feet.

Bruises mar his face, chest, and ribs. Lips split, his eyes blackened. Intricate, intentional cuts line his body, from his chest to his waist. Some clearly old, others new.

Even though I remain expressionless, my chest tightens, breaths stalling, frozen with the tiniest sliver of buried panic. My pulse thunders in my veins, blood rushing to my ears.

I'm thrust back to the dungeon with Witt, and the brutal memories of my time with him flash across my mind. Of being tortured for those long, drawn-out days. I didn't think it bothered me that much, but looking at this male now…

I blink when someone steps in front of me, blocking my view of that warrior, and I drag in a slow breath. Ren tilts my face up, his fingers grazing my chin. Barely controlled rage crawls up my neck, spilling from that crack in his mind.

"He fucking tortured you, didn't he?" he says so quietly that the hair rises on my arms at his tone. Regardless, I step out of his reach.

"I'm fine," I say curtly. "It doesn't matter."

I turn, finding Rydian's jaw clenched. Only I have a feeling it's not because of Ren, but because of the knowledge of what Witt did to me. I've never breathed a word about it. I ignore his reaction and stride to their side, swallowing my emotions.

Ivy sets down a swirling crystal; something that looks exactly like the crystals King Elion had in his archives. My stomach coils, my eyes now shooting to the other crystals laid flat, side by side—orange, yellow, violet. A variety of shapes, sizes, and colors.

"What are those?" I ask.

"The explosives Ekrin said they're making," Orin informs. "Unfortunately for us, he was right."

"Those are explosives?" My brows furrow, and I reach for one. Cool and heavy against my palm, the magic dances, twisting beneath the surface with a faint shimmer. "Are they memories or an entire essence? How many do they have?"

Ivy huffs, hands resting on her swords. "That's what we're trying to find out, but our captive won't say anything."

"They look exactly like how my memories were stored," I say, almost to myself as I stare at the crystal in my hand. They're each the size of my palm, though long, jagged, and cylindrical.

"That's what we assumed," Orin says, gripping a crystal. "They've figured out a way to create explosives; we just don't know how. Would you be able to pull a few memories?" he asks, and I nod as he makes his way toward the warrior.

"Wait." I hold my hand out and then wince, knowing a confession rests on my tongue. *Shit.* "I've somehow managed to pull memories without someone… touching me."

Rydian stiffens, eyes widening. "When has that happened?"

Another wince. "Once with Anya just yesterday, and the others… I think I pulled one from Cassivene at her estate and then with Mari at the…" I trail off, unable to explain.

"Are you sure?" Rydian asks, though his brows furrow.

I nod and glance up as he processes.

Then he hums after a moment, like it all just clicked into place. "You also pulled one from me."

Alina enters my mind as I recall our training session. My brows pinch. "You were touching me, though."

"But it was involuntary, right?" he asks. "You pulled it without meaning to."

"Yes." I exhale. What does it mean, though? "But I could try again—from here. No need to bring him down."

Everyone steps back, and I catch the flicker of wariness between them as I inch forward, my boots slick against the cold ground. The warrior's breath rattles, head dipping as blood trails along his body from his nose and ears, down to his fingers.

I focus just as I had with Anya yesterday and pull warmth up between my eyes. I focus on his pain and the buzz of his mind, and after a moment, my brow begins to tingle. Warm, inviting, and curious.

I yank on the connection.

Images race across my mind, pulling me deeper and deeper into his. My breath catches, my body frozen, when disfigurement and creatures and darkness consume me.

So much darkness.

Detailed training flies through my mind—training held in a large clearing while warriors keep the creatures at arm's length by heavy chains, testing their creations and their control.

Grokees and Wraiths and Nightlurkers. Fae, even.

Their eyes glow red, and it's then that I notice shards of crystal embedded in various places along their bodies. Some replace teeth, others replace eyes and fragments of exposed bone.

The Wraiths rise with thin, gray bodies, towering over seven feet, glancing around with lifeless eyes. Nightlurkers slither across the ground, horned with serpent like faces and bodies, thick-scaled and downright menacing. All controlled by slivers of crystal.

All missing their essence.

Nothing but hunger mars their features, eager to be used. My stomach twists when more images race over my eyes—humans and Fae coming into view. Chained against their will, then whipped when disobedient.

King Elion is creating an army of slaves.

Witt strides toward a weak Fae female with matted hair, her eyes hollow. He grips a pulsing crystal, his palm hovering over her head. White, sparkling light twists toward the crystal as he drains her essence, and her body goes limp. More fires and explosions rise in the vision, and I quickly recognize the location.

I gasp and loosen my grip on the warrior's mind, jolting back and stumbling into Rydian behind me. His hands tighten on my shoulders, but I squeeze my eyes shut as I fight the urge to retch all over my boots. My head spins.

"What did you see?" Ren asks.

I take a long breath, swallowing the bile rising in my throat.

"Everything," I rasp and open my eyes. "I think they burned Nymara."

I explain in vivid detail what I saw within Elion's legion, and how I believe they're draining the creatures and Fae of their essence for those explosives. That they'd destroyed Nymara in an effort to search for more Siphons. Silence settles in the dungeon, a buzz of fear and uncertainty tainting the air. And I think, perhaps, that this is the first time I've witnessed true fear in Ivy and Orin's gazes.

As we all turn to leave, the warrior takes another rattled breath. He coughs and then groans, twisting in the chains. I pause, staring at the warrior.

Anger tightens my chest.

"End his suffering," I get out, jaw clenching as I push the large steel door open. "And next time, you'll get me first before you decide to torture someone for information."

Only the faint scraping of a blade and a quiet grunt pierces the air as I stride down the darkened corridor. But I don't need to watch to know that Ren was the one to end his life.

40

Cold mist hits my cheeks as waves crash below me, beating against those black rocks, completely devoid of color. Sand lines the lush, green vale with milky foam and waves breaking on the shore.

Darkness continues to bleed over the horizon, a glimmer of moonlight spilling across the ocean, and I take a long breath. Hours before the sun rises, I stand here, with Kalde watching my back, in an attempt to calm my racing heart.

Elion had yanked on my oath in the middle of sleep.

Unable to deny the call, I had arrived in nothing but my night-slip, no weapons in sight. Not even a dagger in my grasp.

Perhaps that's how he wanted me—unarmed and without company.

Elion only wanted an update, prying for more information about Rydian's legion, the progress of the stone, and our upcoming nuptials. Thankfully, he didn't ask specifics, more focused on Rydian's legion than anything, meaning the knowledge of Ekrin is still safe... for now.

I told him what I could, and with strained focus, was able to weave a few lies. He didn't question my reports—didn't even sense the falsehoods—even though sweat broke across my brow. He also didn't ask about Ren. Surprisingly, no one else was there, not even Witt.

But if Elion's focus is on Rydian, it means he's pushed aside the search for the Veilstone. That thought terrifies me more than anything, because I fear his focus lies on the war he's planning.

Another thought rises... What if he already has the Veilstone?

"You're coming with us today," I say to Kalde, my eyes level with his. After weeks of being in Aurelia, he now stands shoulder to shoulder beside me. "Ekrin has a list of... items for us to search for. Can you track them?"

He growls, hackles rising, when his deep voice enters my mind. *"I'll be able to track anything now."*

Kalde has remained near the castle, venturing off here and there with Ire close by. With only a few months out from being an adult, he's large enough to aid in tracking the herbs Ekrin demands. Large enough to rip a few trained warriors to shreds, should we need.

A comforting thought.

Either way, we'll be using him as Rydian and I search for the herbs, giving Wayd and Kaeda a break. They'll be doing other things though, like tracking Milena down before Elion does.

With an annoyed grind of my teeth, I Veil back to my chamber. I glance at Rydian peacefully asleep on my bed, completely unaware of my absence at three in the morning.

The moon casts pale streaks across his face, the sheets tangling at his hips. Rydian's going to be angry when he hears about my meeting with Elion, and I know that I need to speak with Ren soon.

I release a strained huff and then pull out a blank leaf from the stack on my bedside table and scribble out a quick note. Staring at the summarized letter, I light it with a single spark along my finger and send it off. Perhaps Ren will find it in the morning after Rydian and I leave. I'll avoid an awkward conversation if he does.

But just as I crawl into bed, slide beneath the quilts where it's warm, Ren enters my mind with a low growl. Gods, why is he awake?

"You went there in the middle of the night?" he clips, tone sharp. *"Why didn't you get me?"*

His angry words send my teeth grinding again, and my head hits the pillow. I wanted to avoid telling him about the summons at all, but it was inevitable. Without warning, my wrist flares, glowing bright just as an ache throbs beneath my skin. I quickly cover it to keep Rydian from waking.

A damn annoyance is what it is.

Ren was the reason it hurt so much in Elderheim. The reason it ached as he tugged on our bond at odd times; the only evidence that our mate claim existed apparently. I had realized just last week what he was doing as he attempted to gain my attention in a council meeting.

I stifle a groan and turn on my side, tucking myself into Rydian once more. He mindlessly wraps an arm around me, his steady breaths hitting the inside of my neck.

"You act like I have a choice," I say finally.

My heart races as I wait for his reply, yet nothing brushes my thoughts. He doesn't need to say it, not really.

I do have a choice, the words echo over and over.

Regardless of how many times I meet and work with Varrin and Cassivene, I can't seem to hold that thread long enough to sever it. That unnatural itch in my veins, much like a spider crawling along my skin. Even as I push my magic forward, it slithers away, just out of reach. But as the days go on, I feel it fraying little by little.

Fear is what keeps me from severing it, though.

Keeps me from grasping onto it like I should, as the ache of losing my mother tangles in my chest. Even though I don't know her, I want to. Because once I sever it, I could lose her entirely, and this war will begin. A war I desperately want to avoid altogether.

A knock raps on my door, and I stiffen, knowing exactly who stands on the other side.

Against my better judgement, I reluctantly peel away from Rydian and answer the door, greeted by a familiar low-set brow and a clenched jaw. He appears more assassin than mate, at the moment.

Ren stands furious in the corridor, shirtless, anger rippling off his shoulders. But I blink in the dim light, realizing that even though he stands with calm, practiced composure, it's his fury I feel along my neck.

"You can be angry and ignore me all you want," he says calmly. "But don't go to Elderheim by yourself, not when both of us remain in Aurelia."

Both of us, meaning him and Rydian.

"What does it matter?" I clip in annoyance. "It's not like I can waste time and fetch you every time he calls for me. The result is the same whether I go with or without you."

"Because the last time—" He snarls in frustration then takes a steady inhale. He stares off, head shaking in disbelief. My stomach plummets, ice coating my veins as it sinks in. He'd left the castle on a mission days before I showed Witt my marks.

"They took my memories when you were gone, didn't they?"

He says nothing, but his gaze finds mine, and I know then that I'm right. My palms rest against my eyes, and I force myself to take a deep breath. Why does this all have to be so complicated?

"I don't care who you take with you," he says quietly, pulling my hands off my face. "Just don't do it alone."

"Tell me what happened and I'll agree." I clench my jaw, my words biting as I step back. The door remains ajar. *I want to hear it,* is what I refuse to say.

His nostrils flare in the lingering silence before he sighs. "I made the mistake of agreeing to one last mission near Nymara before we decided to leave. I wasn't there when..." He cuts himself off, shaking his head like he can't say it out loud.

He wasn't there when they took everything from me, and I know just by looking at him that he blames himself. Despite my urge to slam the door in his face—return to the warmth beside Rydian beneath the quilts—guilt presses down on me.

"Please," he says softly, brows drawing together. Pleading words I've never heard him breathe before. Ren doesn't plead for anything.

I mindlessly nod when he turns on his heel. Yet my hand shoots out on impulse. I grip his hand in mine—a voiceless question. I don't want him to leave.

Gods, what am I doing?

One brief conversation in the middle of the night, and my restraint is fracturing. His eyes shoot to our joined hands, brows furrowing once more. He glances behind me—toward Rydian.

"Do you want to stay?" I whisper, hardly managing the waver in my voice. The uncertainty.

For a moment, I think he'll deny the request and shrug me off. Embarrassment warms my cheeks, feeling foolish for asking when Rydian sleeps just feet away. But then he nods and steps in, crowding me, before quietly shutting the door with a soft click.

"I'm still mad at you," I say breathlessly, chest heaving, craning my neck only to catch the amused tilt to his mouth. Honestly, I didn't think he'd say yes. Gods, now what?

"I know," he murmurs, hesitating momentarily. "Can I kiss you?"

"No," I blurt. Yet... doubt laces my tone.

I blink in the darkness as my heart thunders so loudly I fear it might wake Rydian. An awfully bold question for so late in the night. Perhaps he's tired of waiting.

He steps closer. "Are you sure?"

"No." I'm not sure, actually.

All I've done since our time together weeks ago is think about his mouth on mine. The way he kissed me—slow, unhurried, and lingering. As if he savored the taste, seared it into his mind like he'd forget it.

Like *I'd* forget it.

And yet... it was the one thing that brought me back—that pulled the memory of us to the surface. All it took was a simple kiss. If only he had done it sooner. Why didn't he do it sooner?

You hated him, remember? The thought echoes in my mind, and my face warms. I did hate him—treated him as such—and he'd been my mate the whole time.

Sensing my doubt, he leans in, sliding his hand into a solid grip right beneath my ear. If he wasn't holding me steady, I'm positive my knees would give out. His mouth hovers over mine, and I release a defeated sigh.

"I'm still mad at you," I repeat, my voice cracking, hands trembling. The comforting scent of him floods me, and I instinctively inhale.

His lips graze mine, feather-light and barely there, like he's waiting for a firm answer. Against my better judgement, I carefully close the distance. My pulse flutters, lips parting as the taste of him consumes me, my mind dizzy with confusion and *want*. He deepens it, and his tongue sweeps over mine in a delicate, slow dance.

A small sound slips from me, desire running down my body in a delicious shudder. Yet I pull back and release another disbelieving breath. I realize now how much of a hold Ren has on me, so consuming it terrifies the very blood in my veins.

That damn bond between us.

Ren's brows lower, his gaze tracking me as I back away, inching closer to the bed. Without another word, I turn and dive beneath the quilts, pressing myself against Rydian's chest as if his warmth can pull me from my rising emotions. My skin buzzes.

"All good?" Rydian says groggily, wrapping an arm around me once more, and I stiffen in his grasp. His amusement brushes my mind, but with that, a tiny sliver of annoyance and a prickle of jealousy. *"Took you long enough."*

I jab my elbow into his side. He grunts, chuckling in my ear, and tightens his grip. I begin to wonder how much he heard as he doesn't appear angry at my departure, meaning I'll have to tell him tomorrow.

Then Ren carefully settles on my other side, the bed dipping under his weight. He rests on his back, one arm behind his head, the other grazing the tips of my fingers in a gentle caress. Warmth settles there, rising up my arm and into my chest.

He's close enough that he invites me to rest against him. Another voiceless question as he lifts his arm and peers down at me. My eyes linger on the curve of his lips.

After a silent moment, I adjust so that my cheek sits flush against him, my arm flung over his body, a leg grazing his thigh.

And... for the first time in what seems like a long while, Ren slowly exhales, his chest rising and falling steadily beneath me. Something that sounds awfully close to relief as my eyes drift shut.

Alone in bed, I graze cold sheets with my fingertips before the chamber door creaks open and the scent of breakfast hits my nose. My brows pinch, my eyes squeezed shut.

"Oh, gods," Lettie musters, her voice wavering with what appears to be discomfort. An awkward beat of silence follows—so awkward, I can almost taste it.

"I didn't realize..." She trails off, and I dare peel my eyes open.

Rydian greets Lettie in the doorway to my chamber as she holds a tray of food. The warmth in her cheeks rises to a dark flush in the dim chamber. Embarrassed or flustered?

Lettie looks at Ren just as he enters from the bathing chamber and pauses. Shirtless. He runs a hand through his hair.

"Set it over there," Rydian grumbles under his breath, gesturing to the table, and moves to the side.

Dawn hasn't even filtered through the windows yet, meaning we've only been asleep for a few hours before Lettie came with breakfast. Her eyes skim over Ren in the doorway, then she quickly sets the silver tray down, uncomfortably clearing her throat.

"I don't think I brought enough," she says sheepishly. "I'll be right back."

She vanishes into the Veil, not bothering to use the door as Rydian clicks it shut and sighs. Ren chuckles quietly and reaches for the food, already helping himself.

Rydian huffs, jaw feathering. "Lettie seems to be aware that you eat enough for seven."

"If you ate more, I'm sure you'd be somewhat..." Ren pauses and then arches a brow. "...bearable to be around."

Rydian's lip curls, but before he can snap a retort, Lettie appears with another full tray. Without so much as another look at either of them, the Veil consumes her.

"It's too early for this," Rydian grumbles, reaching for a plate. "Perhaps we should just enter a fight and get it out of the way."

The fighting rings in Voltros enter my mind, and I recall how Orin mentioned that Rydian would place a bet on me. I stifle my rising amusement and settle deeper into the quilts, hiding my face as I watch them.

"I'd hate to embarrass you again," Ren adds as he sits. "I suppose I could teach you a few things. Show you how to aim for the heart." He arches a brow. "My aim is good."

A warning laces his tone and I hold my breath, glancing between them. It's barely dawn and they're already arguing.

Rydian's knuckles whiten, though a dark chuckle brushes the air. "You can't kill me."

"Maybe not." Ren smirks, the tiniest lift to his mouth. "But it'd give me thirty minutes of silence."

The air plummets, cold and furious, and shadows skim Rydian's hands as he stands frozen at the table. His plate thuds against the wood and he leans forward on his palms and growls. His annoyance pounds against my temples. Ren's grin only widens, though, as if daring him to do something.

"Don't kill him," I tell Rydian, and he straightens.

He inhales a steady breath, his shock and amusement brushing my mind. Then his gaze swivels to me, a smile curling his lips as if they hadn't just been arguing.

"Are you hungry?" Rydian asks.

Ren says nothing as he looks at me, but I rise to an elbow.

"If there's any left after the brute eats."

Even though Ren remains expressionless, his amusement threads my thoughts before he begins eating his pastry dripping with jam again. It oozes down his fingers.

I stifle my surprise from feeling his emotions and sit at the edge of the bed, planting my feet on the floor. Feeling Ren's emotions so freely now is quite jarring.

Rydian smirks and walks over to me, stepping between my legs.

He settles his hand below my ear, forcing my gaze up with a tiny smile. My heart races when his lips brush against mine.

"Firstly, good morning. Secondly..." he says softly, sliding his hand to my throat. His features harden, and my breath catches when his grip tightens. "I'm furious with you."

My lips part in confusion. "For what?"

"For leaving for Elderheim last night without waking me," he says, eyes narrowing. *Oh, is that it?*

Looks like they had time to discuss my whereabouts before I could tell him this morning. Despite myself, I smirk, and my body treacherously arches, hoping for another squeeze as warmth consumes me.

I whisper, "Any tighter and I'll consider disobeying more."

Rydian only growls, though his pupils dilate, and the faintest trace of his arousal hits my nose. I gasp, eyes fluttering when he yanks me up by the back of my neck. Heat builds in my blood, knowing that Ren is watching.

"A glutton for punishment," Ren remarks, almost to himself.

My chest grows hot at his comment, as if he has experience with that—*with me*. He remains sitting at the table, the food in front of him completely forgotten, with his eyes locked on me.

Ren arches a brow. "You'll only make it worse."

Rydian ignores him, but his eyes soften as he stares down at me. *"Promise me you won't do it again."*

"I already told Ren I wouldn't," I breathe. "But I promise."

"Good." He kisses me once more before releasing me. I stifle a shuddering breath—the shiver of need coursing through me. Gods.

"When do we leave?" I ask, clearing my throat.

"As soon as we're dressed," Rydian says, stepping away to prepare an assortment of eggs, pastries, and a variety of sharp cheeses for the both of us. Though Ren's gaze skims over my thin nightslip before landing on my face. A flicker of *want* settles in his stare, but only for a moment before he smooths his expression.

"Are you jealous?" I prod, and his breathing stalls.

"Yes," he says without an ounce of hesitation, and a sliver of

shock snakes down my spine. I wasn't expecting him to answer so honestly, let alone at all. I blink, unsure what to do.

"And if you... kissed me?" The question has my heart racing. I probably shouldn't have asked.

A beat of silence passes between us.

His brows lower. *"I wouldn't stop at kissing."*

I knew I shouldn't have asked, because now I'm wondering what exactly he'd do if I allowed him to kiss me now. But it's then that I realize that he isn't holding a Veil coin, and my eyes narrow.

"Where's your coin?"

A knowing smirk grows on his face before he rises, wiping his hands, bare chest rippling in the low light of dawn. "Our essence is tied to each other... I never needed a coin. I need one to speak to the others though." He looks at Rydian, who rolls his eyes and pulls on a fresh tunic. Even though it's the most casual tunic he owns, it still fits like luxury.

"Trust me, I'm thinking of taking it back," Rydian gripes as he rolls his sleeves.

Ren only huffs. "I'll meet you back here after I get dressed."

I exhale sharply. "You're going with us?"

"Of course," Ren says, reaching the door and throwing me a devilish grin over his shoulder. "I can't leave you alone in the woods with only a king and a Howler for company."

Just as the door clicks shut, a leaf flutters in front of my face. I catch it, turning it over to find a list of herbs from Ekrin—locations and colors and specifics on what to search for. But within those words also lies a warning not to arrive at his estate, now or in the next few days.

Witt is visiting.

41

Days pass, though the air is warmer here. Thicker.

And although snow still blankets the realm, the further north we travel, the less we see of it. As if the heat of the Veil's Edge bleeds into the expanse, leaving us sweating as we continue to climb the frost tipped mountain.

We're far beyond the cities now.

Into the realm so deep, the mountains and the forest expand on every side of us and our use of the Veil has become draining. We're able to jump locations but only in small bursts, and walking has saved our energy. Though, I know the real reason Rydian wants us to walk—in case Elion calls for me while I'm gone.

Kalde trots ahead, nose to the ground as we near the top of a peak—one of many we've climbed only to travel back down.

My thoughts snag on Ekrin though, and I can't help but wonder what Witt needed from him days ago. Whatever it was, it's bound to stall our current... progress.

The possibility of Ekrin betraying us might have crossed my mind once or twice. Perhaps more, if I'm being honest. Regardless of my current hatred of him, he's been helpful. Working diligently with Bess without complaint—creating a new elixir almost every day. Failed elixirs, but elixirs nonetheless.

The tracking herb Ekrin requires is one that can be used in both realms. *Coladinseal.* He believes that if he uses that herb, it might make searching for the Veilstone easier. But as Kalde tracks the herb, he pulls us closer and closer to the Veil's Edge.

My only worry is what we might find there if we get too close—Elion's legion of human miners digging out that magic-deflecting metal.

Human miners or slaves? The thought echoes in my mind, and I'm unable to shake the growing dread twisting in my stomach. I hate that there are slaves.

I sigh once we reach the top of the mountain, stopping to peer into the peaks. With a bow strapped across his chest, Ren wipes his brow, his eyes skimming the depths of the forest. Shirtless, he tucks his tunic in his back pocket so it hangs down. From this vantage point, we can make out which paths are safer to travel, even with the trees blocking most of our view.

Rydian stops on my left, also sweating, just as Ire lands on his shoulder. Ire shakes and ruffles his wings, puffing his chest out.

"We should be getting close," Ire says, clicking his beak.

"Miles still," Kalde chimes in, his golden eyes meeting mine. *"But we're almost there."*

He faces forward, dark fur rippling in the wind, but remains standing there. As if he, too, needs a break. He agreed to carry our packs, strapped to him like a saddle, including our tent.

"We'll need to stop at some point." I look at the expanse below, searching for the river that runs down the center of our realms. The one that spills into the sea in a violent, glorious waterfall. The Evermoore.

"I need you to fly down and look for Elion's legion," Rydian demands, scratching Ire under his beak. "And a resting spot. Preferably near water."

"On it," Ire squawks, wings stretching before he dives. He vanishes among the trees, their canopies so high, they graze the clouds.

"We should follow the river." Ren says. "We can hunt on the way, before sunset settles."

We've been eating rabbits here and there, along with whatever's left from our packs. I reach out, gently squeezing Rydian's hand as a wind brushes past. It cools the sweat slicking my neck, and I sigh, lifting my braid.

The forest stretches out, endless and dark as the sun's light dims to a honey-gold. It pours in fractured beams across the trees, melding from reds to oranges to yellows.

"Kalde can find the herb tonight while we camp, so we can leave in the morning."

Rydian tips his head back, drinking from his flask before passing it to me. The crisp water slides down my throat.

"As long as I can take these bags off." Kalde shifts his weight, so the packs clink against each other.

A few dragging minutes go by, the three of us standing in silence while we wait. Ire finally ascends from the trees ahead, and then swoops in a wide arc before landing on Rydian once more.

"Half a mile north east," Ire says. *"A small clearing near the river. Humans work five miles ahead, though. Still hours away."*

"Enough shelter not to be noticed?" Ren asks, shading his eyes. His jaw works in annoyance.

"Correct." Ire flies off. *"Stick to the trees."*

I fill Rydian in, and we begin our descent in silence. Rock and sediment crunch beneath our boots, and by the time we reach the bottom, trees hide us once more.

The Evermoore's wild current cuts through the air, and we follow its sound as Ire flies above. Kalde takes the lead again, and after a while, the trees begin to thin.

I sigh in relief, eager to rest after hours of travel, when we come to a stop in a lush clearing, padded thick with clover and moss. Humidity hangs in the air, steam curling along the edges of the Evermoore. Interesting.

I stride toward it. Perhaps the Veil's Edge holds more heat than I thought. I crouch, dipping my hand in, and am surprised to find the water comfortable enough to bathe.

A shiver runs down my spine though, and my blood curdles, my magic itching to be released from Elion's hold.

I've continued to grasp our bond, successfully holding it as the days pass. Even if it writhes, even if it's only for a few seconds, it's progress.

Progress I didn't expect to make at all. I haven't mentioned it to either Rydian or Ren for fear of being pressured into severing it while we are so far from the castle. If Elion can't feel me grasping our tether, surely he'd feel me severing it.

A risk I'm not willing to take at the moment.

We'll find Ekrin's herbs, head back, and hopefully by then, Cassivene and Orin will have found a way to break the runes along Elion's hidden chambers.

Eagerness to find my mother has only grown in the last few days. My fingers graze the pendant with her memories, warm against my touch. I turn and find that Rydian already has the tent halfway up as Ren sparks the wood and then shrugs on a shirt.

"Will they notice the fire?" I ask and remove the packs from Kalde as he impatiently shuffles his feet.

"Not from this far," Rydian says. "The trees will conceal us. And even if they do, I doubt the humans will seek us out."

A low, satisfied groan—part huff, part grumble—leave's Kalde as the packs hit the ground. He shakes, hackles rising before they settle.

"Stay out of sight," I warn.

All I receive is a low growl before he disappears into the fading golden light ahead. Ire flies above, following his trail.

An hour goes by as Ren cooks a few rabbits over the fire and we all sit down to eat in silence. Smoke curls lazily in the air, the crackles of the fire mingling with the violent rush of the nearby water. And for the first time in what feels like months, Ren pulls out his dagger and a block of wood.

"Why do you carve?" I ask, wondering what he does with all those pieces. Does he keep them or toss them out when he's done? I've never seen him hold a finished carving.

"I've already told you," he replies, his voice laced with exaspera-tion. He continues to scrape his knife along the block. Delicate shavings curl before falling to his feet.

"And I don't remember," I snap.

Rydian slows his eating, quietly eyeing us. Even though we're on speaking terms, I've hardly said anything to Ren the last couple of days.

"Sure you do," Ren says with a sigh. "Now, if you could quit pretending you don't know anything, perhaps we could talk more. Or, better yet, sever that oath."

His eyes flick up, and rage builds in my palms.

After traveling all day, I don't particularly feel like arguing. Though Rydian's awkward tension pounds against my temples, followed by a sliver of annoyance. He scratches the back of his head, eyes fixed on the ground with a slight clench to his jaw before tossing the remnants of his food to the leaves.

"I don't know how to navigate... this." I stress the words and look between them. "I hardly remember anything, and I definitely don't know where either of you sit in my life."

"Yes you do." Ren pauses his carving. He straightens, arms folding across his chest. "Which ones did you get back? I can practically feel them surfacing."

My face warms, yet I remain silent.

"I can only tell you so much," Ren continues, "but the memories with me in them shouldn't be a problem for you. Maybe search for that one and you'll remember it." His tone comes out slightly sharp.

I narrow my eyes. "This would be so much easier if you would just share them with me, instead of pissing me off."

"And what fun would that be?"

A beat of silence passes between us when a knowing smirk rises on his lips, and my stomach dips. I know that look. Nothing good comes from that look. It thrusts me back into the Brotherhood when he'd push my buttons until I snapped. Yes, definitely a look I'm used to seeing from him.

Before I give him the chance to open his mouth again, I rise and storm into the direction of the Evermoore. The crunching of leaves behind me reaches my ears, and I know I'm being followed.

I walk until I'm glancing down at the current. Wild but not

strong enough to sweep me away. Rydian steps beside me, and I relax, though his silence stretches a beat longer.

"A swim?" he asks finally, his brow arching as if reading my thoughts. I glance over and release a sigh, staring at him as darkness looms closer and closer.

I shrug. Without a word, Rydian casts aside his clothes, now fully naked before me as I follow suit and strip down. The fading light ripples across his skin, sending a deep shadow over one side of his face. Hard lines and taut muscles. A sight to behold.

My heart leaps as Rydian steps back with a menacing smirk, turns, and then drops into the water with a quiet splash. It settles just above his thighs.

Even though it's shallow, he dips below the surface, rising to slick his hair back, the copper hues gleaming in the light. His eyes skim over me, water dripping from the point of his nose as he begins to wash. I stride forward and he extends his hand, leading me in.

I step down and water kisses my feet, met by stones as thick as chairs. Another step and the warm waves collect higher, reaching my hips.

He sinks down, tugging me to him with a grin and a chuckle. His arm wraps around my back before he dips me down, soaking my hair, then nuzzles his face into my neck. He lets out a low hum, and my eyes flutter as his teeth graze my skin, just barely, before pulling back.

Though now, I'm not so sure it would be wise to indulge in each other at the edge of the forest with Ren nearby. Not that it would matter, but still.

"How's Mari?" I ask in distraction, and run my fingers through the tangles in my hair.

After the night in the ballroom, I didn't quite discover where she ended up, but knew that she was placed somewhere in the castle. Alina is training her with a few new house-maidens.

"She's in the kitchen for now," Rydian says, splashing water on his chest. "After that, I'm not quite sure. I still think you should have executed her."

"I don't think she'd try to kill me again," I say. "Maybe we could use her later for something else."

Rydian looks past my shoulder and his eyes narrow. I turn to see Ren perched against a nearby tree. He secures his dagger, eyes fixed on us. Though I ignore the way my face heats at the sight of him watching. Regardless, I sink so the water comes to my chest.

He pushes off the tree, reaching the bank with that same menacing look etched onto his face. His voice dips. "Do you remember our first time together?" *Gods.*

My eyes flash, hands curling into fists beneath the water.

"Drop it," Rydian snaps, pressing into my back, though I know he's only doing it to stifle whatever thought surfaced in Ren. Apparently, he's bound to spill whatever it is.

"Would you like to hear it?" Ren says, fighting a smile. "It did involve more than one person."

My lips part, but before I can protest, Rydian's curiosity blossoms in my mind. I can practically hear the question in the silence that follows.

A small chuckle from Rydian. "Wait—"

"No." I growl, shooting Rydian a glare behind me. He only grins, slow and fascinated, then arches a brow.

"Well, now I'm curious."

Ren lets out a breathless laugh, stepping closer. Though an embarrassing flush rises in my face, and I stifle the urge to slink back and disappear beneath the water.

Ren folds his arms. "We were on a mission, too focused on our set goal to... cross that line." His eyes meet mine. "But one of those long nights, we found ourselves included in a rite of sorts—a pleasure night—testing out a new enchanted wine, similar to what brothels do. Only you had me believe I drank some and then lured me to one of those rooms with another female."

"Good gods," I grouse, grinding my teeth as I frustratingly scrub my arms. "Is that it? Are you done?"

His eyes glimmer. "You'd gotten that female to agree to your plan, and had her suck me off, claiming you wanted to watch."

Even in cool, brisk water, my entire body flushes, from my feet all the way to the back of my neck. I have no words, rendered completely fucking speechless as droplets trail down my collarbone. A slow, devious grin lines his mouth as he tracks those droplets.

Rydian smiles. "I don't think I've ever wanted to see someone's memories more. Who was it?"

"You're lying. I'd never do that," I get out, the words coming out rushed. Flustered. I peer up and blink. "Not if we were mates."

"Actually, that sounds exactly like something you'd do." Rydian laughs.

Ren hums, agreeing. "We didn't know we were mates at the time, but... I'd be willing to share that memory with you—to prove it."

Rydian stiffens as if realizing what exactly that would entail. He steps out from behind me. "I don't think you should do that..." His head tilts, eyes narrowing as they speak in the Veil. His jaw tightens, attention solely fixed on Ren.

"I'm sure it'll be fine," Ren says, casual yet sure. "She won't pull any more than what's necessary... right?"

His memories and my ability surface in my thoughts.

My lips part, and for the tiniest of moments, I hesitate. Granted, I want nothing more than to see those snippets he keeps to himself, yank on that thread to show me everything. Still, hesitation consumes me, a sliver of fear and uncertainty that Rydian is right.

Even if I did my best not to yank too hard, the times I've taken memories have mostly been involuntary. If our future is dependent on my not knowing details until I sever my oath, it could risk everything.

I stifle a groan, fixing my eyes on the trees behind him as I battle with indecision. Of all the things he could show me, it's an intimate one. Intimate, yes, and something of our past...

I sigh in defeat after a moment and return my gaze to Ren who has a menacing grin tilting his mouth. Like he knew what my decision would be. He pulls his shirt off, and my heart races as it falls to the ground.

"What are you doing?" I ask.

"I can either show you in the water, or you can get out fully naked to see it." He arches a brow, as if he wouldn't mind my getting out. Either way, I'd be naked before him as his hands settled on my face.

"Fine," I say, turning away to stare at the darkening sky. A nervousness coats my insides at the faint sound of discarded clothing, rustling in fallen twigs and leaves.

"I have a feeling this is about to get..." Rydian brushes his lips against the shell of my ear. "...very interesting."

"Hush," I snap.

The sound of rushing water cuts the air before it's muffled, interrupted by splashes and scraping rock and then... silence. The current slows until it's barely running past.

I blink and pull away from Rydian. A partial dam redirects the flow toward the back edge, as if Ren created a makeshift pool out of stone. Darkness shrouds the sky, stars gleaming before tiny, twinkling orbs take over. They hover above, reflecting off the now-still water of the Evermoore.

I turn to Ren, who sits on one of those large stones beneath the water, knees spread wide, waiting for me. His chest ripples, the scar below his collarbone staring at me. Then my eyes shift down and warmth settles in my stomach.

The water rests just below his navel.

He laughs quietly, and I snap my eyes up. With an annoyed huff, I rise and step forward, stopping between Ren's legs. His breath catches, his eyes fixed on my breasts as they peek through my hair. My thighs brush against him, though Rydian's uncertainty enters my thoughts. A flicker of worry.

Ren exhales, brows lifting. "Only what I show you."

I nod, and his hands settle on my temples, his fingertips warming against my skin. The tingling buzz of my magic forms between my brows. Then his entire being consumes me, the faint scent of cedar and crisp rain flooding my senses. My heart races with anticipation.

I inhale sharply when images race across my mind.

Dim lighting, flowing curtains, and ecstasy swarm my thoughts. Not in Alvonia. No, we're somewhere different. Dark and luxurious. Not as grand as a castle—an estate perhaps. Only he keeps the location to himself.

Another female comes into view, masked and dark-haired much like myself, but she leans in to whisper in my ear. A smile grows on my face. Pure deviousness settles behind my eyes.

Through Ren's eyes, I look ethereal, dressed in a sheer, creamy fabric, the neckline plunging to my navel. I sip from a golden chalice, my eyes locked on Ren as I hand him the rest. He swallows the contents, and a dark grin lines my face. Suspicion settles in him before it's gone, replaced by a mixture of annoyance at being there and his infatuation with me.

Infatuation he's fighting.

Images flicker to him tracking my scent after being separated, ending up in a room with split curtains. A circular bed rests in the center, similar to brothels. He sees me and stops, watching as the female trails her mouth down my neck. My eyes fly open, landing on Ren in the doorway.

Another flicker of images.

Then I'm at his side with a menacing grin. The other female drops to her knees, working the ties at his hips as his cock strains against the fabric. His chest heaves, his blood spiking with arousal.

"Let me watch," I say, my voice sultry and smooth, my eyes fixed on his mouth. Looking everything like the cunning assassin Elion created me to be.

"You set me up," Ren snarls, his grip locking in my hair, jerking my head back. I only grin. "I told you I'm not participating."

An unrecognizable laugh escapes me, dark and devious. "Funny you say that. The enchanted wine only works if the emotions are *shared*." I rise to my toes, tugging against his grip on my hair, inching closer to his mouth. "You wouldn't like it if you didn't want it. Now let me watch you fuck her mouth. I want to see it."

My heart races, chest heaving when more images fly across my mind. The female leaving, him barking orders at me, us tangled on the bed together, him silencing my cries with his hand as he unabashedly pounds into me. Rough and hard.

Our first time together.

Shock electrifies my blood when Ren's hands drop from my temples, thrusting me back into the water between his legs. Only now, my own arousal consumes me, warmth pooling, leaving me to rub my thighs together. I blink, staring at Ren with wide eyes and yet...

Yet, pieces of that night flood me.

Fragmented, yes, but enough to know that I did in fact, do that. I set him up because I knew he wanted me. Only he'd been fighting it, refusing to cross that line between us. We were on a mission together, and our friendship shattered that night. I made sure of it.

My chest heats with something wild, brows lowering as I hold his steely gaze with a tiny smirk. I admit, it was amusing.

He gives me a small smile, his fingers gently brushing a tendril of damp hair off my lips as he leans in.

"There she is," Ren murmurs, then his gaze darts behind me.

"I really want to know what he just showed you with an arousal like that," Rydian whispers, low and throaty, and my breath catches. "It's intoxicating, little fawn. Tell me... what did you see?"

He stands against my back, the hard length of him pressing into me. His hands roam before threading my nape, before pulling my head to the side to drag his tongue up my throat. Towering over me, he tugs my head back, and I gasp.

Caught between the two of them, Rydian bends and captures my mouth with his, a low moan escaping me when his tongue sweeps over mine. Not a single ounce of their jealousy consumes my thoughts.

One minute I'm fighting for breath as Rydian devours me, the next I'm pulled from Rydian and gathered in Ren's lap by the backs of my thighs. Forced to sit on him—straddle him.

His hand curls around my jaw and my knees tighten at his hips, his cock brushing against me. Stiffening. With panting breaths, he holds my gaze—waiting. Searching. I know he'll make no move toward me, not unless I allow it.

Ren says nothing, but Rydian pushes closer, trapping me. So close that his breath brushes against my neck when he leans down. His cheek presses into mine.

"Tell us it's what you want and we're all yours," Rydian says softly, nibbling my ear as a breeze rushes past, a tease lacing his tone. His teeth graze my jaw as I sit with another decision. Ren remains perfectly still—hardly breathing as my own shallow pants fills the space between us.

Blood pounds at my temples, a rush of anticipation and warmth and... *need.* The need to have both of them barrels through me like a violent rush of water, stealing my breath. But with that is a want I never expected to have, not really.

I *want* both of my mates.

The ones carefully crafted only for me, in both realms. No one has ever had two mates before, yet here I am, bound to both of them. I'd be a fool for not wanting to accept it.

Ren was right. They haven't forced me to choose—I'd come to that thought all on my own. Even though they argue and bicker and compete against each other, their feelings for me are the same. And despite what I believe, they're completely fine with sharing.

Clearly, if this is any indication.

"Yes," I declare, and release a shaky breath, even though my answer came quickly.

Now, as I stare at Ren, I realize how easy it is to say it.

Yes, yes, yes.

Twinkling orb lights of orange and yellow reflect in Ren's gray eyes as they skim over me, wild and unbearably feral. His gaze holds my own, and a slow, yet hungry smirk curves the corner of his mouth.

Part of me knows I should hate the idea of this. Part of me wants to, and yet... I don't.

Not as my own hungry smirk reflects in Ren's eyes, staring back at me like a dark witness. That wildness beneath my skin surfaces with sheer force—so forceful, my own breathing stalls temporarily.

Without thinking, I roll my hips, the friction almost unbearable as my skin meets his. Ren hisses, low and sharp, and his hands tighten on my thighs as if to keep me steady. I smile when the hard length of him pushes up. Pushes against the warmth between my legs, sending a ferocious ache down the center of me.

I pull Ren's mouth to mine, my fingers tangling in his hair, lips parting as my tongue darts inside. I devour him, and he groans, deepening it when he pushes his hips up into a forceful grind. A small, whimpering noise slips from me, and I hurriedly reach between us.

Ren quickly pulls back though, gripping my wrist with a grin. Halting my touch. Hunger blazes in his stare.

"Not yet, little fawn," Rydian says behind me. "We're going to take our time worshipping every..." I'm pulled off Ren. "Single..." I gasp as he spins me around, water splashing. "Inch of you."

Rydian smiles as he grips my jaw, and Ren rises to stand at my back.

The faint sounds of Ren adjusting himself behind me heat my blood, my body humming with need and anticipation. Rydian strides forward until my back grazes Ren's knees. Though it appears Ren is out of the water, now atop the clover and moss at the edge.

Rydian glances over my shoulder and within a single breath, I'm lifted and placed back on Ren's lap. I'm facing the water and Rydian, trapped in Ren's grasp. My nipples tighten, skin on fire, when a painfully desperate ache forms low in my core.

Ren pushes me forward, his hand snaking up my spine to fist my hair, dragging me flush against him. He rolls his hips, grinding hard, and I gasp. Rydian's eyes darken as he inches closer.

"Tell me," Ren whispers, and his other hand firmly grips my hip, fingers biting into my skin. "Have you ever been fucked while being eaten?"

A soft, whimpering cry slips from me.

"Spread your legs," Rydian says with a low, devious chuckle. His eyes skim over me, and I squeeze my thighs together.

"Make me," I say breathlessly.

Ren's free hand runs down my leg before forcefully prying my knees apart, using his knee to hold me open.

Rydian hums in approval.

"So disobedient," Ren grumbles. "You already know what I do for disobedience. Do you remember?" His lips brush the inside of my neck, amusement in his tone. "Warm her up first or she won't be able to take me."

"I gather she's already there. Aren't you, princess?" Rydian's finger drags up my inner thigh until he meets my swollen clit, swirling over me in taunting circles. I whimper, my hips rolling until he stops the movement.

"Greedy little thing. Didn't someone teach you to savor the moment?" Rydian tsks and inclines my head with a tight squeeze to my throat and a push of his thumb.

A roaring heat pulses down my center, a throbbing ache so insufferable, and another whimper escapes. Pure torture.

Rydian steps back, assessing. "Lift her."

Ren reaches my jaw with his hand first, before tilting my head to trail his nose down my neck. He bites and grinds into me again, his cock hard against my ass.

"You are ready, aren't you?" Ren breathes. "You're practically dripping."

He lifts me by my hips, lining himself up before slowly, painfully lowering me onto his cock. My mouth falls open on a silent gasp, and Ren groans, the sound tangling in his throat. Inch by glorious inch, he stretches me, and I have to grip his forearm, grip the back of his neck, to steady myself.

"Fuck," I pant, and my eyes squeeze shut.

"That's it. A little more," one of them says, only I'm too blinded by the pressure of Ren filling me to know who's talking. A hand comes up to my breast, nipples pinched between hungry fingers. My legs quiver, and I writhe.

"Breathe."

"Look at me," Rydian growls, and my eyes fly open.

Damp auburn hair falls to his brows as he lowers his head, hands meeting my thighs to spread me further. A low chuckle escapes him before his tongue moves against my clit in torturous circles, over and over and over.

A shocked cry escapes me as sensation rips down my spine, low and explosive. Eyes fluttering, my hips roll, chasing and writhing under the tingling warmth of pleasure as it encompasses me. Pleasure so wild, my vision flickers white. Rydian watches me, groaning against my skin in approval, and the sound alone almost shatters my control.

Ren holds me still as he drives his hips up, slow and deep. The tiniest amount of friction and yet, he fills me so much my breath catches. *Fuck.*

I moan, pushing back, the heat of his body overtaking mine as Rydian works between my thighs. His tongue circles me again— licking, teasing—then sucks. Another moan. My leg drapes over

Rydian's shoulder, heat surging through me. He groans, and stars explode across my vision, my clit swelling.

"Gods." I quiver. "Don't—don't stop."

Ren guides my hips, now moving solely by him alone as he controls the pace between us. His panting breaths distract me, as if the tiniest bit of friction between us is fraying his control.

"I want to hear you break." Ren's breaths stir the hair at my neck, now slick with sweat as my thighs tremble. He growls, lips against my neck. "Show the king how your voice trembles when you're wrapped around my cock."

A hard thrust—*gods*.

With a breathy moan, my hips roll wildly between them. I chase my release as it builds with ferocity, coiling low and fast. Ren's speed picks up, his panting breaths stirring the hair at my neck. Then a hard flick of Rydian's tongue has my climax ripping through me, my body trembling, a sharp moan tearing from my throat.

Ren sharply hisses, his hands tightening on my hips as if to keep me from clamping down. To keep himself from losing his control.

Head dizzy, I hardly take two breaths before I'm flipped around, now straddling Ren. I hover as he braces on his elbows in the lush clover, breaths shallow and ragged. A buzzing, heated silence settles between us, but his gaze sears through me as I stare down.

Rydian's hands on my hips pull me back to reality, his voice dipping. "I think I like this side of you, little fawn. It's amazing what can happen when you allow your queens to flourish. And you, my queen, are flourishing."

Rydian's hand roams my skin before it's between my slick thighs, and his fingers swirl over me again. I gasp as my hips buck forward.

"Are you ready?" Rydian asks, and a slow smirk lifts the corner of Ren's mouth. "You're going to fuck him. I'm going to watch. And then… then I'm going to ruin you," he declares, dragging his finger down my back, then halts the movement. "Say 'Yes, Your Majesty, I'll fuck him like you want.'"

My breath stalls entirely, heart racing with a new type of adrenaline. "Yes, Your Majesty," I echo, eyes locked on Ren as I inch closer. He glances at my lips. "I'll fuck him like you want."

"Good. Now sit." Rydian guides my hips down and a small cry escapes me when Ren's cock slides in again. Eager to feel him stretching me, a delicious need coils my spine.

I waste no time picking up speed, withdrawing only to slam into him with desperate intensity. Slam into him as the shroud of our desire hovers like a thick mist. Ren captures my mouth on a groan, his fingers curling around my throat to steady me, eyes hazing over.

"Gods," Ren says against me. "You're perfect."

My breasts graze his chest, our bodies writhing, moving together as I sink down over and over and over. His grip tightens, hands trembling, undone by the feel of me riding him.

My breath turns heavy.

I glance over my shoulder, my skin hot at the sight of Rydian slowly fisting his cock with both hands, his ragged grunts slicing the air.

His hungry eyes are fixed on us—intently watching.

His lips part, head falling back with pleasure as he strokes himself two more times. Then he stops and stalks forward before bracing a knee in the clover and moss beside me.

I slow my movement with Ren, heat rising in my face as I realize what he's doing. Oh gods. His cock brushes my backside, a hand gripping my hip, and my eyes flutter. Ren grips my jaw, forcing me to look down my nose at him.

"Trust me," Ren breathes. "You can take it."

"You will need to relax for this to work," Rydian says breathlessly, and pushes his hips forward. A sharp moan slips from me as he carefully pushes in. With agonizing slowness, he sinks himself until he's buried. Ren's grip tightens on my face as my mouth falls open in shock, and I blink.

Yet, the pleasure between the both of them is... explosive.

"I hope I'm buried inside of you when I die," Rydian breathes, his fingers tightening. He begins to move—slowly at first and then...

"You're doing so well," Ren says, voice gruff, and guides my hips down with a smirk. "Taking us like a good little wench."

Although a growl rumbles up my throat, desire floods my veins, blood scorching as it settles in my core again. Very quickly we find our rhythm, almost too overwhelming to handle. I roll between the two of them—Rydian pounding from behind, the sound of flesh against flesh, as I continuously ride Ren.

Wild moans fill the air, and Ren's cock firms, his abs working, seconds from losing his control. Then his fingers dip between my thighs, circling over me until I'm panting for breath. He picks up pace, my clit swelling as another release forms, heat searing my blood.

"Fuck... yes. Yes, right there," Rydian groans, pleasure consuming him as he pounds into me, fingers gripping to the point of pain. Yet I welcome it as his control slowly fractures, his moans uncontrolled and wild behind me.

"You sound so pretty when you're breaking." Ren's hazed eyes focus down, watching himself enter me, his cock slick with my need. He groans, hips rocking, and pushes himself deeper. Filling me so fully, so deeply that I feel him everywhere. Then darkness skims my knuckles, seeping onto Ren's chest. He quakes beneath me.

"Gods, I'm coming," Rydian gets out, his movements unrestrained as he pounds faster—once, twice, three times. He trembles, spilling himself, roaring his release to the darkened sky.

Whimpered cries fall from my lips as my climax follows, clamping Ren so tight that he hisses, his teeth baring. He thrusts so hard that he immediately finds his release, mouth falling open, eyes closing as he shudders. I collapse, panting heavily on his chest, our bodies slick with sweat and need.

A minute goes by before we finally catch our breath, and Ren sits up—me cradled against him—with Rydian still submerged in water. Ren pulls away slightly as Rydian sweeps my hair aside and kisses my neck, unhurried and tender.

"That was the most beautiful thing I've ever witnessed," Rydian confesses. I exhale, tilting my face to him with a small smile. *"But*

Wayd and Kaeda are close enough to speak in the Veil. They'll be meeting us at the camp shortly, I think. Clean up and meet me there."

My brows furrow in confusion, but I nod. He rinses and then exits the river, leaving Ren and me at the edge. I move to rise, but Ren's grip tightens, refusing to let go.

My heart lurches, but before I can muster a single word, his fingertips brush my temples. I rapidly blink as images race through my mind, stealing my breath. His memories.

Us, together.

Some beneath the trees in Elderheim, others on missions, in taverns, and late-night visits. The joyful discovery of our marks. Then the fragmented images linger on something that isn't a memory, but perhaps one made up in his mind.

A future together—somewhere discreet. Happy. One without killing. One with... children. My heart races, adrenaline pumping as I realize what he's showing me. It's what he longs for—with me. Us.

They vanish as fast as they come.

Yet the moment his fingers fall from my face, I release a sob, the broken sound slipping from my lips. And an emotion I never expected surfaces—grief and heartache. My lungs claw for air.

"Why did you show me that?" I attempt to bite out, but my voice wavers on a broken cry, my head shaking in confusion. His forehead dips to mine.

"I've always loved you," he confesses, lips brushing against my temple, and my heart leaps. "I wanted to remind you what freedom looks like. That you can still have it, if you want." My vision blurs, tears running down my cheeks. "I should have broken our friend-ship the moment I realized I had feelings for you, and if I had... maybe we could have had more time together." He cradles my face as another sob wracks through me, unable to stifle it. "I'm no stranger to grief and pain, Isa. It felt like I was suffocating all those years without you, so I dealt with it the only way I knew how. I thought it was my punishment for not protecting you like I should have—for not being there when it happened." A wrinkle of pain forms between his brows, and he takes a shuddering breath. "I should have *been* there."

I choke back another sob, and my arms wrap around his neck. Our foreheads touch again, and his thumbs swipe over my cheeks. Though I have no words—nothing to add as he confesses what I already knew.

But what can I possibly say now as his words dangle between us? Where do I even start?

"I still want it—with you," he confesses, and his fingers tangle my hair.

He pulls back, and I can almost feel his heart shattering as it beats against my chest. A wave of his heartache slams into me, pounding relentlessly as his grief surfaces. But with that is a love so deep my breathing stalls, as if threaded into the fabric of his being, written in blood. Marked by fate.

"I know you're worried about the repercussions of severing that oath, and what I'm asking of you is unfair." His eyes search mine before he gives me a grim smile. "But I'm your family, Isa. We're yours if you want us, because I want you. I've *always* wanted you— you were just out of reach for a while."

"I don't want to give up on my mother—to make that decision," I admit, my voice wavering.

"I know," he says, pausing for a breath. "Will you try, though— to sever it?"

Another desperate plea as he searches my face.

Tiny twinkling orbs still hover, sending a fiery glow to our damp skin. He watches me, a silent minute going by as I ponder his pleading request. And despite my instinct to say no, despite my heartache and worry, I nod—a tiny dip of my chin.

He releases a breath, a sigh of relief, before pivoting us. My back hits the clover as he towers over me, propped on an elbow. A shiver snakes down my spine.

"Say it," he murmurs, and his hand skates down my waist, past my thigh and to the back of my knee. He raises it over his hip. "Say you'll break it."

"I'll break it," I whisper.

His hand captures my wrists, pinning them above me. Desire burns through his gaze, and my core tightens, already slick with renewed need. I arch into him, lips parting on a soft exhale.

"Say it again," he demands, and very, very slowly, he pushes his hips forward. My breath catches when he enters me.

"I'll break it."

His lips brush mine, soft and reverent, before deepening the kiss. Devouring my mouth like I'm the last thing he'll taste. Warmth blooms in my core, spreading as he moves, steady and sure. All consuming.

His mouth tenderly trails my jaw, my throat, my collarbone. And as darkness engulfs the forest, the worship between our bodies collides—sacred and reckless.

Together, we become rapt in our movements, a practiced dance between lost lovers, breaths and limbs tangling on the clover. Tangling beneath the glimmering stars and soundless moon as it bears witness to my promise. It's not until my whispered cries of his name caressing the night air that we slow our pace, each quick to find our release. My hand finds his face when he props himself on an elbow, brows pinching.

He pants heavily, and then whispers, "I missed you."

Hearing the torment in his voice makes my chest ache, my heart cracking under the weight of it. Despite that ache, his mouth meets mine again, if only to savor the moment.

Something like guilt wraps around my heart, knowing that I'm the reason for it. Deep down, Ren's torment is because of me— because I wouldn't give Witt his name. And he kept it to himself all those years, lived his own nightmare in the very castle we shared knowing he may never have me again. He watched me live my life, all while he was suffering.

After a few silent minutes of lingering stillness, we quietly dress and walk back to the camp. Wayd and Kaeda sit with Rydian around the fire, and to my surprise, Kalde and Ire hover nearby. Only Kalde is pacing, his bushy tail swooshing across the ground in frustration. Wayd, of course, has a smirk plastered on his face, arms folded as if fully aware of what we were doing, despite the tension hanging in the air.

Confusion ripples through me.

"Kalde is... frustrated," Rydian explains, and looks at the Howler. "We can't hear him, but he found the herb."

"What's the problem then?" I ask.

Kalde halts long enough for his golden eyes to hold mine above the fire. "*That* king *is at the Veil's Edge.*"

Blood drains from my face, palms damp, heart thumping erratically in my chest. Oh gods. Ren stiffens beside me.

"That's impossible," Ren says. "It would take him weeks to arrive there, and Isa just saw him a few days ago."

"What?" Rydian demands, now fully alert.

"Kalde said he saw Elion at the Veil's Edge," I explain as Kalde huffs again. The group collectively snaps their heads to the Howler just feet away.

Kalde tilts his head and asks, "*Would you like to see for yourself?*"

43

Unsure of what we'll discover, I quickly strap on my weapons in silence, as do the others. My hood sits low over my brow, and my eyes meet Kalde's before he turns to lead us.

Adrenaline floods my veins as we quietly follow in the darkness, hidden by the coverage of the surrounding trees. They tower above, silhouetted against the full moon. A breeze rushes past, leaves rustling, carrying the scent of burnt oil and the faintest trace of smoke. Yet the further we walk, an orange glow rises in the distance.

After a few jumps into the Veil to gain ground, the trees begin to thin and I glance at Rydian beside me. He gives me a firm nod, and I grip Ren's hand, entering the Veil once more.

Kalde crouches, hiding himself as much as he can once we reach the edge of the trees. We halt our steps, peering across the vast expanse of the Veil's Edge.

It appears much like a mountain towering in the distance, only black rock and golden sediment rise along the sides, as if the realms collided at this one specific location.

It pulses with power, so strong that my breath catches in my throat.

The Evermoore roars through the center of the clearing, though no waterfall exists at the top of the Veil's Edge, almost like the Fates forged a spring beneath it—splitting our realms.

Unease coils tight in my stomach, skin prickling as if my body knows who lingers there. I fight a shudder. Ren gently squeezes my hand though, and I exhale.

Even as darkness blankets the realm, human miners continue to work in the dim glow of lanterns nearby. Glowing orbs hover above the Fae, who appear to be monitoring their work. The clinking of metal on rock echoes from an opening near the base, shouts and calls mingling inside.

"Where is he?" Rydian murmurs, only loud enough for Kalde to hear.

"Near the right edge," he says, and I repeat it to the others. Our eyes roam over the tight crowd, where a pointed tent rises among them. Higher than the others. Heavily guarded.

Minutes go by before two males finally exit, and my stomach drops, pulse pounding in my temples. Ren's grip tightens.

I don't need the glow of daylight to know who it is.

King Elion walks side by side with Witt, deep in conversation as an orb follows them near the center of the clearing. Even from a distance, I can recognize Witt's soft brown hair.

"Are you sure you saw Elion in Elderheim?" Rydian clips.

"How is that possible?" Wayd hisses. Even though his words are sharp, a hint of fear and worry laces his tone.

Nausea twists my stomach, and I'm unable to reply. How *is* that possible? A good question, because he shouldn't be here. I saw Elion just days ago sitting at the edge of his council table as he pestered me about Rydian's legion.

That *wasn't* a dream... was it?

Then, as quickly as those questions come, I have my answer.

A red glow emanates from Witt's hand as he raises something— a crystal, perhaps. His other palm hovers over the ground, siphoning, when a wide portal appears in the center of the clearing. Through it is an image of Elion's council chamber that ripples like pebbles being thrown in a motionless lake.

Dread runs through me, breaths speeding up. They've figured out a way to jump locations similarly to the Veil. Our one leverage against Elderheim. My pulse pounds against my skull, fear surging. Witt and Elion enter the portal, vanishing within seconds before it disappears entirely, winking out with a faint crimson spark.

As if it were never there.

"What the fuck," Kaeda mumbles aloud, unable to stifle the shock in her tone. The fear. "How?"

"We need to leave." Rydian turns sharply, the beat of steps fading among the trees. "Now. Let's gather our things and head back."

His anger thuds between my ears, mingling with mine on our walk back to the camp. Not a word is spoken in our sheer determination to arrive back in Vyria. To inform the others.

We pull the tent down in minutes, snuff the fire, and load our packs on Kalde. But just as we finish up, a leaf flutters in front of my face and my stomach sinks. That clawing panic in my chest rises as it lazily floats down, and I grasp it with trembling fingers, refusing to turn it over.

Frozen with fear.

Ren straightens near Kalde, his head snapping to me, surely feeling my panic.

"Isa," Ren says, stepping toward me. "Isa, what does it say?"

Rydian stalks toward me, spine straight, brows lowered. The determined gaze of my king—my mate. "Show me what it says."

I swallow, flipping it, and my eyes skim over Elion's writing.

I'll allow you ten minutes to gather what I requested. Captain Demaris is to accompany you. A reward for your loyalty awaits your arrival.

My mother or my memories perhaps?

I extend it to Rydian, hands trembling, palms sweating. I had just seen Elion days ago, so why exactly, would he be calling on me so soon? I anticipated a few more weeks, not *days*.

We decided that they were going to search the castle, attempt to break those runes, while Elion and Witt are distracted. Only we had anticipated this happening weeks from now in hopes that I could master my grip on the oath.

Rydian forces my gaze up, though rage marks his face. His jaw feathers before he takes a slow breath, his eyes never leaving mine. "Kaeda, prepare Ivy and Orin for what was planned then meet us in Elderheim."

She vanishes, and I realize that saving our energy in the Veil was a good decision. For this exact moment. Ren meets us, hands curling into fists as his rage blankets my mind.

Rydian exhales, speaking slowly. "Give him what he wants, do you hear me? You need to sever that oath."

I nod even though fear crawls up my spine. What if I fail? What happens if I can't sever my thread, and Elion destroys every part of me? I'd never see Aurelia again, and I would lose my mother.

I would lose *both* of my mates.

"You can do this, just as we practiced. We will not leave you—"

I cry out, fingers curling as heat scorches my veins, followed by that all too familiar itch beneath my skin. Hair rises on my arms as it crawls up, pounding against my ribs, my skin prickling as that oath turns my blood hot. It writhes within me.

My eyes grow wide, lips parting. "No... no, it hasn't been ten minutes."

"Shit," someone mutters.

Rydian grips my face. "Look at me. You will sever that oath— you *have* to sever it. Tonight. Now is our chance."

The forest closes in, darkness flooding the edges of my eyes as the Veil slowly consumes me. Hurried rustling echoes behind me before my pack is thrown to Rydian. He stuffs it in my hands the moment someone grips my elbow, the uncomfortable crawling sensation jolting in my blood.

"We're right behind you," Rydian assures me, and then I blink.

I'm no longer staring at Rydian as the darkened forest disappears before me. Weightlessness of the Veil takes over, and the feeling of falling into nothing engulfs me. Within seconds and a hard thud of my boots, I stare at the shining pale stones of Castle Alvonia. Its towering spires rise in the sky, silhouetted against the moon above us.

Yet my heart settles, my worry easing, when I glance beside me and Ren's composed gaze meets mine.

He gestures to the castle with a firm nod, and we enter.

44

A shudder of disgust runs through me, my body recoiling the moment my boots hit the cold steps leading us into the castle. Damp earth and musk fills my nostrils.

How could I have ever called this place home? It's built on nothing but nightmares and revenge.

Our steps echo across the stone, an eerie silence settling in the corridor. Ren walks quietly beside me with a convincing scowl as we're escorted to King Elion's council chamber.

"We're here." Rydian enters my mind within minutes of our arrival, and I breathe a small sigh of relief.

I'm unsure what to expect, and a flicker of worry threatens to rise the farther we walk. I quickly stifle it though and continue to follow the lone guard ahead of us.

After a few minutes, two guards with metal helmets swing the council doors open on a soft creak. I blink in the dim light, and take a long, controlled breath. Neutrality slides into place—the face of a weapon.

Upon entering, my eyes land on Elion, flanked by Witt on his right and three council members to his left—one of whom is Ekrin and another I haven't seen before. My eyes narrow.

Two long golden braids cascade down to his chest as he focuses on the map in front of him. A thick golden-furred cloak sits on his wide shoulders, a sword strapped to his back, as if he's lived in the mountains all his life.

Kiev Blackwyth. I'm sure of it. The Duke of Eldryn sits next to Drakon Esmyr, the Duke of Nymara. I stifle my shock and force my shoulders back.

If Drakon is still a duke... considering what's left of Nymara. What does he think of the destruction of his city? Where was Drakon during that?

Kiev's pale-blue eyes lift, meeting mine from across the chamber, and his spine straightens—a small rise to his shoulders.

"Kiev Blackwyth is here with Drakon Esmyr and Ekrin. Guards are stationed at the doors. Witt sits beside Elion." I push the thought out, and a jolt of shock enters my mind. I wonder if Ekrin had known about Kiev visiting Alvonia.

"We've been awaiting your arrival. I'm eager to see what you have for me," King Elion says, clasping his hands. "I've given you more than enough time to find something about the Veilstone."

I toss a book onto the table with a loud thud and a tight smile. Something to satisfy him.

"What is that?" Witt grumbles, leaning forward as I slide it down the table. He catches it.

"The Book of the Fates," I explain, casually taking a seat as Ren stands near my left shoulder. Orin, Cassivene, and Varrin took the time to copy the book to perfection, identical to its original save for a few misinterpreted sections. "It took some planning, but I was able to take it before leaving the castle. It's untranslated, but from what I've gathered, it has information regarding the Veilstone. If you're able to read it, it should give you what you need."

For a brief, flickering moment, Elion's eyes shine with satisfaction. Then his jaw tightens. "Is that it? And what about that person you were tracking? Last I heard you had found someone to track the stone for you. That book isn't all you have, is it?"

My stomach sinks. *Last he heard?*

"Break that oath," Ekrin hisses, jaw grinding.

I fight the urge to clench my fists, my hands warming, blood crawling as my excuses form. My lies. A cold sweat breaks across my brow as I grasp for that thread tethering me to Elion—grasp for that sliver of magic. It slinks away, just beyond my reach. *Shit.*

Frustration builds in my chest, but I force a grin.

A full truth and then a partial truth—that's how I did it before. That is how I wove those lies a few days ago.

I tap my fingers on the arms of my chair. "We're still looking for the stone." My blood dances in satisfaction, the crawl in my veins simmering down. "And I'm sure you'll be pleased to hear what I found out about the royal coronation." *A distraction.*

Elion sighs. "Continue."

A cold smirk lines my face. "The King of Aurelia's life is forfeit once the royal essence is passed to me during the coronation." *Forfeit because his life will be tied to mine.* "The only way to spare his life is if we join our blood through a marriage bond, which is why he wanted that bargain in the first place. But why would I take Aurelia *with* him when I can take it for myself and give you whatever you need without stealing ancient texts? Even though he's agreed to aid Elderheim, most of his council has put up a fight, which has led to recent hesitations. King Rydian won't even allow me into their meetings." *Partial truth.* "They don't want to share everything with you for fear of repercussions, which is why I stole the text."

"What are you suggesting?" Kiev asks, voice gruff yet hesitant. I shift my attention to him as he rubs his jaw.

I shrug. "I could kill him—wait until the coronation or do it sooner, either way, I can do it while he sleeps."

Witt shakes his head. "You won't be able to kill him."

"And why not?" I ask, arching my brow. "I'll already be there, and it could be quick—I wasn't trained to be a weapon for nothing. He would never see it coming. Not with me sleeping beside him, anyway."

I release a careless chuckle, heartless and devoid of feeling. A mask. Sweat drips down the back of my neck.

"You don't have the blade," Witt says, like I should know what he means. "The Veilblade—the only thing capable of killing a king or queen of Aurelia."

I blink. "Where can we find it? Maybe it'll make searching for the Veilstone easier if he's gone. I can control the council."

"I hate to agree, but it would make overtaking Aurelia much easier," Ekrin says, casually waving his hand. "Push us to find that stone before the winter solstice. Then by spring, we could create your new realm and perhaps prevent a war."

"A war is inevitable," Drakon says numbly.

Though Elion leans forward, elbows resting on the table. "You won't be getting that blade—I need it for the ritual."

My heart leaps, pulse racing as his confirmation rings in my ears. But what of the Lumen sword? Ekrin's eyes meet mine.

I sigh. "So what then? Marry the King and risk prolonging the search? What if we never find it?" Witt's eyes slide to Elion before he leans back.

"Yes. That was the agreement, was it not?" Elion clips, shifting his attention to my left. "What do you have, Captain? Kiev has been updating us on the work near the Veil's Edge and the mining of Nullium steel. Hopefully, your news will be better than that of the slow progress of our workers up north."

My blood turns cold, knowing he was just there an hour ago.

Ren walks toward the middle of the table beside Witt. He lowers his brows and pulls out a map hidden beneath his tunic. They all rise, hovering over the table.

"I took the time to learn about their army while I could, just as you ordered," Ren says. "More camps rise in the north, but their legion is weak. Since signing the agreement, their forces do not expect any advances from you."

"You're sure?" Elion hums, his mouth curving into a menacing grin. His fingers drum the table.

My heart pounds as I scan the chamber.

As everyone focuses on the map, I use the distraction to tether my mind to the King. My brow tingles, mind buzzing as I focus. Heat sears my mind, and I force back a gasp, sensing nothing but a wall of fired steel. No reaction from him, though, unaware of the invasion.

Ren continues. "I took this after a council meeting with his second. Right now, they have around ten thousand soldiers separated into groups throughout the realm. Not enough in one location for it to matter."

"King Elion is mentally blocking me." I push the thought out, feeling a shiver of understanding a second later.

"Try the others," Rydian replies. *"We're in the chambers, Isa. I need you to hurry."*

Adrenaline surges through me, my stomach twisting into uneasy knots. *They've gained access.* We're one step closer.

Witt leans over the table, too focused on what Ren's pointing at to pay me any attention. Their words fade to a dull hum as I cling to Witt's mind, dark and ominous. Easier to crack than Elion, images hit me all at once.

I force my breathing to slow, deciphering the storm of memories flooding through me to find the information I want.

Crystals. Weapons. And finally, Theo.

Torture consumes my thoughts, and I swallow the pained lump in my throat to maintain my composure.

"Chamber three."

Ren points to the map again. "This is where most of them sit. There's strife within his council, and he's been having difficulty controlling them. You might even be able to sway a few."

Elion hums, stroking his beard. "There's division."

More images fly across my mind, landing on Milena's cottage and the destruction left behind... but no Milena. My heart pounds against my temples as relief floods me. Where is she?

"Milena's not here."

"Good. We have Theo, Ivy took him to the castle. We need Elynor, Isa. Kalde can't track her for some reason," Rydian informs, urgent and clipped.

Ren grunts his agreement. "With more than a few council members."

"Isa," Witt says, his attention shifting to me as if he can feel me sifting through his mind, clawing at his memories. My eyes snap to him as everyone's gazes fall to me. "You've been awfully quiet."

"What would I have to add to that?" I ask tightly. "The legion is the captain's job, not mine."

I rise from my seat, striding to the other rounded side of the table where Kiev stands. Drakon inches closer to Elion, making room beside Ekrin. Kiev eyes me from down his nose before focusing on the map again. A beat of silence follows as I cross my arms directly across from Witt with Ren to his right.

My lip curls. "I've been a bit preoccupied with this stone to care about legion movement and whatever else you're searching for."

"Isa," Ren warns.

Witt's stare grows hot, the air thick with tension as Elion's jaw works. He braces his palms on the table with a slow, menacing smile.

"*Did* you tell her what we're searching for?" Witt asks quietly, brows lowering as he shoots a look at Elion. My stomach twists.

"*You're about to ruin this,*" Ekrin hisses.

Though Drakon remains silent next to Kiev, his features taut with tension, his eyes focus on the wall across the chamber. But the way he stares, so fixed on that wall, leads me to believe he wanted nothing to do with the destruction of Nymara.

Did he have any involvement in it? Was he angry?

Elion tilts his head, eyes narrowing. It takes everything in me not to step back, shoulders rigid, but I keep my chin up.

"Where's the Siphon?" Elion demands.

Unease crawls up my spine at the mention of the Siphons. I hope they don't realize they're currently missing one. I settle my emotions, forcing myself to maintain composure while holding Elion's gaze.

"What Siphon?" I slowly exhale.

Elion throws me a cold, knowing grin. "You know exactly who I'm speaking of. At the time, I thought you used that boy to restore your memories, but it didn't quite... add up. It's been brought to my attention that Milena still walks this realm." Elion chuckles, assessing me. "So, where is she?"

I huff in disbelief, and a smug grin spreads wide on Witt's face. The same calculating expression he gave me in the arena the day I called him by his full name. He must have realized I knew exactly who he was when I said it, only I was too angry to catch my mistake. Now I'm cornered into telling them what I know.

"Last I saw her, she was hid deep in the Whispering Woods with a couple of Howlers."

"She's not there, but I have a feeling you know that. You knew where she was but you didn't tell us." Witt huffs. "And if you had told us, perhaps we wouldn't have gone looking for her in Nymara."

"Or Alvonia," Ekrin adds with a raised brow. "Though I do wish you hadn't used fire. It's been... difficult to rebuild."

"You didn't ask." I clip. "If she's not there, then I don't know where she is."

"I don't believe you." Elion growls, turning away to pace.

"I cannot lie to you, remember? Even if I wanted to, you have something I want." I laugh in disbelief. "I'd be a fool to risk what I want because of some unimportant Siphon."

"Watch your tone, Isa," Ren warns again.

My eyes leap to him. "Fuck you. I've been diligent in searching for the Veilstone while they burn cities and build an army. So all of you could have at least included me in your plans. Tell me, did you know about Nymara? Because I sure didn't."

"No one knew about Nymara," Elion clips, and plants himself by the windows.

Drakon's eyes flash with fury at the mention of his city, his nostrils flaring, hands clenched into fists. Oh, he's furious.

My own fury builds in my chest. It coils, squeezing and squeezing against every quick breath I take as my adrenaline rises.

And yet, beneath that is an ache, deep and raw, settling in the hollow part of me over the absence of a father I never had. One I didn't know I wanted until Ren mentioned it. A small part of me knows he was right, only because I was here, living within the same stone walls as Elion the whole time.

The same walls as my mother.

The very same walls as my *mate*—stripped away, as if he were never a part of me. A part I missed and desperately ached for.

What else will he take from me? What else, what *else*?

The heat of my skin grows to a burning simmer, magic rising, and our oath writhes in fractured pulses beneath the surface. It beats relentlessly, over and over, frightened into submission. It slinks back.

I angrily gesture to the window, where Aurelia sits across the continent, my voice rising with bubbling fury. "Meanwhile, *I'm* the one running through foreign territory, playing the perfect distraction so no one notices what you're really doing. That's what this is, isn't it?"

"Watch it," Elion snaps finally, voice sharp, and strides forward. His long silver hair falls to the sides of his face as his patience thins.

"You don't even want me here," I bite out. "You had no choice but to keep me around. I'm only useful because of the blood I carry, otherwise, you would have just wiped my memories by now."

A heavy silence settles in the air, everyone's gaze on me. But something flickers in Elion's eyes, a mix of admiration, disgust, and pain, perhaps. As if looking at me reminds him of what he lost with Elynor.

And for a short moment, the wall in his mind falls and his memories flood me—the heartache he felt when she left. Betrayal by a love he lost. An enemy.

Then it quickly rises, shutting me out.

It would normally surprise me to find anything other than malice in Elion's eyes, but he fixes that with the hatred that follows. A cold grin tugs at his lips, but before he can reply, Witt lets out a dry laugh from across the table.

"Make no mistake, Isa, no one wanted you," Witt says quietly, brows set with distaste. "Not even your mates—especially not when we pulled those memories years ago. No one came running when the magic in your veins dulled to a hum beneath your skin. You're worthless, and we did you a favor by taking you from that realm. You were never supposed to live after that battle in Aurelia. Andre had—"

"Quiet!" Elion shouts, his hands slamming onto the table.

Witt clamps his jaw, if only to keep from spilling any more information, but the hatred in his cold stare remains. I look between them, aware of a hidden secret I was apparently never meant to find out.

Yet, I hate to admit how much his words affect me. Hate how my stomach churns with its own disgust and heartache. But I force a long inhale, refusing to let it show on my face as I crawl into Witt's mind again.

With sharp focus, I reach for that connecting thread, like the web of a spider, and ground myself to the truth he was about to spill. Memories rise with quick efficiency, a flash of images searing across my vision as it all begins to snap into place.

King Andre. A sealed letter. *Informant.*

The truth almost has me staggering back, but I brace my palms against the table while locking my narrowed eyes on Witt. A cold laugh escapes me when his eyes flare, as if he feels me pulling out those precious memories of his. And yet...

I've lost all sensibility to care.

There's no proof. What's he going to do, say something? Risk revealing to Elion that I know what happened twenty years ago? That I know what they're planning?

"I think we're done here," Elion clips, and his fingertips spark with his growing power, too close to losing his temper. I've pushed one too many buttons tonight. "We can revisit this conversation later. What you've delivered is more than enough to acquire what I need for now and I believe you will be an excellent asset in the future."

Skin prickling, my cold eyes swivel to him, feeling not only the power of Elderheim beneath my skin, but Aurelia too. "And what about what you promised me—my reward? Where is Elynor and where are the rest of my memories? That was our deal."

Kiev, Drakon, and Ekrin inch back, leaving me to face the king all on my own. From the corner of my eye, Kiev's left hand slowly hovers over his sword, but I fix my gaze on the king prowling forward with a scowl.

"I think you know I can't give you those." Elion dips his hand into his pocket to withdraw a swirling crystal, setting it on the table with a thud. "And I recall you only asking for her location."

My chest heaves. *I asked for her location?*

Oh gods, I asked for her fucking location and not her. I suck in a slow breath, pulse climbing, adrenaline pumping as a chilling realization washes over me. He was never going to give them back, and I was a fool for ever trusting his word.

"You lied to me," I say numbly.

Elion releases a huff of disappointment. "You should know better than to make bargains with a king who's never followed through with his promises. Quite naive of you. You're no daughter of mine if you're so easily persuaded with pretty words. Take that as your first lesson. You're too attached to what doesn't matter, which is why you'll make an awful queen. That will change though."

A disbelieving exhale escapes me as I straighten, but that raging calmness pebbles my skin again. Everything fades, a ringing so loud in my ears, his words become muffled.

I blink. "My memories matter. Elynor matters—she's my mother. Why can't you give them to me? It would cost you nothing to return them."

"Oh, but it would have cost me everything," Elion tsks in a tone without care—nonchalant even. "I might have given you your memories back at one point... if I had them."

Dread settles in my stomach, the weight of his words slicing through me like a freshly sharpened blade. Unable to prevent the onset of nausea, bile rises in my throat.

"What do you mean?" I demand.

Ren's eyes widen across the table, spine straightening, shoulders rigid as his hands twitch at his side. Watching—waiting. The first time he's broken his composure since arriving, and Kiev stiffens out of the corner of my eye.

Elion sighs. "I don't have them—your memories from Aurelia... of your mother. When you were captured during that battle, we pulled those memories from you upon your arrival. I had no intention of ever giving them back, so they were destroyed shortly after you were placed in the Brotherhood." He heaves a regretful breath, as if pained. "What you stole out of my archives was all I had."

That means…

That means I've been at full power since Milena returned my memories weeks ago, and my essence has been slowly replenishing over time. Just as Milena said it would. A lump rises in my throat, the knowledge of it sitting like a weight on my chest. There's no more waiting—no more pieces left to uncover.

Nothing, nothing, *nothing*.

My breath catches, and my eyes squeeze shut as I fight the sting of tears building behind them. The burn of betrayal and grief and heartache, cracking into a million tiny pieces.

I won't be getting anything else.

I won't be getting the rest.

Not the memories of her voice, or the feel of her hands when she held me and caressed my cheeks. The way she used to say my name or laugh or cry. The emotions she stirred in me as a child— my *love* for her. Of her taking me to see the flowers.

I wanted to see the flowers.

Gone, as if she had never existed. And the truth of that shatters a piece of me I fear I won't ever get back.

My eyes snap open, landing on the crystal. "What is that, if it's not my memories? Is it to taunt me because you can?"

Heat builds, so stifling that static hangs in the air, as if I could set this castle on fire and watch it burn. The collective alarm of my mates pulse through me, but I ignore it as my fury rises and rises and *rises*.

"Isa," Rydian chokes out. *"We're coming to you. We have to leave. She… she's not here. Not anymore. Break that oath!"*

The hair rises on my arms, my eyes now locked on that swirling crystal. Swirling as if it were… sentient, like it has a mind of its own. I blink, realization sweeping in.

"I had no choice," Elion declares. "And I'm truly sorry for the pain I've caused you. But at the time of your capture, I felt like your mother was my only option since Andre died during the battle, and we needed a royal essence to complete the ritual."

No, no, no. It can't be.

"Her essence is in that crystal... isn't it?" I say the words surprisingly even, masking my unraveling fury. Thread by fucking thread, my rage builds, hot beneath my skin.

This whole time, she wasn't even alive.

It was an illusion, her in that crystal, crafted by the Scry King of Elderheim in order for me to comply with his demands—all for control.

A simple pawn in his game.

"I'm sure you understand the reason for it," he says so casually, as if her life meant nothing. "I'm quite impressed with your ability to find what we needed for the Veilstone, and will reward you to make up for what I cannot give. Am I correct in believing you want more recognition on this council? We could use another person to relay information."

"Yes," I breathe and lift my eyes slowly, though the words leaving my lips don't sound like mine.

Hollow and devoid of feeling. Bland.

And yet my blood boils, and black swarms my vision. I lose focus on who stands in front of me, my chest tightening, my pulse climbing higher and higher. My fingers twitch.

Elion throws Witt a glance. "Good. Now that we're all on the same page, we'll send you back to Aurelia to finish the search, but we cannot afford you having any more distractions. It's the only way to keep you on track."

He looks at Ren.

The air compresses, confinement settling over the chamber, too thick to breathe as Witt's eyes glaze over. A single blink and his expression shifts from casual council member to lethal weapon. My breath catches, and my heart stops as I register what Elion said.

Before I can scream, Witt's blade plunges through Ren's back, right through his chest.

45

Ringing explodes in my ears, everything around me fading.

A silence so stifling, my lips part on a noiseless cry, the air stripped from my lungs. My heart shatters and pain erupts behind my eyes as I watch in horror.

The sword rips through his chest.

Ren chokes, eyes flaring as he glances down. His hands fly to the slickened metal as if to prevent it from doing further damage. Witt grins, twisting the blade, and Ren's gray tunic seeps black as blood rushes down his front.

"Mates only cause you pain and strip you of your focus on duty. He was useless to you anyway," Elion says and snaps his fingers.

I stumble back, hands trembling.

Mate, mate, mate. The word becomes an echo in my mind, over and over, as blood pools onto the table. Onto the floor, collecting on Ren's boots. *He* had relayed the knowledge of my mates to Elion, leaving him to believe I was distracted.

I wasn't distracted; I was—

Ren staggers, bracing himself on the table, breaths ragged and uneven. His eyes lock with mine, a gaze full of apology.

Then a ripple runs down his body and the magic dissipates. The image of Ren fades, replaced by someone entirely different—Wayd.

The sharp angles of his face come into view, green eyes holding mine as blood flows from his chest.

Even though I see that it's not Ren, heartache and pain consume me, tangling with a flicker of relief knowing that my mate is alive. My chest caves, and I choke on a sob as guilt replaces my relief.

Wayd is family—*my family*.

And he took Ren's place tonight, feeding Elion misinformed knowledge of the legion. It slipped past me. I missed it because I was too worried about severing my oath to realize that it was Wayd who had gripped my elbow and not Ren.

Witt kicks him and frees the blade with a squelch. Wayd falls back. Then realization flashes across Witt's face as he collapses to the floor with a thud, arms limp across his body.

A scream tears from my throat, a flood of golden light and darkness igniting in my palms, fury eager to be unleashed. I let it go, and Witt jolts right as an arrow hisses past my ear.

Time slows.

Witt's eyes widen, his hands grasping at his throat as the arrow punctures clean through his neck, the tip bursting out the back. He stumbles, choking and gasping, then he falls to his knees with wide eyes as blood slips past his fingers.

Ren stalks forward, brows lowered, his bow raised high.

Rydian stands beside him and relief crashes over me at the sight of my mates. Kaeda stumbles forward, her shock palpable. She releases a mangled cry, staggering to where Wayd remains lifeless on the ground.

Shadows swirl in Rydian's hands, swiftly lashing out as guards storm through the council chamber. Fifteen? Twenty? A handful of guards' necks crack in unison, and they crumple to the floor.

Chaos erupts.

Elion roars with fury, and his magic surges, light flooding from his hands as he spins toward us. With a flick of his wrist, his light cracks through the air like lightning, aiming for me.

I spring to the side as the electrifying arc connects with the columns behind me. Debris rains down as I roll, chest heaving. Another crack of power, and I duck behind a remaining column. I whip my head to where Drakon and Ekrin hide behind their own, eyes wide with fear. Shouts and mangled grunts fill the air.

"Break that oath!" Ekrin shouts.

Kiev draws his sword, twirling the blade as he backs his way toward me. I whirl around as he lunges, but to my surprise, he takes down the approaching guard with one swift motion.

My vision blurs, electric energy thrumming and rising and twisting as it surges. I ground myself to every drop of my power as it floods my chest. The faint clinking of metal brushes my ears, and I peer around the corner, narrowing my eyes on Elion.

I step out, and he releases a whip of golden light.

I sweep Elion's power aside with a wave of my hand before curling my fingers into an upturned claw. Rage and sorrow and hatred meld with the power in my palms. With a growl, I yank on that worthless air he loves so much, and the walls begin to tremble.

His expression twists into rage and then fear, as he dangles in my grasp. Panic flickers in King Elion's eyes.

My smile drops, and I sweep my eyes over him before holding his cold, heartless gaze. Rage consumes me as a roar tears from my throat, shaking the walls of this very castle. Everything around me crashes down in the midst of chaos—the weight of uncovered truths.

I throw my hands forward, and power explodes from my palms, a flood of darkness and pale light twisting around my arms. Ropes of light and shadow slam into Elion's chest with a thundering crack, hurling him into the windows.

He crashes, glass exploding out like deadly rain, and drops into a heap on the marble.

My head tilts, and a small grin tugs at my lips, magic writhing hot beneath my skin as I finally grasp that oath between us. The only thing tethering me to him.

It burns me as my mental grip tightens, breaths ragged with strained focus, and he manages to rise to his knees. Pain is etched into his features, brows pinched, chest heaving as if he has something to say.

After a tattered breath, I tighten my grip on the oath, squeezing until he writhes. Until the veins bulge on his neck.

Our oath fractures.

I squeeze again—another crack.

Golden light veins out and rises up his arms like a web. Up his neck. His eyes fix on me. His lips seep purple, parting with a strained inhale as he fights against me. His fingers claw at his neck and satisfaction settles in my chest.

"I'm sorry," he rasps, just barely, and my grip falters. "I was only doing what I thought you needed—as your father. I wanted to save you the heartache."

His hands curl into fists, and he braces himself. He bleeds as I twist my magic, tightening my grip on our oath, and it drips from his eyes like golden tears. Yet rage engulfs me, and I scream as I make that final crack.

It explodes out in a burst of light, our oath severing.

His mouth falls open in a silent scream before he crumples to the ground. I stagger forward with a single step as an overwhelming sense of grief takes over me. *Grief*.

Why do I feel *grief* when I had only severed our oath?

A small cry slips from me, even though chaos rings clear across the room. Grunts, groans, and the clinking of metal and stone. Glass shattering, walls trembling.

Kaeda's sobs echo as she grapples with Wayd's crumpled body, vanishing with him into the Veil. Then I'm tugged back by my arm, and I pivot to see Rydian in the midst of it all. Relief runs through me at the sight of him unharmed through his blood-crusted features. Blood slips down his cheek, his clothes splattered with it.

"Where is she taking him?" I ask breathlessly.

"To the Menders." His eyes leap to mine before surveying the battle. "Isa, we have to go. We don't have the Lumen—"

Rydian freezes in place.

His eyes grow wide, and I turn toward those windows once more. My panic rises as Witt crawls to Elion's lifeless body, blood dripping from the hole in his throat.

Did I... did I kill Elion? That's not...

The walls tremble as Witt's menacing eyes graze mine, and then he smirks, his palm extended over Elion's unmoving chest. It glows white, and golden light swirls in the air, writhing and twisting, before it's sucked completely out of Elion lifeless body and forced into Witt.

The royal essence.

He placed it in himself.

Witt's neck wound heals right before my eyes, and he tilts his head—the movement eerie and downright menacing. Adrenaline and fear flood me—so consuming, I choke and stumble forward. He has my mother's essence in his grasp.

No, no, no.

By decree of the Fates, Witt just became the king of Elderheim.

A bellow of rage erupts from Rydian, and he thrusts his hands out, darkness exploding from his palms. But before it has a chance to tear Witt to shreds, he steps into a crimson portal, vanishing from sight.

An eerie silence settles, and I realize now that Ren has braced the council chamber doors with steel and stone, preventing any more guards from entering.

Shocked eyes meet my own, my breath ragged in my chest.

I swivel to see the dukes' shocked expressions. Ekrin's face is pale and clammy, as if he just realized what this means. His frightened eyes find mine, head shaking in disbelief.

Witt is now king.

"Are you all coming or not?" Rydian growls, pivoting to Kiev and the others with a hardened stare. "We need to leave before he comes back."

Confusion settles over me, but Kiev gives Rydian a curt nod. I wordlessly reach for the others and, in the span of a heartbeat, we all land in the council chamber in Aurelia.

Gasps ripple as we all appear. Orin stands at the head of the table and shifts back into his true form. Collective murmurs pierce the air as my vision clears. As my adrenaline fades into shock and then...

And then it hits me—a blistering surge of rage.

The kind of rage that burns cities, leaving nothing but ash in its wake. The kind of rage that severs the heads of traitors. My chest heaves as I pivot, eyes skimming over the room. Whatever shock I felt moments ago evaporates, drowned out by the primal piece of me.

The piece that's out for blood.

The crowd parts, making way for me to move as I search for the one I want. Our eyes meet and his face pales. He knows that I know. *Good.*

I stride forward, my body taut with barely controlled restraint when I finally reach the edge of his boots. My hand snaps out, and I grip Rafe by the collar of his tunic and slam him against a nearby pillar with a feral growl. Stone cracks, the sound echoing across the chamber.

"Tell them!" I scream, and he winces—trembling and cowering into the stone. "Or I'll cut off your fucking head!"

"Isa." Rydian's alarm breaks my focus, and I swivel my gaze over my shoulder as he inches forward. "What's going on?"

"Rafe was Elion's informant." I get out with a dark laugh.

Rafe's chest quickly rises and falls, breaths ragged, eyes widening as his head shakes. His sweat permeates the air, thick with fear, as if this wasn't always going to be the end result.

"I—I can explain, Your Majesty. Please." He begs.

"Tell me it's not true, Rafe," Eldric says in disbelief, pushing his way through the crowd. Rafe's frantic pleas only fuel my anger, leading me to slam his head against the stone again. His eyes roll as he grasps at consciousness.

"Tell them what you've done," I growl. "Everything, including Andre, and all those lies you told."

"What does she mean?" Mikal asks.

"I—I was sworn to secrecy by Andre," Rafe whimpers, nervously wringing his hands together.

Rydian tugs me back by my elbow, but with a glance over my shoulder, the fury written across his features forces me to obey. Almost instinctively, my eyes find Milena across the room, and her expression softens. Relief floods me before my eyes land on Luke and Malrik beside her. My stomach drops. Both are rugged and worn, as if they'd endured a long journey together.

Rafe straightens and nervously scans the room.

"Elynor didn't tell him about Isa until after they were married," he says. "He… he knew what blood Isa carried after he found one of Elynor's journals. Andre felt betrayed, and couldn't fathom Isa taking over Aurelia. He orchestrated her capture, and I helped him. Andre was going to pull back the order, but it was too late," Rafe confesses with a sharp exhale.

Rydian stalks forward in silence, his eyes fixed on Rafe.

"But Elion went back on his word and killed Andre during the battle." Rafe swallows. "Elion has never kept his bargains. They captured Elynor and Isa after that."

Dark tendrils of shadow flood the floor, cascading from Rydian's entire body as he prowls forward, each step slow and calculated. He stops near Rafe's feet. Yet his eyes show a lethal calm, his expression unreadable save for a twitch of his lip.

It's the kind of gaze a god would give you right before shattering a world into unrecognizable pieces.

Rafe slinks into the pillar, the air thick with power, and silence falls as we all gather to listen to the betrayal leaving Rafe's lips. He trembles.

"You're telling me you and Andre killed half of Vyria, conspiring with Elion this whole time?" Rydian whispers. "Were you the reason we couldn't find Isa all those years? They were mates, he wouldn't have done that."

"No. No, I swear." His palms rise in submission. "I—I didn't even know she was alive. I believed they had plans to kill her but didn't. You were never supposed to be Aurelia's king, because Andre wasn't meant to die, but Elion went back on his promise."

"Oh gods," Anya chokes out, her voice cracking, but Rydian's eyes never leave Rafe. "Was that why Andre was so focused on finding a tonic for those who lost their mates? Was it for Elynor? Did Andre know he was going to die?"

"I—I don't know," Rafe admits.

"He was still working for Elion," I add. "He told them I was claimed to Ren. They thought I was distracted."

Rydian ignores me. "Anything else?"

Rafe frantically shakes his head and Rydian's power draws back into his body, leaving the floor bare of darkness. Rafe's shoulders droop with relief. I look between them, confused...

Then I feel him through our bond, stealing the breath from my lungs as one emotion overwhelms my senses—ice cold fury.

"Good," Rydian says.

His shadows lash out in a sickening crack, and Rafe's head falls to the floor—lips parted, eyes open. A dreadful silence encompasses the entire council chamber. Rydian turns slowly, brows lowered, gaze deadly as he assesses the room. *My king.*

"Prepare for war."

46

An hour passes and I find myself racing across the halls as everyone disperses, searching for Ren as we had all lost ourselves to the fray. Lost ourselves to the shock of Rafe's confession, and the staggering truth about my mother's stolen essence.

Witt is now king, and Andre had conspired with Elion for my capture. I was betrayed by someone who I had considered a friend once. I was betrayed by a king—my step-father—who I had believed loved me alongside my mother.

The ache in my chest threatens to pull the air from my lungs, but I stifle the thoughts for now and swallow those emotions. I just need to see Ren.

To get the answers I crave so fiercely.

As dawn filters through the long castle windows, spilling across the dark marble in shiny rays of light, I'm dragged closer and closer to his chamber on the second floor.

Within moments, I'm standing frozen in the corridor, unable to bring myself to knock. My breaths slam to a halt, my fist hovering, pulse racing because I know he's in there. Because I know the answers I need are inside that chamber.

I grip the handle, cool in my grasp, and let myself in.

It's grander than I expected, with a large bed chamber on one side and an entryway to a bathing chamber on the other. Another doorway leads to what appears to be a sitting room, held for meetings. I'm left wondering if he and Rydian had ever met in his chamber without me.

His bathing chamber door is shut, and I assume he's washing off our battle in Elderheim. I release a heavy exhale and settle near the windows, impatiently waiting for him to step out.

His weapons rest on the table beside me, and I drag my finger down a few of the sharp edges, daggers of stone. Warm, golden light dances across a carved wooden box in the center, so out of place in the midst of all his weapons.

Unable to stifle my curiosity, I step closer.

My breath catches as I slide the lid off. Dried flowers, carvings, glass vials, jewelry, and letters.

Letters all addressed me.

Each one is written in his familiar writing, unopened, as if he had left to be forgotten in this delicately carved box. Forgotten until now. Yet, he has them here... in Aurelia.

He came with me, knowing I might never remember what we lost, and he brought them anyway. Like he knew my memories would eventually resurface? My heart races as I reach for the most recent one—dated four years ago.

One year after our marks appeared.

With trembling hands, I unfold the worn parchment with silent tears as I read the first line. And the next. The words slice through me, a grave reminder of the time I lost with him—time that was stolen. I continue to read, frantically skimming over the lines I'm not sure I was ever meant to see.

Was he ever going to give this to me? Is this box mine?

The bathing chamber door creaks open behind me. My tears hit the page, smudging the ink grasped between my trembling fingers.

"What is this?" I whisper, refusing to turn. "Why did you write this to me?"

His steps thud closer, and a quiet exhale brushes the air. For a moment, I think he might not reply, giving me that deliberate silence he's so good at doling out.

"I didn't know how else to get it out," he says.

I laugh—a chuckle of disbelief, perhaps—and pinch my brows. My head shakes as I scramble through possible reasons for him not telling me the truth.

Five years' worth of silence.

"Why couldn't you tell me?" I choke out and face him. "I broke the oath—I did what you asked. Now I need answers."

Ren battles with his composure, searching my face, his breaths speeding up. For a brief, flickering moment, his mask slips.

"Because I love you," he confesses, and my heart flutters.

I exhale, sharp and unrestrained, my chest tightening with the weight of his words.

"And I never stopped, Isa." A wrinkle of pain forms between his brows, and his voice softens. "When our marks appeared, I knew from the beginning that I'd have to eventually share you. I was angry, but as time went on I... I was just happy to have any part of you that you were willing to give me. Even if you hated me. Even if it meant watching another male touch you—love you the way I wanted to. I knew you would eventually come back."

"What does that mean?"

Ren looks away, his eyes filling with a torment I don't quite understand as the silence lingers.

"I wanted to tell you," he says. "There were a few times that I'd almost slipped, regardless of the consequences that came with it. I was going to tell you in Nymara when we fought—when I witnessed your power. But then Rydian arrived, and I saw his hair color. I knew I had to wait."

Shock races down my spine.

"Did you know Rydian was my mate?"

"I had my suspicions..." he admits. "I wasn't sure, though."

"I don't understand—what does *this* mean?" I hold up the letter before tossing it aside with a huff. "Why couldn't you intervene?"

"We went on a mission to Eldryn the same year our marks appeared. We stayed at the estate."

Realization sweeps over me.

It was recognition in Kiev's stare when his eyes met mine in the council chamber. Was that our last mission together? Was that where we were in Ren's memories? Then, very quickly, a flash of images flood my thoughts, and I blink.

"Our marks appeared when we crossed Mount Pyre together, and I was told it was a sign of the Fates by one of the wardens. When we arrived in Eldryn, I met an Oracle. She works closely with Kiev and Selphira."

"An... Oracle?"

My brows furrow, though wariness pebbles my skin. The term is unfamiliar, and yet...

"They are what's created when Shadovar and Aetheri bloodlines mix—sometimes, but not always," he explains. "She told me that I'd lose you and would eventually get you back, but you'd be bound to another. That you were bound to a future far bigger than we could comprehend. I didn't believe her because I didn't understand what she meant... but then you couldn't remember our claim when I came back from that mission in Red Hollow. It was a fate I couldn't intervene in or I'd risk you doing the opposite of what you needed to do for the realms. So I waited for you."

Silence stretches. His gaze drags over me and a sharp inhale drags through my lips. Because now...

Now I understand the reason for his silence all those years. That it wasn't just punishment to himself for what we lost, but purpose. *My* purpose.

Do *what* for the realms? What does that mean, exactly?

My heart clenches, pulling tight against my ribs. He hated me because he felt like he had to—because fate cornered him into suffering. But the Ren I remember was the one who steadied my fire. The one who quieted that raging storm in my veins, itching for a fight.

But he let me bloom into something lethal—deadly—knowing that I could handle myself. It was why he left for that mission in the first place. A grave miscalculation on both our parts.

Then our lives ruptured.

The wind howls outside, a heavy rain beating against the paned glass, drowning the realm alongside my sorrow. Pain and heartache cracks in my chest, and I glance at my hands.

"They tortured me for two days in that dungeon. Witt came in as I was preparing to leave—I didn't want to be separated from you for so long and I—I'd shown him my marks by mistake," I whisper. "He dragged me to the dungeon after that. I tried to swallow my fear because I didn't want you to feel it."

His eyes squeeze shut, torment stretching over his features. His chest rises sharply on an inhale. He drops his head, gazing at the floor, a dark halo of hair forming around his face. Heavy guilt floods me—a pain so forceful, my hand flies to my stomach, nausea over-taking me.

"Please tell me what happened," I plead. "I have to know what I did to you."

He nods, slow and hesitant, but says, "When we came back from Eldryn, we were going to leave. I wasn't sure how long we had before the Oracle's prophecy came calling, and I didn't want to risk losing you. Even if I didn't believe her." His eyes lift, but his brows furrow. "I convinced you to leave with me, but I had already agreed to one last mission in Red Hollow. Toward the end of my mission, I felt an intense wave of your emotions. I wasn't sure what I was feeling since it was so new, but then your panic flooded me."

His jaw clenches at the memory, tight enough to tremble. A storm brews behind his stillness, like a thousand regrets press down on his shoulders. And for a moment, I feel every emotion he keeps from me. It consumes me.

"Our bond went quiet, and it felt like I'd been cleaved in two. I couldn't breathe, and the pain..." His voice wavers, his shoulders rising with a fractured breath. "I was momentarily lost to madness —there were repercussions."

A quiet sob escapes me with the flood of his emotions. I did this to him—I caused him this pain and torment—the same dull ache that I've felt for the last few weeks. Then a wave of understanding washes over me, stealing the breath from my lungs.

"Why did you take me with you to Nymara this past fall?" I ask softly, fearing the answer he might give me.

He had taken me with him to get Theo and had told me it was because he disliked Luke. At the time, I hadn't believed him. But now...

"Because the last time I left you, they took your memories, and I leveled an entire town trying to get back to you. Red Hollow no longer exists because of me, and I didn't—I didn't know what I would have done if something had happened to you while I was gone again. I couldn't risk it."

Oh gods. I had wanted to spare his life, not realizing what would happen if I refused to give him up. How many had died because of me? I should feel guilty for it, and yet...

Yet I don't, because all I feel is heartache and a flood of relief knowing that he's still here with me.

"You were captain then, weren't you?"

He nods. "I was demoted for losing control to what Elion assumed was bloodlust. Most of my missions were stripped from me because of it."

"It's not your fault."

"Isa–"

"It's not your fault, Ren. It was my fault that happened—*mine*," I hiss, inching closer. "Witt wanted to know who bore my marks, but he knew I was lying. I refused to tell him, and so they took everything. They took my feelings. They took every emotion and knowledge of my marks, which included everything we did together. The mark was tied to *you*. They took you—"

"Do you love me?" he interrupts, his tone laced with a fleeting brush of hope.

I hold his gaze, my shoulders dropping on a sigh. He closes the distance between us, his boots quietly thudding against the marble. Thunder cracks outside as the rain beats harder, and lightning flashes over his face.

"I don't want to wait any longer," I say, though my heart races.

A dark hunger forms behind his eyes, skimming my face before settling on my lips. "Wait for what?"

He crowds me, forcing my head back.

I lift my eyes to track his careful movements. The space between us hums, charged with something wild that prickles my skin. His scent sears my nostrils, hitting me all at once, relaxing the tension in my chest. Replacing it with something softer.

Something safe.

I raise my hand and brush my fingers over the scar on his brow, knowing exactly where it came from—who gave it to him. His warm breaths caress my cheeks, soft and steady, as he reaches up with his hand. His thumb brushes over my lip.

"For you," I breathe, barely a whisper. "We've already lost too much time, wouldn't you agree?"

His chest rises sharply against mine, as if he's waited his whole life for me to say those words. Waited a lifetime for me to remember what we had—what we did in Eldryn together. That's what he wanted me to remember—our beginning.

His hand slides to the back of my neck, weaving into my hair before gently tugging my head back, and forcing my gaze upon him.

"And who am I to you?" Gray eyes blaze down at me, searching and waiting for my answer. He leans closer with a small grin, his mouth coasting over mine.

"My husband," I whisper, brows drawing close together. "And I never stopped loving you. It was just quiet for—"

His mouth quickly claims mine with a low rumble, hungry and certain, my soft gasp swallowed by the warmth of his kiss as his tongue dances with mine. As my magic dances with his, melding together as if we had never been separated.

Home.

He was always my home, and I had been a fool to think otherwise. My feelings of being tethered to Elderheim weren't toward the realm, but toward Ren. He was what kept me there, and I hadn't realized it, but my soul did. He was right in front of me.

As he pulls back, his forehead dips to mine, and he exhales a shaky, relieved breath.

"Welcome back, wife," he says softly.

The warmth of his words settle in my chest, sinking into every corner of my mind, every corner of my soul like a long, forgotten lullaby. Only now, the silence between us isn't sharp, but soft and whole. I missed his steady presence in my life.

Though peace never lasts long—after all, chaos follows our every step. The air shifts into something heavier, feeling it before I hear the familiar footsteps in the corridor.

Rydian opens the door and steps through, his eyes dark with exhaustion and the weight of betrayal in his own realm. His own council. My chest aches at the sight of him. Though Ren stiffens beside me as Kiev steps in behind him.

"She's here," Ren says, almost to himself. His hand meets my shoulder as if to steady me. Or perhaps steady himself.

My lips part with a question when my attention shifts behind them. Shifts to the unfamiliar person who steps past Kiev and Rydian with a certain air of confidence.

Dark, silky hair spills over her shoulders. Delicate, pointed ears poke out from beneath the soft tendrils of hair, her eyes a shade of violet and amber.

"Who are you?" I breathe.

My skin warms with a recognition I can't quite decipher. Ren straightens, his grip tightening. Kiev nods in encouragement. Rydian only sighs, jaw working before his hands slide into his pockets.

"I'm Fanora," she says finally, and the points of her canines gleam in the light. Longer than the others. A wrinkle of confusion forms between my brows. "I'm an Oracle, working closely with your... mates." A small, tight smile. "But we've already met."

My stomach twists with unease. Is this who Ren met in Eldryn?

"Why are you here?" I ask, dreading the answer.

"You are our future," Fanora says, tone sure and concise. Though my stomach drops, hating where this is going. "And you need to meld your essences with both males to join the realms, Fate of Unity. We have important blades to forge."

EPILOGUE

REN

As the castle looms in darkness, everyone asleep save for Isa and Rydian, I stick to the shadows. With hardly a scuff of my boots, I remain eerily quiet.

I should probably leave them be—let them perform their own sacred claim in peace, and yet... I can't help but want to watch. After all, I spent years in these very shadows, unable to keep my eyes off her even when our bond had quieted. Tracking her every movement. Knowing I didn't do what I should have to protect her from Witt.

Raw fucking guilt pounds between my ears.

Though anger is quick to follow, flooding my chest, leaving my hands to clench as I weave through the corridors with my hood drawn low. I thought I'd killed him—I should have killed him in that chamber, and yet that fucker had gotten away.

Turned himself into the King of Elderheim.

Was *that* a part of the prophecy Fanora spoke of? She failed to mention anything—vague in her answers like the last time we spoke. As always. A shudder of unease rolls through me.

That Oracle makes me uncomfortable.

I stifle an annoyed growl and veer toward the council chamber, stopping only to glance around. The door creaks open on its hinges, and I glance over my shoulder one last time before striding through.

Shadows bathe the room in near blinding darkness, save for the moon's pale streaks shining through the curtains. With a deep breath, I reach the large-paned balcony windows and look into the courtyard, my chest aching at their silhouettes in the distance.

An ache I hate carrying.

Dread and jealousy so stifling, they force me to place that wall up in my mind, if only to keep Isa from feeling it. I'd hate to ruin what little happiness she has right now. She'd also hound me with questions the moment my feelings brush her mind, I'm certain of it.

Hand in hand, they share whispered words under the waning full moon, too far for me to overhear even if I cracked open the glass door.

After a few minutes, a sting of hot pain cuts through my mind, and I know it's hers. I grind my teeth, knowing it's a faint gash to her palm—same as ours when we had exchanged our blood in Eldryn on the Equinox.

Exchanged our essences.

Memories of our own claim flood me—the oath I swore to her—as if it had happened days ago, not years. That day plays over and over in my mind like a rippling dream, unable to let it go.

Unable to let *her* go.

The greatest piece of me—and yet, my ruination. She utterly ruined me. Still, I'd crawl through the ashes of her rage, bathe in it if it meant she'd never forget me again.

I had even told her it was her destiny to join the realms, risking the very thing Fanora told me not to do. I couldn't help it, though—couldn't keep it to myself after our mission in Eldryn.

Only Fanora had been right; Isa hadn't believed a word I'd said at the time. *They were only dreams,* I had told her after I saw that fear shining in her eyes. That doubt and worry.

A responsibility she clearly didn't want.

She would have fled. Would have left without me, or worse, would have done the complete opposite and aided Elion. Turned into something that would have destroyed our realms instead of fixing them. I had feared she'd done it when she swore that oath to King Elion.

My blood grows hot. Then it writhes as a flood of Isa's arousal coils low in my spine, forcing me to grit my teeth and fight the stiffening of my cock.

Gods, I hate feeling that.

They tangle themselves below, hidden by tall pointed bushes near the elaborate stone fountain. But the faintest *whoosh* in the air breaks me from those emotions.

I whirl around with my dagger, flush against a delicate throat that bobs on a swallow beneath my blade. Though no fear shines in her eyes, just calm assessment.

"Foolish of you to sneak up on me, *Oracle*," I warn, narrowing my eyes on her frame. "Do you forget what I am?"

"My apologies." She breathes a laugh and steps away. "You've been quite patient. I'm impressed."

I scoff, sheathing my dagger. "I had no choice, thanks to you."

She hums a little and nods, her eyes swiveling to the glass. "They've completed it."

"Clearly. What do you want?"

She clasps her hands in front of her, shoulders back, chin high. "It won't be long until his power rises, the same as yours. I'm surprised you haven't leveled the castle yet."

My jaw tightens, and I ignore her as I turn and fix my gaze below. That thrum beneath my skin hasn't stopped simmering since Isa regained her essence. It's the same feeling I had right before it was snuffed out by Witt. When I'd destroyed Red Hollow in the span of a single breath—lost to madness and heartache.

"You did well protecting her."

My lip curls. "I failed."

"Did you?" she asks. "She's here, after all. You kept her safe in that castle until he came for her, as I said."

I ignore her again as my annoyance surfaces, recalling the words she'd muttered to me all those years ago. That I needed to let the one with auburn hair come for her, and once he did, fate would be set in motion.

"She is very powerful, as are you, Stone Shaper."

"I'm not," I huff, watching as Isa and Rydian clothe themselves between drawn-out kisses and Veil out of the gardens.

She breathes out a chuckle. "Before the Scry's took over the Aethralis bloodline, the Stone Shapers ruled for many centuries—created Elderheim itself. Built its very castle. Royal essence can be passed to other nobles not just by marriage, but by the sacrifice of a ruler's life should they choose to give up their throne. But you already knew that, didn't you?"

I stiffen, my blood turning cold when her gaze finds mine. A dark shadow blankets one side of her face, her sharpened canines glinting in the moonlight beneath her smile. A shudder runs through me.

"That means nothing now," I clip, and turn on my heel to exit the council chamber, my boots beating against the marble. Though annoyance grates on my nerves when a question surfaces—one I don't want to ask. But I need to know.

I pause, half turning toward her. A small, amused smile tugs at her lips. "When the realms rejoin... what happens?"

"With you?" she asks, head tilting, and another slow smile rises as I stare in silence, waiting. She strides closer, her dark robes brushing the ground. "Fate has a way of changing based on decisions, you know. I fear if I give you that answer it would prevent the outcome we need."

"Did you lie to me?" I growl, hands curling into fists, the stone quaking beneath our feet before I force a long breath. The trembling subsides, and my voice drops. "I can't lose her again... it will destroy me."

"You want her to choose," she says casually.

My lip curls in frustration, though I can't bring myself to deny it. I never wanted to share, and I even came to terms with Isa finding something with Rydian if it meant her coming back to me, but... I want her. *Only* her.

I'd be willing to set aside my grievances if it meant that much to her, but only if she asked me to. I could deal with it, I think, like I have for the last five years.

"You will never ask her, but you want her to. But perhaps when the realms rejoin, balance must hold, and you cannot have balance with two." She arches her brow. "So, that is the question isn't it—who will she choose?"

I fucking hate her vague answers.

"I'm done here," I snap, shaking my head as I push for the doors. I don't even look back at that wretched Oracle—the one who ruined my life. The one who ensured my suffering with knowledge I never asked for.

But just before the door sways shut, I hear her, barely more than soft echo in the air.

"Prince or king?"

ACKNOWLEDGMENTS

I want to extend my heartfelt gratitude to everyone who supported me during the writing of *Markings of Fate*.

To my family, thank you for your encouragement to publish. To my editor, Kyro Dean, thank you for your patience and attention to detail. Without the support of my readers and everyone behind the scenes, I'm not sure it would be what it is today.

When I first started this series, I had this wild idea: a couple who lost each other, only to find their way back over time. A love marked by longing, sacrifice, and determination to claim the future they once promised each other even if it caused suffering in the process. I never expected that idea to grow into a story that would quite literally consume my life, or shatter my heart along the way.

I hope you fell in love with Ren, Isa, and Rydian with the complexity of their journey as much as I did while writing them. If you have a moment, I would be incredibly grateful if you left a review on your preferred platform. As an indie author, every review makes a difference!

Thank you again for reading, and I hope you enjoyed this book.

TO MY SISSY

Dear Sissy,

I just want to say thank you for entertaining my blab sessions. Your encouragement has meant everything to me since I began writing, and I love you so damn much. From wheezing in the kitchen late at night as kids, to sharing a dorm room, to crying over hot tea sick with grief—you've always been there.

I'm not sure I could explain, even in the slightest way, how much you mean to me. In truth, you're the reason I kept going. You always knew when I needed comfort and when I needed honesty, and you somehow gave me both.

You've nudged me from the very beginning to publish when I didn't want—or plan to. Not once have you made me feel like a weird burden when I needed to work out the kinks in my writing. You've squealed when I did, and you've pushed when I didn't want it but desperately need it. This series exists because you believed it should, long before I did.

To put it simply, you taught me how to believe in myself, and I know mom would be proud to see how well you're doing. Thank you for loving me.

So please don't stop being the sunshine in everyone's life, because mine would be a lot duller without you in it.

And, in Mom's words, I love you more than Oreos.

Love, Candi-Bear

ABOUT THE AUTHOR

C.J. Blaire was born and raised in Texas where she developed a love for storytelling. With a creative background in wedding photography, she has always been drawn to capturing moments—both through a lens and on a page. When she's not weaving wild, intricate stories, she enjoys reading, sewing, and staying active. A wife and mother of two with lots of animals in tow, she finds inspiration in the quiet moments of her everyday life.

https://www.threads.com/@author.cjblaire

CONTENT & TRIGGER WARNINGS

Markings of Fate is an adult romance fantasy with explicit content, intended for audiences 18+. There is on and off page violence, and the romance is explicit. The trigger warnings below are solely to prepare readers for what they'll be reading. I trust that you, as a reader, know what you can or cannot handle.

May contain minor spoilers.

- Explicit sexual activity (consensual)
- Explicit language
- Torture (on/off page mentions)
- Forced Loyalty
- Violence & assassination (on/off page)
- Memory loss & identity manipulation (central to her arc, emotional consequences)
- Psychological trauma: PTSD-like symptoms
- Parental abuse
- Political Oppression (power struggles between realms & slavery)